# MADNESS
# BEHIND THE
# MASK

MIRANDA GRANT

# BY MIRANDA GRANT

## WAR OF THE MYTH
Elemental Claim
Think of Me Demon
Tricked Into It
Rage for Her

## FAIRYTALES OF THE MYTH
Burn Baby Burn
The Little Morgen
Bjerner and the Beast

## DEATHLY BELOVED
To Have and to Lose
Death Do Us Part
For Better or For Worse
To Love and To Perish

## BOOK OF SHADOWS
Madness Behind the Mask
Cursed to be Mine

# MADNESS BEHIND THE MASK

This is a work of fiction. All characters are products of my imagination and should not be seen as having any more credibility than fake news does. Any resemblance to organizations, locales, or persons living, dead, or stuck in purgatory is entirely coincidental.

Copyright © 2023 by Miranda Grant
ISBN: 978-1-914464-21-8

authormirandagrant@gmail.com
mirandagrant.com
Facebook: Author Miranda Grant

All rights reserved. No part of this book may be used or reproduced in any manner whatsoever without written permission by the author, except in the case of brief quotations embodied in critical articles and reviews.

Edited and published by Writing Evolution.
Cover design and interior artwork by Writing Evolution.

### *To Heather G Harris:*

Who wouldn't stop pushing me to 'write to market' while also sending all her friends to be my clients so I could actually afford to do so.

So if anyone needs a fun urban fantasy palette cleanser with little romance (ahhhh! I know, but hear me out), check out her work. This book, this *series* wouldn't be here without her.

---

Though to be fair, this series also wouldn't have been created if it weren't for all the dicks who kept reporting my TT and telling me I should stop writing because I was horrible at it simply because I *deliberately chose* to write a 'bad B-movie romcom satire' rather than the 'serious fantasy' they wanted because I love that genre (like, *Beaster Bunny: Here Comes Peter Cottonhell* is my favourite movie, hands down), but fuck them. I'd much rather dedicate this to Heather. She's amazing; they suck. Arienna is obviously TSTL and thinks about sex 24/7. She grew up in a happiness-sex cult. Like, duh.

# TRIGGER AND CONTENT WARNINGS

(These are also spoilers)

**All the triggers.**

This is not an exaggeration. If you get to a point and think, it can't get worse…it can. There is no light in this. No happy times to counter the dark. Sau's story is just brutal pain because being a woman in the Shadow Family is not easy. She is a survivor, just like too many of us are...

**But she will force this world to bow to her.**

*Find the full list on my website:*

*"Just when you think you can't take any more, when life has already brutalized you, it will take from you again."*

- Sau Shadow

# ONE
## HER
### 30 APRIL 1917

A belt cuts through the air, the sharp snap as it rises making me tense instinctively. I know doing so will make it worse. I need to relax my muscles. I need to –

A scream rips around my skull as harsh leather pelts across my back, knocking out my air, making my left lung feel as if it's collapsing beneath a heavy weight. I slam my teeth shut as I collapse to my knees on the blue-and-white tiles of the kitchen floor, biting through my tongue in an attempt to stay quiet.

*Don't cry, Sau.*

*Don't cry.*

Men don't cry.

Tears burn my eyes as the copper tang of blood fills my mouth. I might not be a man, but I *am* a Shadow, and we are the leaders of this Family. It is our shadow magic that makes us infamous, that makes others tremble in their beds.

*Don't cry, Sau...*
*Don't cry.*
And yet, I hear my little brother crying beside me.
Sobbing.
Begging dad to stop as he raises the belt for him at the same time Uncle David does for me.

I tense despite not wanting to, despite telling myself to relax. It'll be so much better if I just relax. Blood trickles down my mouth as I remove my tongue from between my teeth.

My heart beats rapidly in anticipation of the next sting.
I want to get up and run away.
I want to turn and fight.

But the belt whips down on my naked back, landing on one of the bruises it has already given me, and all I do is groan. A small whimper begs to escape, but I swallow it down, refusing to cry, refusing to break.

The next slap cuts across my skin, opening me up to a flurry of pain that stings in the humid air. The force of the next blow makes me fall forward, and I throw my hands out to catch myself before my face hits the tiles.

My muscles scream in agony as soon as my palms make contact. My arms buckling beneath the pain, I hit my head hard, my lip busting, the hole in my tongue clipping on my teeth, making my eyes water.

"Stop!" Luther screams as he curls up in a ball beside me. "Please, Dad! *Don't!*" He ends on a high-pitched wail as Father hits him again and again, the *crack* resonating in my skull, making me flinch as if gunshots are going off beside me.

I want to tell him not to cry as it only makes them hit us harder, but I can't open my mouth without screaming. I can't tell him that soon we will pass out from the pain and blood loss and that when we wake, the pain will be gone, healed by Mama.

This has been my night for the last eleven months, and not once have I cried. I cannot do so now.

All I can do is watch him with tears in my eyes, my jaw clenched tight in pain, my hands fisted, my tongue bleeding through my lips as I lie sprawled out on the kitchen floor.

The belt hits harder and harder, slicing open naked flesh and leaving bruises and blisters everywhere else. My throat works hard as Luther continues to beg and scream beside me.

"Please don't!

"No more!

"Stop!

"Please!

"Dad, *please!*"

Two men pin him down because he keeps trying to curl into a ball. They stretch his arms over his head and keep his legs straight, opening up his back to Father's blows. Not allowing him to protect himself in any way. Blood oozes down him in ugly criss-cross gashes that mirror the ones on me.

Luther twists his head side to side, trying to look at Dad as he begs for mercy.

His screams are thick with snot and pain, and I tremble as I listen to him. Father's belt whips down on his back, making me flinch a half-second before Uncle David's bites down into my own flesh.

"*Please...*" My little brother's cries are weaker now, his words desperate pleas he knows will never be answered. I want to tell him it's almost over now. To go ahead and drift into unconsciousness.

My own pain pulls at me, wanting to drag me to that sweet surrender. But I won't go until he does. Won't leave him to suffer this on his own.

As the belts rain down on us over and over and over again, Luther finally passes out. Only the *snap* of the belts are heard. Only the *thumping* and *ripping* of flesh. I watch Father hit him a few more times, then he stops and looks at me.

His dark steel gaze catches mine, then lifts to Uncle David's in a silent command. The belt hits me harder.

And harder.

Aiming for the same damn spot.

Again and again until my skin breaks.

Until the muscle beneath is torn.

Until the rib beneath that is broken.

I want to scream.

I want to beg for mercy.

Instead, I hold my father's gaze.

I am a Shadow, and I know they do this out of love.

My eyes drifting close, I pass out into oblivion.

---

I wake up in my bed, covered in sweat but with my wounds healed and the pain gone. I open my eyes to the darkness of my shared room and breathe out heavily as the sounds of the belt still make me flinch.

Phantom noises I can't escape.

So stupid of me.

But despite knowing it's stupid to be afraid now when the threat is gone, my body still shakes, still trembles, still flinches at every imaginary slap of Uncle David's belt.

Keeping my eyes wide, I stare at the floral wallpaper decorating the room. The pink flowers are simply gray in the dark, but their familiarity still helps calm me. Father never hits me in here.

Eventually, my pulse calms, and I raise my hand to my face, trying to concentrate on the feeling in my fingertips. But they feel the same as they always do – no tingling, no numbness, no feeling of magic flickering beneath the skin.

They're my usual powerless fingers, and I drop my arm in annoyance.

"Come on," I growl as I bang my head against my pillow.

"Do you still not have it?" Jade whispers from the other side of our room. She's the youngest cousin on Mama's side, but she won't inherit the Shadow magic like I will, Mama having married into the family. The darkness hides my cousin's features, but I can envision her leaning up on one elbow, facing me as her long blonde hair –so different to my black– hangs in front of her face.

"No," I groan loudly, then sigh. "Maybe it will come before tomorrow night." Before Luther and I are whipped again as they try to trigger our ascensions – that moment when we'll be able to access and control our magic – both our innate power that is personal to us and our family's genetic shadow magic that gives us our last name.

"Does getting whipped hurt?" Jade asks.

"Of course it does. That's the point," I say. "The pain is supposed to release the magic."

"Why?"

"It just does."

"But –"

I roll my eyes. "No buts. And stop asking, 'Why?' all the time. It's annoying."

I turn on my side, wincing at the memory of being hit there.

"But I thought it comes when we bleed?" she pushes. "Why don't you just wait?"

"Because we don't have time. We need more soldiers *now*. Antonio just ambushed Father a few months ago and tried to kill him, remember?"

"But you're twelve. That's two years older than when Ma started. You're already way late."

*Really? I didn't notice.* I roll my eyes. "It's different for everyone, Jade. Now go to sleep."

"So could I get mine tonight?"

"No."

"Why not?"

"Because you have to be older than ten."

"I turn ten tomorrow. So it could be tonight."

"You turn seven. You're six now, dummy. Seven comes after six, not ten."

There's a moment of silence, but I don't dare hope that means she's falling asleep. She's most likely trying to count on her fingers.

"If I get mine before you, will I marry Caden?"

"No," I snap, sitting up and glaring daggers in her direction. "He's mine." Ever since I was conceived, he's been my destiny. When we marry, our Families will unite and fight against the werewolves and vampires plaguing St. Augustine together.

Which is why it's so important I get my ascension soon. The vampires' blood and sex trafficking is messing with our Family's business of blackmail and extortion. We can't exactly get weekly or monthly payments of hush money from people if they are being bled dry by the vampires or having most of their earnings taken away by their pimps.

As for the werewolves, we know they are planning something big, their new alpha having tried to lure my father into an ambush with talks of 'peace' three months ago. Everyone knows the only way for there to be peace is if the vampires and werewolves are dead.

"But I want Caden," Jade whines.

"Too bad. He's mine. Now go to sleep."

"But –"

"Now, Jade," I snap.

She sighs grumpily but doesn't make another sound. In another few minutes, she's snoring softly, and I turn on my side to look out the window, wondering how long I have before I am next disturbed. The stars shine brightly, meaning I've been out for a while and don't have long; maybe half an hour, if that, before Uncle David visits me to teach me how to be a good wife.

*A good wife uses her tongue. Just like that. Just like that! Gods, Sau. Now swallow.*

I'm not a fan of the end, the saltiness not a flavor I enjoy, but if I bob down deep enough, his cum will miss my tongue and it's bearable. Plus, he always gives me some candy afterwards, and I love candy.

Rolling onto my back, I wonder what he'll give me tonight. I really like gum, but there's a shortage of it with the war going on across the ocean. I haven't had a piece in months.

I wrinkle my nose, hoping he doesn't give me licorice. I hate it; it's absolutely awful, and I would rather taste his cum, but a good wife never complains about the gifts she's given, meaning I'll have to eat it.

This is my duty as a female Shadow – please the men who protect us, make their home life good to counter the nightmares they face on the streets they patrol. It's also to bear children, to create the next generation of soldiers, and I press a hand to my belly as it flutters at the thought of swelling with my husband's children. I smile.

Although Florida requires a woman to be eighteen to marry, if I get pregnant, I can marry at any age. There's also Georgia just a few miles up that allows one to marry at ten. I'm two years older than that, so we have options in case Caden can't get me pregnant before he's drafted. There are talks about such happening in the next few months with the war over in Europe heating up. My chest squeezes at the thought of losing my love before I even get the chance to marry him.

*Please gods, don't be that cruel.*

The bedroom door opens, making my pulse thud at the sight of a broad silhouette that's easily recognizable even in the dark. Uncle David shuts the door behind him, and I swing my legs off the bed in excitement. I love learning how to be a good wife. I'm going to make Caden so happy and my father so proud. I lick my lips, wetting the area as I kneel on the cold floor. When my uncle sits down and spreads his thighs, I shift between them, my hand eagerly reaching for him in the dark.

Hard fingers close over my wrist before I can suck him into my mouth though. He pulls me towards the bedroom door as I'm left confused about what's happening.

"Uncle David?" I ask once we're in the hall, knowing better than to have made a noise that would've woken my cousin. A good wife never disturbs those sleeping.

He raises his other hand, and the confusion mounts at the sight of blood on his fingers.

"You're hu..." I start.

But then it hits me, how he might have got that off my sheets as there's no cut, and excitement mounts as I drop a hand between my thighs, beneath the white nightgown I'm wearing. Sticky wetness meets my tips, and I raise my hand in excitement. "I'm bleeding!"

The beating finally worked, triggering my puberty, and soon I'll get my ascension. My pace picks up as we head towards my parents' room, but before we reach their door, Uncle David stops me.

"Don't tell them I was in your room." He digs out a stick of gum from his pocket. My eyes light up as I take it from him. "It'll be our secret to surprise your husband, okay?"

I nod, absolutely delighted about how this night is going. When Uncle David starts to walk away though, my smile fades a little. "Aren't you coming in with me?"

He shakes his head. "This is your moment, Sau."

He disappears down the hall, but I'm too excited to think much of it. This *is* my moment. This is the moment I become a woman, when I can do my duty as a woman of this Family. I'm going to get married to Caden. I'm going to have my own babies and raise them as strong soldiers. I'm going to make Father proud, help him win this war against the werewolves and the vampires.

Excitement buzzing down my fingers, I open the door and rush in.

# PART ONE:
## A HATED ENEMY

# TWO
## ANTONIO
### 8 MAY 1917

The young witch is dressed all in white, so pristine, so pure, her rosy cheeks the only color beneath her veil. She smells of a false innocence, not sick-like with stress or fear burrowed deep within her pores. She's too young to know such harsh truths.

Oh, she knows of the monsters in the dark, has most likely been told of our sins. Be good or the werewolves will get you. Eat your food or the werewolves will eat you.

Nothing but fairytale monsters that speak not of the true monstrosities we can be.

I breathe in her scent. A small smirk curls my lips.

But she will learn it soon.

And so fitting on her wedding day too – that moment where a girl becomes a woman. Where young Sau, the first born of the Shadow's newest generation, will learn what it means to be afraid.

To fear.

To never sleep again without her heart racing in her scrawny little chest.

# MADNESS BEHIND THE MASK

I lick my lips, trailing my tongue across my canines as I watch her from the roof of the next building over. The witches think they're so smart, spelling the venue so other supernaturals (sups) can't enter on her special day, this binding of witch Families, this creation of pacts that will see their numbers grow. But I don't need to enter to be able to kill a witch. My rifle aims over the side of the roof, angling down to point at little Sau's head.

Then it trails over to her father's.

Her fiance's.

Eeny, meeny, miny, moe.

I'm liking these guns the humans made. The previous alpha of the Death Hunt, my gang of wolves, thought they were useless, un-honorable. We should only kill people with our teeth and claws and natural strength. Blah, blah, blah. Pathetic thoughts from a pathetic man. There is no honor in war.

I learned that the hard way when I once thought I could bring peace to the three gangs of St. Augustine just by talking through our differences. But there is too much hatred on all our sides. Too many vendettas unpaid and uncollected. All everyone wants is to fight and kill, and so I will join them in their madness.

I will end this war with their corpses hanging in my halls and splayed out on my dining tables. Perhaps then they'll realize the folly of their mockery over my attempts at peace.

Nestling the butt of the rifle into my shoulder, I aim for the little girl. She is the only daughter of Delun Shadow, and although the Shadow Domain does not allow their females to fight, she is more important than any of his sons; with her marriage, their Family will easily double in size overnight.

So despite how much effort they put into her white dress and veil, despite the armed men there to protect her, Sau Shadow will never know a man's kiss.

My finger on the trigger, I follow her down the aisle.

Then I exhale.

And fire.

She lifts her head just as the bullet hits her, coloring her white dress red. Her eyes fly up to mine as she falls to the ground right in front of the altar. The venue explodes into action. Her father throws up a shield around her, a shimmering blue that is as useless as it is pretty given her mother is running towards them, white healing magic flowing around her hands, and I'm training my gun on her.

With inhuman speed, I fire.

She falls to the ground, a river of life flowing out of her head. The light fades from her hands... Is gone completely. She lies on the floor with one arm out as if reaching for her daughter, who is on the ground in her father's arms, bleeding out from the wound in her neck. They will soon be reunited.

Their soldiers rush around, trying to figure out where I'm shooting from, wondering why their wards never activated to tell them of my presence. But the invisibility charm hanging around my neck hides me from magical sight as well as from normal vision.

Delun Shadow should have been a bit more observant when I killed his youngest brother three weeks ago. He should've noticed Jack's magical charm was missing from around his neck.

I feel the little translucent stone pulsing with power against my chest, consuming the magic thrown at me as the Shadows search with their useless scries. I dart around the roof, firing into the venue at different angles, taking out every woman and girl in attendance.

The men might be soldiers, but the women are their breeders, and with their deaths, the Shadow Family will stagnate, then finally fall.

It's dirty tactics, but as the alpha of my pack, I do not

have the luxury of keeping clean.

Aiming my rifle, I blow out the brains of a little baby in pink. I jump onto the next roof, skidding across angled tiles, working my way to a new vantage point to target those now hiding behind the cover of the pews. I skid to a stop at the edge of the new roof, line up a shot through a new window, and then freeze, my senses blaring.

For just a moment, for the barest of seconds, gone too fast I would have missed it if not for my heightened wolf awareness, was a glimmer inside the wedding venue. Like a heat haze that disappeared as soon as I really looked.

*Like a mirage created by fucking magic...*

*To keep me distracted while someone –*

Cursing, I swing my rifle around, having just picked up the scent of a man behind me. The charm around my neck suddenly burns white hot against my chest, and I hiss in a breath as it brands my skin, overheating with magic. *The bastard can see me.* I yank it off, snapping the chain just as I clock the ball of green fire being thrown at my head by Delun Shadow.

Falling backwards, I tumble off the roof as flames lick the air above me. The rifle falls to the ground as I flip in the air, my bones breaking, my skin and tendons tearing. Claws rupture from my fingertips as canines extend in a newly formed muzzle. Long red fur sprouts across my body everywhere but my chest, which fills in with white.

My claws dig into the edge of the roof as I catch myself from falling. Slamming both furred feet into the side of the building, I launch off the wall, jumping back onto the angled roof, my maw open in a snarl.

Delun throws up a wall of blue magic just as I reach him. I bounce off it, my neck snapping to the side as my teeth close over air frizzling with magic.

Standing upright, I bare my teeth as he readies another spell. His fire is a pain to deal with as it doesn't just burn one's skin, which would be easy enough to ignore given how quick my body is to heal and how naturally resistant werewolves are to most magic. His fire, though, burns one's soul, and if it hits me, I'll be crippled in an instant. There is no defense against soul magic. Only black-out agony.

I dart forward just as Delun's infamous whip of flames extends from his left hand. It barely grows a few inches before I'm on him, the slope of the roof making him react slower than usual as he struggles to keep his balance. His shield goes down. His whip goes up, growing another few inches in the time it takes me to snap my teeth around his other arm as he fights me off. The coppery taste of his blood flows across my tongue as I jerk my head, wanting to throw him off balance so he doesn't have time to –

I release him on a howl as his fucking whip hits me in the back. I drop to my knees, my vision narrowing into pinpoints of black as the pain resonates in every part of my body. Lurching down the side of the roof, I roll off it just as his whip slams down where I was. I tumble down the three stories, my normal grace stolen by the flair of agony ripping apart my soul. The ground hits me in the face, and I want to take a moment to breathe, but I know if I do, I'm dead. Delun can jump from the roof and shift into his shadow form, taking no damage. And once he shifts back, he's going to kill me with that damn whip.

So I force myself to my feet and stumble forward. A witch tries to stop me, standing in my way as red light builds around his hands, but my attention is over his shoulder, on the gray wolf that follows me everywhere. She's my own little shadow, my lifelong mate, and the love of my life.

I growl at her, ordering her back to her position on the perimeter watch, but Siome launches herself at the back of the witch. Screaming, he falls beneath her weight as her teeth close around his neck.

My ears twitch at the sound of flames crackling behind me. Lunging to the left, I catch the sight of green fire whipping through the air. But it isn't aiming for the position I was just at nor the position I am dodging to. My heart stutters as the whip of soul fire lands fully on the back of my mate.

Siome collapses to the ground, her howling whimper a cut I am defenseless to. Throwing my head back, I howl my own pain and give the rest of my pack, which is hanging back on the perimeter, the signal to attack.

Pivoting, I take a step towards Delun as he pulls back his whip, but another witch gets between us, throwing red bolts of crackling magic at my chest. It hits and fizzles out, making my fur stand on end but doing no damage, my natural resistance to magic strong, even for my kind. The only thing I've come across so far that can hurt me is Delun's fucking whip.

My sight on the head of the Shadow Domain, I charge at him, ignoring the little gnat witch completely until I'm passing him. Then my arm snaps out. My hand wraps around his face, my claws sinking into the back of his skull and my palm crushing bone beneath my grip. He's dead by the time I lift his body and throw him at Delun.

He dodges to the right, away from me, rather than choosing to create a blue shield. Although witches have an infinite amount of magic, to use it in great quantity or quality will leave them suffering the consequences. It is a tactic we use often – force them to use as much magic as possible in a short time and watch as it kills them for us.

A shadow of red fur darts in from the right, aiming for one of the witches that have poured out of the wedding venue to join the fight. Although we wouldn't normally be so bold as to travel in our wolf forms during the day, the whole area around the wedding venue has been cloaked from human eyes. Neither witches nor werewolves want to be spotted by the humans, both of our kind having suffered for such visibility all throughout history.

A low whine rumbles from my throat, and my left ear twitches at Siome's responding noise. She is in a lot of pain, and I want to go to her, but to turn my back on Delun would be a death sentence for both of us.

As my pack deals with the other witches, Delun and I assess each other with eyes that speak of all of our sins. I wanted peace. I *begged* for peace. I tried to set up a talk between Delun, Aleric (the vampire leader and head of the third gang, the Blood Fangs), and I in the hopes that we could finally overcome millennia of ancestral crimes.

I was ready to forgive him for killing my parents, his coven for all the other deaths they've dealt. I was even ready to give up our claim to the portal (the only place in the U.S.A. where supernaturals can be smuggled into this world, coming from Blódyrió, one of the Seven Planes the humans know nothing about), and talk about the splitting of territory. I wanted peace. I wanted the pups in Siome's belly to grow up in a world so different to my own.

I wanted a foolish wish.

For the only way we can ever be at peace is with the witches and vampires all dead.

Lunging forward, I keep myself between him and my mate, ready to intercept any cracks of his whip. He raises his arm just as a little girl yells, "Dad!"

In my peripheral, I catch his daughter running out of the wedding venue, white magic from her hands matching her beautiful white dress but contrasting to the shadows swirling around her feet. She pulls his attention for the barest of seconds, the quick flick of widening eyes, but that's all I need for my opening. With a burst of power, I close the gap between us.

His eyes fly back to me.

His whip swings down.

But he's too late, too slow, and my teeth sink into his neck as I grab both his arms and pull. My muscles strain as he fights me with his magic, desperately trying to keep his body whole even as his life bleeds out between my gums.

"Let him go!"

A little fist hits me, and a pleasurable heat flashes through my body, radiating out from my side. The brat's a healer, and she's unknowingly taking away the pain her father dealt with his whip earlier.

Ignoring her, I snap my head left and right, trying to rip out Delun's throat, but his magic pulls at me, holding my teeth to his skin, forcing them to act like morbid little dams. As soon as I let him go, he will bleed out quickly, nothing there to stop the flow.

Suddenly, I can feel magic seeping through his blood, feel it heating my mouth. Sau's a strong little witch, and I glance down to see her with her hands wrapped around his arm, white power pulsing around her fingers.

Growling, I release my grip on Delun's left arm, blood spraying as I pull my claws from his flesh and backhand her across the cheek. She flies back and slams into Siome, who just tried to rise to her feet. My mate catches her, but before she can sink her teeth into Delun's daughter, Sau fully fades into her shadows.

Siome growls her frustration.

And then she screams.

Stopping my heart in a moment of disbelief.

I wrench back around so I can see what's wrong, and my eyes instantly widen with the force of my fear. I drop Delun as I run for my mate, but Sau's shadows are already enveloping her, the monsters that lurk inside them eating away her flesh.

I whine as I barrel forward, an agonized plea to the gods that have long abandoned us. It goes unanswered, as it always does, and I watch, helpless, as Siome drops to the ground, her legs gone. She reaches for me just as I reach her, and our fingers clasp around each other. Pain streaks down her face and erupts from her lungs as she places her other hand over her belly, a futile attempt to protect our pups.

There is nothing she can do to save them.

Nothing I can do to save her.

The only hope I have is by dragging her away from here and praying Sau lets go in fear of being taken away from the protection of her Family. Howling the signal to retreat, I race away from the wedding venue, dragging my mate behind me on the ground.

Her whimpers cut harsher than any whip of Delun's, and the feel of her weight decreases with every step. She's so light to carry, about half her weight. *No...*

Panic overtaking me, I flee down the street, not caring when I near the magic shield hiding us from the humans. The air glistens up ahead, a shimmering wall that is barely noticeable, separating me from the crowd of people a bit further down the road. As soon as I pass through, they will see me, but they cannot hurt me any more than I am already hurting.

I can't lose her.

Can't lose her and our kids all in one day.

Whimpering, I race for the wall, knowing it's my best chance to get Sau off her. She's still wrapped around my mate in her shadow form, clinging like a disease. I want to plead with her to let her go, to tell her she might be able to save her father if she goes back now, but we can't speak in our wolf forms. Can't bargain. Can't beg.

All I can do is run for the magical wall and hope there is enough of Siome left by the time we get there that she can heal at least somewhat. That she can close the wounds of her missing legs and survive as an amputee.

Just *survive*.

*Please.*

I can't lose them all in one day. In one hour. One damn moment.

One damn *mistake* in thinking that I could take the Shadows by surprise. She can't die because of *me*.

Howling, I near the wall.

I glance behind me and catch those beautiful red eyes I have woken up beside for the last decade. They are dim and distant in her pain. I squeeze her hand and whine low, letting her know we're almost there.

The shadows have consumed her up to her waist now.

The pups are gone, our children eaten by the monsters called forth by Sau Shadow.

A little girl.

A murderer.

Heartless and cold like her father.

Siome and I had names picked out.

A nursery completed in our excitement.

But Sau has taken all of that from us, molded by the sins of her father.

Turning my head around, I burst through the wall, my red hair rising as the magic shimmers around us.

It takes a second for people to notice our blurred forms. Our speed is too fast for them to see clearly but they can clearly see something is here. Double glances turn into open mouths, but I ignore them all as a white wolf darts past me to take care of them before they can scream and alert more people to our presence. Throats slit, they sink to the ground, useless witnesses to a world they should have never seen.

Their deaths are on my hands, but in the end, they are mere innocent bystanders I value less than my mate. I would sacrifice this whole fucking city if it meant I could save her.

My fingers tighten around Siome's hand as it slackens completely. I look behind me, fear in my every breath. She's in her human form. She can't heal as well in it. She has to heal. *Baby, you have to heal!*

Whimpering, I turn down the alley set up as our fall back. Wolves stand in both buildings, keeping an eye out, and a hidden door lies flush against the wall on my right.

Slowing, I watch with terrible hope as the shadows finally fall off my mate, but it quickly turns to sheer agony when I see the damage they have wrought. She has no legs left, just a bleeding hole that's pouring organs and partial four-month-old fetuses out onto the cobbled street. The monsters in the shadows have eaten too much of her, the life flickering out of her eyes making me howl as I cradle the upper half of her body, the only part left.

An answering howl of pain comes from the end of the alley, and I lift my head to see the white wolf from earlier now sprayed in the red of his kills, blocking Sau's exit. She's back in her human form, huddled against the wall, her eyes wide, her arms down at her sides, exhaustion all over her face. The wolf shows his teeth as he advances on the little witch, and I let out a whine as I'm forced to let go of my love. If he gets to Sau before I can, he will kill her for harming his baby sister, and as much as I wish her dead, I need her alive to heal Siome. The only hope of my happiness lies in the hands of my enemy, and it is a terrible position to be in.

Laying my mate down as gently as I can, I jump over her body and entrails, over our pups that never got a chance to breathe, to rub their noses against ours before we chased them around the yard. Forcing down my desire to fall into his arms and share our grief, I face off against my brother-in-law. Pain hits the air in high-pitched notes that resonate inside my chest as he begs for the chance to get around me and rip Sau to pieces.

I want to let him.

I want to let him so fucking much.

But Sau is a healer and Siome's only hope.

I tackle him, my teeth going for his throat for a quick pin, but he dodges, so I only get his shoulder, and we roll across the street. My claws rake into his side, his dig deep into mine, but the sudden pain is nothing under the agony already breaking me apart.

Needing to talk to him, I start to shift despite how stupid of a decision it is. In human form, I'll heal slower, and if he doesn't back off, he could easily kill me. But I cannot lose him today too. Cannot lose the last of Siome's family; he is my brother too.

As my body rips itself apart, tearing flesh and tendons and bone, he rolls on top of me and bares his teeth in my face. The stink of his breath is the first thing to fill my human lungs.

"Vance," I rasp as he looks up, preparing to jump off me now that I am too weak to hold him back. "She's a healer."

His muscles tense, then start to shake before he drops his head to mine. A low whine rumbles from his chest, and I press my forehead against his wet nose, the comfort of touch as dominant to us in our human forms as well as when we're our wolves.

He moves off me, and I twist onto my stomach to look at Sau. She's still huddled against the wall, her eyes wide and bright with tears unshed.

"Heal her," I command as I pull myself to my feet, my body aching and bruised and in more pieces than I know what to do with.

Siome and I are childhood sweethearts. Every memory I have is deeply entwined with her. She is the reason I became alpha, the reason I fight for a better world. She is my better half, and I am not above begging to save her.

"Please," I say as I drop to my knees in front of Sau. "Heal her."

She looks at me, her green gaze so terrified and young. "I

don't know how."

The pain in my chest twists under the drips of acid that are poured from the honesty of her words. Today is her wedding day, meaning she's only just hit puberty, only just had her ascension. She's barely come into her powers, hasn't learned how to control them, but I don't care about logic and truth.

I just want her to heal my mate.

Grabbing her by the arm, I yank her over to Siome.

I try not to look at the beautiful red eyes that used to be so bright. But their dullness calls to me like a flame to a bug, and I cannot help but stare into the eyes I fear will never light up again. They watch me with so much pain, and I shove Sau down onto her knees.

Dropping beside her, I snatch both her hands and press them over Siome's heart.

"Heal. Her," I growl, my voice cracking. "Or I swear to all the gods, I will cut you apart piece by piece so your Family can hear your screams. When they come for you, I will butcher them until everyone you love is dead. Their blood will be on your hands."

Her head bows down, her shoulders trembling as she sucks in harsh breaths. "I...*can't*," she whispers.

"An..." Siome rasps, and my eyes thin with the twisting of my face, my heart.

"Don't talk. Save your strength," I plea as I release one of Sau's hands to cup my mate's cheek. It is cold and too pale, a woman dying.

*No.*

She can't.

"I love you..." Struggle lines carve deep into her face as I rub my thumb over her cheek, begging her to stop, to not give up. Not yet. We have a healer. We can save her.

"Siome..."

"But our babies..." Her face twists in the manifestation of

my own pain, a mirror, a painting of terrible emotion with crashing waves and drowning men under the gray skies of a winter storm. "They...need me..."

"Siome...no, *I* need you. Our pups...they're all gone." I crack. Break. Utterly fucking shatter as those words are ripped from my lips, the truth hitting the air, the grief hitting every part of me. I want to yell at her for breaking from her position. I want to ask her why she fucking put herself in danger while carrying our pups. She should've stayed back. She should've stayed *safe*. For me. For them.

My eyes lift to the partial fetuses behind her, resting under the red twists of her intestines. A few of their faces are frozen in pain, and my heart jumps into my closed throat on a rising scream. I want to yell at her for doing this to us. I want to shake her with my grief.

But instead, I drop my gaze back to my mate and roll my lips in, trapping the cries building in my chest. She needs my strength right now. She needs –

"I must go...to them..." Her eyes drift close, and I dig my fingers into her face as a low-pitched whine comes from me. Vance joins me in my vocalized grief as he paces back and forth, his claws flexing every time he glances at Sau.

"No, Siome. You have to stay here. *Please*. We can heal you."

She doesn't say anything as she holds my gaze, but I can see her answer, the fading of the last rays of light that steal all the warmth from this world.

My heart trips over my words as I beg her to stay. I need her to stay. "Siome, I can't do this without you. Don't leave me. *Please*. Please don't leave me." Leaning forward, I touch my forehead to hers. "I need you, baby. I need you."

She stays silent, and I cling to her, rubbing warmth into her cheek.

"Siome, Siome, listen to me, baby. You have to change back into your wolf. You'll heal faster."

*It won't work.*
*It will.*
*It has to.*

"Siome, baby, change for me." My voice cracks as I hold her, praying she listens.

But she doesn't move. Doesn't breathe. Just lies there in utter stillness as I desperately try to convince myself she isn't gone.

"No...no, Siome... Please, baby."

A broken howl screams from Vance's lungs, and I can no longer hide from the truth when it's so clearly ringing in my ears. Cannot pretend she will wake by keeping my eyes on her face instead of the rest of her body... *The rest of her body...* All gone. Taken by monsters in the shadows of a little girl.

My right hand tightens on Sau even as the left loosens on my mate's cheek. I hesitate for a second, then reach up and close her eyes, her beautiful red eyes I will never see again.

Turning from Siome, I stare at the little girl.

A murderer.

A witch.

A monument of all my grief and anger.

I wanted peace.

I wanted peace...

My hand crushes hers.

But I will settle for revenge.

# THREE
## HER
### 8 MAY 1917

I can't take my eyes off the babies resting in their mom's intestines even though he's hurting my hand. Only one of the three looks whole, their translucent body curled in tight, so small it would fit in the palm of my hand. The other two have been gnawed in half, their head and body crushed between teeth and pincers. Or maybe they were ripped apart by claws.

I've never entered the Plane of Monsters. I have no idea what the creatures look like. When my family travels as shadows, we flit on the edge of that place, not looking in, just opening it up to this world. Only strong witches can hold the portal open long enough for monsters to eat those who touch us in our shadows forms though, and excitement hits me that I'm one of them, momentarily overcoming my utter exhaustion and fear about being alone in the presence of wolves. Today was my first day using magic, and I can't wait to tell Father I –

My rising smile crumbles as the pain slams back into me. A burning cry lodges in my throat as Antonio turns to stare at me, and I remember his teeth around my father's neck.

"I hope she suffered," I say bitterly – suffered like my dad did, suffered like I am, and his face twists with a pain that spikes the pounding in my chest and between my ears.

Sucking in a sharp breath, I try to scoot away from him, but the white wolf grabs my shoulder, his claws stabbing into my flesh like knives. I scream as the agony hits me – so different to when Father beat me to trigger my ascension. Although the pain is similar, the fear inside me isn't. I always knew Father would stop when he beat me, knew the pain had a time of expiration and I would be healed immediately after.

But there is no knowledge of that in this moment.

No sign of the pain easing, no limitations to what this wolf will do now that the female wolf is dead.

"Get off her, Vance," Antonio Garcia says, but those words don't sound as protective as their meaning. They sound like a promise of his own pain that he'll soon be inflicting on me. *Don't hurt what's mine to break.*

My heart knocks behind my teeth as I finally realize that I'm alone in an alley with over a dozen wolves. Only the white one is in his monster form, but the others all emit a power that says they're not human.

"Let her go, Vance. Take Siome and our pups home."

A low whine comes from the white wolf as his claws dig deeper, making me cry. But then he's releasing me and gingerly moving towards the half corpse and her babies, where he drops to his knees as I scramble back as far as I can. The cracking of bones cuts through the quiet of his stare as the wolf shifts into a burly man with long blond hair. A few jackets are shrugged off and offered to him, and he uses them to gather up the organs of the woman.

## MADNESS BEHIND THE MASK

As Antonio rises to his feet and strides towards me, I glance up and down the alley but see no allies. My heart thunders inside of me as I realize I'm not going to survive this.

I'm going to die on the same day as Father.

Tears run down my cheeks as terror shakes me. I try to call on my magic, but a sharp pain explodes inside me and I scream. Father told me what would happen if I used magic while being too exhausted to control it – it would eat away at my organs, killing me rather than doing what I want.

Falling to my side, I curl up on the cobbled ground, my eyes rolling back in my head as I spasm in sharp jerks, my jaw locking so I can't scream. Voices shout around me, some familiar in the distance, but they can't pierce the agony rushing through my skull.

Heavy hands grab me.

And then I'm gone, lost to the world of the living...

---

I jerk awake, not dead but wishing it as I find myself sitting up in a dark room full of wolves. Their howls are what woke me, and I scramble away instinctively, only to cry out at the sudden pain flaring through my hands.

Tears burning my eyes, I look at them stretched above my head, overlapping. A large spike with a bulky head has been hammered through my palms. I can't control magic without my hands, and if I can't control it, calling on it will kill me.

My breaths come in sharp gasps. My eyes fly around the room, only to realize I am in the woods and it's long into the night. I've been nailed to a tree, and the wolves of the Death Hunt (for we all have trusted humans in our gangs) are in their animal forms, snarling and howling. They're circling around something on the ground, but between their rushing bodies, the sliver of the moon, and the tears blurring my vision, I can't make out what it is.

Biting my cheek to try not to sob, I wiggle my thumbs and pinkies. The rest of my fingers are useless, severed by the metal stake pushed through them. Even if I can find the courage to shove my palms deeper onto the spike to reach the head, I won't have the strength or movement to rip the thing out of the tree.

I am stuck and helpless.

A sob breaks through my bloody barrier of teeth and cheek, and then they're rushing free of me as I start to suck in quicker and quicker breaths, struggling to get the air in against the flow of pain leaving my lips.

*Don't cry, Sau. Don't cry.*

I'm a Shadow, and we don't...

We don't...

Rolling my lips in, I struggle to be the son my father wanted. But then I finally catch a glimpse of what they're doing, and a feminine scream ruptures from me, raw and with nothing to hold it back.

Antonio is in his werewolf form and is ripping apart the female who died in the alley with his teeth. The white wolf is tearing chunks off her arm. My stomach churns, but I can't take my eyes off them as the other wolves sit back and howl, their cries raising the hairs on my neck and arms.

Bile ruptures up my throat as her face pulls free, then disappears down Antonio's throat.

They loved her, but they're eating her.

So what will they do to their enemy?

# FOUR
## ANTONIO
### 8 MAY 1917

I have consumed many of our fallen, keeping their spirits alive inside of me, but the pain of eating my mate and children, having their blood all over my face, their bodies sitting heavily in my belly, it twists the purity of this ritual that is done to forever keep our loved ones with us. By consuming their flesh, we are granted their power, but I never should've outlived my children. Never should have tasted the flesh of their corpses.

Never should have let Sau fucking Shadow get to my mate.

My eyes snap to her as a tremor of rage rips through me. She sits with her skinny arms above her, her hands bleeding onto her dirty torn dress, her eyes frantically searching left and right for a savior that will never come. We are deep within Death Hunt territory, in the woods to the north of town. The witches chased us through the alleys of St.

Augustine, too slow to catch us even in our grief, but they stopped as soon as we entered these woods.

They will not come for her.

They will only wait for us to dispose of her body, and it will be on the doorstep of their home. They might have their entire street protected by magic to keep us out, but it won't stop me from throwing the pieces of her corpse through the barrier.

I wanted her death to be quick, a shot to the head she didn't even feel, but I know now there is no breaking this cycle of revenge, this two thousand year war that was triggered by her Family's greed to own the portal. There can only be death and suffering, and Sau will know both those things tonight.

My maw dripping with the blood of my family, I drop to my hands and knees as my body tears itself back into the shape of a man. My senses dwindle, still sharper than a human's but nowhere near that of a shifted werewolf. The smell of death isn't so strong, the rich copper taste of blood no longer overwhelming. My ability to see through the dark fades until I am forced to walk towards Sau to see her clearly.

I stop in front of her, heaving through all my pain.

She stares up at me with a child's fear, a knowing that lacks true comprehension of what horrors might befall her. Her imagination is limited by experience. Mine has been crafted by all the torture I have seen, the bodies I've consumed after they've been butchered by the witches and vampires.

I've seen skinned pups whose pelts were used to make jackets, bodies emptied of all their organs so they can be used in spells that kill more of our kind. I have witnessed grown werewolves being bled dry by a horde of vampires, unable to save them due to the vast quantity of enemies. Like a pack of hyenas against a male lion, outnumbering us twenty to one.

And then there are the werewolves that were made into examples, into warnings when we ventured too close to their business or killed someone too dear to the leaders. What was done to their bodies made them impossible to consume, their spirits forever lost to us.

Sau will be my message to the Shadow Domain.

*I am coming for you all.*

Slamming my hand into the spike, I hammer it deeper into her palms. She screams, throwing her head against the tree as her green eyes roll back, flashing white.

The pain shudders through her, convulsing her limbs, and my stomach twists at the sight of it. I never wanted to join the witches and vampires in their madness, never wanted to continue this pointless war. I killed the previous alpha in an attempt to lead us into peace.

Yet, here I am causing pain for the sake of pain.

My hand stills in the air, ready for the next blow as I look at her.

At the real *her*.

Not Sau fucking Shadow.

Not Delun's daughter.

Not an enemy to my people.

Just *her*.

A little girl in a wedding dress, forced into a life she can't truly comprehend.

She's a breeder.

A tool to create more soldiers.

Brainwashed into hating every werewolf, into wanting to kill us for reasons she doesn't understand.

Her life is not her own.

Standing here in front of her, naked in every sense of the word, I hesitate even as my pack howls for retribution. Her screams shift into whimpers as she shakes with her arms above her.

"Go ahead and kill me," she hisses, but the words are shaky and weak. "I will die with pride over having killed that bitch and her pups."

My eyes close briefly as the sorrow wraps me fully in its arms. Then my eyes snap open, and I hammer the spike all the way into the tree.

Her screams grind against the hairs on my arms and neck, but I no longer hesitate. No longer give her the benefit of the doubt about just being some victim to this madness like me.

Gripping her wrists with one hand, I yank them down hard, tearing the spike through the rest of her flesh until her hands split down the middle. Two fingers fall uselessly to both sides, a fountain of red spurting through the Vs I have just given her.

Jerking her up by her arms, I slam her against the tree; my other hand wraps around her throat. Her scream shifts into a sharp gasp as her eyes widen, then fades completely as I squeeze her neck.

"Her name was Siome." I lean forward, my face almost touching hers. "And her pups were *my* pups."

Her legs kick as I choke her. Her face goes red, then blue. I want it to go still, but death this way will be too quick, a mercy she doesn't deserve.

I drop my hand from her throat. She sucks in a great gasp, color flooding her cheeks as she heaves and coughs. Spittle flies as her eyes widen and narrow, the shock of not dying written all over her face.

"You ate them," she wheezes, still so much fight in her.

"You know *nothing*," I growl as I pivot and throw her into the center of the small clearing. The wolves in my pack pace restlessly, their eyes on her small body as it hits the ground and rolls. Their heads are low; their teeth are bared. They want blood, and I want to give it to them.

"All you know," I seethe as I stalk towards her as she lies

sprawled out on her stomach, "is how to spread your legs and be the good little whore your father taught you to be."

"I'm not a whor—"

I fist her hair and rip her head up off the ground. My other hand backslaps her across the face as I hold her still, not letting the energy pass naturally through movement, forcing her to take it all. Rage feeds my muscles, making them twitch with a need to hit her again. I want to tear her to pieces. I want to rip her apart like she ripped apart my mate, but that doesn't feel like enough. She needs to suffer more, be *punished* more. She needs to feel what it's like to be helpless, to have everything she's ever loved taken from her.

"You want to breed little witch soldiers?" I growl as I slam her head to the ground and grind her face into the dirt. She tries to twist free, clawing at the earth around her face in a desperate attempt to remove it so she can breathe. But her hands are all but useless, bleeding holes that fill with dirt.

I sit on her ass before yanking her head up, and she coughs loudly, flecks of brown shooting from her lips as half-decomposed leaves stick to her face. I pull her hair harder, arching her nearly in half so she can look up into my cold eyes.

"You want to be the good whore your father wanted?"

Her gaze widens, her little brain finally understanding where this is going. She starts to thrash against me, her small body carving gashes into the ground, but I'm easily twice her weight and many times her bulk.

There is nothing she can do to save herself just like there was nothing I could do to save Siome, nothing my mate could do to save our pups.

My anger pushes blood through my cock, lifting it and making it hard. I focus on the feel of my rage rather than Sau's body, which looks so different to Siome's. Although werewolves are rarely monogamous, and the alpha is able to sleep with all the females in his pack, Siome was my first and only. She was all I ever wanted.

But now she's been taken from me.

And I'm left with this poor substitute who all I want to do is make bleed.

"Get off me!" she screams, her voice high-pitched and frantic, and I hover over her for a quick moment, just long enough to turn her over onto her back, hike up her dress, and tear through the fabric of her undergarments. Then I am back on her, my naked thighs hitting her naked flesh.

Concentrating on my hand, I shift just it into the form of my wolf, claws extending from my fingers. Dragging them down her ass, leaving red lines of rage, I line one up with her pussy.

"Sto–aaaaaaaaah!" She screams out in pain as I push a claw into her, making sure to be rough, cutting as much of her insides as I can. She tries to drag herself across the ground, away from me, but my weight is fully on her legs.

My pack howls their approval around us, and Vance charges over in his white wolf form. He stops beside her head, his eyes on me as he waits for my permission to join. He is four times her size in his current form, and if he fucks her, he'll kill her.

"Shift," I demand, not wanting her to die that quickly even though the damage she would suffer through broken bones, a snapped spine, and a force heavy enough to pop her lungs would be nothing short of what she deserves.

I want her to suffer more.

More than she can ever fathom.

Vance does as demanded, then kneels beside her face. Sau hasn't looked at him yet, probably hasn't even noticed him, her entire world focused on the pain inside her. I curl my finger, hooking my claw into more flesh, and she cries out as tears flood down the sides of her eyes.

Her entire purpose in life is to breed; that is the only thing she knows, and I am taking this from her. Breaking her in more ways than one.

I pull my finger back, then shove forward again, and she jerks on a scream as my claw ruptures through the front of her pussy.

"Stop!" she begs, but she doesn't get to say another word as Vance fists her hair and angles her head towards his naked hips. He shoves his cock into her mouth and fucks her hard as he growls out his pain and anger.

She jerks between the two of us, desperately trying to get away despite not knowing which way to go. Her body is a twitching mess of blood and tears, and I lift my head to look at the rest of my pack.

Although the majority of them are females, there are six other men watching us punish the woman who killed our queen and future heirs.

Not one of them looks willing to help her despite the talks of peace just three months ago, of not continuing the cycle of abuse in the name of revenge.

Their howls quiet as they watch me, the only noise the wet sucking of Vance's dick and his harsh breaths as he moves.

"Shift," I say to them, and they instantly drop to the ground to turn back into man. "Then come here and make your own holes."

A few of the women glance at each other, but all the men move without hesitation. They're betas, submissives; a wolf pack full of testosterone-filled budding alphas will tear itself apart. But the women have the freedom to be anything they want, and a few of them look uncertain with what we're doing. I hold the gaze of a red wolf with a black patch between her eyes. She bares her teeth, then she turns and snaps at the women beside her, giving her own commands. A few glance at me in uncertainty, but as one, they turn and disappear into the trees.

My eyes scan the remaining women. "Find a stick," I growl. They shift into their human forms, then start to look around the forest floor for thick makeshift dildos that will allow them to participate with the men.

I turn my attention back to Sau as the first men reach us. None of them can partially shift, so I raise my free hand and flex my new claws. "Pick your spot," I say.

Hands grab her everywhere, her body too small to take them all at once. Chest, side, throat, stomach. I shove a claw above her left nipple, opening up a hole, and she cries around her moving gag.

The men shove each other to be the first, but just as one's about to enter her, I growl a warning and they all still. Removing my claw from Sau's pussy, I shuffle to the same side of her body Vance is on and twist her onto her side so I can line up my cock with the hole I made in her pussy.

"You want to be bred, you little whore? Want your stomach swollen with seed?"

My tip pushes past the tear in her skin, and she jerks on a whimper, trying to get away from me. The edges of the hole rip further, delicate skin shredding beneath my hard thrust.

"Then you can bear my fucking children, and watch as they kill the rest of your family," I growl, slamming inside her with one smooth stroke. She spasms beneath me, her pain evident in the shaking of her body. But I'm not in all the way, the back of her pussy stopping me. In a moment, I'll cut her deeper with a claw, tearing into her anal canal sideways, but for now, I'm content to just fuck away my frustration in the hole already there.

The men scramble, hands on their cocks, in an attempt to shove into the hole I made in her chest. A couple grab the flaps of her hands and wrap them around their cocks. But just as the females join us with their sticks, a warning howl cuts through the woods.

My eyes snap to Vance as we all freeze. The howl was warning us of witches, our variation of pitch and length giving us a limited range of communication while in our animal forms.

"*Shift!*" I roar as I drop Sau's body and start to change myself. As naturally resistant as we are to magic, we're more vulnerable in our human forms. Vance screams as a spray of bullets pepper his shoulders and neck. They're using magic-enhanced guns to be able to fire so accurately and around the trunks of trees. The fuckers might not even be in the woods. Caden Davenport's telekinesis has a long range, which is why I hoped to end their marriage before it began.

I whip my head around as my maw extends and fangs drop through my gums. My claws dig into the earth as I release Sau's broken body to search the trees around us. Long range or not, Caden can't aim without eyes on the area, and there isn't a whiff of another type of animal nearby. So if he's not using a familiar, then he has to be using a scry.

My gaze darts through the branches until I spot a sheen of the air flickering like a summer haze above us and to the right. So slight, it was easily missed in our overconfidence that they would not enter these woods. Growling, I run towards a tree beneath the scry even as another warning howl is sounded by the same wolf, which means the witches are not aiming for her.

They're focusing all their magic on the wolves around Sau, the majority of whom haven't finished their change. It's a process that gets faster with age and power, but very few of us live that long.

Launching myself at the tree, I jump at another and push off that one too, zigzagging up to the scry. Bullets curve around branches to aim straight at me. I reach out a clawed hand, only needing a single swipe through the scry to break it. Pain explodes in my side as a bullet enters and starts to burrow towards my heart.

Growling, I slash my claws through the rippling air, hoping the fucker can see the murderous promise in my eyes. A chill raises the hairs on my arm as I start to fall back to the ground, and the rest of the bullets continue upwards, no longer moving at unnatural angles. The one inside me stills too. The scry broken, I land on all fours and turn towards Sau. They're not going to save –

*She's gone!*

Snarling, I run over to where she was, but I don't need to sniff the area to tell who was here. There's only one way they could've managed to rescue her. David Shadow came in under all our noses, using the camouflage of night and moving branches and sucked her into his shadow. If he took anyone else into the Plane of Monsters, they'd already be dead, but the Shadows are somehow able to enter that plane and survive. The bullets were merely a distraction, not meant to do much damage. The scry was in the exact right position to get me away...

"Anton..." Vance's voice cuts into my thoughts and building rage at losing Sau just when I was about to have her.

Twisting on my feet, I turn to him, my eyes widening when I see he's still in his human form. He should have changed by now. He knows he'll heal faster as his wolf.

And that's when I smell it.

That's when I see it too.

And *feel* it.

The slight burn in my side. The weakening of my muscles. The retreat of my wolf. They've laced the bullets with a potion that smells of bitter almonds and the sick sweetness of death. One dosage does not feel like it is enough to kill us –the poison inside me is weak– but there are six in my brother-in-law, and each hole has green lines branching out from it.

My heart racing, I dig a claw into my side, fishing for the bullet. I drop it on the ground as I shift and fall to my knees beside him. I turn him over to see glassy blue eyes staring up at me.

"Just hold on, Vance. I'm going to get these out." My throat tightens, and I shift one finger back into a claw, but he shakes his head ever so weakly.

"No time... Kill them, An..."

My arms tighten around him as I feel his life bleed out onto the damp ground. His body stills. His chest no longer moves, and I scream out my grief, which doesn't seem to end.

I've lost everyone and everything. My entire family in one day. My past wishes for peace, my future hopes for what could be. There is nothing inside me but this hole that is filling all too quickly with a rage that feels good enough to keep.

"I will, Vance," I promise as I kiss his forehead before laying him on the ground and standing. "I will kill every last fucking witch in the Shadow Domain."

Howls ring out all around me as the rest of the wolves realize Vance is gone. Circling, I address them all, my body shaking with the force of my emotions. "There will be no more talks of peace," I hiss. "If anyone is against that, leave now."

I still, waiting for someone to make a move, but no one does. Even the women who left earlier, who've since come back, stand strong with the rest.

My people.

My Family.

The only one I have now.

Opening myself up to all the rage, I snap out orders to reinforce our borders. As everyone scatters in groups to do as commanded, I turn back to Vance's body.

There's too much of a risk to consume it. The poison might still be potent. His spirit will be lost to us forever, unable to join us in this fight.

I kneel beside him, look into his eyes one last time, and then close them to give him a false semblance of peace.

"I will kill them all, Vance," I vow.

And among their scattered corpses, I *will* get my alone time with Sau.

# PART TWO:

## A LOVING SPOUSE

# FIVE
## CADEN
### 31 NOVEMBER 1908

*Twelve years ago...*

"She's going to be yours one day, Caden."

I can barely hear my father's words over the wailing baby. He stands beside her crib on the opposite side of it to Delun Shadow, who doesn't smile, his gaze hard on mine.

The man is intimidating, his dark-brown eyes nearly black. It doesn't help that all the stories I have heard of Delun have either ended in a gruesome death or the person wishing for it. He's the Boss of the Shadow Domain, and he has been wanting us to join his Family for years, but Father wants it to be on equal footing rather than just as disposable soldiers. Our family is rich, and we're just as infamous as them up in New York, but we're still not in the same league as the Shadows. We need a bargaining chip to join their table, and that chip is me.

## MADNESS BEHIND THE MASK

It is rare enough for a witch to have natural talent in telepathy, telekinesis, or astral projection, but I am a witch prodigy, gifted in long range telekinesis. With her genetic shadow magic, our children will be a new generation of unstoppable...if she lives long enough to bear them.

Without them, my family can't take over the Shadow Domain. The Boss can only ever be a Shadow or a father of one, so our alliance banks on her surviving the next ten or so years.

I'll be twenty-three then... That seems like a long –

"Caden," Father says, a tightness around his words. My eyes snap to him as adrenaline floods my body, expecting a slap or some other form of discipline. But he just smiles at me, which makes me feel more on edge.

"Yes, Father?" I ask over the baby's wails.

"Come see her."

"She's crying."

"She's a baby. She won't cry forever."

I glance at Delun and suck in a breath as I slowly take a step forward. The dark wood of the crib seems ominous in a way I can't explain. Almost like dark clouds rolling in the distance. A crack of thunder sounds in the depths of my mind as my hairs stand on end.

But I don't stop walking, don't dare ignore my father's orders and Delun's clear expectancy. The Shadows are in the middle of a war, and he needs our magic to win it. He would not be pleased if I refused this agreement...not that I really have a choice in the matter.

Father told me very clearly that if I refused, he would kill Myers and Dermont, my two younger brothers. They aren't as gifted as I, aren't as valuable, and he knows I love them. Will do anything for them.

Swallowing, feeling the electricity in the air sharpen, I take those final steps up to the crib.

Suddenly, the thunder clouds break, pierced by a ray of

sunshine as I look down at the little girl's face.

*She's so tiny...*

Not much bigger than both my hands.

She stops crying as she looks up at me, lying on her back in a blue onesie that matches her light-sky eyes. She is the ugliest baby I've ever seen, but there's something about her, something soft and sweet that makes me smile.

"What's her name?" I ask, not looking up, not wanting to break the connection pulling us together.

"I haven't named her yet," Delun says, his voice like rumbling gravel. "Pick."

I glance up in surprise.

"She is to be yours," he says simply, and I glance back down, studying the little baby once more.

*She is mine...*

I like that.

Reaching forward, I bop her nose. Her eyes followed my finger until they couldn't, and now she looks silly as well as ugly and sweet.

"Sau," I say softly, not sure where that came from but liking it.

When Delun doesn't say anything, I look up at him, shifting on my feet.

"Why?" he asks.

I shrug.

"'Sau' means 'defender,' and she is a woman."

*But she'll defend a part of me no one else can.*

And I'll be her defender too.

My tongue heavy, uncertain under his gaze despite the strong, sure beat of my heart, I shrug again. "I like it."

He studies me a second longer, then nods.

My smile spreads wide across my face as I look down at her again.

"Sau," I say softly.

My little sweet Sau.

## MADNESS BEHIND THE MASK

*I will cherish you forever.*
*And protect you forever too.*

# SIX
## CADEN
### 16 MAY 1917

*Present day...*

"Is she awake yet?" David Shadow asks as he settles in the chair beside me. It's been eight days since we rescued my wife from the wolves. When David brought her out of his shadow –his family able to use it as an etheric storage unit– I thought she was dead. She was so still, and the amount of blood covering her looked too much to survive losing.

But her mama and two other healers worked on her for three days, and on the fourth, they assured me she was stable and all her injuries healed. They even managed to put her hands back together so she can access her magic without it killing her.

And yet, she hasn't woken.

Hasn't once fluttered her green eyes open, them having

changed from the baby blue of her birth, before going back to sleep.

I slouch in my chair, staring at her blank face, my long legs stretched out in front of me in the most comfortable position I can manage, yet still my muscles ache, cramped from being in this same black chair, in roughly this same position for the last eight days.

"You need to get some rest, Caden," David says.

"I have been."

"In a proper bed." He turns to me. "Delun's passing is tomorrow, and you're expected to give a speech."

I glance at him, my eyes narrowing. The Shadows don't do funerals, instead sucking the bodies of their fallen into the Plane of Monsters, then hosting a service afterwards called a passing.

"My Family will not join yours until we have an heir," I say. I'm not going to let this situation manipulate me into turning my Family into disposable soldiers. Until my seat on the Shadow Domain throne is secure, they will not get our undying support.

He raises a brow. "You'll let the werewolves' crimes go unpunished?"

Anger rises at the dishonor he's hinting at. "This is your war."

"She is your wife."

My fingers twitch with the urge to use my magic to snap his neck. His shadows won't save him from me; my power affects the atomic levels, so whether he's man or shadow, I can kill him.

But he is Sau's beloved uncle, and my Family will not win a war against them. The humans have started to take over our home turf in New York as we cannot compete with their numbers without revealing our magic. We have suffered too many losses as is.

And despite what I told David, I will not let Antonio get

away with hurting my wife. I will kill him; it just won't be for the Shadow Domain. No one hurts what's mine.

And Sau is now mine in every sense of the word, not just in a future promise between our fathers.

"I know what she is," I say slowly, letting each word ring in the air between us. "And I know what she *isn't*. And what she *isn't* is something for you to try to use against me. Treat her as a pawn again, and I will kill you with my own fucking hands."

His jaw locks, and my magic hums in my every vein, waiting for him to do something stupid. He has at least fifteen years on me, all of that hard experience, but he is a second son who's found himself in the role of leader. I was trained for it since the moment I was born. He will not kill me easily even with his infamous shadow magic and his illusionary spells – spells that won't work on me given I can use my telekinesis to discern what's real and what's not, and he knows it.

Relaxing his clenched teeth, he bares them in a devil's smile. "I only wish to protect my family. I'm sure you can respect that."

I nod subtly, not giving him anything more as my gaze moves back to my wife. Whether I can respect his reasons or not, that will not stop me from killing him. Something he now knows.

"If you bed her now," he says casually, shifting in his chair to face me fully, "we can tell if she's pregnant in a fortnight. Then will you pledge your loyalty and those of your Family to the Shadow Domain?"

My eyes snap to him. My jaw clenches at what he is suggesting. "She is still in a coma," I growl.

"She would be willing if she were awake. It is what she is for."

"What the wolves did to her –"

He leans forward. "And that's exactly why you should do

it now. So she doesn't relive any of that trauma."

My jaw starts to ache with how tightly it's locked. I saw the horrors of her experience through that scry. Saw Vance fucking her mouth as she cried around him. Even though Antonio would have been the more strategic kill, I could not leave the white wolf alive after watching him take what's mine.

My hands clench, my fingers wishing they were around that fucker's neck. I wanted to jerk his corpse out of the woods with my power so I could desecrate it further, but Antonio destroyed my 'eyes,' and using my telekinesis that far out requires me to 'see' in one way or another. Otherwise, it gets too hard for me to distinguish what's what with too many atoms in my way.

"We need your support soon if we're to survive this," David presses. "Antonio has lost his entire family, and he will come for us. I'm surprised he hasn't already."

"He's not reckless," I say. "He'll make a plan first."

Over the last eight days, I've had my two brothers find out everything they can about Antonio and the rest of the Death Hunt. Although when we join the Shadow Domain, I'll be fighting the vampiric Blood Fangs as well, Aleric's gang is not my priority. I want Antonio's head mounted on my wall and his pelt laid out in a rug on our floor.

There are whispers of Antonio planning something big. He wants nothing less than to have the entire Shadow Domain wiped from existence. But he will wait years if he needs to, dangerously patient. Then again, he could strike tomorrow if all is how he wants it.

Time is not a luxury we have. And if Sau wakes and is too traumatized by what they did to her...

"Do it now," David says as he stands. "I'll make sure you're not disturbed."

Heading for the door, he leaves me alone with my wife.

# SEVEN
## CADEN
### 16 MAY 1917

She doesn't move when I stand.

She doesn't move when I sit on the edge of the bed.

She doesn't move even when I drag the covers down her small body, revealing her white nightgown.

She just lies there, completely dead to the world, and I reach forward to check her pulse, pressing two fingers to her neck. It beats steadily beneath my tips, and I take solace in the fact that she isn't *completely* dead. She just looks it with how still she is. Even her chest barely moves.

"Wake up, Sau," I whisper as I watch her expressionless face. Not a flicker of an eyelid. Not a twitch of the brow. She looks entirely peaceful.

Perhaps what David said *is* for the best. Perhaps she would rather get pregnant this way rather than when she is awake.

My stomach twists, not on board with this at all. She is

so small, so young, and so utterly voiceless. What if I do something she doesn't like? What if I go too fast? What if she wants me to stop? She is a virgin...

The churning intensifies, bubbling up my throat as I stare at the woman I vowed to defend. Who I promised I would take it slow with, let her lead on our wedding night when I found her shaking with nerves the night before.

She wanted our first time to be special.

*I* want that too...

But if I don't do this, I could lose everything my father wants for this family. I could lose what I was promised all those years ago – control of one of the most, if not *the* most, powerful witch Families in all of the US. Worse...I could lose my two young brothers. I am not naive enough to think Father will not punish them for my reluctance.

At the thought of him, my spine grows rigid. I have seen the bruises he leaves on Mother, the fear he ruptures in her eyes. I swore I would never do those things to my wife.

But here I am.

My hands tied.

"What do you want me to do, Sau?" I ask, tracing my fingers up to her cheek. "I need to get you pregnant." Not just for my seat on the throne but for hers. If she doesn't give this Family an heir, David will become Boss, robbing her of her birthright. Then Father will kill Sau so I can become a widow and marry again. Perhaps to Cara Jervis or Terra Harrison – two powerhouses in the Midwest who are currently at war with each other; either will benefit from our alliance.

"I can't lose you, Sau," I say, having come to the only conclusion that's available to us. Leaning forward, I kiss her forehead, then hover over her lips. A bolt of desire shoots through me as my eyes flick to them. I haven't kissed her since our wedding. We didn't get the wedding night we should've, and my need for her starts to thicken my cock. I lean forward...

Then snap back, shame filling me.

She is asleep.

She can't say no.

It would be wrong.

But I have to get her pregnant, or the both of us will lose everything.

Standing, I strip off my clothes, keeping my eyes on her face. She doesn't move, doesn't wake. Naked, I crawl back onto the bed, my cock soft. I hike up her thin gown, dragging it slowly up her thighs. With it bunched at her waist, I kneel over her and grip my cock, stroking it to get hard. I don't need to actually fuck her to get her pregnant. I just need to push my come inside her. This way, our first time can still be special, and we can have the heirs we need.

But my hand isn't feeding my arousal. My cock stays limp regardless of how many times I pump it.

Frustration building, I drag my eyes off her face and linger on her small breasts. Perhaps if I saw them...

My lips part and my cock jumps at the idea. I can imagine the feel of them beneath my hands, the lightness of her skin that's never seen the sun. Bared just for me.

My cock hardens even as guilt and shame slam into me. It'd be wrong to strip her without her permission, but...I can't get her pregnant if I can't get hard.

Hesitating for just a moment longer, I use my magic to sit her upright. Then I pull her nightgown over her head. She still doesn't wake, doesn't bat a single eyelash, and I drop my eyes to her naked chest.

A groan rumbles from me at the sight of her bared for my pleasure. I reach a hand forward to cup one. It's so small, so soft, and entirely mine. Lying her back down with my magic, I fondle her breasts as I grip my cock. It's a lot harder now, arousal pumping through me as I play with my wife. I pinch her nipple in between my fingers as my other hand strokes myself. Another groan is pulled from me as my cock becomes sensitive, now reacting to every brush of my palm.

"You're so beautiful, Sau," I say as I look back up to her face. She still hasn't moved at all, and I take that as this isn't hurting her, isn't registering any differently to when I sat over in the chair. My arousal building, I lean forward to kiss her.

Her mouth is so soft, and I rub my lower lip against hers, kissing her gently as I hold myself up on one elbow and pump my cock with my other hand. I imagine her virgin pussy gripping me, and I groan once more. My tongue pushes past her lips, sweeping inside to taste her. *It is my right*, I tell myself. *I am her husband. She would want this. It's okay...*

And I'll take it slow. Be gentle.

Pre-cum wetting my hand on the upstroke, I hiss in a breath. Then I trail my lips down her neck, sucking and licking as I imagine her as she should be, arching up into me, her hands in my hair, her breaths coming fast as she begs me to fill her.

"I'm going to kill Antonio for taking this from me," I whisper as I kiss my way down to her breasts. I lick one fully, swirling my tongue around her nipple. "From *us*," I say as I take her into my mouth. The small pebble of hers grows hard beneath the caresses of my tongue and lips, and I groan as I tighten the grip on my cock. Pumping myself harder, I suck on her gently, then move over to her other breast.

My cock throbs on the verge of release, and I remove my hand from it to pull down her undergarments. Moving my lips back to her first breast, I swirl my tongue around it and grab my cock again. I pump it faster, in tune to my quickened breaths.

Feeling myself about to come, I angle my hips to line

myself up with her pussy.

But at the feel of her pussy lips caressing the head of my cock, my mouth pops off her breast, and I lean up to claim her lips once more. My arousal builds tight in my balls, the tip of my cock becoming blindingly sensitive. Too much. Too good. Too *wrong* in its further demands.

I don't want to just come on her thighs and push it into her. I want to bury my cock inside my wife. I want her legs to wrap around me as I slam into her. I want to take what Antonio tried to, to make her fully mine, to wipe his touch off her.

Groaning against her mouth, I concentrate on my magic. I need her to kiss me, and she does, directed by the power of my telekinesis.

Her tongue strokes mine, demanding I fuck her. One of her hands comes between us to cup my balls, and I hiss against her lips. "That's it, Sau," I say even though I'm the one controlling her, the one making her do the things I want. "Show me you want this, sweet girl."

Her other hand wraps around my cock, and she slides my head back and forth between her lips, wetting herself with my precum and me with her own arousal. She wants this so fucking much, she's reacting even inside her coma.

My cock thickens so hard it hurts, and I want to ram into her, bury myself in her fully. But her hands come up to my head and push me down, demanding I take it slow like I promised. "I'm sorry," I say as I shudder, reigning my desires back under control. Kissing my way down her throat to her breasts, I suck on each of them before going further south. She arches against me, her fingers tight in my hair as she guides me where she wants me.

Spreading her legs, I stare at the lips wet with precum and desire. Groaning, I lean forward and kiss one inner thigh, then the other, taking my time, going slow like she wants me to.

Her fingers dig deep into my scalp, and she rocks her hips up against me. I wish I could hear her groan, but my magic can't get her to do that, so I am left with the silence of her coma as I kiss her right in the center

The taste of her rocks me, and my cock jerks with a flair of desire too demanding to resist. Burying my head between her legs, I lick the full length of her over and over and over again until she's soaking the bed beneath my chin. And still, I can't get enough.

My cock painfully hard, I push it into the mattress to relieve just a bit of the pressure. I don't rock my hips much though, knowing that I am only a few pumps away from finishing.

And still I keep my head between her legs, my fingers holding her open as I eat her out until I can't remember what it's like not having her taste on my tongue.

My cock throbbing, my balls pulled up tight, I finally pull my lips away from hers. If I don't bury myself inside her right this moment, I'm going to waste my cum all over her sheets.

Kissing her again, spreading the taste of her pussy all inside her mouth, I groan against her lips as I reach down and grab my cock. Lining it up with her soaking wet hole, I push in just the tip. Pleasure explodes inside me, arching down to my balls, and they pull up so tight, I can't help but growl, needing to express my desire.

Feeling her pussy spread for me, I lose all control and slam in. She whimpers beneath my lips, and I raise my head to see her face twisting with pain. Horrified, I pull back to slide out of her, but the movement has her feeling too good against me, and my body shaking, I slam back in, unable to help myself, to stop myself.

Burying my head against her neck, I kiss the base of her throat. "It's only going to hurt for a moment," I rasp as I pull back out, convincing myself her whimper was one of pleasure. "But I can't stop now, Sau. You understand that, don't you?"

Cupping one of her tits in my hand, I push my cock back into her. "You understand you make me feel too good to stop?" I rock my hips, groaning at the blinding pleasure that flairs through my cock and balls as her pussy slides against my length, wet and tight and *mine*.

I pinch her nipple, all my weight on my other arm as I suck her skin into my mouth, marking the base of her neck.

She whimpers again, but it's not as loud this time and sounds more like desperate need. "That's it, sweet girl," I growl against her. "You take my cock inside you like a good little wife. You feel so good. So *fucking* good. You're going to make me come so quick." I groan as I thrust into her harder, slamming all the way in before pulling back just to slam in again. "Fuck," I hiss as the pleasure builds to unimaginable heights.

My breath ragged, my body slick with sweat, I thrust in one more time and come all inside my wife. Throwing my head back, I growl as my cock pulses, shooting out cum in the strongest orgasm I've ever had.

I collapse against her, my chest pounding, my cock still going, filling her up until it leaks out to my balls. I kiss her neck, then lift my head, hoping she's awake.

But her eyes still stayed glued shut. My sleeping beauty who cares not to be woken by her prince.

My heart squeezing, I kiss her gently on the lips, then pull out of her. Rolling her onto her side, I crawl in behind her and wrap my arm around her. Sliding my cock back into her soaking wet pussy, I kiss her shoulder, then close my eyes, following her into sleep.

# EIGHT
## HER
### 16 MAY 1917

I can't breathe.

There's a weight on my chest.

Or maybe it's my punctured lung still.

There was a warmth that flowed through me...at some point... *I can't quite...*

Everything is fuzzy, wrapped in layers I can't break, and it's making me breathe rapidly.

I whimper, feeling the pain of Antonio's claw all over again.

*Wait...*

*Over again?*

Does that mean it's not happening now?

My eyes burn with tears, but I can't feel them on my cheeks. Are they falling or just pooling behind my lids?

My eyelids are closed.

For some reason that matters.
But I can't...
I can't figure it out.
Why it matters.
More tears pool.

I want the pain to stop. I want to push them off me. Vance's dick is in my mouth. Antonio's hand...is there. In me. Tearing me. Making holes in my body so the rest of his pack can fuck me like the whore he's trying to make me. His golden eyes glare down at me as his lips curl.

"You're such a whore...my sweet Sau."

*I'm not a whore.*
*I'm a wife.*
*I'm Caden's wife.*

I want to scream, but I'm helpless and unable to move as Antonio's body presses down on me. His hands grope me everywhere now, not just down *there*. I want to kick him off. I want to shove him or hit him with my magic, but not a single muscle listens to me.

His lips are on my neck. They're soft and moving with words I don't yet hear.

They're fuzzy, like he's far away.

But that can't be right.

Because he's on me.

I can *see* him.

*Feel* him.

Antonio's on *me*.

*"Get off me! Get off me! Get off me!"*

His hand covers the left side of my chest, but it isn't rough, and there isn't any pain of a claw this time. No hole in my lungs. It's easier to breathe. His palm rubs against my small breast, and a burst of something other than terror shoots through me. I don't want to feel any pleasure though. I don't want to turn into a whore.

But he's rolling my nipple between his fingers, and my

breath catches as heat floods me. I tremble with disgust and desire, torn between the two of them.

"My sweet, sweet Sau." Antonio's other hand trails up my thigh, causing me to tense. Light paths stroke against my skin though, gentle caresses that make it too hard for me to hate.

Even though I want to hate him.

Hate his touch.

Keep myself pure for Caden.

He's my husband.

I'm not a whore.

*I'm not a whore...*

*I'm not.*

A small whimper escapes my lips, the first noise I have managed to make. His body presses more firmly on me. His lower hand travels up as his lips graze across my skin. He licks up my neck as his fingers reach me *there*, and I tense on another whimper.

And then I scream, but my lips don't move anymore, the noise just inside my head, loud and shrill and full of panic and desperation for him to get off me. I can feel his claw ripping me apart as he pushes deep, then draws out.

"You're so wet," he murmurs as he sinks back into me.

*"I'm not a whore."*

"You're such a fucking whore."

His mouth closes over mine, and I can't stop his tongue from entering me. It strokes against mine, feeling too big for my mouth. I don't like the taste of him. I try to turn my head, but it doesn't move. He groans against me, his finger moving faster, and I squeeze my eyes shut, as well as my thighs, hoping to push him out.

When his hand moves away, I nearly sag with relief, but then there's a sharper pain, a bigger thing filling me down there, and I cry out against his lips.

"Sau?"

I freeze at the sound of Caden's voice even as my body trembles.

*What is he doing here?*

I don't want him to see me like this. Don't want him to think I'm some whore getting fucked by a wolf.

"Squeeze me, sweet girl," Antonio says as he thrusts into me. I turn my head, but my gaze finds Caden's as he peers out of the woods suddenly surrounding us, his green eyes wide in disgust.

*"Don't look at me!"* I scream, but the words don't leave my throat. They just sit there, suffocating me.

I can't breathe again.

My pulse pounds in my ears as I try to fight Antonio off me.

But none of my muscles move. I'm completely helpless. All I can do is scream words no one can hear.

*"Get off me!"*

*"Caden, don't look."*

*"I'm not a whore..."*

*"I'm not a whore."*

Antonio's lips are on my mouth again. He pushes his tongue into mine, swirling it around mine as his cock slams into me. It hurts so much but not more than the pain of Caden's stare.

"You're a fucking whore," he says, breaking my heart. "So enjoy it like one."

I cry as Antonio's thrusts get faster.

"Just relax and enjoy it."

*But I don't want to.*

*I don't want...*

*I'm not a whore...*

I turn my head from Caden, unable to bear looking at him while Antonio fucks me, his hands everywhere on my body – squeezing my nipples, rubbing above where he's entering me, grabbing my hips and lifting them up so that I now meet him with every thrust.

He circles his finger on my clit and groans against my neck as he pumps faster into me. An unwanted, shameful heat builds inside my belly despite how much I wish to keep it down. I know what it is, know that a girl should enjoy sex, but I don't want to enjoy it with him.

*Don't want to...*

I whimper as I squeeze around him, feeling sick as I'm dragged to the edge of my orgasm.

Mama told me I would like it.

All the other women in the Family agreed.

But I don't like it now.

Don't want it.

Squeezing my eyes shut, I cry in the silent prison that is my own body even as that heat floods through me, the dam opening as my hips lift of their own accord, faster and faster until I pulse around his cock.

Antonio falls against me on a groan, kissing my neck, then my lips, his body slick with sweat. Sex fills the air, and when he pulls out of me, his cum trickles down my thigh. Reaching between us, he pushes it back in, his finger lingering against me.

I want him to leave.

I just want him to leave.

My eyes wet behind my lids, I cry without shame when he finally goes, though where, I'm not entirely sure.

But all too quickly, he returns.

And his cock rams into me.

Over.

And over.

And over again.

*Please just make it stop...*

# NINE
## HER
### DATE UNKNOWN

It all feels different this time. There aren't any leaves beneath me. No twigs digging into my neck and back. No damp earth rubbing against my thighs as I'm shoved into the ground by the weight on top of me.

I'm on something soft. Something that creaks as I'm moved in forceful thrusts that burn between my thighs.

Someone is in me.

But it's not Antonio.

He doesn't smell like him. Isn't as heavy. Doesn't move the same or punishes me like the werewolf does. He's just fucking me, groaning against my neck as he gets himself off on my body.

My eyes flicker open.

There's a ceiling above me, not the open sky blocked by the moving of trees. I don't understand. Where is the sky? Where is Antonio?

But then I notice it. The floral wallpaper. Dusty blue with pink flowers and dark-green leaves.

I'm in my bedroom.

I'm home.

*I'm...home.*

Tears burn my eyes as I focus on a pink flower, using it to pull myself out of the sluggish fog filling my brain. My eyes trail back and forth as I'm moved, and the man on top of me groans.

My blood chilling, I finally put the pieces together.

I'm home...but I'm still being raped.

My Family saved me.

They *saved* me, so why am I still being raped?

Screaming, I try to throw the man off me, but my limbs are heavy. So confusingly heavy like I've slept on them or they've not been used in a long time. But I *just* used them to fight Antonio...

The man's head snaps up as he stills inside me. His dark-brown eyes widen, his mouth dropping open in a small gasp.

"Geovme!" My voice is broken and raspy, my throat seemingly unable to make the words in my head. Thunder roars between my ears as panic squeezes the air from my lungs.

"Shhh. Be quiet." He lifts a hand, and knowing it's to go over my mouth, I lift up with all the energy I have and bite his nose.

He screams as he jerks beneath my teeth, but I latch on, locking my jaw as tears roll down my cheeks. This can't be happening. I won't let it. First Antonio, and then this man. Caden will never want me...

The man's hand closes around my neck. My eyes bug, and my teeth start to fall off his nose, but I dig my teeth into him deeper and wrench my head sideways. The wet tearing of flesh is followed by his savage roar as I spit out the chunk of flesh from between my lips. Blood squirts all over my face from his gashing hole as he squeezes the air from me on heavy whimpers. I gasp silently as my vision starts to fade...

And then he's screaming as his hand explodes without blood and he's wrenched straight up. He hovers over me, and I scoot back until I hit the wall, my chest heaving with the same terror in his eyes.

I scream again as he's flung to the ceiling and pinned there.

"Sau!" a man shouts, demanding my attention, and I turn my head to the left, seeing someone who looks like...

*"Mr. Davenport?"* I rasp, the words intelligible as they meet the air.

"Caden," he murmurs as he walks towards me, his cold eyes softening, and my heart thunders louder with every step he takes.

I press my back against the wall as close as I can, a small whimper escaping me as I bring up my knees. This can't be Caden. He's too old. Almost the same age as my father.

I shake my head, but my gaze doesn't leave him. "You can't..." I swallow, trying so hard to make the words sound right. "Be..."

He sits down slowly on the bed, his green eyes on me. They're so familiar to my husband's... Tears blur my eyes as I continue to shake my head. But he can't be. He *can't*.

"Dad?"

A man rushes into the room, and my gaze flies to him. He freezes as soon as our eyes meet, the tense mien of his face slackening into one of disbelief.

"Caden?" I squeak, scrambling off the bed towards him, finally realizing that Mr. Davenport didn't call himself Caden but called *for* him. My feet hit the ground and take none of my weight, my legs collapsing in an instant.

The man lunges forward, opening his arms to catch me,

but I'm frozen long before he reaches me, caught by his telekinesis.

"Leave us, Leon," the man behind me says.

"But –"

"Take him and find out who let him in here."

The man on the ceiling is flung at the door, his screams turning into pleas of mercy that don't reach my heart. I don't care what happens to him. I just want to go to my husband...who for some reason has changed his name to Leon?

My mouth opens on a cry as I'm pulled back onto the bed. Caden/Leon leaves me, dragging my rapist behind him, his knuckles white in a grip promising death.

"Sau..." the man behind me says, a tinge of familiarity in his voice. "My sweet, sweet Sau."

I shudder at that phrase, my mind going back to my wedding just the other day. Caden said those four words as he cupped my cheek and kissed me.

"Sau, sweetheart," he murmurs again as I'm set on the bed, the force of the telekinesis lifting from my limbs. He shifts in front of me, forcing my gaze off the door and onto his green eyes.

My mouth drops open further as I look into them, tears blurring my vision. "I don't...under..."

"Shhh," he says as he scoots further onto the bed and pulls me into his arms. A rough hand strokes my hair as his lips kiss the top of my head. He pulls my nightgown down my thighs, and my gaze drops to the movement, but I'm immediately distracted by the size of my chest.

Yesterday, my breasts were small triangular mounds, but now they'd overfill my palms if I had the strength to lift my hands to them. I don't understand how they could have grown this fast overnight.

*I don't understand anything...*

Clutching my fists into Mr. Davenport's shirt, I shake

against him, finding comfort in his warmth.

"Sau, you've been asleep a long time," he says, kissing my head. "After what...happened to you, you went into a self-induced coma."

My mouth moves wordlessly before closing on a tight jaw. I shudder as I rub my cheek against him.

"The healers say you did it to save what remained of your fractured mind, giving you time to heal."

My eyes land on my hand gripping his shirt, widening at the sight of it in one piece. The last time I saw it... The last time... I shake my head, closing my eyes. This can't be real. This can't be anything more than a dream.

A sob escapes me as his hand continues to stroke my hair.

"I'm so happy you're finally awake, Sau. I tried to wake you, but all the healers said that forcing you out of it could damage you permanently, so I've waited so long..."

He lifts my chin, his thumb brushing away my tears. "I'm so sorry I couldn't keep you from being hurt. But look at me, sweetheart."

I shudder against him, but he waits patiently for me to obey.

A female Shadow always obeys. Always listens to her husband...

Swallowing, I open my eyes and am instantly reminded of my wedding day. The lifting of my veil. The smiling green eyes that looked down on me.

"Caden?"

He smiles at me – that same smile but more hardness in his eyes. More experience of a dark world. Do mine look the same?

"It's really me, Sau," he says as he presses his forehead to mine. "And I'm so sorry I thought you were safe here, but I promise I will never let you get hurt again."

Tears roll down my cheeks as I feel the truth in his

words. I throw both arms around him and cry until there is no more water left inside me. He holds me patiently, stroking my hair and back as I struggle to come to terms with everything.

Finally, I lift my head and look at him. "How long?" I croak. *How long was I asleep?*

He holds my gaze, his eyes full of a sorrow that sucks away my breath. My heart starts to pick up speed as I wait for his answer.

"Thirty years," Caden eventually murmurs. "You have been lost to us for thirty years."

I jerk from him, dropping my head into my hands and squeezing at the roots of my hair. My eyes widen as I catch the length of it. It's no longer just at my shoulders. It's down to my waist and so luxurious and shiny, like it's been brushed every day like Mama said to do.

"Mama..." I ask, looking up at him, needing him to just know the rest of the sentence: *is she alive?* My throat is weak from not being used for thirty years and sore from being overused now even though I have such strong, clear memories of using it recently.

I screamed so much. I begged Antonio so much...

To find out none of that was real is fucking with my head. It's still so real to me. I want to ask Caden if he killed Antonio yet, but first I need to know if my mama is okay. If Luther and any of my other brothers survived. If my cousins...

Tears burn my eyes as the silence tells me the answers. But even still, I hope that Caden hasn't understood what I'm asking. I need someone, anyone I used to know to still be here.

"Where's...Mama?" I push again, and his eyes darken with a pain that cuts me into pieces.

"I'm so sorry, Sau, but a few years after we rescued you, the Death Hunt attacked our guards at the portal. I called everyone in for reinforcements."

I clutch at him, praying I haven't lost Uncle David too.

"We killed a lot of the wolves and kept control of the portal, but when we got back home..." He pauses as he strokes my hair, and I wish he didn't stop. Didn't hesitate to look at me like he expects me to break. "The nursery was on fire. They'd thrown torches past the wards on our street. Your mother and cousins...I'm so sorry, Sau."

My fingers tighten in his shirt as I close my eyes, but I don't cry.

I don't break.

I just mourn them all and everything I've lost.

They died because of me.

Because Antonio wanted me to suffer. Just like he'd promised me.

"My brothers?" I ask softly even though there's a part of me that already knows. My Father was 'old' at fifty-two. Although our kind lives to two hundred naturally, the war takes our men far too soon. But if Caden is still alive, then maybe...

"I'm so sorry, Sau."

I bite my cheek as I try to accept his words and the horrible truth my life has become.

"Luther died two hours ago," he continues. "The blood on my shirt is his."

A small whimper escapes me as I finally notice the fresh smell of blood. It's soaked into his cotton shirt and spattered across his face and arms. I've been so used to the smell, so flooded in it in my dreams that I didn't notice. I should have noticed my brother's blood. "How?" I whine, the word a broken plea.

"Antonio bit his arm off. We tried to heal him, but we only have one healer, and she is young. She couldn't –"

"I want...to see..." I say as I try to rise, but he holds me down.

"He is gone, Sau. David already consumed him in his shadows."

A low rasp escapes me as I still in his arms. "He's alive?"

He nods, his eyes softening.

"Where..."

"He can see you after you rest."

"But –"

"Don't argue with me, Sau. You've been in a coma for a long time. Self-induced or not, you need to rest." He smiles as I frown at him. "I understand the irony, but David will be here tomorrow. You can catch up with him then."

My frown tightens, but I don't say anything. As my husband, he knows best.

Kissing the top of my head, he strokes my back, then lays me down on the bed. "Before I go though," he says, "I need to clean you."

His jaw tics as he presses a hand to my thigh. Panic rises, slamming against my ribs as I stare up at him. As my husband, he has the right to touch me whenever he wants, but I want to scream at him to stop. Even though I know he won't hurt me like Antonio, I don't want him to touch me like he did.

But I bite my cheek as Caden pushes my thighs apart and hikes up my dressing gown, being the good wife I was taught to be. He holds a hand out towards the door as he keeps his eyes on me. "I'm just going to clean you of Bert's filth, my sweet Sau," he murmurs softly as a bottle of rum flies into his hand, pulled by his telekinesis. "But this might sting a little."

Uncorking the bottle, he presses it into me, the glass cold as it enters. I bite my cheek harder but don't look away from him, telling myself he's my husband and knows best.

But then the alcohol hits me, and I yelp at the burning pain. I try to wiggle back, away from it, but his magic wraps around me, holding me still.

The liquid burns everywhere, and I cry out, begging him to stop.

"I need to get his touch off you, Sau. No one but me ever gets to touch you. You understand that, don't you?"

I nod, tears glistening in my eyes – whether from the pain or the sentiment though, I don't know. I *do* want that man's touch off me. I want Antonio's off me too.

"And you don't want his cum staying inside you. You don't want to carry his children, do you?"

I shake my head.

"Because that's *my right only*. Isn't it, Sau?"

I nod again.

"Say it. Tell me you want his touch off you."

"I want..." I swallow. Close my eyes briefly, then open them again. "I want to be clean. I don't want him inside me."

"And you want me?"

"Just you. Only ever you."

My thighs shaking, I embrace the agony between them. He presses the bottle deeper into me, the cold glass a slight relief from the burning liquid. His magic pulls my thighs further apart, opening me to the bottle. His eyes leave mine as he looks down at what he's doing. His lips part on a harsh breath.

The bottle pulls out, then pushes back in.

My eyes widen as my breath catches in my lungs. *No,* I want to scream. *I don't want you to do that. I want you to stop.*

But the words are fuzzy even in my head. A familiar warmth is starting to fill my body, and I'm reminded of that one time Father let me drink from his cup, but this is happening faster, and I can't limit my intake. Can't put down the cup so I can think.

I don't feel the burn of the liquid anymore, just the thrusting of the bottle. Maybe it's all poured out. Or maybe he's holding it back with his magic. My head is too fuzzy to figure it out.

Reaching up, Caden pulls down the top of my dressing gown, bearing my breasts. I glance at them sluggishly, seeing them as they are for the first time. They're so big...so different... His mouth covers one quickly, sucking my nipple in, and my body arches of its own accord.

No...not of mine. Of *his*, manipulated and controlled by his telekinesis.

He moves my hands into his wavy red hair, curling my fingers as I hold him to me. My thighs spread further apart. The bottle is removed from between us completely, flying across the room to settle on a low dresser with a mirror over it. The door to the bedroom closes, giving us privacy as my husband settles between my hips.

My legs wrap around him. One of my hands releases his hair and reaches down to dig his cock out of his pants.

I shake inside the prison of my puppeteered body even as I tilt my head back to meet his demanding lips.

"You're mine, Sau," he says as he kisses me. "You're only ever mine." His tongue strokes inside me, and I'm forced to kiss him back. Then he pulls away and looks into my eyes. "Say it," he demands.

I swallow as my hand strokes his cock without my permission. But I'm his wife, so this is okay...

My mouth moves silently for a moment before I can push the words past my weak vocal chords. "I'm your wife," I rasp. "I'm yours."

I pull his cock to me and arch as he enters on a groan. My hands grab his ass, guiding him into me. His muscles flex beneath my palms. With every thrust, I meet him, my body no longer my own.

But he is my husband, and this is his right...

He's all I have left. I don't want to upset him with my no's, especially since he's being so kind by ignoring the fact that I've been dirtied by all those werewolves and that man I woke up to. I left Caden alone for thirty years... I can't deny him anymore. This is my duty as a Shadow woman, especially if I'm the only one of my bloodline left. There's no one else to continue our name, and I want to do my part in making soldiers to kill the Death Hunt.

"I'm your wife," I say as strong as I can, and he groans, then stills against me.

*I'm his wife...*

Someone alive still loves me, and it would be wrong of me not to love him back however he needs me to.

He kisses my neck, then lifts off me. "Get some sleep," he says as he scoots off the bed. "No one but me will ever touch you again."

The mirror glistens, its surface turning into a scry. I try to take comfort in how my husband can watch over me even when he's not here, but there's a knot in my belly that doesn't disappear even when the alcohol-induced sleep takes me.

Because I'm back in the nightmares I still can't escape.

*Antonio, no!*

*Stop.*

*Stoooop!*

# TEN
## CADEN
22 JULY 1947

As soon as I leave her room, I pivot and trace a hidden ward on her door, imbuing it with my magic. Anyone who opens it will instantly disintegrate into dust, their body ripped apart at the atomic level – something I want to do to Bert – the bastard who hurt Sau.

He did it in my house.

Without me fucking knowing.

Turning on my heels, I head left towards the basement, where Leon has most likely taken him. We have various places of business to do our dirty deeds –butchers, docks, warehouses– but Leon will want this dealt with quickly. At eighteen years old, he's just seen his mother's eyes for the first time, and he won't want to be that far away from her.

I take the stairs down, then open the door to the rich smell of copper and the sound of breaking bones beneath heavy fists.

Leon slams his knuckles into Bert's jaw, snapping his head to the side in a spray of teeth and blood. The man hangs limply from the meat hooks in the ceiling, the metal barbs stretching the skin on his back into little tents. They aren't new additions to the place, neither is the large grate beneath him that will allow for an easy clean-up.

Humans are often sacrificed in our darker magic, and the basement is our spellroom. A closed dark-mahogany cabinet that spans to the ceiling sits along the back wall, hiding our jars of ingredients, athames stained with the souls of the dead, and candles ready to be burned in future spells.

"Leon," I say as I enter, a single word that has his fist stilling in the air. His muscles strain beneath his control. Then his arm drops as he pivots to face me.

"Father."

He inclines his head briefly as he steps back. He is a spitting image of me – wavy red hair, green eyes, and pale skin, so different to his darker brothers and sisters who take after their mother's side of the family with their dark hair and brown eyes. The only difference is his lack of a beard. Clean shaven but with a well-trimmed mustache, Leon is particular about his appearance. So young, yet already so serious.

Then again, he's the firstborn and the one set to inherit the Shadow Domain once he marries and finally becomes a real man. He might not have been born with the weight of responsibility, but he carries it proudly on his tattooed shoulders.

"How is she?" he asks.

"Your focus should be on Bert." I nod at him as he hangs from the ceiling, drooling blood. "Did you find out who he's working with before you knocked him out?"

"Uh...he's not –"

"Of course he is, boy. Why would he have risked death just for some pussy that doesn't move?"

Leon frowns as I step up to the man in question.

"There's only one reason to risk that – get her pregnant and kill off all her offspring." Like a new male lion taking over the pack.

"Giving him the right to rule this Family," Leon says slowly, finally catching on.

Although Sau and I are married, if another man gets her pregnant, I will be pushed aside. The throne of the Shadow Domain can only ever be truly held by a Shadow who has inherited the gift of their family name.

I glance at my son over my shoulder. "And does *Bert* here seem capable of killing us on his own?"

Leon's jaw tightens as his eyes drift to the coward hanging before us. "No."

"Exactly, my boy. So he's working with someone."

"I'll find out who." He steps up beside me, raising an arm to punch Bert back to consciousness, but I place a hand on his chest, holding him back.

"No." I smile, my eyes on the bloody face of my enemy. "He hurt my wife. This pleasure will be mine."

Raising my other hand, I trace runes in the air between us, channeling my magic to turn all of Bert's clothes into dust.

I shake him awake with a grip on his jaw, then smile as his hazel eyes first open slowly, then widen sharply as he sees me in front of him.

"I'm so–*aaaaaaahhh*!" His apologies turn into screams as I tear apart his testicles with my telekinesis.

He jerks on the hooks, ripping skin and flinging blood as he cries for a mercy that will not come. My fingers twist in the air, lifting his detached sack up to his lips.

"The thing with torture," I say to Leon, "is that people will tell you whatever it is you want to know regardless of whether it is true or not. You must be able to discern what's factual and what's desperate pleas of a dying man, told to stop the pain."

He doesn't respond, but I know he's listening, ever the dutiful student.

"The trick is to only ask questions you know they have answers to. For instance, I *know* Bert here isn't working alone. Isn't that right, Bert?"

He whimpers as I take a step closer to him. His fingers have all been broken; it's the first step anyone takes when going up against a witch; even the weakest of us can kill with a spell. Dark magic is always easy to cast; the hard part is only in controlling it so it doesn't kill you too.

"Yes," he cries, knowing how this works. He cleaned up many bodies for me before.

"I want a name."

"I don't know –" He cuts off on a gag as I press the open end of his sack to his lips and squeeze a ball free. He tries to turn his head away from me and close his mouth, but I hold him where I want him. One small ball falls onto his tongue, and he gags again.

Holding his gaze, I twirl the fingers on my free hand, pushing his testicle down his throat. I stop it halfway, blocking his air supply as his eyes bug wide and become bloodshot.

He kicks wildly, moving himself back and forth on the hooks, but though he can't suck in any air to speak, I can hear his pleas all the same.

I enjoy 'listening' to them for a couple minutes, letting him fully panic before releasing my hold on his testicle. He swallows it immediately, then gasps and gags.

"If you know nothing, you are useless to me," I say calmly.

"Please," he rasps. "I don't know his name." As the other ball starts to squeeze from the sack in front of him, he turns his wet eyes to Leon as if he thinks he'll help him, as if my son will have more mercy than I. But I raised my boy right, and I know he will not crack.

"What *do* you know?" I ask, pulling his attention back to me. "You make it good..." My eyes dip to his bleeding groin. "And I'll leave your cock attached."

"I...I..." He flounders, panic widening his eyes. "I paid a man to have fifteen minutes with her."

"How did you contact him?"

He swallows. The ball pushes against his lips.

"I didn't. He contacted me!"

I still, as does his testicle.

Out of all the things I expected, that was not one of them. I expected Bert to have a stronger partner, a witch that is actually capable of taking my children and I out. What this sniveling fucker doesn't have in magical ability, he has in money, and buying 'loyalty' is something he can easily afford. My other theory was along the lines of him paying someone to fuck my wife, that a much smarter witch than him managed to set up a little side business pimping her out.

But a pimp wouldn't approach their clients. Scumbags come to them.

"How?" I ask, rage coiling in the tips of my fingers.

"He left a card in my room."

"I want to see it."

"I burned it after...as instructed on it."

My jaw tics as I rein in my anger before I explode his remaining ball all over his face. Losing control is a sign of weakness, and there are too many sharks in this Family who don't like how I run things. How I'm too 'clinical' in my thinking, not letting my emotions rule me.

If they get even the smallest *sniff* that my wife is my weakness, they'll feast on her like an injured fish.

"And let me guess," I say slowly, "you never met the man who left it?"

He whimpers as his testicle pushes all the way out of his

severed sack and lands on his tongue. He doesn't have any more answers for me. I can see it in the panic of his eyes. Whoever used him was smart enough to cover their tracks. I just don't get *why* they used Bert. Why they gave *him* a card to rape my wife. Something –

I pull his testicle back out of his mouth as my gaze sharpens. "You trusted the card you got not to be a trap. Why?"

He whimpers, his gaze going to my son, at the ceiling, at everywhere but me. And then it finally does, and I can see the moment where he loses all hope of survival.

"Fuck you."

I smile cruelly, enjoying these moments. Where they think they're too tough to break. "No, Bert... You're the one being fucked. But tell me how long this...*business*," I say distastefully, "with my wife has been going on, and I won't make another hole in you."

I move his sack to right between his eyes. He flinches when I run it over his cheek in a gentle caress. "But waste any more of my time, and I will carve parts off you until the day I die."

His courage deflates until it's as flat as the empty sack. "I don't know."

"When did you hear about it?" I hiss, knowing this is not the first time someone has fucked my wife. Otherwise, Bert wouldn't have had the courage to go through with it. He wouldn't have trusted the card to be real. He's weak, but he isn't completely fucking stupid, just a coward who needs others to go first. To make sure that it's possible for him to get those minutes he was promised without getting caught and castrated for his crimes.

"Two...two..." He whimpers, and I have to fight back the desire to ask if he means days or weeks. You should never give the person you're torturing answers, never hint at what you *want* to hear. Otherwise, all they say is that rather than the truth.

I wait, my silence pressing on his throat just as much as his ball did moments ago.

Another pathetic whimper leaves his lips before he blurts, "Two years ago."

My body chills, but it doesn't snuff out the white-hot rage boiling inside me. It just changes it. Makes it colder. Makes my plan to choke him on his last testicle dissipate under a need to hurt him further.

For at least two years, my wife has been sold like some piece of meat at the butcher's, and this lowlife *fucker* knew about it.

"Where did you hear it?" I ask, my voice cold and flat, not revealing one ounce of my rage.

Bert would have come to me with this news if he was the only one to know of it. He is a sniveling weasel who licks the boots of whoever he thinks can lavish him with rewards. For him to have not come to me two years ago means the business of raping my comatose wife is well and truly entrenched within the Shadow Domain, kept secret by the johns who visited her while I was otherwise preoccupied, further hidden by a strong witch – the secret mastermind pulling all the strings.

He shakes his head, tears falling down his cheeks as he rolls his lips in. His body trembles, but there is a strength in his eyes, a moronic bite of courage so he doesn't die as the coward everyone knows him to be.

My smile curls as I hold his gaze. "I respect that you've finally grown some balls," I say as I push his testicle deep into his mouth, rolling it across his tongue. "So I'll honor my promise of not making another hole in you."

Fear trembles at his lips as his ball lodges in his throat, stealing his air once more. But before he can go red with the lack of oxygen, I release my hold on it, and the idiot swallows quickly with relief. As if he doesn't realize I can pull it back up if I want to. I can pull up his entire fucking stomach.

But instead, I step back.

Then I hold out my hand as the large cabinet behind him opens, and a funnel and a glass jar fly through the air towards me.

His eyes widen as he screams and jerks on the hooks, desperate to get away from me – or rather, from the little creature in the jar now hovering in front of his face. No bigger than two of my fingers touching end to end and not much wider than the width of one either, it doesn't look like it should warrant Bert's level of fear.

Although brought over from Blódyrió by the Shadows' ancestors when they entered the portal to St. Augustine, the ainska can easily be mistaken for a centipede found somewhere in the uncharted jungles of South America with its electric blue body and black splotches running down its back. Its hundred legs click-clatter across the glass as it rears up in anticipation of being fed. It's lived its whole life in the dark cupboard depths, only seeing light when it is to eat, and it has been conditioned well. If it were a dog, it would be salivating as it looked at Bert.

"I overheard Chris–" he starts to scream, but I cut him off by forcing his mouth closed. The muffled noises of his throat sing alongside the rattling of the hooks' chains.

"Don't revert back to your cowardice, Bert," I say as I pluck the funnel out of the air and grab his floppy dick with my other hand. Lining up the tip of the funnel with his urethral, I push it slowly inside him, wiggling it into the tight fit.

He screams and cries behind lips that won't part for him. He thrashes like a land-stranded fish, but I know it is not over the pain of his stretching hole. It is over fear and understanding of what is to come.

With the tip of the funnel inserted fully inside him, I

bring the jar over to it with my telekinesis. I don't want to be within jumping distance of the ainska when the lid comes off. As beautiful as it is, it's fucking vicious and will go after whatever it can catch.

Pointing the jar to face down the funnel, I quickly uncork it, then slam it against the open hole, sealing its rim and giving the ainska only one way to escape.

It raises its head and hisses, its black antennas moving back and forth as it picks up the scent of its meal. Lunging forward, it scuttles out of the glass and down the funnel, and within a second, it's gone.

Within one more, Bert is convulsing on the hooks, ripping his skin without care. His feet kick as he bucks wildly and his damaged hand swipes at his naked belly. He whines, loud and painful, like a dog that's just lost its master. Heartfelt and full of grief.

This will not be a quick death for him.

The ainska will eat its way to his chest, where it will burrow inside and lay its eggs. It won't kill him though; it needs him alive so all six thousand of its offspring have something to eat as they grow.

Eventually, all but sixteen will burrow out of him, the rest plugging up their holes with special secreted saliva. He'll be kept alive and aware, full of pain both physically and mentally as he's trapped in his own body, controlled by the sixteen ainska as they move around his brain. It's exactly what certain wasps on Earth do with caterpillars and cockroaches. They will use him as a bodyguard until they are finally ready to consume the entirety of him.

"I appreciate you talking to me, Bert," I say as I pat his cheek. "I really do." Stepping past him, I make my way to the stairs as he convulses in agony, increased by the pain of his knowledge.

At the bottom step, I call out over my shoulder, "Figure out which Christian he was talking about, son, and see if he knows who the boss is. I want his head on my desk in the morning."

"Can I see Mother first?"

I turn around, my eyes softening as they land on him. "I've not told her she is a mother yet," I say softly. "She needs time to adjust."

He isn't pleased, but he nods, understanding that her health comes first.

# ELEVEN

## HER
### 22 JULY 1947

I can't escape.

I've been rescued from Antonio's sick, twisted desires, and I *still* can't escape the gold eyes glaring down at me in the darkness of my bedroom. They loom over every aspect of my reality, painting it all in red even though I'm now home.

I'm now safe.

My throat tightens as I recall the man I woke up to. Another witch like me. Not a monstrous werewolf who uses his claws to dig holes into me so he and his pack can fuck me in all the wrong places.

A whimper claws its way past my clamped throat as pain explodes below my belly button, phantom pain from his cock ramming down a hole that is no longer there. I place a hand over the front of my pussy, my bony fingers skittering across the fabric as I convince myself the pain isn't real.

But tears glisten in my eyes as my nails dig through my nightgown and into my flesh.

Because the pain is all too real.

I lost thirty *years* because of him. I missed my father's passing. My mother's and cousins' and brothers'. I missed seeing Luther one last time because I woke up two hours too late. I've missed thirty years of mourning, and it is hitting me all at once.

Pulling my knees up to my chest, I wrap exhausted arms around them, hating how fragile I am even though I'm now an adult. I'm older than Dad was when he died. When Antonio killed him for protecting me. And yet, I still feel like a child, wishing to hide in his arms until the darkness fades to light.

Until the werewolves are dead and it is finally safe to come out from under the covers.

A tear tracks slowly down the side of my face as I accept that I will never feel his arms again, never feel that safety I so desperately want. I am awake, alone in a dark room, with nearly everyone I know already gone. All I have left now is Caden and Uncle David.

But even they don't feel real – just two ghosts that've yet to realize they're already translucent. And when they do, they will pass over to the underworld they worship. I don't even know where they will go. If either of them will meet up with the dead members of my family. And for some reason, that hurts the most – the knowledge that I know nothing about them anymore. Is Uncle David still as kind? Is Caden still mine or has he taken another?

That boy...Leon, he looks too much like Caden to be anyone's other than his. Perhaps that boy is Jade's son or Mama's before Antonio killed them all. When a husband dies, the woman is passed along to his brother or cousin or uncle or nephew or some other male relative of theirs. Perhaps the same is for when a wife is stuck in a coma for thirty years. Maybe my cousin, Jade, got her wish after all and filled his bed and birthed his children.

Rolling over onto my side, I push my pillow to my face and scream. My muscle-starved shoulders jerk back and forth beside my ears. I suck in another breath and let loose a sob that damn near breaks me.

Thirty years.

He took from me thirty years.

But worse…

Worse thing is I let him.

I was too much of a coward to wake up. I was too weak to face what he'd done to me. I wanted it to be a dream. I wanted it to be a dream so much that I stayed stuck in them while my family died all around me.

Tears blistering my heart, I sob long and hard.

Alone.

In the dark.

With nothing but my guilt and grief to consume me.

"I'm so sorry," I rasp into my pillow, clutching it tight. "I'm so sorry."

For everyone I've failed.

For soiling the Shadow name with my cowardice.

For not being the perfect gift to Caden like I was meant to be.

And I'm sorry…

I'm sorry I survived. Sorry someone had to take care of me for thirty years while I wasted away in this bed.

I think about biting out my tongue and just ending it – the grief and shame– in a desperate need to stop feeling. I can either choke on my severed tongue then or die from bleeding out; it matters not as long as I'm gone. As long as everything stops.

My body shaking, I open my mouth and stick out my tongue between my teeth. My heart pounds inside my skull, making my jaw jerk with every pulse. My teeth skitter along the bottom of my tongue, and I whimper in fear at the scrape of death lingering at the edges of my decision.

I don't want to die. I don't want to die alone and in the dark.

But I don't want to live either.

Tears pouring into my pillow, soaking it with my pain, I squeeze my eyes shut, hesitate for a few seconds, and then chomp down hard.

Blood floods my mouth, filling it up as my teeth close behind a severed muscle that flops down onto my pillow. My mouth opens instinctively on a gurgled scream as my eyes pop open, slammed into action by the sheer agony radiating behind my lips. I roll onto my belly, my hands reaching for the side of the bed, but I can't see it in the dark.

Thunderous thoughts rain down on me. Desperation claws at me. Horrible breaths are barred from reaching my lungs by the mass of blood pouring down my throat and out past my chin.

I try to scream for help, but it's nothing but a choked cry that burbles red bubbles of panicked regret.

I don't want to die.

*I don't want to die!*

I just wanted the pain to stop.

My lungs squeeze tight, raking invisible talons across my chest that try to open me up to breathe. But they can't help me. They just make it worse, make me panic more. Make my brain spasm as it runs left and right, tugging on padlocked doors as a fire rages behind it.

I can't breathe.

*I can't breathe!*

I don't want to die.

Alone.

And in the dark.

Drowning in my own traitorous blood.

I finally reach the edge of the bed and fall off, my body

hitting the ground with a thump that slams my teeth together, intensifying the pain in what remains of my tongue.

I've landed on my back though, and I cannot spit the blood free, cannot let it drain down my chin. I can only lie here and continue to choke, my vision narrowing as my panic explodes, covering every part of my world.

I don't want to die.

I don't want to die.

Someone please help me.

I want my daddy.

*Daddy!*

*Daddy!*

The door opens like a prayer, and a man rushes in, but I can't focus on him, can't tell who it is as he turns me onto my side and angles my head down to drain the red from my lips. I gag as the blood in my throat and lungs is pulled out by an invisible force, the liquid sliding past my shaking teeth that can't clamp close despite how much my gag reflex makes them want to.

"Dammit, Sau, *breathe.*"

The rich timbre makes me cry.

For a moment, I imagined Dad holding me in his arms, but it's only Caden. Only a man I don't know and who is probably no longer mine. Who isn't ours.

That pain I tried to escape when I bit off my tongue comes back to me, and I shake with uncontrollable wails, so much louder than they were now that my air pathway is clear.

He holds me close, his hands cradling my head as he rocks me back and forth. "Shhh," he rasps, a shakiness to his tone, a tremble to his hands. "It's going to be okay, my sweet. You're going to be okay."

But his fingers leave me, and that makes me panic. My mouth is forced open with his telekinesis. I rear back, but he doesn't let me move, holding me open, my teeth wide apart as something is shoved into my mouth.

I cry on a jerk I can't make as pain ruptures all over my mouth, open nerve endings pushed upon by a severed tongue held up by magic.

"I'm so sorry it hurts, Sau. I'm sorry, but I need to reattach it." His words are strained in his concentration as he holds me still with his power and pulls snapped nerves and blood vessels and muscles back together at the same time.

Streaks of tears, no longer singular in their fall, cascade down my cheeks as the pain strengthens to the point of blessed black –

"Stay awake, Sau," Caden rasps.

*"A good wife never disobeys her husband," Mama tells me as she braids my long black hair.*

*Mama?* I blink at her, standing inside this reality in the adult body I now have.

*Mama!* I shout as her and my younger self, sitting in front of a mirror, are pulled away in a pinpoint of black.

I want to go to her, back to that time of innocence, back to that time when she was still alive and my future was bright and perfect. But I'm running through pitch-black molasses, and my feet are sinking, holding me still, ripping me back into the world of the living. Of the now. Of the nightmarish reality I can't escape.

I shudder as my tears increase like two waterfalls that are joined by rapids of snot and pain.

"Sau!" Caden's voice is strong, his tone an order that I don't dare disobey. "Heal yourself. *Now!*"

My magic pulses out, flowing into my mouth, or maybe he's pulling it from me because I don't feel in control of it. I don't feel in control of anything.

But my tongue heals itself, guided by the connected paths he created, holding my severed parts together.

His arms come around me now, his fingers no longer preoccupied with guiding his own magic, like a conductor guides an orchestra. Without such strict control, magic can easily kill its user.

He pulls me to him as I shake and shudder and retch and cry.

"I didn't...want to...die," I sob against his chest, his naked flesh now wet with my tears.

He holds me close, stroking my hair, his body vibrating beneath me, like my shaking fits are affecting him just as much, just as terribly.

"I won't ever let you," he says as he kisses the top of my head. "I'll never let you leave me again, Sau. You're mine. Till the sun dies and the heavens fall."

"But you...you have a...a son," I cry, the words barely understandable beneath the tearing chasms of my heart. I can't explain how much that hurts. How much it tells me I failed in everything Dad wanted me to be. I was raised to be a good girl, engaged to Caden before I was even born, promised to him as a good wife. And instead I failed him. I failed my family. Failed at being a woman. A mother. I should've been a mother.

"With *Jade*," I say, spitting my cousin's name out even as I mourn her loss, her never-ending questions, her cute little screwed up face of concentration. She had a sweet voice and so much spirit. Even if her constant questions were annoying, I want her back. I want them all back.

But they're gone from me. Ripped away, making me feel so utterly alone and wrong for being here when they are not.

"Sau, my sweet, look at me," he says, cupping my chin and lifting. He shakes his head, and as my bleary eyes stare up at him, he wipes his thumbs across my cheeks. "Sau...I've never broken our wedding vows."

I sniffle. "But that boy...Leon. He looks..." My throat

clogs with words I don't want to say.

The thumb on my left cheek trails down to my mouth. It presses against my lips, shushing me. His sharp green eyes soften as he murmurs, "He's *ours*, sweet girl. And he's not the only child we have."

My jaw drops behind his thumb; wordless questions flow across his pad. I slept through my entire pregnancy? Pregnancies, I correct as that second sentence of his hits me. My mind reels. My breath catches. I clutch at him with muscle-bare fingers, hope so hesitant to bloom.

"You didn't...?" I swallow hard. "They're mine?"

Something *good* came out of these last thirty years?

He nods. "All six of them."

"And they're healthy?" I ask, breathless and afraid they're about to be ripped from me all too soon. Although the War to End All Wars was across the Atlantic, there was a more dangerous war brewing between two families not long before my wedding. Terra Harrison and Cara Jervis – two heads of powerful Families in the Midwest, both specializing in the creation of disease, started to fight over the expansion of their territories.

A curse that mimicked influenza blossomed, allowing them to take lives mercilessly without getting caught by the SCU – the only governing body of us sups on Earth. But as is common with dark magic, it spiraled out of their control and started taking lives they did not personally mark. Dad feared what a curse crafted by such powerful witches would turn into, and there were already hushed whispers of thousands of deaths by the time Caden and I married. Dad suspected it might rise into the tens of thousands, its dark reach spreading across the world.

"They're all healthy," Caden says.

A sigh of relief escapes me, turning into a soft sob that worsens with every breath. I almost took my life before I met them. I could have passed from this world without speaking to them. Without hugging them. Without ever letting them know they were loved by their mother.

My chest squeezes the air from every part of my body, making me dizzy. My limbs feel heavy, my lungs sore.

Caden sits me all the way up and rubs his hand in circles on my back, murmuring words I don't quite catch. Something about breathing and it being okay.

But it's not okay.

I almost robbed them of a mother. I almost did what vampires and werewolves have long done to us – crimes that we've demanded blood over. So how am I any better than them?

"I'm…sorry," I rasp around air that won't fill my lungs. It just sits heavily in my chest along with the tears and the pain and the guilt for both being alive and trying to die.

"You have nothing to be sorry for, Sau." A small noise of pleasure escapes him. "Do you know how often I've dreamed of saying your name? Sau…" As his one hand continues to stroke circles on my back, the other grips my hip and squeezes. "Sau." He burrows his face into the side of my neck and exhales, his soft breath tickling a path of goosebumps up to my ear. "Sau."

I still in anticipation of hearing my name again. In all of my dreams, I never heard it, and hearing it now, said like a prayer, a word of awe cuts through some of my pain and panic.

He sees me. Wants me despite all the broken pieces, the shameful parts of me I let get marred by the touch of a werewolf.

He sees *me*.

Even though I can't see myself anymore beneath all the cuts and bruises.

I grab hold of his belief in me like a piece of driftwood in a tumultuous sea. Grasping with cold fingers, numb with disbelief that there's anything worth holding on to all the way out here. That I am worth *saving* despite all my faults...

Tears burn my eyes as he says my name again.

"Sau... Don't let Antonio take anything else from you. Don't let him take you from *me*. You are mine, sweet girl."

I cling to him, turning into his embrace and wrapping my arms around him.

"I understand if you don't think you are strong enough, but you don't need to be, Sau. I will be strong for you. I will take care of everything you need. I will wash you when you don't have the energy. I will feed you when you forget to eat. I will keep you safe from ever getting hurt again, and it will be an honor, a pleasure to keep you as mine. Let me do this for you, my sweet Sau. Let me be your everything."

I nod against his neck, my tears making his flesh wet. I need his strength. I cannot do this on my own.

He glides his fingers into my hair, tilting my head back all the way so he can kiss me. I keep my mouth closed, my tongue too sore to want to dance. He doesn't push. Just rubs his lips against mine in soft gentle caresses. "Thank you, Sau," Caden murmurs, and those three words nearly break me. He's thanking *me*. When I've done nothing to deserve it.

I got myself raped, forever tainted by the touch of wolves. I stayed asleep like a coward while my family died all around me. And I nearly killed myself upon waking, too weak to live in this new world.

There is nothing he should be thanking me for.

But I stay quiet, trusting that he knows more than me.

That he can see something I can't when he peers into the shattered glass of my soul.

Clinging to him in the darkness of my bedroom, I tell myself I am not alone.

*I am not alone...*

# TWELVE
## CADEN
### 23 JULY 1947

She sleeps beneath my desk, her head resting on my lap, her frail body curled against my legs. I can feel her shaking as she hides from the world, and I know she still can't escape the torments of her mind – a twelve year old now suddenly awake in a forty-two-year-old body.

All night she thrashed with little whimpers, waking up sporadically to scream in fear and launch herself off the bed to crawl underneath it. I brought her back out with my telekinesis and held her until she fell asleep. She didn't close her eyes until she was in my arms, until she felt safe. But even then, she could not find peace.

I stayed in bed with her for as long as I could, but work pulled me up a few minutes after sunrise. She scampered up behind me, her green eyes wide with terror, her lips silent as she struggled to ask me not to leave her alone – that Shadow pride still burning bright after all this time.

But she'll never have to ask for another thing again. I will simply provide.

And so she hides beneath my desk, not yet able to face the world, finding a small comfort in my touch, my leg pressed against her cheek, my fingers combing her hair – just enough to lure her back to sleep.

Back to her nightmares.

Where *he* rules her everything.

My jaw tightens as my pen moves across our coded ledger, checking the payments we collected overnight from people wanting our protection (those who live on the streets where our war with the other two gangs rage), our product (the drugs we sell – both to other supernaturals and humans across America), and our silence (those we blackmail and extort into being part of our business). The tip of my pen digs into the page, nearly tearing it before I force myself to relax.

Antonio does not own her.

He is not her husband.

He might have left his mark on her, but I will wash him from her memories, give her new ones to sleep to, to find comfort in rather than pain.

I wish I could promise her his head on a silver platter – nothing less than what she deserves to be given, but the fucker is wily.

Soon after we rescued Sau, he went into business with a witch coven further north, far outside our territory. They supply Antonio and his higher ups with charms to counter our scrying, so we haven't been able to get a pinpoint on him in years. Although he still fights on the front lines, he never lingers when it comes to exchanging blows, using his natural speed to strike hard and fast before running away. He doesn't even have his tail tucked between his legs when he does so, instead carrying an arm or a leg or even the fucking head of a witch proudly in between his teeth.

But one day I will get hold of him.

And he will regret ever hurting what's mine.

As will Bert and anyone involved with fucking my wife these last two years.

"Caden?"

My name is a soft whisper in the quiet of my study, and I look down at her cheekbones that need filling and her sad green eyes that need laughter.

"Yes?" I murmur, stroking my fingers through her long black hair –the only part of her that looks vibrant and full of life– as I have done many times over these last three decades.

"Is Antonio dead?" There is so much hope in that soft murmured question. So much agony.

Cupping her chin with my fingers, I lift her gaze up. "He will be, my sweet."

She's quiet for a long moment as she stares at me. Then so softly I can barely hear the words, she asks, "Am I safe here?"

My chest tightens, as do my fingers, and I lay my pen down on the ledger so it doesn't snap in half. "Yes, Sau," I say. "That man you woke to will never hurt *anyone* ever again."

"Is he dead?"

"He surely wishes it."

She shudders, no doubt remembering all the times she wished the same.

Pushing my leather chair back, I reach down and pull her onto my lap. She tenses now that she's out of cover, her muscles so tight, they tremble. Her head swivels fast around my office, searching for danger in the brightly lit room, the rays of the sun already strong despite the early hour. Her eyes latch onto the window, its curtains on either side, and her heart rate increases, thumping hard at the base of her neck.

With a flick of my fingers, I close the dark-red curtains while also turning on the light with my other hand. The room is dimmer now, but there aren't any monsters lining up shots through an open window. She is safe.

Swallowing, my wife ducks her head against my neck. "Aren't I in the way of your work?" she murmurs.

"This morning's work is depressing anyway." The damn vampires, the Blood Fangs, are bleeding us dry, turning those we've blackmailed and pressured into working for us into bloodbanks – humans that are passed around like a tray of hors d'oeuvres. They've even kidnapped a couple of our human members to be sired under Aleric.

For the first two and a half decades after Sau's rescue, they were quiet. We thought they were simply letting us and the Death Hunt duke it out, but Aleric, their Boss, was actually turning humans en masse, building an army of sired vampires. Now there are hundreds of the fuckers, and for every one we kill, another five seem to rise. And another couple of our suppliers and business partners go missing.

"And I am not?" my wife asks.

A smile pulls at a corner of my lips. She will need time to heal and a safe space to hide to constantly run back to, but she is a fighter, and one day, she will walk these halls with the confidence of a queen.

"Never to me," I say, and she glances up at me, a quick widening of surprise before her eyes dart low again.

"Luckily for you we're already married because that was awful." She mumbles the words so low I barely make them out, but when I do, my grin spreads unhindered.

"A woman without an interest in flattery?" I tease.

"I would rather the truth."

"The truth is, sweet girl, I have waited thirty years for you to wake up. Every time I fed you with my telekinesis, every time I cleaned you or just sat at your bedside and talked, I hoped you'd open those pretty green eyes of yours and smile at me like you did on our wedding day. The truth is, Sau." I tilt her chin up so she can meet my gaze. "I will never seek distance from your company."

Her cheeks and neck turn a pretty shade of pink, but she doesn't duck her head, doesn't hide from me in any way. She just stares, seeking the truth, so much fragility in her eyes. So much fear that it is just flattery.

It isn't.

And eventually she must realize that for her muscles finally relax against mine.

She drops her head back against my neck, but it isn't a retreat. It's a seeking of comfort, and I tighten my arms around her.

We sit like this until there's a knock on my door that causes her to jump. She jerks around in my lap, already moving to disappear beneath the desk. I wait until she is fully settled, her body pressed against my legs, her knees pulled in close to her chest before I call out, "Come in."

Leon strides in to stand in front of me, speckled and sprayed in flesh blood that stains his gray button-up shirt, his sleeves rolled up to show red crusted hairs on thick forearms. The severed head of Christian Gale hangs from short black locks twirled in my son's fingers. He lays the traitor on the stretch of dark-red vinyl inlaid into the front of my mahogany desk – the wipeable fabric makes it so much easier to clean.

"And the boss' name?" I ask, my lips flattening at the sight of my son's frustration.

"He didn't talk."

"Not a single word?" I glance at the dead man's mouth, seeing if his tongue is still there; I wouldn't be surprised if the mastermind behind this all had cursed it to explode if he so much uttered a word. "He still has his tongue. You killed him too quickly."

His jaw tics. "He tried to kill me."

"I see no wounds on you."

"Because I killed him first."

"Clearly. Leave me." When he reaches for the head, I shake mine. "Leave it."

He hesitates, then turns, and I watch him as he walks from my office until the door clicks shut behind him. Sau looks up at me as I push my chair back and gesture for her to climb back onto my lap.

My wife does so slowly, her muscles too weak to move much faster. She sucks in a breath when she turns to settle comfortably on my thighs, her head in the direction of the one on my desk. "Who is that?"

"Christian Gale."

She shakes her head. "I don't know him."

"He was a capo." A man I personally gave orders to and trusted to make sure they were followed. I expected Christian Boyle to be the head on my desk this morning. He is a falcon –one of the eyes and ears of the streets– but he is also only an associate, not a full member. His true loyalty is his and no one else's.

But Christian Gale... I would have trusted him with my life.

"What did he do?" she asks, and I hesitate, finding my words carefully. But there isn't a nice way to tell her she's been raped an unknown amount of times by an unknown amount of people in a place she should feel safe.

There's a knock at the door, giving me an out, but I don't take it. As much as I wish to protect her from the cruelty of the world she lives in, my hunt is not ending with Christian Gale. When I castrate all the men who hurt her, she and everyone else in this Family will hear their screams. There will be no protecting her then.

"The man you woke up to... Christian was an associate of his."

She sucks in a breath, a choked sob. "Did he *touch me*

too?" she asks, her voice raw and shaky.

"I don't know."

"Did they take it in *turns*? Or did they...*rape* me at the same time? Did they *cut* me, make *holes* in me?" She shudders as she places a hand on her left breast, then trails it to her lower abdomen. "Was it just the two of them or were there *more*?" Her words come out fast and high-pitched.

Wrapping her arms around herself, she digs each set of nails into her elbows and rips five deep lines down to her wrists, clawing at her skin. I grab hold of her hands as she collapses against my chest, sobbing and screaming out questions I can't answer.

"Was it just once?"

"Was it just them?"

"What did they do to me?"

"What did they *do* to me!"

She jerks away from me, wanting off my lap, but I don't trust her enough to let her go. Don't trust she won't hurt herself even more. I can imagine her bleeding out in front of me, lying on her back and gasping for air just as I found her last night. My heart quickens to the same pace as her panicked breathing.

"Sau, listen to me," I say, turning her around to face me with my magic. I cup her face, using my telekinesis to keep her hands still. "They can never hurt you again, Sau, and I *promise* you, if anyone does again, I'll kill them all."

"Like you have Antonio?" she asks, her eyes red and puffy and accusing in their grief.

"Like I did Vance."

She looks away from me, her eyes darting to the side, not quite ready to trust me like a wife should her husband. I haven't earned it yet, but the gods as my witness, I will spend every day of my life proving to her she can. No one will ever hurt so much as a hair on her head and live.

"I want them to suffer," she finally whispers, looking back at me. "I don't want it to be quick for any of them."

"It won't be," I say as I stand with her in my arms.

The knock comes again, but I ignore it until she nods, showing a sign of trust. She tries to crawl back beneath the desk, but I hold her on my lap. "It's your uncle David."

She tenses, freezing with the decision of what to do. As much as she wishes to see him, shame is clear in her eyes.

"You are not responsible for what Antonio did to you."

"But I hid like a coward in my dreams."

"You survived, Sau," I say strongly. "There is no shame in that."

She glances at me, then looks quickly away, chewing on her bottom lip. Breathing out, she wiggles against me, getting comfortable as she faces the door. Another soft breath passes her lips. Then she fists her hands in her lap and nods.

"Come in."

The door swings open, and I can see it in her body – the tensing of anticipation. The little jitters of excitement.

He is the man who means the most to her.

Not I.

Not fucking I.

# THIRTEEN
## HER
### 23 JULY 1947

Uncle David looks exactly the same as I last saw him, and my breath catches in my chest, ballooning out against the cavities until it hurts. Air shouldn't hurt. I have a flicker of a thought of Jade asking me how it can, and that only intensifies the pain until tears fill my eyes.

I want to run to him as he enters and throw myself in the only arms left of my past, but my legs are too weak. Even though Caden kept me fed with his telekinesis –not wanting me to wake up to tubes– my muscles have not been used in years. Walking has been hard. Running is currently impossible.

"Uncle David…" I say, my words faltering as too many emotions fight to be heard. He is now the only father figure I have, and I am desperate to be in his arms, to have him hold me and tell me everything will be okay. Tears burn my eyes, and I blink them back, telling myself a Shadow doesn't cry. He must think I am embarrassingly weak already, a shame on the family name. I will not sully it further.

He stops in front of the desk. His dark-brown eyes do not even drop to the severed head in front of us. They hold mine, but I cannot read anything in them. "You're really awake," he says. "After all this time..."

I flinch, wondering if he hates me for all those years I was asleep. "I'm sorry –"

"For what?" David cuts in. "You did your duty to this family, Sau. You gave us the next generation of Shadows."

I swallow, my lips pressing together under his praise. There was a time were that would have left me bouncing in happiness for days, but today, guilt hammers against my throat. A part of me wants to just accept that I did what I was created for – birthing six healthy children, so I have nothing to apologize for. But that is a coward's way out. It is because of me that my family is dead.

"I could have saved them if I were awake," I say. "I'm a healer. I could've saved Luther if I just woke up earlier. I could've saved Dad –"

"There was no saving them, Sau. Their wounds were too great."

"But Luther only lost his arm! I could've –"

"It wasn't just his arm that was the issue. They tried to turn him into a vampire. His blood was too infected."

"What?" I bolt upright, my mind reeling from the pain he must've suffered. "Why would they do that? You can't turn another sup into a vampire without making them Crazed." Their mind would fracture, and they'd become a rabid animal that would have to be put down.

"That's what they wanted. They hoped he would be their Trojan Horse."

I shake on Caden's lap as I turn to him. "Why didn't you tell me this?"

His jaw is tight as his eyes move from Uncle David to

me, softening slightly but still holding their edge. "I didn't want you to think of him like that," he says.

"So you let me think I could have *saved* him if I just woke up a bit sooner."

"I didn't know you blamed yourself."

"How could I not? He was my *brother*, and I just *slept through his death!*" Closing my eyes, I push my palms against them. "I slept through all of their deaths. I could have saved some of them if I just tried. I could've –"

"Sau!" Uncle David's voice is sharp and authoritarian, and I clamp my lips shut instinctively, bowing my head as I did all my childhood. "That is *enough*. You are making a fool of what it means to be a Shadow."

I flinch but keep my head bowed, knowing he is right.

"Get out, David," Caden says softly. "And be thankful your tongue is still in your fucking mouth."

"She is my niece."

"She is your queen."

My cheeks burning, I don't dare lift my head. My new status is one I was trained for all my life, but hearing it used to chastise my uncle makes my skin itch, especially since it is a position that is and was always known to be temporary. I am a woman, and we cannot hold power. As soon as our eldest son turns twenty-two, he'll gain the seat of Boss – the chair only ever permanently going to a true Shadow. If our eldest was a girl, then she would've been bred as soon as she hit puberty and her son would take the throne once he turned of age...if she wasn't killed first. Having two generations of first-borns being female is seen as a curse, a thinning of the Shadow name, and the second one rarely lives long enough to become a mother.

My head snaps up as the door closes behind an exiting David. Although I hate his absence, my attention is solely on my husband, Leon's age pounding in between my ears. He can't be more than twenty – ten years younger than I slept.

"How many?" I rasp.

The firstborn is a moving title, passed to whoever is the oldest. With Father's death, David would have become the firstborn, meaning he would've become Boss unless I was already pregnant.

There was a condition in our marriage contract though because we needed the Davenports' support. Caden would have a month to get me pregnant if Father died before he could take the throne. But Leon is not thirty.

"How many of our children have *died*?" I demand, my body shaking from all the loss I suffered without knowing.

"Eight." The word is clipped. Factual. Without a hint of remorse, and I close my eyes as my heart wails in close-mouthed silence. His arms tighten around me, holding me together too because the Boss of the Shadows does not cry. My father never did it – even when Antonio's father made him watch as he raped and then murdered his first wife and two bright-eyed toddlers.

He'd had his fingers broken and his tongue ripped out so he couldn't use his magic. Uncle David said they had been about to kill him when he and their younger sister, Adri, had arrived. Despite being a woman, she'd refused to stay at home, and together, the three of them –Delun tying his hand to the sword Adri had brought with her– had killed the wolves.

Dad did not cry as he cradled the mangled bodies of his wife and two children. He did not cry when Adri was the one who had to wrap her shadows around them, pulling their corpses into her domain and robbing him of their presence in his because he was too broken to do it himself.

Because Shadows do not cry.

*We. Do. Not. Cry.*

I hold on to that rule so fucking hard as I dig my nails into my palms and shake on my husband's lap.

"What were their names?" I whisper.

With every name he says, I carve their essence into my heart. His tone never fluctuates, just stays as a monotone monument to factuality. A grieving father pretending to be strong. A grieving mother trying too.

When he finishes, we sit in silence, their names on repeat inside my skull. Eight names... Six boys. Two girls. I don't ask how they died or at what age, my heart too sore with the knowledge already gained.

I simply close my eyes and take a deep breath before opening them again. "I want to see Leon," I say, "and the others."

"Leon is out," he says. "The twins, Bonnie and Molly, are at school with their younger brother, Jonathan, but you can see Olivia and Ryo."

My throat tightens as he stands, holding me to his chest. I try to picture what the two will look like, but all I can imagine are the faces of the dead staring back at me, morphed into the young faces of my children.

My mouth runs drier with every step he takes to his office door, then down the green wallpapered hall. They're not going to recognize me as their mother. They might be afraid of me – this haunted figure carried in their father's arms. Do they have another woman they call Mama, even if it's only in the darkness of their dreams? Will they cry for her, wanting her to save them from *me?*

I swallow hard for all too soon, we are standing outside the door to what is assumingly the new nursery. Giggles come through the wood, and my heart slams hard in my chest. When Caden reaches for the handle, I make a soft strangled noise he is somehow able to decipher.

*Not yet. I'm not ready.*

He stills, then moves his hand back to my right hip. He squeezes me slightly, giving me time to catch my breath and still my nerves.

"Put me down," I say despite knowing my legs are too weak to hold my weight on their own. He hesitates for a second, then takes a few steps back before placing my feet on the hardwood floor. My muscles don't feel connected to my brain, my knees buckling almost instantly, but I don't drop far. It's not even noticeable to anyone but us, Caden's magic catching me just as fast.

"I've got you," he murmurs. My legs shift under his telekinesis, allowing me to seemingly walk on my own, and my heart blossoms into my throat, pushing tears up that I hurriedly blink back.

"Thank you," I whisper, words so soft I can barely hear them, but he wraps his arm around my shoulders and kisses me on the temple.

My hand lifts to the handle.

I take a deep breath.

Then enter.

Only to immediately wish I didn't.

---

The woman's laughter rings out like a ray through the clouds of a storm as she stands in front of a white wooden crib pressed against the wall on the left. She's wearing a purple flower-patterned dress as she holds a blue bundle in her arms. She's a bit older than me – older than I *was* before I woke up. Though not older than I am now, and that knowledge settles heavily in my stomach. My mouth tastes bitter as I swallow the sudden increase in age, the lost years *she* gets to enjoy. My eyes burn, but I lift my chin, wondering who this woman is who holds my son like she's his mother.

The love between them is as obvious as their lack of shared blood –her skin a few shades lighter than the rich Asian-like bronze of our family– but it makes up for any traditional titles she might not have. I am a mother, *his* mother, and yet that title falls flat in the face of their bond.

She looks up at me, that radiant smile dimming a bit. Her eyes dart over my shoulder to Caden, then back to me before growing wide, the smile now gone completely. She opens her mouth to say something as I wet mine to do the same, but neither of us get the chance.

The blue bundle in her arms says, "Mama," breaking my heart as he looks at the woman who isn't me.

My feet move forward, commanded by Caden even as I want to turn and run, to find somewhere to hide before this beautiful woman watches me fall apart.

*I am a Shadow. I am a Shadow...* I tell myself.

But I am not his mother.

Not in any way that matters to him.

My chest tightens.

My throat constricts.

I dig my teeth deep into my cheek so I don't scream out my torment at the sound of his words.

"Mama," he says again, and blood floods my mouth as I bite back the tears.

"Yes, Ryo," she says, finally looking at him, snapping the last fibers of my heart. I'd fall to the floor in grief if Caden's magic wasn't holding me up. Instead, he walks me to them, not realizing that I want to go in the other direction.

Or at least just stop to take a moment to compose myself, to hide the anguish surely cracking through my skin.

A tear falls down my cheek as I stop an arm's length away. I want to wipe the sign of weakness off, but my limbs are too weak to fight Caden's magic, so instead they reach out to the boy in blue.

The woman looks at me, and my heart jumps in fear that she'll pivot away, shielding him from a lioness who wishes to steal another's cub, but her smile comes back, a lot softer this time. "Yes, Ryo," she says again, shifting her arms to keep him safe as he tries to twist to face me. "It's your mama."

He reaches for me, his pudgy fingers ripping the air from my lungs. I stare at her, then him, watching in silent awe as he's placed in my arms. He smiles up at me, his wet mouth moving up and down as he places his hands on my face. "Mama."

My heart breaks, a shudder ripping through me as I draw him to my chest. "He knows me?" Shock quiets my words to a mere whisper.

Caden moves around to my side, his fingers working discreetly down at his hips as he has me walk towards an arm chair. He sits me down on it, then crouches down in front of us. Ryo looks at him, then back to me, and my chest grows tight at the preference in his little blue eyes. At least in this moment, he wants *me.*

"They all know you're their mother, Sau. Every night, I read to the younger kids in your room. Jonathan, Bonnie, and Molly all read to you on their own now too. It's the first thing the twins do when they get home, and Jonathan would as well if he didn't have his training, but he always sees you first."

His face blurs beneath my lashes, and I blink quickly, but that doesn't stop a tear from rolling down my cheek.

He squeezes my leg as Ryo tries to climb further up my body, grabbing hold of my hair and pulling. I don't even feel the pain I know should be there, my emotions too strong for anything else to penetrate.

"Olivia is only two months, but look at her crib, sweet girl." He nods to the right of my chair, and I twist my neck to look at it. My eyes first fall to the sleeping infant lying on her back. Dressed all in white, she looks like a precious dream, and my eyes are already misting strongly by the time I look at the handmade wooden mobile above her.

Tears fall down my cheeks as I stare at the toys that used

to be mine. My rattle. A Raggedy Ann doll looking as tired as I feel, with her bright red hair no longer there, having been accidentally burned off when I got her a little too close to the fire as Mama and I made potions... The black cotton blanket I used to carry around until it became tattered has been cut and sewn into a little stuffed fox – my favorite animal. And in the middle of all the dangling memories is a photo facing down, watching over my baby girl as she sleeps inside an ornate gold frame. I don't need to see the picture to know it's me. All I wonder is if it's one of the photos they took on my wedding day or if it's one of me asleep, dressed up and propped up like a family member who's just passed, like they used to do in Victoria times.

"Thank you," I whisper, turning back to the man I love. His face is blurred too much for me to see the emotions settled there, but the soft press of his lips tells me them all the same.

"I will give you the world, Sau," he murmurs against my lips. "I just need you to want to live long enough to see it."

# FOURTEEN
## CADEN
### 12 AUGUST 1947

She gave me her promise that day in the nursery room that she wouldn't try to take her life again, but I still find myself watching her, worrying myself every time she's somewhere other than where I left her. She's not quite able to move around normally yet, but she is getting her strength back bit by bit. Just this morning, I woke to the *thud* of her body hitting the ground. As she stared up at me, annoyance flashed in her eyes, and she refused to let me help her on the way to the bathroom. She crawled half of the way to the ensuite, staggered up by holding the door frame, and then muttered under her breath when I caught her from falling with my telekinesis.

Her fire is coming back, that reckless determination I fell in love with all those years ago. She is relearning to walk alongside Ryo, taking comfort in his gains whenever she becomes too frustrated with the slow pacing of hers. She reads with Molly and Bonnie in the afternoons. They sit with her on our bed so she can see the words, teaching her what she doesn't know. Her reading level was higher than theirs before our wedding day, and so I teach her more in the evenings.

She is constantly exhausted and sleeps a lot during the day. The children know better than to wake her. Jonathan, in particular though, is getting more and more annoyed as she is often asleep just after he's done with his training after school. He's learning how to handle his innate magic of super strength and speed, how to fight in various styles – knives, swords, bows, guns, and bare-knuckled– and is being educated in our Family business. So he often sits outside our bedroom door, peeking in every so often to see if she's awake yet.

But Leon...for all of his desires to see her earlier, has been avoiding the entire house these last three weeks, staying instead at his private residence at the other side of the street, which is where I am now, in his kitchen.

His knuckles are white as he digs his nails into the four-seater table. His jaw is locked as he stares at me, seated in a chair across from me. His broad shoulders are rigid, and the rage boiling off them is palpable in the cold night air. He leans forward, his weight on his palms as he grits out, "I told you I can't see her until I catch the fuckers who were working with Bert."

Since he beheaded Christian Gale, the leads have been non-existent. No one is talking, either to Leon or to me even though Bert no longer hangs alone on the hooks in one of our fishmongers. Orien and Paul hang there too – trusted falcons who were supposed to have their eyes and ears on the welfare of our Family.

"I understand your guilt," I start, "but she asks for you every day. I will not keep lying to her about how busy you are."

"But I *am* fucking busy," he spits out as he digs his nails deeper into the stone, carving gashes out of the counter. His magic gives him the strength and speed capable of stopping a tank in its tracks and grabbing an arrow out of the air. He is working on catching bullets; give it a few years and he might manage yet – making him a damn strong leader for this Family.

When he takes over my position in four years, on his twenty-second birthday, I will sit proudly at his side. I do not let my thoughts wonder to how many times I thought such things for my other children...before burying all their bodies...or whatever remained of them. I simply focus on the now – a tactic that has allowed me to handle my grief for decades.

"Katie Wilks disappeared at lunchtime," he growls. "One fucking guess where she is."

I still, my words slicing like shards of ice. "Did Aleric send a gift?"

The fucking vampire has a love for leaving his kills on our doorsteps. Although he can't phase –or teleport– past the protective wards surrounding this street, he takes full advantage of the postmen, who are completely unaware that they are delivering boxes of various body parts.

Leon shakes his head. "Not yet. But it's only a matter of time if we don't get her back. He'll break her."

I snort. "He'd have a better chance of trying to sire her."

Given how strong of a witch Katie Wilks is, she won't have a chance of surviving the siring process. She will die in absolute agony, the innate magic in her blood warring with Aleric's. Massive organ failure. Bleeding from every orifice. Rapid seizures one after the next, hour upon hour until she died. Alone. The only creatures a born vampire can sire reliably – well, '*reliably*' are humans without any slither of magic inside them.

And still, the chance of that happening is more than her

breaking under his torture. She's a strong bastard who I highly respect and is capable of hypnosis that can get a man to chop off his own fucking penis – something I've had the pleasure to witness when some scumbag tried to feel her up.

If Aleric is dumb enough to stay in her presence long enough to torture her, he'll be dead before sunrise.

"Maybe she won't," Leon says, "But is it worth the chance given all she knows?"

My eyes narrow on him. Katie is our regional hotel manager for all of Florida. She runs the twenty-five hotels we own, promoting our penthouses to people of interest, offering them ridiculous deals just to get them in so we can then clean up after them. A violent boyfriend wins a holiday he never entered. The mayor of St Augustine gets a discreet service that keeps his name off the paperwork and the women he pays for in through a back door. Katie even got a few stockbrokers from Wall Street in as they holidayed down in West Point Beach.

She gives them excellent service, makes sure they have everything they need before they leave, none the wiser that their lives are already owned by the Shadow Domain. She cleans their rooms personally, collecting loose hairs and cum off the sheets in little bags marked with a code that is coded again when I add it to my ledger.

So when an associate of the boyfriend's ends up dead, beaten to death in an alley not far from his work, and his hair is found on her body and his dried cum is found on her thighs, hurriedly wiped off so only small bits remain, he takes the fall for our crimes.

Mayor Reynolds is blackmailed into greasing political hands for our gain and our enemies' losses.

But it is the stockbrokers who give us the most back in that set of three.

What we do with their collected DNA is the heart of our Family. We use it in spells to spy through their senses, listening in on shady deals and quiet conversations. I can also mix it with my telekinesis, allowing me to control them without need of a scry, regardless of range.

Although Katie doesn't know the full picture of my plans, only being told which targets to bring in, her last one was President Harry Truman himself. He had a lovely holiday in Key West.

"You should kill her before she talks," Leon says.

All those in my trusted circle –the capos and advisors and top-level associates– were required to gift me with a few strands of their hair as an offering of loyalty. And a warning of what'd happen if they ever broke that trust.

I lean back in my chair, my eyes on my son. "Is that what you would do as Boss?"

His eyes don't waver as he nods. "If not to keep her silent, then to stop her suffering."

My lips tighten. Aleric is a sick bastard, more even than Antonio. A death by my hand would be a kindness.

But the spell required to reach out to her, to use her as a scry to guide my telekinesis wherever she is in this world will leave me vulnerable and drained for days. It's a last resort, used for dealing with traitors or for gleaming information we can't move forward without. Such strong magic always comes with a high price.

"She deserves at least that kindness," he says. "Given her unwavering loyalty over the years."

Her unwavering loyalty.

Something about that settles harshly in my stomach.

Christian Gale had unwavering loyalty, and his head ended up on my desk three weeks ago.

Pushing my chair back, I stand and grab my suit jacket off the back of it. "Come see your Mother," I say, needing to be out of this house and back in mine, where Sau is. I want to make sure she is sleeping soundly, safe in our bed.

That no *trusted associates* have entered our fucking

room.

The knot in my stomach tightens as I turn my back on him and walk towards the door.

"How is she?" he asks softly as he follows me through the house.

"You should see her for yourself." I glance at him as I open the door into the night. "Come have dinner with us tomorrow. She asks about you every day."

He looks away, so much guilt on his shoulders for not yet having caught all those who've hurt her.

"The blame is mine, Leon," I say softly. "*I* failed to protect her. Not you. And given she can still bare to see me, she'll love to see you."

He doesn't say anything, but there is a new tightness to his jaw. A battle between shame and desire to speak to a mother he never thought he'd get a chance to know. I wish to ease the weight caving his shoulders in, but the one on mine is urging me home. *Now*.

"Come to dinner tomorrow, son," I say, clapping him on the shoulder before stepping out.

"I can't," he says behind me, his words twisted and raw. "I have to t–"

"That wasn't an invitation," I call over my shoulder. It was an order as Boss of this Family. I promised Sau I would take care of her in all things. If she wants to see Leon, I'll damn well make sure he's there.

And if anyone has hurt her in my absence again, I'll burn this whole fucking city to the ground.

"Yes, sir," Leon says, but I'm already at the end of his front lawn, brisk strides carrying me towards home. I offer a two fingered wave without looking as adrenaline pumps through my veins. Although my house is only a couple down from Leon's and I am well inside our wards where no witches or vampires dare come, the night has always been owned by our enemies, and the hairs on the back of my neck and arms stand at rightful attention.

The air is hot and muggy despite the presence of the moon above, and I leave my jacket draped over my arm. The pavement is hard beneath my feet. The lamps cast circles of light beneath them, leaving the rest of the world hidden. A movement flutters off to the side, a whisper of wind, and I glance in its direction, my pace not faltering, my telekinesis reaching out, searching the shadows to see what's there.

Nothing.

But the uneasiness in my stomach builds with every step I take towards home. My eyes flick to the roof of our house, the only bit of it I can see from here, and my throat tightens at the thought of Sau in danger either from others or from herself.

My pace picks up at the thought of her bleeding out on the cold tiles of our ensuite.

I'm through the front door, having swung it open before I even reached it. It closes behind me as I quicken down the hall. I'm in our bedroom a moment later, staring at her in relief as she sleeps quietly in our bed. No blood. No pain. No one else in the room.

I lean against the doorframe for a moment, catching my breath and giving my heart a chance to settle. The pounding of my pulse starts to slow as the panic twisting my stomach starts to unwind.

Walking over to her, I strip out of my clothes, dropping them on the floor as I go. The door shuts behind me, and I crawl into bed with my wife.

She turns to me, her eyes popping open. The first look is that of terror, but then she realizes it's me and where she is – safe, and that fear fades beneath a slow smile.

I lean forward and kiss her, my hands running down her body to squeeze her breasts. She stills beneath my caresses, her mouth freezing against mine. There is still fear inside her, still an uncertainty of trust, but I need her too much right now to back off.

"I need to make love to you, Sau," I say as I palm her through her thin nightgown. "I need to bury my cock inside you and feel your legs wrapped around me. Can you hold me, sweet girl?" I slide my hand between her thighs and run a finger against her underwear. "Can you hold me right here?"

Sliding aside the fabric, I push a finger in.

# FIFTEEN

## HER

### 12 AUGUST 1947

I squeeze my eyes shut at his finger's penetration, the pain of Antonio's claw ripping through my memory.

"Open your eyes, Sau," Caden says as his finger moves in and out of me. "I want your eyes on me while I fuck you." His thumb presses against my clit, a soft contrast to what my body remembers. "Can't you feel my love for you?"

I roll my lips in to stop a whimper, and I hate myself for needing to. For letting the filth the wolf left on me taint this special moment, taint him.

"*Don't think about him,*" my husband hisses, curling his finger. The scratch of his nail sends a bolt of electricity through me, and my eyes snap open wide even as I flinch instinctively, expecting to see a gold gaze so full of anger.

Instead, I see the soft green of fields I dream to run through, where life is just the love of grass beneath bare feet and high-pitched squeals as your love chases you. I want to believe that fairy tale. I want to get lost in its bed of soft summer heat. Where this is good and safe and *wanted*.

But the clouds roll in dark and hateful, and lightning strikes, setting the earth on fire until nothing but gold flames stare back at me.

"Concentrate on me, Sau," Caden murmurs gently. "Let me wash his touch away."

My heart thrashes in my chest as my body remembers something so different to what my ears are hearing. I try to focus on the now, on the loving green eyes waiting for me.

But my throat is constricting.

My heart is racing.

And a small sob escapes before I manage to catch it on an inhale.

Caden's face softens as he tilts my chin and presses a kiss to my clamped lips. "Don't hide your tears from me, sweet girl," he says. "Come to me to dry them."

His thumb slides across my cheek, brushing away the wetness. And there is a weight of a thousand promises in that gesture. A strength that I cling to. A trust that he'll carry all my burdens to the cliff edge and toss them into the sea.

"I'll kill him for you, Sau. I will kill every single person who has ever hurt you."

Grabbing my hand, Caden places it beneath his on my pussy. He curls my own finger inside of me, and I flinch despite still holding his gaze. "But first we're going to get rid of his touch together. You're going to come on your hand, then squeeze around my cock. You're going to find your own pleasure, Sau. You're going to *own* your body. It won't be his anymore. It won't be theirs. It'll just be *ours*."

My lips trembling, I nod. I want what he's offering so badly. To no longer be owned by *him*.

So I try not to tense when Caden guides my finger under the pressure of his. I try not to back away when he tells me to keep curling it just like that while he moves his own fingers, pumping them in and out.

The friction of our fingers makes me hot, the heat building with every movement, but my mind is trapped in a cold asylum nothing can break. It makes me feel even more broken, and I struggle even harder to feel something *good.*

But all I'm feeling are fingers. Like when Uncle David would have me touch myself while he taught me how to be a good wife. Just movements that mean nothing. That bring no pleasure, just wetness.

Caden grabs my free hand and wraps it around his cock. His head dips to my neck, trailing kisses down to the collar of my nightgown. Ripping the fabric apart with his telekinesis, he then licks my left breast.

Right where Antonio made his second hole.

My eyes slam shut.

My finger stops moving.

But Caden's don't. His fingers fuck me faster. His hand holding me to his cock pumps in a similar rhythm. When his lips close around my nipple, I cry out, and he sucks on me harder with a groan.

"I'm so sorry, Sau," he rasps against my skin. "I thought I could wait. But I need to be inside you. Need you tight around my cock."

He pulls his fingers out of me and places his arm beside my chest, leaning on it as his hips push forward. He holds my hand around his cock as he lines it up with my pussy. I try to remove my own finger from between my lips, but his magic holds me still. Then makes me curl it. Over and over, hitting a spot that sends jolts of electricity through me.

He sucks on my nipple harder, rough growls emitting from his chest as he rubs the tip of his cock between my lips. "I need you to tell me you want this, Sau. Make this moment *ours.*"

A whimper claws at my throat, not letting anything else

out. But I want to tell him to take Antonio's touch away. To please take it all away.

"Sau," he groans as he moves to my other breast, and the tip of his cock pushes in just enough to start spreading my lips. He sucks on my nipple, his tongue flicking it back and forth as he jerks my hand up and down his cock.

He rocks in a tiny bit further, and I spread my legs in silent invitation, still too numb to speak.

Groaning, he sinks in all the way, sending pain and heat flaring through me. "That's my good girl," he rasps as he rolls us on the mattress.

I'm suddenly sitting up, straddling him with my hands on his chest as he holds my hips. He lifts me up and down, rocking me sensually on his cock. "You feel so fucking *good*," he hisses, his green eyes on mine, half-hooded in his honesty. "I want you to use me, Sau. Ride me for your own pleasure."

His hands leave my hips, giving me the power, the control.

I still, not sure what to do. What I *want*.

But he doesn't rush me, doesn't force me to be ready before I am. Now that he's inside me, he's fully content, comforted for some reason just by the grip I have on his cock.

"You're so beautiful sitting there," he murmurs. He cups both my breasts, rubbing me leisurely as he keeps his eyes on mine. "Now own your beauty, my sweet, sweet girl," he commands. "Use me to wash every part of him away."

I nod jerkily as I let my tears fall freely, trusting him to catch them, catch *me* as I splinter apart on top of him. I rock forward and back, not having the strength to bounce up and down, and his fingers pinch my nipples a second before his mouth closes on the right. He kisses me as I cry, murmuring sweet comforts I'm not quite ready to trust.

How I'm beautiful.

Strong.

Worthy of being queen.

This last month, I have struggled to keep up with Ryo crawling across the nursery. I have read slower than my two twin girls, them having to wait for me before they can flip the page. I have fallen asleep more times than any elderly human. I am nothing but a burden.

A burden who can't even enjoy this simple moment with my husband.

My throat clogs as I grind my pussy against his pelvis more desperately. Squeezing my eyes shut as the tears fall, I try to feel *something* good. Something that is not just numb motions that make me want to curl up into a ball and weep.

I wrap my hands around his head, holding him to me as if that will hold me together. His red curls slip between my fingers, entwining with them, making us one, but all I want to do is break away and find my own corner.

I don't want him touching me.

No...

*That's not the truth, now is it?*

My shoulders collapse as the truth hits me. A thousand whips that rip me to shreds.

I don't want him touching me like *this*.

Reverently.

Cherishingly.

As if I'm some queen.

Instead of the whore I am.

And that's what is disgusting me the most. Knowing that I *can* come, I *can* find pleasure...if only he fucks me like a whore.

Like Antonio did all those nights in my dreams.

Sobs breaking freely, I cling to my husband in utter shame, no longer moving, no longer pretending I can take back what Antonio fucking stole from me. That I can heal myself through the man I love.

His arms come around me, holding me up as he pumps into me, still murmuring those sweet words, still telling me I'm strong, how this is *our* moment. He kisses me with little pecks of love, having no idea that each one, each promise of his lips is breaking me even more.

Because this isn't *our* moment.

It's still Antonio's and always will be.

He has a grip on my neck I can never remove, a dog with a collar whose chain leads back to him.

Crying, I bury my face into the top of Caden's hair and finally accept what I am.

Antonio's.

Dirty.

Little.

Fucking.

*Whore*.

# SIXTEEN

## HER
### 13 AUGUST 1947

I hate myself. I hate everything about me as I lie in Caden's arms with his cock still inside me as he seeks comfort in the lying warmth of my body. I can never tell him the truth. Never break his heart over knowing that it isn't just Antonio's torture that has a grip on me. It's some sick, twisted part of *me* that has a grip on *him*. I might not have come that night in the woods, but I came over and over in my dreams. Even just thinking about how he brutalized me. How he took without asking. How he degraded me and stole every bit of my control... It makes me wet, my pussy squeeze. And I hate it. I hate *me*. What the fuck is wrong with me?

I am nothing but a horrible, terrible person with needs no woman should have. I am a *disease*, a blemish on his purity.

Caden groans as his cock jerks inside me, reacting to my involuntary kegel. "I love you," he murmurs as he kisses my shoulder, and I only manage not to flinch due to how numb my body is. How it's been for the last hour as Caden tried to make this moment *ours*.

My heart too broken for any more tears, I stare with tired eyes into the darkness of our room. "I love you too," I whisper, hoping that is enough. Hoping that my love for him will make up for the terrible, horrible wife that I am. For the sick, disgusting woman that I am.

My stomach twists, and the taste of bile fills my mouth. Gods, I hate myself so fucking much.

I run my tongue across my teeth...

Wondering if I'm stronger this time. Less of a coward so I can actually go through with it and leave this world, remove my sickness from the lives of my family.

They'll be so much better off without me...

"Trauma doesn't heal immediately, Sau," Caden says, turning me around to face him, his cock finally slipping free of my body. "Don't blame yourself for needing time." He cups my cheek, a dark desperation in his green eyes. A terrifying understanding about where my thoughts went.

"You promised me," he whispers softly.

I close my eyes on a shudder.

I nod jerkily, then look at him and nod again. "I'm sorry –" I start, but he cuts me off.

"Don't apologize for your pain, sweet girl. I don't just want your happy smiles." Grabbing my hand, he raises it to his lips. "I want all of you, Sau. All the broken jagged pieces. All the glints of sunlight. I understand you need time to heal. I'm just asking you not to push me out while you do it."

I glance away. A shaky exhale leaves my lips, but my nod this time is stronger.

*I can do that...*
*I want to do that...*

Leaning close, Caden kisses me. "Now get some rest. I

apologize for keeping you up so long." I start to close my eyes on a yawn when he swings his legs out of bed and stands.

"Where are you going?" I ask as he picks up his shirt from the floor.

The question lingers in the dark, and for a moment, I don't think he will answer, but then he turns to me on a sigh. "I need to go talk to Christian's wife."

My heart skips a beat at the name of one of my rapists. "Why?" I demand, pushing up on an elbow.

"I just have some questions I want to ask her."

"Do you think she knew what he was doing to me?" The question is a soft whisper, but it isn't fear that quiets it. It is rage. Cold, vengeful rage that wishes to see them all dead.

He pulls on his under shorts, then his pants. Doing up the zipper and button, my husband finally turns to face me. "Christian sacrificed his hand saving my life when he shoved it down a wolf's throat."

My jaw drops on a gasp. "But that's... Why would he do that?" Losing a hand is never a light matter regardless of one's species, but for a witch, you're not just losing a hand. You're losing a conduit needed to access and control your magic. Very few people manage to survive learning how to wield it one-handed.

"That's exactly what I need to find out," he says. "I've struggled to make sense of his betrayal."

"Maybe he regretted losing his hand?"

"Perhaps... But Christian learned to control his magic verbally." That's no easy feat, the binding of words a lot harder to master than a few twists of the hand. "And he lost it nearly fifteen years ago. So why did he decide to betray me now?"

My mouth opens and closes wordlessly as I collapse back onto the bed. I don't want him to be innocent. I don't want justice to have not been served, for another victim to have joined me in this darkness. Finally, I manage to ask, "But then why did he attack Leon?"

"I don't know."

"But you think his wife will?"

"I think I need to talk to her." He sighs. "She's also good friends with Katie Wilks."

"The regional manager?" I ask, my brow furrowing. I only met her once, when I was up past my bedtime while Father had her over for a late night meeting. They were discussing whose hair to sneak into evidence to get the police off our back for a crime we'd definitely committed. She looked up and saw me peeking through the crack in the door. I stumbled back, terrified of being caught and outed to Father, but she never ratted me out. I still remember her sneaky, friendly smile.

"What does she have to do with it?" I croak, my throat suddenly dry. My stomach twists at the thought of her having anything to do with Christian and Bert.

"Nothing as far as I'm aware. But she was loyal to me and has gone missing."

"Missing?" It's a question I already know the answer to. Many members of this Family have gone "missing," only to turn up in pieces on our doorstep, delivered via postmen with no idea of the dark messages they carry. My heart breaks over the loss of her, and I hug a pillow to my chest.

"She might be lying low, or she might be with Aleric," Caden says. "Leon wants me to kill her with my magic before she gives any of our secrets up."

I look up at him, my eyes wide. "You can do that?" I've only ever known a telekinetic to be able to kill those in sight. Father told me how strong of a witch Caden was, but he never went into the details. He just talked about how their family would be a great asset to ours. How our children would all be forces to be reckoned with.

"I have a strand of her hair, so theoretically, yes, but she's a powerful hypnotist. She might be able to fight off my telekinesis so I won't be able to use her own body to kill her."

"Oh." There are a lot more questions I want to ask, but my eyelids are suddenly real heavy. The disruption to my sleep is catching up to me, and I've been so constantly exhausted ever since I woke up from my coma. But there are still so many more questions...

"Now sleep, sweet girl."

*But I don't want to...*

There's a light touch of his lips on my forehead. My body snuggles deeper into the mattress of its own accord.

I struggle to open my eyes to see him off, at least, but they're so heavy...so resistant to opening, and as the door clicks shut, I quickly fall asleep.

---

The screams wake me, loud and shrill, and I try to jerk upright, only to find I can't move. A weight presses down on me, squeezing my chest closed but my eyes wide as I thrash beneath invisible binds.

Antonio's golden gaze looms down at me in the dark, but I can't see the rest of him. Can't smell him. Can't feel the pain of his claws. I can only suffocate under his bulk as my mind struggles to shift from dream to reality.

Sucking in air to scream, I throw my whole weight off the bed. My breath exits on a hard whoosh and a small gasp as I hit the ground, but I'm so desperately happy to finally be able to move, I don't care about the bruises. A half-sob, half-whimper escapes me as I crawl beneath the bed. Shaking and terrified, I stare out into the darkness of my room, waiting for a wolf to bend down and drag me out.

But when no wolf comes, when no one comes at all, I finally manage to hear past the pounding of my heart.

The world is quiet.

I'm all alone.

Squeezing my eyes shut, I'm hit by just how real that statement is.

Everyone I love is gone.

*That's not true...*

I struggle to make sense of that subconscious thought for a minute before it all comes back to me. Caden loves me, and he's still here. Uncle David is too even though we have barely seen much of each other because all my kids wish to spend time with me, and I always end up falling asleep before he's back.

I'm a mother, I remind myself, drawing strength from that statement, my lungs shaking as I breathe.

*I'm a mother.*

I am not alone.

Swallowing hard, I shudder beneath my bed, my cheek pressed against the cold wood of the floor.

*I'm a mother.*

And that is when I hear it, ever so softly, ever so muted, a child's midnight cries.

"Olivia," I rasp as I finally find the strength to reach an arm out from under the bed. My nails dig into the floor as I pull myself out. "Olivia," I say again, working my way over to the door. I need to see her. Need to see she's okay. Need to hold her and give comfort as much as I need to take it.

At the door, my arm shakes as I reach up to grab the knob. I clumsily haul myself to my feet, swaying slightly but my legs solidifying over the sound of another cry.

"I'm coming, baby," I whisper as I struggle out the door. Leaning one shoulder against the wall, I stumble in the direction of the nursery. Exhaustion wants to pull me to the floor, but I place one foot in front of the next, listening to my baby's cries.

I need to go to her. I need to comfort her. A door up

ahead is open a crack, and for a moment, disappointment hurts me at the thought that Abby, the nanny, has already reached her, stepping into my role of mother as she's done all these years.

But then that disappointment morphs into something worse as I realize that isn't the nanny's room. It's the Underboss' – Caden's right-hand man and the second in charge.

It's Uncle David's room.

My throat constricting, a flood of emotions suck me down into a whirlpool of panic. My legs move faster. My heart beats harder. I'm suddenly drowning in a pool of vomit that burns my throat. Uncle David loves me. He never hurt me. He gave me candy and told me I was a good, quick learner.

*It isn't wrong.*
*He.*
*Told.*
*Me.*
*It.*
*Isn't.*
*Wrong!*

But it *feels* so fucking wrong.

I don't want him to touch her like he did me.

*She's only three months old!* I scream inside my head as I imagine cradling her in my arms, keeping her safe from him. *She doesn't need to practice!*

Horrid rasps leave me, as do bits off my shoulder that scrape across the wall due to how hard I'm pushing, how desperate I am to keep moving forward as fast as I can. I pass Uncle David's room. My stomach drops with the last bit of hope that he might be in there. That he might have just accidentally left his door open as he fell into bed.

But his room is dark and empty, just like my lungs are now. Struggling to breathe, I move forward. *I can't be too late. I can't be –*

Gasping, I trip over my feet and hit the ground hard. I crawl with aching fingertips and exhausted limbs to the nursery, not stopping for a second to look at my own injuries.

Light comes from under the door I am desperate to get to, but the cries have now stopped. Utter silence under the rasps of my breaths and the pounding of my heart reigns. And I hate it more than the cries.

Has he finished with her?

Am I too late?

Or is he muffling her mouth with his hand?

With his...

A flash of Vance fucking mine hits me with the force of a hundred belts flaying into my back. I cry out silently, my throat too constricted to manifest even the smallest of sounds. I dig my fingers into the carpet. I haul my body forward.

Nails rip, leaving blood across the dark wood.

My limbs shaking, I reach another arm forward.

I can't be too late.

*I can't be too late!*

Dragging myself up the wall, I open the door.

Only to immediately crumble at the sight before me.

This is a room of innocence. Of the bubbling words of a baby learning to speak, of them finding delight in the little things we've all forgotten to croon over. This is a room of peace, of inner sanctuary. Of children too young to know the horrors of the world.

And yet, there is Uncle David...

Standing in front of her crib...

With his hands...

*His fucking hands!*

Below her naked waist.

And Olivia is still screaming, her face bunched up in

blotchy red pain, but I can't hear her over whatever magic he is using to keep her quiet.

My stomach drops as I throw out my hands without coordination, grasping at anything around me to hold me up. But instead of latching on to the door frame or knob, my fingers twist and curl in front of me, magic shooting out of them, uncontrollable in my rage.

David twists, his eyes widening as his arms come up, erecting a blue wall of energy to counter the red flames of mine. They shoot towards him and slam into his shield, but the force throws him back hard into the wall behind him.

"Get away from her!" I scream as I hit the floor on my knees. Scrambling to stand back up before him, I struggle to control my magic. But it has been thirty years since I used it, and the last time I did, I couldn't control it either. It rushes away from me, greedy in its desire to see him bleed, and my heart slams in my ears as I fear for my little girl getting caught in the crossfire.

The red magic rushes to her, splintering apart her crib until each wooden slat explodes at once. I scream as I watch her get embedded from all sides in my mind, and I stumble forward, praying that I can make it to her before she passes away. I can heal her. I'm a healer! I can save her even though I've never saved anyone before.

My legs shaking, I trip over something on the ground.

But then I realize I'm not falling. I'm sinking.

Sinking into unnatural shadows as they wrap around my body and pull me under.

I flail for a purchase in this world, but David's shadows wrap around me, pulling me into the realm of darkness even as I scream for him to stop. He is the only person who can get me back out of the Plane of Monsters, my family the only ones capable of controlling its portals, and I do not trust him to do so.

"Please!" I beg as they twist around my neck. I try to tap

into my own power, try to command them as is my birthright, but they do not listen to me.

He does not listen to me.

He simply stands over me, his eyes cold, blood trickling out of his mouth.

And then I am gone, sucked into a nightmare that will end all others...

Worst for the fact that I've left my baby girl with a monster of her own.

# SEVENTEEN

## HER

### DAYS DO NOT EXIST HERE

It is pitch-black in all directions. If only it was quiet too. But there are animalistic screams and the sounds of ripping flesh coming from right in front of me. Something thicker and warmer than water sloshes around my hands and knees as I kneel in this new world.

My pulse slamming inside of me, I jerk my head up, but my eyes can't pierce the complete darkness. I tremble despite knowing that the pact an ancestor made with a djini long ago keeps us Shadows safe in this place. No one knows or perhaps cares to remember what the exact deal was or if it was ever collected. Perhaps it still might be, and my time will soon be up, a debt ripped from my flesh by whatever monster is in front of me.

Breathing as softly as I can, moving just as quietly, I shift backwards under the cover of the screams of its prey. My magic doesn't work here. Whether a part of the deal with the djini or just the limitations of this plane, I don't know. Nor do I care to think about it.

I just want to get away from this monster.

Get away from Antonio's golden eyes looming at me from its position in my mind.

And get back to my daughter.

*Olivia...*

Trying to drown out the slurping, crunching sounds of death, I scurry further away. Then I'm standing upright. Then running. A direction picked randomly in the dark.

I stumble and fall multiple times, but I just keep getting back up again. The clicking of crab-like feet chases me. The thumps of hooves in a two-step beat. The soft thuds of clawed feet. The hisses and frustrated sounds of predators that can't bite the prey, but that doesn't stop them from trying to get close. From saliva dripping on me. From the air beside me being sliced apart by talon and claw and pincer.

I run for what seems like hours before I see a light up ahead. A pinprick at first that makes me flinch, thinking it is the reflection off a pair of golden eyes.

But then it grows bigger, and I heave with relief as I stumble ever closer. Only to realize it's coming towards me.

I throw my arms up as the world of light envelopes me, certain it is some ungodly beast that has finally figured out a way to eat me on this nightmarish plane.

"Sau!"

My arms fall at the sound of Uncle David's voice, and I crack open my eyes to see I'm back in the nursery, the signs of destruction, of wayward, uncontrollable magic in every splintered piece of wood. The crib, the walls, the floor, even the ceiling. None of it was spared in my fear.

"Where is she?" I cry as I look around, trying to spot the blood beneath the wreckage.

"She's safe," he says as he crouches down in front of me.

I flinch away from him. "What did you *do*?"

"I had to stop your magic." His lips tighten even as his eyes soften. "You're a very strong witch, Sau. It was the only way I could save Olivia. Probably this whole fucking house. Your father would have been proud."

I tremble, a manifestation of me not knowing what to think. "But you were hurting her," I say slowly. "I heard – saw her screaming."

"She's a baby, Sau," he says, chastising me for being stupid. "They cry when they need their nappy changed."

I shake my head slowly, trying to remember what I saw. He had his hands below her waist... But I can't see what he was doing, my mind too fractured by the events on the Plane of Monsters. Every time I try to think too hard, I'm back there, terrified and alone. I just want to curl in on myself, stop thinking about anything at all, but my daughter needs me.

Right?

She needed me?

I look around at the destruction of her home. Her crib is gone. The mobile above it too. The entire room is just a shrine to chaos and pain. Trembling, I wrap my arms around myself. I could have hurt her. I could have killed her because I am too broken to understand not everyone is to be feared.

"I'm sorry," I say, my eyes burning as I look back at my uncle. "I thought you were..." I don't say it, but the change in his eyes tells me I don't need to.

He rears back, disgust curling his lips. "Let's just get you back to bed. I'll come up with a story that caused this wreckage, and you keep your fucking mouth shut about what you *think* you saw. I'm not going to have you talk shit about me to Caden. I have cared for every single one of your children while you slept like a fucking baby. Fuck, Sau, I was *changing her nappy.* Just like I've done every fucking night she needs it. I'd *never* hurt her."

"But you did it to me," I say as he hauls me to my feet, his fingers digging into my arm.

"I *trained* you because I love you, Sau. Though lot of fucking good that did, didn't it? I bet you haven't even once sucked Caden's cock. Wasted all my fucking time, didn't you?"

I flinch, my words beat back down my throat by his. He drags me to the door. I stumble behind him, trying to keep up, to stop being the burden I am. I tried to save Dad and only made matters worse, making Antonio slaughter nearly my entire family. I tried to save my baby girl, only to nearly kill her. If it wasn't for Uncle David, I would've. And if it wasn't for him advising Caden and giving him his support as his Underboss all these years…would the Shadow Family even still be here?

"*You know* nothing." The memory of Antonio's words slaps me hard.

I didn't believe him then, so sure in my purpose that I was doing the right thing. That I was being a *good* soldier despite being a girl. Doing what my father wanted. What every witch wanted.

I struggle to remember Antonio's mate's name, my first kill… Or rather, my fourth kill, her three pups having died first.

My heart breaks at the thought of Olivia being dead, at the thought of the pain that mother went through because of *me*.

That *mother…*

Not a werewolf.

Not a fucking mutt or an enemy.

Not even just a woman.

But a mother.

A mother who didn't even get to know the love of her children.

Because of *me*.

Tears burning tracks down my cheeks, I mouth the words, "I'm sorry." A genuine wish to say those words to her...and Antonio.

Perhaps if I had the knowledge and compassion to have done so all those years ago, my family would still be alive, and I wouldn't have nearly killed my darling little girl, thinking the worst of people because that's all I've ever known. Perhaps...perhaps it would be a much different world, where I wouldn't have to worry every time Caden or one of my children goes outside our protective wards.

Perhaps, we could have had peace...

Stopping suddenly outside of my bedroom door, Uncle David collects himself. His rage dissipates from his rigid shoulders, and his mien turns to one of calm and concern. He knocks on the door once, but when no one answers, he opens it himself and then drags me in, his rage back at the forefront of his actions. His lips twisted in a sneer, my uncle throws me down on the bed.

"Not a word," he hisses as I struggle to right myself, my limbs severely exhausted from their use. "You say one word to Caden about what you *think* you saw me doing, and I swear to all the gods, Sau, I will kill you. And no one will care either considering we already spent thirty years without you."

I flinch, absolutely believing his words.

He turns to the door, then closes it softly behind him.

Trembling, I fall back onto the bed and curl up into a ball. Perhaps the world *would* be better off without me...

# EIGHTEEN
## CADEN
### 13 AUGUST 1947

"What do you think?" I ask my younger brother Myers as we approach our car, parked in the slab driveway of Christian's widow's house. Although I wanted to talk to her alone, I can't dismiss the impact Myer's presence had on her willingness to divulge information. He is the reaper of the Shadow Family, the one tasked with killing traitors. When the time comes to kill Bert, Orien, and Paul, it'll be at his hands. It was not a position held within our own Family when we lived up north, which is why I'm so quick to get my own hands dirty and, in his words, 'sneak out of the house like some goddamn teenager,' but it is a family tradition for the Shadows.

A reaper protects the Boss and the Family, putting his own desires and friendships last. He is the black twisted hand of vengeance. With David being my Underboss, one of my own brothers had to take the empty position as the previous one was killed on our wedding day. Dermont, our youngest brother, would have been far too soft for the job even if he was still alive today.

Nyra's eyes kept flicking to Myers as he stood behind me as I questioned her about Christian's last few days. She started trying to lie, talking about how he'd regretted losing his hand to protect someone who wouldn't protect him. Then she looked at Myers and swallowed, trailing off before bursting into a whole different story.

"About hinting that someone high up threatened her children if she didn't convince us Christian was dirty?" Myers asks.

"No. About the tea she offered us. Do you think she's secretly a Red Coat?" I say as I open the car door. "Yes, about the fucking traitor."

He grins as he slides into the driver's seat. "That was some pretty damn good tea. She could be a Red Coat." Raising his voice an octave, he quotes Paul Revere's famous line, "The British are coming! The British are coming!" and then follows it up with, "You know Paul never actually said that?"

"I'm going to kill you."

Laughing, he turns on the car. "You can try, little guy."

"You're *one* inch taller than me," I hiss. "And that's *if* you round up by one inch."

He snorts. He's exactly 0.1 inches taller than me, and he's been lording that over me since he turned thirteen.

Reversing out of the driveway, Myers peers over his shoulder at the road. A car honks. He ignores it, and not for the first time I wonder if he's trying to kill me with his driving. His body's innate healing magic is a lot better than mine...

Glancing over at me, he laughs. "There was loads of space!"

"You drive like a maniac."

"Eh. It's a good thing I'm crazy, no?"

I don't comment, knowing damn well he used to be a lot more sane before he took the job as reaper.

I give him a subtle nod, and he grins at me. A moment of silence descends between us. Respect, gratitude, and a giant fucking dose of paranoia about who this higher up who threatened Nyra might be.

*He has access to my wife...*

He could be with her now...

My hands fisting, I order, "Drive faster."

He glances over at me, but there isn't any humor in his light-blue eyes that nearly verge on lilac. "Not to throw accusations around," he says slowly as the car picks up speed. "But I think it's David."

My head snaps to him, wondering why the fuck he's never voiced this suspicion before. I've trusted David for these last thirty years. Trusted him alone with my wife. With my kids. He is their beloved great uncle; him being the traitor will rip this family apart. Not the Family, the Shadow Domain, but *my* family.

My jaw tight, I hiss, "Why?"

He shrugs, but it isn't one of flippancy. It's a calculated move that expresses an unease in his gut. "Perhaps I've read too many books because the gods know he's never done anything to warrant suspicion... Hel, he was the one who wanted you to become Boss, and he has given you decades of support."

"But?" I grind out. His job as reaper has him constantly watching those around me, and thinking about it, it's been years since Myers has left me alone with David.

He quiets for a moment, no doubt trying to find the right way to voice his suspicions. I want to snap at him to speak already, but I know that'll do nothing to hurry him up. This accusation might damn well lead to a full-on war within the Family. Such matters cannot be spoken of lightly.

"But not once has he ever acted like he wanted to kill you."

"What?"

He looks at me askance as if he can't seriously believe I just asked that question. "You're a dick, Caden. Everyone hates you."

"Thanks," I say dryly.

"Nah, not like that." He tilts his head. "Well, also like that, but I mean... You're too calculated when it comes to people's lives. Sacrifice a few here to save a few there. You're too callous, not having favorites –"

"How is that too –"

"Your own children," he says softly. "You had Mack and Jack hold position at the portal rather than to retreat to meet up with the backup and retake it."

"It's too strong of a position to lose." Although the portals were closed by decree of the archangels ages ago, the Seven have looked the other way recently about them being reopened to smuggle sups across. A good portion of our income and off-world alliances come from it. "Getting it back would've cost more lives. They –"

"I know," he cuts in. "*I* know. I was there when you opened a scry to be with them the whole way through, trying to help where you could. And I was there when you broke down and cried over their loss." He glances at me, and I don't even get on to him for taking his eyes off the road for so long. There are some moments you just can't avoid. "I've been there every single time you've watched David take their bodies into his shadow domain, hating that you couldn't," he says softly. "But they don't see that. They see a father who sacrificed his children."

I look away, the buried grief in my chest banging at the lid of the locker I chained it inside. "What does this have to do with suspecting David?" I ask, my voice soft but not cracking in the slightest.

A leader cannot bend.

And he sure as hel cannot crack.

Not if he wants to keep his family alive. If I die under the blade of a traitor, so will all my children. Like a lion clearing out the pups to make way for his own.

"David has never once questioned an order or shown even the tiniest bit of frustration with your rule, and you and I know both know you've made mistakes. He's not kissing your ass, but his emotions are hidden beneath a mask of loyalty when *no one* is that loyal. I know he's heard the whispers of discontent concerning you. They like him. He's a born Shadow. He could easily claim the throne."

I shake my head. "He loves our children."

"Does he? Or is he luring them over to his side, happy to put Leon up as Boss?"

"Then he could just wait four years. I'm not holding tight to the throne." At the start, when I was young and groomed to take Sau as my wife and take control of this Family as my own, yes, I wanted the power and respect that came with being Boss. But after thirty years of losing eight children, of watching my wife suffer in nightmares I was helpless to save her from... I just want done with it.

"I know that. But there are whispers about why you are so quick to sacrifice your children."

"Quick?" The word explodes out of my mouth as I turn to him. "Two of them died from the flu! I spent two weeks beside their bedsides, guiding water down their throats so they wouldn't die of dehydration. I did *everything* I could to get Eric and...George –" I choke on his name, on his particular death before continuing, "back from Antonio. And Aleric already hit the portal three times in three days the week before Jack and Mack arrived. No one thought he would try again so soon with an even larger number of sired –"

He reaches over and grabs my shoulder. "I know."

I stare out the window, trembling under the pounding of the grief wanting to get out of its cracking cage. "They died heroes," I whisper, "not victims."

"I know."

My throat works as I struggle to work through what my brother is telling me. I've never been foolish enough to believe the Shadow Domain appreciates me as Boss. I am and always will be an outsider. But I was foolish enough to think that they understood the choices I've been forced to make to save more than we've lost.

"So if David just wants to kill me, why would he need to have others rape Sau?" I finally ask, breathing out as I find my control. My logic. A calculating Boss rather than a grieving father.

Myers releases his grip on my shoulder and puts it back on the wheel. We turn onto our street, the dark of the night only broken by the cut of our lights. "Bert said he was approached, right?"

"Yes, but he still had to pay for it."

"Like an exclusive club fee?"

I swear, then silence descends, heavy and thick with the warning of a storm. "We have to be sure about this," I finally say. If I kill David and he's innocent, I'll lose a valuable advisor and whatever support I have left in this Family. Hel, I'll probably lose that support regardless of his innocence or not. If Myers kills him, as reaper, he will be trusted to have made the right choice… Or feared too much to speak up against. But I will not let David die by another's hands. If his crimes are true, I will avenge my wife and deal with the fallout later.

Pulling onto our drive, he cuts off the lights. "How do you want to do this?"

"Gather the evidence, then we'll hold a trial."

"You could lose. Charisma matters more than facts."

He speaks a truth that's been repeated time over time

throughout Earth's history, and my jaw locks. "It'll be a family trial only then," I say. "Sau, Leon, Jonathan, Molly, Bonnie, and I, plus the six capos. I'll call them in once we have the evidence." I pause for only a second. "And find out which of the capos are working with him. There's no way he's been doing this alone.'"

He nods, and I open the car door. Leaning down, I add one final thing. "I don't care how many are left standing in this fucking Family, Myers. I want them all dead. If that does what the werewolves and vampires cannot, then so fucking be it."

His lips tighten. His responsibility as reaper says he should kill me for even voicing how little I care about the lives of this Family. But they crossed a line selling my wife. And I will fight even my brother to protect her.

He holds my gaze, both of our bodies tense, seeing which way this will go.

Then he exhales.

"Family first," he murmurs.

I nod. "To the end, brother."

Clasping him on the shoulder, I head in to see my wife.

# NINETEEN

## CADEN

### 14 AUGUST 1947

I'm not surprised to see she's awake when I enter our bedroom (she's been struggling to sleep), but I'm surprised to see her down on her knees in front of the door. Before I can say a word, she grabs my waistband and fumbles with my button and zipper.

"Sau, what are you –"

She pulls me out at the same time I grab her shoulders. But she's already leaning forward and opening her mouth.

Panic fills me at the sight of her desperation to please. A complete change from how she was only a few hours ago when she lay still beneath me, her only movement the trembling of her limbs. I hold her back before she can suck me into her wide lips.

"Sau, *stop*," I say, digging my fingers into her shoulders. I don't want her like this, where she is acting like a paid whore with fake enthusiasm behind the glimmer of tears.

"But I am good for this."

The strength goes out of my arms at her whispered plea, and she is against me in an instant. Her lips close around the head of my cock as her tongue swirls beneath the foreskin. Pleasure pulls a groan from my lips as I haul her close and shove deeper into her mouth. My eyes close half-hooded as she sucks me deep, her nose pressing into my stomach without so much as a gag. Alarm bells ring inside me even as the desire to fuck her pretty little mouth hard and fast has me thrusting into her.

She cups my balls as she starts to bob up and down, dragging out my pleasure with each stroke of her tongue. She sucks the tip of my cock hard, humming vibrations down its length as her fingers stroke between my thighs. I widen my stance with a grunt, then hit the back of her throat on the next thrust.

She teases me, skilled in the ways of her mouth.

But it is all too calculated, too cold for true pleasure.

So despite the ache in my balls, I pull back and grab her chin, squeezing slightly when she tries to suck me in again. I pop out of her mouth, and she looks up at me with a hurtful expression that cuts me deeper than any blade ever has.

"What have I done wrong?" she whispers, and I drop to my knees in front of her. Our gazes level, I shake my head.

"Nothing, Sau," I murmur. "I just want to know where this is coming from."

She glances away, her mouth closing as she wars with that infamous Shadow pride. She shrugs half-heartedly, and ice grips me as firmly as I do her chin. Was this a goodbye? A last gift, a last made memory before she killed herself? The calm before the storm? The bright brilliance of the sun before the eclipse?

Hauling her to me, I fall onto my ass and drag her onto my lap. "I'm sorry I left you on your own," I say, my soft words heavily controlled so they don't split and break apart. So I don't follow them in their grief.

I run my fingers through her hair, taking comfort in the fact that she is still here. I still have time to convince her to stay alive.

I try not to think about how many successful suicides there have been in this Family. How none of them could be saved unless they *wanted* to be saved.

I cling to her, trying to push my desires for her life into her very core.

But magic is not miraculous.

And my heart shatters inside my chest, exploding in all directions like a fucking grenade, imbedding shrapnel in my ribs and lungs, knowing that unless she wants to stay with me...I *will* lose her.

"But I got a lead on the head of your abusers," I say, hoping that is enough of a tendril, enough of a wanted thread to tie her to the world of the living. I hesitate for a second, wondering what will happen to her grief if David turns out not to be the mastermind behind her rape. She could spiral quickly.

But she needs this knowledge now...and I am prepared to sacrifice him for her peace of mind, guilty or not.

Whether that destroys this Family or not...

She looks up at me, her mouth closing on whatever she was about to say. Then she swallows. "*Who?*"

"David Woolman Shadow."

Her mouth drops open, and a part of me fucking purrs at the terror in her eyes, the instant belief that he could hurt her. That she trusts me over him. That perhaps he isn't the one who means the most to her after all.

"Did he..." She trails off, but it isn't due to a tremble of words. It is because of a growl. A flash of anger in her eyes. "Touch me *like that* too?"

Every last molecule of pleasure is ripped from me over

the way she asks. "What do you mean *like that*?" I say, a softer growl than hers, more measured, more controlled but no less promising of pain. The alarm bells ring again about how skilled she was with her mouth, and my grip tightens on her hair, yanking her head back to meet my eyes.

She stares unflinchingly, but there isn't any pain in her gaze, no sign of victimhood or distaste like there always is when she thinks about her rape at the hands of Bert or Antonio. No, this is indifference. A lack of caring, a lack of understanding that what happened to her was just as wrong.

That it was the same.

I trace my thumb across her lips, my jaw tight, and she turns her head fractionally away. "They were just lessons. A gift for you," she says. "Now answer me about –"

A small whimper escapes her, the first knowledge I have about how hard I'm squeezing her. I dig deep for the ability to force my fingers to loosen despite the desire to clench them into fists and slam them into the wall behind me.

"No, he was *abusing* you, Sau," I hiss as I can imagine it all so fucking clearly. She was a virgin when I met her – a stipulation in the contract between our Families – but given how detached she is when it comes to sex now... He touched her when she was a fucking kid. He looked me in the eye all these years. He lives in my house. I trusted him alone with her. He was supposed to look after her, protect her. Instead, he violated her.

*For.*

*Fucking.*

*Years.*

Because a sick fuck like that doesn't just stop. He doesn't 'get help' or suddenly 'see his ways.' He simply continues until his victim either outgrows his tastes or he finds another.

I release her chin abruptly, knowing if I hold her, I'll hurt her accidentally. My hand is already a fist, my magic pulsing at the tips. "I bet he told you to keep it a secret, didn't he, Sau? Special lessons?"

Her pretty green eyes narrow as she searches my face, still not quite sure about why I'm upset. "Yes," my wife whispers, and my whole body goes cold, coiled. My magic sits just beneath my tips, waiting for my command to rip the fucker apart atom by fucking atom.

I move her off me and stand. I don't care anymore about collecting evidence. I don't care what David's death at my hands without a trial will do to this Family. He touched what's mine.

And —I turn for the door— he has been so *helpful* with Olivia lately. So *kind* and *caring* and *It's no trouble at all to change her during the night.*

A sickness claws at my stomach as Sau scrambles up behind me. "I want to come with you."

"No."

"But —"

I turn back around to see her swaying on her feet. My eyes soften even as I grab her arm and haul her towards the bed. "Stay here, my sweet. You don't want to see what happens."

"But I need to see him suffer if he —"

I shake my head, knowing what she wants and what she can actually handle are two different things. It's easy to say we want death, we want violence, we want that special someone to pay. It's a whole different thing seeing their organs hit the floor. Hearing their pleas for mercy. For forgiveness.

She'll be thrown right back in those woods.

I lost her for thirty years. I cannot lose her again.

"Trust me, Sau. Trust me as your husband to take care of you."

She closes her mouth, then opens it, only to look away as

I lower her onto the bed. "Ask him why first," my wife whispers. "I just need to know why."

*Why I wasn't enough to love?*

*To care for.*

*To protect.*

*Why someone I trusted so dearly hurt me?*

She doesn't say those things, but they're clear in the air between us, hidden under that Shadow pride.

Cupping her face, I tilt her chin up. "Because he is a monster, sweet girl. There is something wrong with him, not you. You are not at fault. You are not any less because of what *he* did to you." I lean down and press my forehead against hers as I look into her damp eyes. "You are loved. You are cherished. And you are utterly perfect exactly as you are."

She grabs my hand on her cheek, squeezing my fingers as she exhales roughly. Her eyes glisten as she holds my gaze.

"He's my uncle and the last memory I have of that time..." she says softly, and my body stills as I wait for her to ask me to grant him mercy. I don't want to ever deny her, but in this...

"But don't let that sway you from killing him. Father would have." She swallows. "Uncle David told me not to tell him. I should have known..."

"You were a child, sweet girl," I say softly. "He took advantage of your trust in him. You are not to blame in *any* way."

She glances away, exhales, then looks back at me. A single nod.

I kiss her forehead, then straighten.

David can create illusions strong enough to kill, and his damn shadow magic is terrifying. I think about getting Myers first; that would be the logical thing to do. But for once, I am happy to let logic go fuck itself. David will die by my hands alone. No one will deny me even a second of that pleasure.

As I pivot on my heels, Sau's soft voice calls out behind me. "I still want his head, Caden."

A smile curls my lips as I reach the door. She trusts me to provide for her. "And so you shall have it, sweet girl."

# TWENTY
## CADEN
### 14 AUGUST 1947

Every step towards David's room has my heart racing just a little bit faster. He is a Shadow, and that is more than enough to fear him, but it is the rumors surrounding him that play menacingly in my head. How he's said to always have an illusion up. How he's never where you actually see him. I have tested this theory multiple times over the years, seeking out his flesh with my telekinesis, feeling his atoms with my power to make sure he is where he says he is, and he always has been.

Perhaps he knows my magic is his natural counter. Perhaps he thought it would be too suspicious to play games around me. Either way, only a fool goes into a fight expecting to win, so I need to make sure that when I attack him, he isn't a fucking illusion.

And I need to get him talking so I can find out what happened to Katie Wilks. If she really got taken...or if the fucker killed her for her loyalty to me.

Stopping outside his room, I knock – a quick rap of expectation for him to let me in. Late night/early morning meetings in private rooms are not a rare occurrence in this house. Although normally Myers is with me, tonight he'll be my scapegoat.

The door opens, and I push in, every step that of a confident Boss with no suspicious thoughts concerning his second. "Aleric took Katie," I say as I turn around to face him as he shuts the door. Locking us in, unaware that he's the prey in this little scenario, and my blood rushes hot at the thought of having him where I want him. Alone. With me. And no one to fucking help him as he screams.

"Who?" His eyes glaze over for just a second, and my body tingles with a spark of pride and pain.

"Katie Wilks, the regional manager of our hotels," I snap, hiding my true feelings behind shallow annoyance. He never was one to take notice of those 'beneath him.' And Katie, the clever girl, played on that beautifully. Both times I said her name, he got a distant look in his eye, meaning she managed to hypnotize him – a subtle action he probably doesn't even realize he's doing.

But for her to have done *that*, I realize with a tightness in my chest, he must have been the one to attack her. She wouldn't have marked him otherwise. And if David went after her himself...she's probably dead inside his shadows, ripped apart by the monsters who lurk within.

I turn so he doesn't see the rage boiling beneath my skin, so I don't just kill him where he stands for all the suffering he's caused. Crossing the room, I deliberately show him my back. *I feel safe here. I don't suspect you.*

I stop in front of his window. Despite the stifling heat outside, it isn't open – us witches preferring to keep our rooms a comfortable temperature with our magic. It beats any warm breeze. I casually close the dark-red curtains before turning back to face him.

"Leon thinks I should kill her before she talks."

He nods. "She does know a lot."

My lips tighten as he basically confirms my suspicions about her death. He wouldn't want me to find her if she were alive given she'd then be able to tell me all about him attacking her. But if she is dead and I try to search for her, the magic will drain me enough for him to kill.

But he also just gave me something more – he isn't a fucking illusion. Katie can't hypnotize what isn't real.

Feeling the power coiling beneath my skin, I take a step towards him. "First Christian Gale. Then Katie Wilks. I thought they were loyal, and they showed me the truth behind their masks." I shake my head in disgust. "You're the only person I can trust."

His chest puffs out.

"Even Myers," I say slowly. "I don't trust him after all that's happened with Sau. You saw how he acted on our wedding day."

How he leered at her. How he wanted her for his own.

A boy just coming into puberty, who was close to her in age, only a year and a half older. An innocent, childish crush now twisted to feed David's ego in having played me for a fool.

I hide my smile beneath the mask I always wear as I imagine his snarky pride falling under the realization that I *know*.

He nods gravely – just the right mixture of acceptance and grief in that action to have fooled me into trusting him if I didn't already know his sins. For a moment, I look at the man I believed him to be – my most trusted advisor, a doting great uncle who treated my kids as his own, a loyal second who kept a lot of the wolves in this Family off my back with his support, a *friend*. A fucking friend.

But he is none of those things.

He never was.

Or perhaps he was before something changed.

There is a part of me that wonders what that was. If I had accidentally, unknowingly caused so much hatred to blister inside of him.

But there is a bigger part of me that just doesn't care. Understanding is only required if I plan to forgive him, and I sure as hel don't.

Regardless if our friendship was ever real, he hurt what was mine. He ignored the contract between our Families concerning Sau's innocence for his own selfish gain.

And he *continued* to hurt her – selling her when she couldn't give consent.

Robbing me of that moment she awoke, from being the first to see her pretty green eyes open.

He *took* from me.

And so I will take it all from him.

As he says something about having caught Myer's in her room once, I start to pace in agitation, a plan forming in my head about what I'm going to do to him. I promised Sau his head...but that is too merciful a cut.

"I thought he was just checking in on her, but now..." He trails off, a pitiful expression on his face, and mine twists in displeasure and pain as I pretend to buy into his lies about him having caught my brother fixing his pants in Sau's room. "How do you want to handle this?" David asks.

"You'll have to kill him," I say, finally stopping in front of him. "If I do it, the Family will turn against me."

He nods, a flash of triumph in his eyes, quickly gone. "Of course I will. The Family comes first," he says.

"And Leon," I say, watching him carefully to see if he truly wishes for my son's death or not, if Myer's idea of him wanting Leon on the throne is true.

His jaw doesn't tighten in the slightest. His eyes don't darken with grief. He actually fucking smiles – just the barest beneath his mask but enough for me to see given how closely I'm watching him, how much I already know of his sins.

"And I'll try to find," I start to say tightly, my power building beneath the tips of my fingers, "Katie."

I lash out in that moment his eyes go glazed, lifting my hands to grab the atoms in his and ripping them apart at the wrist. He screams as he staggers forward, both of his hands left behind as they hit the carpet, dropping down two waterfalls of red.

I don't stop the blood like I did for Bert; Sau isn't here to see it.

I don't dismiss him, turning my attention elsewhere for there is nowhere else for it to go. No panicking bride who needs to be soothed. No son who needs orders. Just him and me and the memory of my wife's words.

*"I want them to suffer."*

Stepping into the last of the space between us, I swing a fist into his jaw. My knuckles crack with the force of my blow. His jaw breaks. Blood whips out, splattering across my shirt as he staggers forward. His arms whirl in wild abandon, and I let him hit me, then sneer as he screams as he realizes that hurts him more than me.

As he falls to his knees, cradling his bleeding arms, I pick up one of his hands with my telekinesis. His eyes lift to me as I place his own damn fingers around his neck and squeeze.

I lift him into the air with calm, controlled movements of my hand. His legs kick. His eyes bulge.

He stares at me in disbelief, and I relish in his panic. His fear. His realization that this is the end.

But oh how wrong he is.

For the end brings mercy.

And he will have none of it.

"You took what was mine," I hiss as I squeeze his throat

tighter with his own fingers. "You violated the agreement between our Families concerning Sau's innocence. You violated *her* for your own twisted pleasure."

"*That's*...what this..." he wheezes as sweat beads down his paling complexion. "...all about?"

I have half a mind to crush his vocal chords or perhaps rip them out entirely, but there are still truths I wish to know. *Need* to know so his punishment can fit his crimes.

As soon as I relax the grip on his neck, he coughs and then wheezes out a laugh. "You're risking the Family for some *whore*?"

I bare my teeth. "I would risk *everything* for her. As you should have. She is your fucking niece."

Blood dribbling down his lips, he sneers. "Yeah. She was a fuck all ri–"

I cut off his words with a flick of my hand, controlling his severed one to choke the words out of him. "You sold her. You *raped* her. You fed Leon lies to kill Chris –"

"Fed...him?"

My blood runs cold at the laughter behind his barely heard words. Soft rasps that are only expelled from his lips by pure force of will. A chill running down my spine, I relax his fingers, needing to hear what he has to say.

His eyes light up with cruel delight. "The boy," he spits, "is desperate to get rid of you. He's been in on this since day one."

"You're lying."

"With what purpose?" David croaks, then laughs as he holds up his bleeding arms. "I'm a dead man."

My jaw tightening, I stare at him as his words crawl across my skin, injecting poison with every step they take along my arms and neck. My hairs all on edge, I shake my head as my eyes narrow. "If you're being all talkative, then tell me why you sold Sau."

"*I just need to know why.*" My wife's desperate plea

resonates inside my skull, slicing me apart with her raw desire to be loved by her uncle.

"She's a pretty little thing, isn't she? So many men wanted to fuck her while she was in a coma, wanted to experience what it was like to fuck a Shadow." He sneers. "Wanted to flip you the bird for being such an asshole. So I saw an opportunity, and I took it."

An *opportunity?* That's all this was to him? A fucking *opportunity?*

"She's your niece!"

"She's a spoiled brat who always tried to act so tough, never screaming when I whipped her as a kid to trigger her ascension." His sneer takes on a predatory gleam. "I had to craft illusions those nights so Delun wouldn't see me getting hard. I always fucked her face after while she played with herself and moaned around my cock."

A vile disease claws at my stomach, demanding I eject it up through my throat.

"And Olivia?" I ask tightly despite knowing what his answer already is. Given his detailed descriptions, I know all he's doing is trying to taunt me, to have the last word, to perhaps get me to kill him in my uncontrollable rage.

"Every time I changed her diaper, I would shove my fingers so far up her cunt, she'd start screaming. So, of course, then I'd have to kiss her boo –"

I rip out his tongue with my telekinesis on a scream of rage. I wanted his punishment to fit his crimes. I wanted to know of his sins against my family so they wouldn't have to suffer alone, but I can't listen to such *evil*.

I have no illusions over the monster I am, am not blind to all the blood on my hands, but what David did to my daughter... What he's deriving pleasure in *remembering*...

Pain slices through me, raw and thick, choking in its intensity. As the fucker tries to swallow his tongue, to die quick, I force his mouth open. Blood pours forth like a burst dam.

My heart hammers. His pulses, each pump seen in each new bubbling outpour from his lips. I grab his chin with my own hand and force his mouth open. Blood rises in the air, parting like the Red Sea so I can get a good look at his severed stub.

Sweat runs down me in long trails as I focus on the atoms of his wound, closing it up, saving his life so he doesn't bleed out too easily. I stop the bleeding of his arms too, and then I throw him onto the floor. He hits it with his face, unable to catch himself, and a grunt of agony leaves him – the first of many he will make tonight.

The first of many nights.

Standing over him, my chest heaving, I glare down at his vulnerable body. He tries to crawl away, but I slam a foot onto his back and pin him in place.

"You touched my wife and daughter with these hands," I hiss as I pull his other severed hand to linger in the air above his ass. "So now you will feel what they felt."

I don't use my telekinesis to yank his pants and under shorts down. I do that with my own hands, wanting him to feel like he might have a chance at fighting me off, wanting him to feel that sense of utter helplessness and despair when he realizes he can't, that it doesn't matter what he does. I am simply too strong.

He gurgles and grunts, pathetic noises flying out of his mouth as he bucks beneath my assault. I claw at his clothes, twisting him back over every time he tries to roll. Heaving, I finally manage to pull his bottom clothes off. He tries to kick me in the face, his legs still flailing wildly, his balls squished against the carpet as he desperately tries to crawl away.

Grabbing both his bare hips, I haul him back, forcing him onto his knees. Mine burrow into his calves, holding him down as my telekinesis moves his severed hand to line up with his asshole.

"Which finger was it?" I growl, not caring about the answer as I force the forefinger in, slamming it in to the knuckle. He bucks on a mangled scream as I pump his hand in and out, the rage clawing at my heart nowhere near sated. I shove a second finger inside him, then a third, stretching his ass like he stretched Sau's mouth. Like he stretched Olivia's –

I cut those thoughts off, too sickened by his actions.

A frustrated growl ruptures from my throat as blood leaks from his ass. It isn't enough. The pain he's suffering. The humiliation. The panic. It's. Not. Enough.

He tries to twist away from me again, and I release my grip on his hips so I can lift my arms. I weave a spell in front of me, opening a scry in Myer's room, envisioning it in my mind's eye until the air above his dresser crackles with my magic.

The drawer of Myer's bedside table flies open, and I pull out the knife he keeps there. I'd grab one of my own, but I don't want to open a scry in my own bedroom. I don't want Sau to be able to look in and perhaps paint me with the same brush as Antonio.

I focus back in David's room when he kicks me hard in the stomach. I grunt as he tries to fend me off, having rolled over onto his back despite his own hand still being up his ass. Pinning him down with my telekinesis, I sneer at him. "You like your *opportunities*. Well, here's one for you, you fucking coward."

Looking him in the eye, I hold out my hand towards the door, pulling Myer's knife to me. It flies down the hall, directed by my rage. When it slams into my palm, I point it at his face as he trembles before me. "You can take this *opportunity* to *beg* me for forgiveness."

Jerking his legs apart, I line the knife up with the open wrist of his hand. It fucks him as he screams without his tongue, a gurgling mess of I don't care what. He can beg and plead and swear on his own cock that he will never touch another woman again, but he won't have a cock by the end of this, so such a promise is moot.

Holding his hip with one hand, I slam the knife up his ass blade first. I twist it through the fragile protection of his hand, and he screams again, no doubt waking the rest of the household. I want his pain to resonate through the place like a fucking bell ringing the doom of all those he sold Sau to.

"Beg me, you fucking piece of shit," I growl as I thrust the knife in and out of him. Blood pours from his ass and hand as tendons and severed fingers drop from him. I hold his wet gaze, forcing his eyelids to stay open. "Beg me like Olivia would have begged you were she able to speak."

I pull the knife out, then jerk out the shredded mess that remains of his hand. "Beg me like Sau would have."

I shove the blade in to the hilt, then twist it. He spasms before me, blood spraying out his lips as I clearly rupture his stomach. He won't live long if I don't heal him, and I growl my displeasure at my reckless thrusting.

Leaving the knife in him, I turn my head to the ensuite on the other side of the room. He'll have a healing wand in the cabinet in there – a pre-spelled wand that anyone past their ascension can use. It's not as good as having an actual healer, akin to a doctor fresh out of college rather than an experienced surgeon, but it'll save his pathetic hide.

Standing, I stride towards the bathroom, but I keep my power on David, locking him in place. I don't want him bouncing on the blade while I'm gone, giving himself a quick death he doesn't deserve.

I open the door and step in, my eyes shifting straight towards the cabinet. But they pass over the sink to get there, and a streak of pink running down the outside of the bowl stops me.

The world caves in on me, squeezing me like I'm in a

giant's fist, my rib cage crushing my lungs as I see it for what it is.

Poorly washed off blood.

My head pounds as my vision tunnels on the pink.

It is not uncommon for a man in this Family to come home covered in blood. Not uncommon for his bathroom to have it splattered across its floor and walls.

But there is something about this particular streak that makes every hair on my arms and neck stand on end. It is a sign of a task interrupted. A late night secret hurriedly scrubbed.

My stomach pounding, my heart having been squeezed down there to bathe in its acid, I take a step forward.

My eyes scan the bathroom in a slow, terrible arc.

Until they land on the toilet. Both of its lids are down. A man rarely ever closes one lid, let alone two.

My throat tightens as I listen to David's broken pleas, finally realizing what is missing...

The crying noises of a baby rudely awakened coming through the walls.

I stop in front of the white porcelain, the blood in my face draining at the sight of the blood on *it*. A smudge along its rim. A fingerprint evidencing the crime I'm about to find.

My lips parting as my lungs claw for air, I reach forward and lift the lid.

A broken scream comes from me as I drop to my knees and stare at the crammed, lifeless, wet form of Olivia.

She's been shoved in face first, hidden to be disposed of later, her clothes ripped from her, her thighs rubbed raw, great big patches torn from her skin. I reach in the pool of pink and pull her out, crying and screaming as I hold her to me. Her wet, twisted form reeks of pain and suffering. Her spine is broken. Her rectum has prolapsed, pulled from the rough thrusts of a –

I scream over the thoughts bombarding my mind. The

knowledge. The pain.

She is still warm despite her wet body.

Dead only a few minutes.

Killed, perhaps, when I knocked on his door, David panicking and needing to hide her.

For the first time, I curse my telekinesis. If I was not able to detect David's illusions, would he have killed my baby girl? Or would he have simply hidden her cries and her broken, bleeding body? Healed her after I left...

Has he done that before?

How many times...

Tears flood down my cheeks as I struggle to breathe. I stroke her soft tufts of hair that will never know the full length of her mother's. My throat burning, I scream again as I clutch her to my chest, wishing with every part of me that her little heart will thump against mine.

But it doesn't.

It stays as still as her.

Trapping in the next scream, I plant a kiss on her head. It lolls backwards, unsupported in any way.

Sniffling, I go to place her down on the ground so I can finish punishing David for his crimes, but I cannot bring myself to let her go.

To fail her a final time by leaving her alone in her death.

Closing my eyes, I stand.

Shudder in a deep breath.

The bathroom door flings open, catching me off guard, and I turn on full adrenaline as Myers half-enters. "Fuck, Caden. What have you done to Da–" He stops dead, both mid-step and mid-sentence, as his eyes drop to the bundle of joy now forever silent in my arms.

His face pales.

He pivots on his heels.

I want to call to him, to tell him David is mine. That I don't want him dead. Don't want him to get off that easily.

But the reaper is already gone.
And the door slams shut behind him.
Final.
Lethal.
David screams no more.

# TWENTY-ONE

## HER
### 14 AUGUST 1947

I shudder in relief at the sudden silence. Although I wanted David to suffer, hearing his gurgled screams threw me back into those woods with Antonio. I bring my hands down from my ears, my arms shaking as I try to control my breathing. I don't want Caden to think I am weak, that I can't stomach even the sound of so much pain.

I rub my shoulders, trying to bring the warmth back into my body as I sit huddled on the big empty bed.

"I'm out of the woods," I whisper. "I'm home."

Caden has taken care of everything.

I have nothing to fear here.

Nothing will hurt me as long as I trust my husband.

Swallowing hard, ignoring the rapid pounding of my pulse, I keep my eyes on the door, waiting for his return. Waiting to jump up in joy and relief that the nightmare is finally over.

But when the bedroom door opens, and I stagger to my feet, forcing a smile to my face...the blood runs out of my cheeks, and I stumble to my knees.

Caden doesn't catch me this time, his arms wrapped around a bundle of yellow fabric cradled to his chest.

I hit the floor hard as a sob is wrenched from me. Even though I can't see her face, I know she no longer breathes.

"Olivia..." I rasp past wobbling lips and a throat closed too tight to breathe. "What's...how...?" I ask as I lift my eyes to Caden.

His hands are clean of blood. The fresh scent of soap hits me, and I instantly hate the carbolic smell that clings to him. I hate the silence that sears between us. I hate the color yellow. I hate the helpless look on his face. I hate *him*. He promised me... He promised me that he would protect me. That I would never be hurt again.

My eyes fall to my still daughter, and the most pain I have ever felt hits me all at once. "You *promised*," I scream as a sob rushes from my throat. "You *promised me*."

I reach for her, only to immediately collapse inwards, my arms wrapping around each other. My hands curl into fists, and I bang them on the floor as I scream. My eyes squeeze shut as I remember David in her room. He had his hands below her waist. Was he really changing her diaper then? Was he hurting her? Was he killing her while I watched? While I did *nothing* to help her?

I am her mother.

Was her mother.

*Am* her mother. Even in death, she is mine.

I crawl towards her, sobbing and crying as Caden just stands there in utter silence.

I hate his silence.

I hate *him*.

He was supposed to protect her.

*I* was supposed to protect her.

I hate me just as much as I hate him.

"Did David..." I ask, a worthless question to assuage my guilt. I already know what happened. I already know I failed her in that moment I found him in the nursery. But I let David convince me he knew best. I was not there to raise any of my children, but he was.

I was not there to kiss their grazed knees or rock them as they cried.

But he was.

And they loved him.

And I trusted him...

I trusted him because he made sure I did not know what he'd done to me was wrong.

Tears burn my eyes as I hate that bitter, hard truth. Regardless of what David told me, though, I should've *known*. The fault is mine. I was old enough to get married. I was old enough to know...

Olivia is dead because of my childish stupidity.

I fold in on myself, my head hitting the floor as tears pool beneath my cheeks. Caden doesn't answer me or maybe he does and I just don't hear him over my wails.

I should have known.

*I should have known...*

*My baby is dead because of me.*

"No," Caden finally whispers as he crouches down and touches my shoulder. "No, David didn't..." He swallows as I look up at him, desperately craving his next words. My entire world is held in the Adam's apple bobbing at his throat.

He shakes his head.

He looks away.

"Sometimes babies just die," he says softly. "She died in her sleep. It was peaceful."

"But I saw David..." I start to say, but my throat closes and I cannot speak the words.

He hears them anyway. I can tell given how harshly he flinches. But he shakes his head again.

"She died in Myer's arms, my sweet Sau. David never touched her."

I fall forward, collapsing on the cold floor as waves of relief expel from my lungs on ragged cries. I shudder, my whole body trembling as I thank the gods for this one good thing. I'd go through everything I've gone through again just to hear those words.

*"David never touched her."*

A sob shakes me to my core.

I did not fail my daughter.

Tears falling down my cheeks, I finally reach for her.

He hands her to me, gently placing her in my arms, and then I curl back in on myself, sheltering her from the world that's so horrible and cruel to the women of the Shadow Domain.

I kiss her sweet forehead, closing my eyes to match hers.

My tears fall off my cheeks and drip down onto hers. Each drop carries a mother's love for her to take across the ferry of the Styx or perhaps across the bridge and into Niflhel. I do not know which of the three underworlds she'll end up in, so I pray to Hades, Hel, and Arawn to let her into the good fields. To judge her soul to be worthy of finding happiness in the afterlife.

Holding her close, I kiss her for the last time.

Then take her little body into my shadows.

# TWENTY-TWO
## CADEN
### 14 AUGUST 1947

Each pulse of my heart demands I go back to my wife, to hold her as she cries in her sleep. It has been two hours since we said our goodbyes and Sau wrapped our baby girl in her shadows. A mere half hour since she fell into a fitful sleep. Ten seconds since Myers called me into the hall.

A Boss does not have the luxury to grieve.

It is a lesson I've learned over and over these last thirty years, and I have never been more ready to just burn this entire Family to the ground.

I used to think we could actually be a *family*, us against not just the werewolves and vampires but the entire world that wishes to see us burn.

Instead, the fighting comes more from within our own halls. The betrayals. The pain. The fucking pitchforks and pre-strung nooses.

Myers' eyes are as raw as mine. He stands before me in a

red-splattered shirt, his knuckles dripping both his blood and David's. He beat him unconscious, but he didn't kill him.

"He's going to be a new Family commodity," he said when I finally found the strength to step out of David's ensuite. "For every hour for the rest of his life, he will be sold to be tortured and raped and humiliated."

For the first time, I did not protest the Family getting involved in human trafficking. I still think it is beneath us, fit only for the savage vampires who are too uncouth to handle the finer crimes of blackmail and extortion. But it is a punishment fit for a nobody. A coward who prayed on those too weak to defend themselves.

Exhaling harshly, my brother holds up the tip of a severed penis. "You said you promised Sau his head."

It is not the head she meant, but it is the only one she'll get. I take it from him with my telekinesis, not wanting to touch it with my own flesh. "How did we miss what he was doing to her, Myers?" I ask softly, guilt crushing my lungs, my words, my entire fucking body until I want to just fall to the floor and scream.

He swallows hard, and I can see him struggling to find words to comfort me despite his own guilt. "David creates illusions, Caden," he finally says. "He fooled us all."

"But I'm–" My throat closes. "*Was* her father. I should have –" I shake my head as I try to remember any sign he gave that I just missed. Any lingering touches. Any bad feelings in my gut. Anything at all.

But all I can remember is how much laughter he pulled from my children. How they rushed over to see him every time he came to visit. They love him so much. His death is going to devastate them.

"I should've noticed," I say.

Myers doesn't say anything this time, but I don't turn from him even though silence bangs loud between us. I know this is not what he called me out into the hall for.

He entered David's room for a reason – one he has yet to share.

But I don't push him to speak, too exhausted to want to deal with anything further. Too tied up by responsibility, though, to take my leave until the morning.

As much as I have grown to hate the Shadow Domain, it is my wife's legacy. My *children's* legacy.

I try not to think how many of them have died for that 'privilege.'

"I found Katie," Myers finally says as he glances at my closed bedroom door. Sau's whimpers come from behind the wood, and my heart aches with the distance between us – not just the physical space but the uncertainty about what she saw David doing to Olivia. Did she see him touching her? Did she let him convince her that that was okay? Did she keep quiet when telling me could have saved her? Or did she only have her suspicions? Her lack of knowledge and ignorance?

I can't find the words to ask her.

Can't find the strength of knowing if she knew.

So I focus instead on what my brother is saying. Katie has given me her loyalty all these years; it is the least I owe her. "Where was her body?" I ask.

He shakes his head. "She's alive."

"What?" My attention focuses sharply.

"She claims David tried to kill her, so she hypnotized him to think he did, and she ran. She wanted to get to you personally, but I found her first."

"Is she okay?"

"A bit pale. A bit beaten up, but she'll live. She's tough."

I exhale an empty laugh. That she fucking is. "Does she know why David tried to kill her?" Katie isn't just a run-of-the-mill hypnotist. She's extremely talented, able to use her magic in tiny, indiscernible doses that make her target tell her things they don't mean to reveal.

His jaw tightens. "He was going to stage a coup. He's been getting rid of those loyal to you –"

"Like Christian Gale," I cut in.

His face grows even more grim. "Among others."

"Who?"

"She didn't get their names, but he bragged about their plan being three years in the making."

"Joseph Migor," I growl instantly. He stepped in front of a car and died on scene. But that fucker was paranoid as hel. I've never met someone who checked the road six times before they crossed. His death has never settled well in my stomach.

"Perhaps," he says, not confirming anything. No doubt with David unable to talk or sign, we'll never truly know.

My brother glances away from me, looking off in the distance as he battles something inside him. "There's one last thing..." he finally says with a grimness that hits me hard. "It's about Leon."

"I know."

A silence descends, saying more words than either of us are able to.

I swore to protect my wife.

I swore to protect my children.

Perhaps if Leon had just tried to kill me, I would have stayed still and let him plunge the blade between my rib cage. But he sold out his mother when she was helpless. He allowed his uncle to rape his baby sister.

A part of me wants to give my son the benefit of the doubt.

A part of me wants to believe David only said those things about him being involved to tear this Family apart, knowing that if I killed both him and my heir, my position as Boss would be as solid as a sand castle at low tide.

But there is a bigger part of me that already knows.

That knew it as soon as he dropped Christian Gale's head on my desk. When he avoided his mother after she woke. When he avoided my eyes that night in his kitchen when I asked why he hadn't been to see her.

Leon might not know what David did to Olivia. But there is no doubt that he knew what he was doing to Sau.

My eyes lift up to those of my brother's. "Make it look like Aleric did it," I say slowly, not wanting to give Sau another reason to obsess over Antonio. "And don't let him know it's coming."

A shutter closes over the entirety of Myers' face, and now the reaper stands fully in front of me. "I won't."

My heart shatters into pieces despite the solidity of my words. "But don't do it until after tonight," I say softly. "I want to give Sau at least one dinner with him."

*And me.*

But I don't say that.

Because if I start thinking about it being the last time I'll ever see him…I'll be too damn tempted to forgive him.

"And one more thing," I say, shifting on my feet. "Don't tell anyone what David did to Olivia."

"But –"

I shake my head, remembering the guilt so clear in my wife's eyes. "Let the memories of her bring joy. Olivia has suffered enough."

Pain flashes across his face as he nods.

We hold each other's eyes for a long moment.

Then I turn and open my bedroom door.

Slipping into bed beside my wife, I pull her against my chest. She whimpers in pain, a pain I feel in every atom of my body.

I want to soothe her cries and tell her it'll be okay.

But I can't even murmur the words in the dark without any witnesses.

Because I know them to be lies.

# Madness Behind the Mask

In two days, she will lose two children.
She will never be okay again.
And nor will I.

# PART THREE:
## AN OBSESSED SADIST

# TWENTY-THREE

## ALERIC
### 14 AUGUST 1947

"Cara, my dear," I say with a smile as I step into the beam of moonlight pouring through the open window of her kitchen; the room is the center of any witch's house. Potions and spells are created here, and the power from years of work has seeped into the cream walls of her domain. The air crackles with danger, like the lightning of a storm, raising the hairs on my arms and neck.

She leans against the table, her legs stretched out in front of her. Her full-sleeved tattooed arms are crossed as I open mine in a non-threatening manner. She knows I don't need a weapon to kill her, but I take great pleasure in showing her there isn't a gun tucked into a holster beneath my jacket. There isn't a shirt under it either, and her eyes flow from my pecs to the narrow V pointing beneath my waistband. Her eyes slip lower still, linger, and then rise slowly as she flashes a smile of her own.

"It's not a gun," I say with a light rumble of laughter. Despite her being a witch who would kill me without any hesitation for the right price, I quite enjoy these meetings. The thrill of being this close to death, of being in the presence of someone powerful enough to potentially kill me… It's enough to get my cock hard.

"Aleric." She inclines her head, then eyes me dryly. "I see your choice of words are just as distasteful as always. Has anyone told you you'd be much more desirable if you didn't talk?" She lifts a tattooed hand, a flicker of power arcing between her fingers.

I grin, tucking my thumbs into my black pant's pocket, leaving my jacket open for her to admire the sculpture of my abs as I rock my hips forward. "Aw, my dear," I say as her eyes flick south before quickly rising again. "If you take my mouth with your magic, then you won't be able to haggle a ridiculous price from my lips."

Her eyes narrow. "My prices are not ridiculous. You wish me to go against the Shadows."

"They are nowhere near your territory."

"They are in this world. That is close enough."

Her lips pull down, but there is a gleam of respect in her light-gray eyes. It is a respect I understand. For as much as I wish to destroy the Shadow Domain, I admire their power and audacity to keep clawing back from the bottom of the graves that I and Antonio keep shoving them into.

But this time, I will have the luxury of tossing the dirt over their heads before they can reach up a hand…as long as Cara doesn't screw me over.

Although her coven and theirs are not on good terms, the disease-ridden spell she helped create all those years ago having killed two of Sau's children when it spread out of control, I am not foolish enough to trust the great Cara just because she is the enemy of my enemy.

"But they won't be if your magic works," I say, eyeing

her carefully for any signs of betrayal.

There isn't any glee over playing me alight in her eyes nor any fear about being caught glistening across her brow. No, instead she bares her teeth, insulted.

"It will work. It is *your* plans, simple as they are, that I am not convinced by."

"The best plans are simple."

"The best plans *work*."

I grin as I step towards her, crossing the final space between us. The smell of rosemary and sage tickles my nose, along with the coppery scent of her blood pulsing just beneath her skin. My nostrils flare as I inhale her in, and my fangs elongate at the close proximity of a meal.

Witches have such a delightful flavor – a warm buzz akin to fine wine for humans, and I could use a drink before phasing back home, the teleportation magic so utterly draining, especially given the hundreds of miles between her home and mine.

Adrenaline and hunger rushing through me, I lift a hand to her cheek. Her eyes narrow even as she pushes slightly into my touch, daring me to try something so foolish as to bite her. Were I a sired vampire, she'd feel warm against my palm due to the lack of blood heating mine, but I was born into this life, and my blood pulses as strongly as her own.

Leaning in, I murmur, "Ten thousand dollars, sixteen more hours, a hundred dead…then you will see just how well my plan works."

She looks at me cooly. "Twenty thousand."

"Ridiculous."

"Twenty-five."

She knows damn well I'll go higher. There's no one else I know…who won't just kill me on sight, anyway, who can bypass the Shadow's home wards. Delun spelled them to keep out all vampires and werewolves, and any humans that enter are automatically tagged. With his fucking soul magic,

Delun made the barriers strong as fuck, and not even Cara – the only powerhouse in the middle of the US, having killed Terra Harrison decades ago (though some rumors claim she's still alive, just waiting for her moment of revenge), can break them.

But what Cara Jervis can do is give me a virus that will momentarily weaken a witch's wards.

"Forty," I offer as I rub my thumb across her cheek. "As a show of how much I value our future..." I lean in, my breath whispering across her ear. "*Relationship.*"

She pulls her head away with a snort. "Having seen how you leave your women, forty is not enough."

Staring into her eyes, I lean close, but she smacks me across the cheek, putting her magic behind it to leave a delicious sting. Twisting away from me, she now stands a foot away and raises her hand, power sizzling between her tattooed fingers. "If you even try to charm me, I'll kill you."

"You should know charming is nothing but a modern myth. Even born vampires can't –"

"I am aware. But I'm not talking about that 'look into my eyes' bullshit that humans think vampires have. I'm talking about –"

"My raw charisma?"

"Your arrogant confidence. Strutting in here with your jacket splayed open like a common whore."

I laugh, genuine and carefree as annoyance flashes in her eyes. "Worried you'll succumb?"

"Never."

"Then what's the problem?"

"It's insulting." But though her words are harsh and clipped, her cheeks are a bit flushed and her eyes dart down a fraction before she jerks them back up again.

Grinning, I lean one hip against the counter and cross my arms. My abs tighten to hold the pose, and her gaze wavers again before she narrows her eyes.

"Then let's talk business," I say, my tone flat beneath my smile. I have been waiting a long time to finally kill off the Shadow Domain and take control of St. Augustine. The Death Hunt are mostly concerned with the witches' downfall rather than spreading their own territory, and I am certain after the Shadows go, I'll be able to wipe them out too. But at the moment, I have been flat-out ignoring them. The enemy of my enemy, and all...

But with the corked vial of liquid Cara Jervis fishes out of her robes –a clear, crystal white, best described like captured light to those who can't see magic– the game is about to change in our favor.

"Thirty-nine thousand," she says as she offers it to me, dropping from the forty I offered to show she values our future relationship...but without giving up too much.

My smile for the first time tonight turns genuine – a predatory sneer as I take the vial from her hands.

"Thirty-nine thousand, sixteen hours, and a hundred dead." As I lift my eyes to hers, she shivers.

# TWENTY-FOUR

## HER
### 14 AUGUST 1947

My eyes are so heavy, they feel as if they will tear if I even try to open them. With them swollen from tears thick with grief and caked to my cheeks with what feels like cement, I keep them closed as I wake from a fitful sleep.

If you can even call it sleep.

I don't feel refreshed despite the strong light in the room telling me that I've been out for at least a few hours. I assume it's the sun, but I guess someone could have turned my light on.

My chest tightens with both hate and love.

Love that someone might have realized I didn't want to be alone in the dark.

Hate that I am so grief stricken as to need a light on.

But in the dark, all I end up seeing are the shadows that took my daughter.

My shadows...

My *family's* shadows...meaning *David's* shadows.

And although Caden assured me my uncle didn't touch her, a horrible weight settles in my stomach at the thought of any part of him being near her sweet innocence. He might not have raped her, but he did me.

The knowledge of that has the weight in my stomach seeping into my mouth, making my tongue thick and heavy, my throat constricting at the memory of his cum sliding down my throat. I trusted him... I thought he loved me, that he was teaching me to be a good wife because he cared. But in truth, he was forcing a secret of sin down my throat, and I'm not quite sure what disgusts me more. The fact that he never loved me or my dumb naivety.

The door of my room opens before I can decide, and I know it is Caden who enters despite my eyes being shut. His presence soothes me, and I whimper softly in my need for him to hold me.

He moves to my side immediately, crawling into bed as he wraps me in his arms.

I cling to him as I shake, remembering how cold Olivia was when last I held her. So stiff. So still... Not giggling like she used to whenever I visited her in the nursery. Not staring at me with wide beautiful eyes that radiated so much happiness.

Just gone.

I hope she found comfort in Myers arms' in her final moments.

I hope she looked at his face and didn't die afraid.

I hope it wasn't painful.

Shuddering, I heave and sob as I cry for her all over again. The well of grief is so deep inside me, I feel like I will never know anything other than this pain.

It fills every atom of my existence, weighs it down with a suffocation that squeezes every ounce of life from my bones.

I am so desperate to take her place.

I am her mother.

My little angel should not have died before me.

My shoulders jerking from my wails, I think about how I almost did die a month ago. How I bit out my tongue in an attempt to kill myself, not valuing the precious gift of life at all.

I do not deserve to live.

I do not deserve it.

I want to take her place.

*Please, gods, just let me take her place.*

---

I wake up again, hating that I do. Hating that the gods have ignored my prayer, one of hundreds I've made since I took Olivia into my shadows.

I do not ask again, knowing it is pointless.

I only pray that she'll make it to the good fields of the afterlife. That some dead mother will take care of her for me. Love her for me.

Tears pool behind my eyes as I rub my cheek against Caden's bare chest, seeking comfort.

He doesn't say anything about the snot pouring out of my nose. He just squeezes me tighter and kisses the top of my head.

I want to apologize. I want to tell him I don't normally cry. That I am a true Shadow.

But my tongue is as heavy as my eyes.

And I am already drifting off again in my desperation to escape the living…

---

The next time I wake, I finally find the strength to open

my eyes. Caden is still in bed with me, his arms around me, holding me together as I face the first day without my little girl.

Guilt clogs my throat as I think about the last time I saw her. My magic spiraled out of control. I tore apart the nursery with her in it. Did I hurt her, impale her on the broken splinters of her crib? Did David try to save her but fail? Did he lie about her being okay just so I wouldn't feel this guilt?

Did he…

Did he try to protect me…right before I allowed his torture?

A war of emotions battles inside me, pulling me apart on the blood-soaked fields of uncertainty. I shudder on a gasp, my shoulders shaking under the weight of all this guilt.

It builds even more, crushing the air from my lungs as I suddenly realize who else I might've failed to protect.

Clawing at Caden's arms, I struggle to move away from him, my breaths quick and ragged and raw.

"What's wrong?" my husband asks, his voice sounding as if he's just woken from sleep but is alert nonetheless.

"Ryo," I rasp, begging him to understand as I can't get any more words out. I just need to move. Need to run to the nursery and see if he's okay. How did I forget about my youngest boy? His cot isn't far from Olivia's, but I was so focused on her…so focused on what I thought Uncle David was doing to her…

My body slick with sweat, I fight off the covers as soon as Caden releases me. I don't even try to stand. I just roll off the side of the bed, hit the ground, and crawl.

"Sau!"

My hands shake from the fervor of my mind and the weakness of my body. I'm still not strong enough to move much on my own, but I grit my teeth and haul myself forward.

Feet thud onto the floor behind me, and in another moment, I'm scooped up by two strong arms, but even the thick barrier of my husband's biceps and forearms can't keep out the cold gripping my heart. Twisting it. Freezing it as I think about Ryo lying dead under a pile of rubble that *I* caused.

Uncle David never said anything about my little boy surviving.

"*Please*," I rasp as I look at the door, desperate to get through it.

"Okay," Caden says as he walks forward, and I nod jerkily, my body coiled with the need to be there already. Holding my boy. Making sure he's okay. Not dead like his sister.

*"Sometimes babies just die."*

My heart squeezes, a sharp pain lancing through my body. My throat tight, I gasp wildly, struggling to get any air down my lungs. Is this what Olivia felt like when she just died for no reason? Did she feel like the earth was closing in on her on all sides? Unable to breathe. Unable to escape death's clutches?

Tears thick on my lashes, I swivel my head down to the right, down the hall in the direction of the nursery.

But Caden turns left, and I let out a choked cry. Before I can beg him to turn around, he lifts my chin up with his telekinesis until I catch his eyes.

"They're all in the kitchen, Sau," he murmurs. "Ryo's with them."

I close my mouth, then open it again to suck in the first solid breath I've been able to take for a while. "He's..." I swallow, finally managing to dislodge the hard knot in my throat. "He's okay?"

"Yes."

I breathe out, feeling the biggest of the tremors leaving me, but the small shaky ones still tremble down my spine.

"Can I see the nursery anyway?"

He stops in the hall, and my heart flips on a nervous plummet. Has Caden seen it since I destroyed it?

"What happened in there, Sau?" he asks, and there is a tightness to his voice that causes me to flinch.

I guess Uncle David's illusion fell when Caden tortured him. I take a deep breath, hold it for a second, then let it out, reminding myself that he never touched my daughter. "I heard crying, so I went to go check on her, but Uncle David was already there. He changed her diaper..."

I frown, trying to remember if I smelled a soiled nappy. I shake my head at the smell of a clean nursery. He didn't touch her. I just wasn't paying attention.

"But I panicked," I blurt. "I thought... My magic got out of control and I..." Tears burn my eyes as I stare at him, pleading for him to tell me the truth despite how much it will hurt. "Did I kill her?" The words come out as a mere whisper, but I don't doubt that he hears them clearly.

His eyes glisten as he shakes his head. "Magic didn't kill her," he whispers.

I shudder, my entire body caving in, and I press my cheek against his chest.

I didn't kill her.

A small sob leaves me, but I swallow it down as I close my eyes. "Thank you," I murmur, but whether to him for telling me the truth or to the gods for finally answering a prayer, I am too exhausted to discern.

"Do you still want to see the nursery?" he asks, his arms tightening around me.

I shake my head, wanting to see my children. *Needing* to see them all. "Is Leon..."

"He is here," he says. "He's come to have dinner with you if you're up to it."

"I am," I say despite exhaustion pulling on every bone.

Caden continues walking towards the kitchen, and the

spicy smell of jambalaya soon fills my nose. My stomach grumbles, suddenly realizing it hasn't eaten all day, too full of grief to have noticed before.

Caden's pace quickens, and within seconds we're there. The room is quiet and gloomy, sorrow snuffing out all else. Jonathan is normally asking for seconds long before anyone else has even half-finished their plates, but now he just twirls his fork around the rice, scooping out bits only to dump them back down.

Molly and Bonnie cry as they eat small amounts, Molly with her left hand, Bonnie with her right. No doubt they are holding hands under the table, giving and taking the only warmth in the room.

My eyes fly to Leon, who sits at one end of the table. Ryo is beside him, grabbing a fistful of food and shoving it into his mouth. But even he is doing it without his normal laughing gusto.

My eyes glisten as he looks up and sees me. "Mama!" He reaches for me with a soggy, dirty hand, bits of yellow mush falling off it.

I want to cry and laugh in equal volume as I see that he truly is okay.

They're all okay.

Thank gods because I cannot lose another one.

I might've missed most of their moments due to being in a coma, but this past month, I have come to love each and every one of them more than life itself. They have become my motivations for living, even Leon, who I have not seen much of at all nor talked to once. He's been so busy, but now he's finally here, and I take comfort in that, letting it nudge up against my grief.

He smiles at me tightly, his face white with pain, and I shift in Caden's arms, a silent request for him to put me down. As soon as he does, everyone stands and rushes over to me, as if our pain is pulling us all together, elastic lines snapping back. I hold them tightly, my arms moving around each one, trying to touch them all, taking their pain and finding comfort at the same time.

I turn to Leon, wanting to ask him how he is, what he's been up to, what his likes and dislikes are, if he has a girl, all the questions I haven't been able to ask, just wanting to get to know him, to bask in a mother's love.

But before I can say a word, Ryo starts to cry for me, hating that we are all here while he is left at the table, stuck in his highchair.

My children all step back, albeit slowly, so I can go to him, and I drag my feet, such exhaustive movements that leave me sweating from the effort. Dropping to my knees in front of him, I smile. Not forced but not full. A pang to my happiness.

"Mama!" Ryo says, his tears stopping as he pats my face, the slop on his hands smearing across my chin. It gets in my hair as he fists a bit, and I wince as he pulls, but I embrace the pain.

"Nom nom nom," I say, pretending to eat the fingers of his other hand. He giggles, soft rays that pierce the dark clouds hanging over us all. Chairs are scooted towards the table as everyone retakes their seats, and Caden touches my shoulder to let me know to take mine. My stomach growls as he helps me up and into an empty chair. A fresh plate is laid in front of me by one of our staff, and my belly rumbles again.

I want to eat, but as Caden is here, no one can start until he does. Even Leon stops Ryo from taking another bite. Picking up my fork, Caden places it in my hand. "Eat," he says as he heads for his chair, and the first bite is down my throat before he can settle.

Unlike how they all were when we entered, forks now move with purpose. Olivia's presence still weighs on us as heavily as before, but we all carry a part of her, helping to hold her up so no one staggers under alone.

Once the sharpest of my hunger is sated, I turn to my firstborn, wanting so badly to get to know him. Despite him not actually being the *first* of my children to be born, the title is moved to the oldest surviving to make writing and understanding our laws easier, while also not making him seem weak by calling him a 'surviving heir.'

A surviving heir is one undeserving of the throne who just happens to inherit it due to the death of his brothers. It leads to people asking, "If he got it. Why can't I?"

But a *firstborn* is power. He is one born to lead, and I see that solidified in the strong shoulders and stiff back of my son.

"Leon," I start just as Caden shouts for me to get down.

I turn to him as movement explodes around me. Caden is on his feet, facing the front door, but the stranger enters directly behind him, having phased in, simply appearing from thin air.

I scream as my husband turns too slowly, and the new man with dark-gray eyes bares his teeth to show fangs. He snaps them over Caden's neck, the points piercing skin before he hisses with pain and vanishes as quickly as he appeared. The knife Caden shoved into him with his magic flies to his hand as he swings around.

My heart thudding, I grab my plate of food, the glass China decades old, then fling it at Leon. He ducks just as the air ripples behind him, and the glass shatters across the face that's just solidified. Dark-gray eyes snap to me as the vampire phases once more. I shove to my feet even as Caden pushes me away with his telekinesis, both of us having clocked the man's next move.

But he doesn't appear to rip out my throat. Another vampire comes instead, right behind Molly. My scream just starts to rip past my lips when he grabs her and is gone. The kitchen fills with more bodies, more vampires somehow able to get past our wards.

I don't have time to ask Caden how this is possible, if he detected something breaking or weakening when he shot to his feet before anyone entered. I barely have time to stop my scream when the first vampire appears again, finally in front of me.

I swing at him, my muscles weak, and he laughs as my fist connects with his face. A body falls from the ceiling behind him, one of his men having phased high, and my heart shatters as Molly screams on her plummet. She hits the table with a *thud* that snaps her head in an awkward angle, but before I can scream for her, the man in front grabs me by the hair and jerks my head to the side. I kick out at him as Caden screams my name.

White fangs flash as my children are picked off around me.

My body buzzes with my power. I was asleep for years; worse, it was during the time when I should've learned to control my magic. So now it builds without any training, without any guidelines, running on pure emotion that rips out of my fingers as they dangle at my sides.

My hands turn into smoke that grows out in long lines that shoot to the floor just as the vampire sinks his teeth into my neck. My blood pulses beneath his lips, and on instinct, my magic builds there, denying him the pleasure of drinking my essence, healing itself around his fangs.

He growls as he lifts his teeth to bite again, but by this time my shadows have pushed between us, and although they are not solid enough to shove us apart, he jumps back as if they are.

He knows I can kill with them. Knows that I am one of those progenies.

But he doesn't know I am a grieving mother.

Who will do anything to save her remaining children.

As my eyes flick around the kitchen, seeing the blood of

my babies, I open myself completely, offering up my own body to the monsters I know lurk inside my shadows.

I can feel them coming in swathes. Their feet clicking across a rocky ground that doesn't exist in this world. I can hear their mandibles snapping with hunger, see their eyes glowing with greed.

"Sau, stop!" Cadens screams, but I don't listen, having nothing left to lose. "Sau!"

The vampire's head snaps to the left as his eyes widen. I direct my anger at him, my shadows, knowing he is going to try to phase. Just as his body starts to fade, I wrap a tendril of darkness around his foot, anchoring him here.

He curses as his eyes grab me.

A child's scream breaks my concentration, and I look towards Bonnie as she cradles her sister, but it's already too late for him. I am no longer in control of my magic. The monsters are coming.

My twins fly across the room and into a corner, put there by their father's telekinesis. Ryo joins them at the same time, and Bonnie reaches for her brother. Jonathan and Leon fight back to back in front of them, bleeding from various wounds as vampires hit them from all sides, their claws and knives swiping fast.

I can't see Caden through the thick of bodies phasing in and out of our kitchen, but I know he's here. Still alive. Still fighting. Somewhere…

The vampire who started this all takes a step back, and my eyes snap to him. I won't let him leave. If we are to die, so will he.

Screaming, I fall to my knees and open my shadows up further, hurrying the monsters on like a steak waved in the face of a starving dog. They come. Finally. Gnarled clawed hands, twisted and half-decayed shoot out of the swirling black smoke spread across the floor. Mandibles and open maws slick with blood and drool, bits of rotten corpses stuck between their teeth. Beady black eyes, set by the dozen on furry heads and stalks that swivel. Foul-smelling tentacles that leak an acid that burns the very air.

They come from everywhere, in all their monstrous forms, grabbing vampires and yanking them into the dark world below. Little snacks to chew and munch on, the cracking of bones interrupted only by the screams, as they continue to claw their way into our world.

"Go!" the vampire screams as his body starts to fade. A gnarled hand shoots for him, but he is already gone, and the rest of his men leave soon after, blinking out fast like dying stars, and I am left to scream.

I can't stop the shadows from opening up further.

And now there is no one left to eat other than my husband – the rest of my family protected by our blood.

Tears falling down my cheeks, I turn to Leon, hoping Uncle David instructed him what to do if a Shadow ever fell to the magic we controlled.

His eyes snap to me, then away as his father screams. A tentacle has wrapped around his left foot, and some godsawful bulbous form is pulling itself out of the dark towards him, using him as an anchor. Hisses erupt as more appendages fly towards the only morsel left in the room.

Caden shoves as many of them away as he can with his telekinesis, but his power is waning, drained and taxed hard. His eyes snap to me without any anger, without any pain, and I know he is about to give up. Or perhaps he simply can't hold out anymore.

He mouths, "I love you," just as the tentacle manages to pull him to his knees.

I scream.

And then there is blissful darkness.

My son's shadows having consumed me, hopefully in time...

# TWENTY-FIVE

## ALERIC
### 14 AUGUST 1947

I land in my own house across town, my body buzzing with adrenaline. After such careful planning, after cutting through their guards without notice, after leaving nearly a hundred dead in our wake before we attacked the Shadow family itself, I came so close to death.

Throwing my head back, I laugh, exhilaration escaping my lungs rather than the angry, frustrated curses that I'm sure will leave my men as soon as they phase in.

I have never felt more alive.

A male vampire phases in front of me as if on queue, breathing hard and covered in blood. He straightens as he looks at me, his dark-gray eyes so similar to my own. He inherited them from me, after all.

"Why the fuck are you laughing?" he asks. "We failed in our mission and lost over fifty of the sired."

"Yes, yes, what a shame," I say, but not even the deaths of a good portion of my sired 'children' can extinguish the joy inside me.

For nearly three hundred years I've been alive.

And not once have I ever felt like this.

Sau Shadow... There was such fire in her eyes, such devotion to burning the world down around her.

My cock twitches as I turn from my son and look out the window of my study. Despite the evening hour, the sun is still strong in the Floridian sky. Such a beautiful start to the night...

"What a *shame*?" my son seethes as he stalks over to me, his rage blistering the air so much with every step that I can practically feel where he is in the room.

"Mmm," I say, unconcerned. He's only fifty or so years old, an accidental pregnancy by some woman or another. I'm not even sure. He just showed up crying on my doorstep one day, claiming his mother had sent him to find Mr. Zadar on her deathbed. I never cared enough to figure out which whore she'd been. Even with him being a full-blood and with blonde hair to my black, those clues don't really narrow the list down much.

But her surviving our night together, then long enough to give birth... Now *that* is a damn good clue. Perhaps I could figure out her identity easily enough if I cared. Then again, I don't even care enough to just ask Colton.

Nor did I care to even question his claims about being my son. He served his purpose, marrying Destiny, the oldest daughter of the Laska Family, two weeks after I officially named him my heir. Besides, I doubt Colton will even live long enough to claim my throne. I'm surprised he didn't die tonight, in all honesty. He's too soft, which is ironic given he's supposedly my son and his mother was strong enough to survive my *attentions*.

"Do their lives mean nothing to you?" Colton asks as he

stops beside me, his eyes blazing red in their fury. I can see them in the reflection of the window, and I bet he is just *itching* to attack me despite the respectable distance he's left between us. He knows I do not care for my space to be invaded.

"No," I say, watching our backyard fill with vampires phasing home. "And neither does yours."

Turning, I dismiss him as I head for the door.

But he just follows me – his courage and disregard for authority the only two traits of his that I admire.

"You know, *Father*," he says as we hit the stairs. "If you keep treating us like disposables, you won't have a Family left to fight for."

"You think I fight for this Family?" I chuckle. "A soft heart *and* a fool."

"You used to."

"Be a soft heart or a fool?"

"Mother said –"

"Your mother is dead," I snap, not caring to hear what false stories she filled his head with.

"She died still loving you."

"Then I see where you inherited your foolishness." I'm not a man worth loving, and if any of the women I use for my own twisted pleasure don't realize that, then they are damn fools.

"You're an ass," he hisses.

"No, I'm Aleric."

He seethes in silence, no doubt imagining my death and how the Family would thrive under his rule. Which only proves his further idiocy.

Our nest needs sired vampires to thrive, and his heart is too soft to turn those who don't wish to be turned. But we aren't faster than the wolves nor have their natural resistance to magic. Although we have a relatively good chance against most witches one on one, it only takes one good spell to kill us. Only takes one damn good witch to hold us off. Like Caden did as he protected most of his fucking children, I think with a scowl.

My rage morphs into a smirk. *Or Sau.*

Such fire.

Such passion.

My cock twitches again as we reach the bottom of the stairs.

I'm looking forward to seeing her again. I'll cut off her hands and fuck her until she dies.

I wonder if she'll still have that light in her eyes by the end. That utter defiance.

A groan builds in my chest, but I squash it. As much as I want to think about her as I wrap my hand around my cock upstairs, I have men to see. Morale to build. Yada yada yada, blah blah blah.

I open the door to the backyard and step outside. The air is thick and muggy despite the hour, the summer heat causing nearly instant sweat to build on my skin. There are tall hedges all along my property to keep the nosy neighbors from spotting us popping out of thin air and walking around covered in blood.

Or dragging bodies out in the middle of the night, fully drained, their corpses shriveled to a sack of bones.

Scanning the yard, I look for the redheaded lumberjack who has sat at my right-hand side for the last thirty-two years. I spot my son-in-law, Vlad, Destiny's older brother, holding up a young sired missing his left foot.

"Who'd you lose it to?" I ask, nodding at the wound gushing all over my lawn. In normal circumstances, he'd regrow it over time if he feeds from me, but that damn reaper of the Shadows has a cursed weapon that stops our natural healing process. If he was cut by that, there's no saving him.

Vlad narrows his eyes. His jaw tight, he shifts between

us, no doubt knowing what's on my mind. But unlike my soft heart of a son, Vlad understands the laws of nature. Just like a mother will leave her runts to die, there is no point wasting resources to try to save someone who won't survive.

"He stepped on a mine," Vlad says.

I quirk a brow. "Good reflexes." The guy looks military, shaved head, clear brown eyes if a bit pale, and I probably turned him for that reason, but there are a lot of humans I've sired recently, and they've all merged together.

But I don't need to know his name to heal him. And he will thank me for it, convincing himself that I care despite not showing him basic courtesy.

Bringing my wrist up, I sink my fangs into my flesh. The sired's eyes turn a muddy red as his hunger pulses quicker in the vein at his throat. The other sired around us shift with the same need to feed, like addicts sighting their dealer coming down the street.

But not one moves towards me or shoves another out of their way to be the first in line. Such rudeness will get them killed, and they have witnessed that enough to know I will not hesitate to kill them any more than I hesitated to turn them despite their screams. I have no patience for true addicts.

I beckon to Soldier Boy, and he falls forward out of Vlad's grip, dropping to his knees in front of me as he lifts his head. I hold my wrist over his open mouth and let my blood drip down his throat. He swallows greedily as I turn my attention to Vlad. "Did you kill that girl?"

"I don't know. I wasn't able to check after I dropped her from the ceiling."

"Mmm." A whimper from below tells me my wrist has stopped bleeding, my natural healing having kicked in, but I do not reopen it to continue his feeding. He only needed a few drops to kickstart his own healing; I've been more than generous – not that Colton would agree.

Turning my head, I look for him. "Colton."

He tenses, his back to me as he talks to his wife. She's covered in blood, having joined us in tonight's fight. Her brown eyes find mine, a harsh glare within them. Slowly, my boy turns to me. "Yes, Father?"

"Go out and let word get back to the Death Hunt that the Shadow's wards are weakened for another hour or so."

Although I want Sau for my own, if she can't survive this attack, she isn't as strong as I thought, and it will be no loss to me.

"Yes, Father." With a last glance at his wife, he phases away.

"The rest of you get inside." No one hesitates, having waited for this very command. Within seconds, the yard is cleared until it's just Vlad, Destiny, and I.

But when Vlad cocks his head at his younger sister, even she leaves to feast on the buffet I had prepared for our return. Unfortunately, it won't be the celebratory meal I had in mind, but well, it's still an open bar full of fresh meat. The humans that survive tonight will even be given the fantastic opportunity of becoming bloodbanks – those in our gang who feed us in exchange for a position at the kiddie's table.

"Count how many we've lost and find replacements by the end of the week," I say to Vlad. "Do you know who fought Myers?"

I was hoping he would be at the main house, having dinner with the family, but no one came across him by the time we struck. Either we got damn lucky, or the fucker has come back with us. He is a shapeshifter, able to take another form, and he could be one of the sired (he can't phase) inside my house right now. He'd have to be crazy to have returned with us, but reapers are rarely sane.

"Egrin said he saw Myers fall."

"Is that right?"

I turn my head towards my house and inhale. I don't smell a witch's wine-like blood, but a shapeshifter can replicate even that. Myers would've needed time to study Egrin though, and unless he'd planned to take his spot from the start, I doubted he would have bothered. We had been well on our way to slaughtering the entire Shadow Domain, having caught them with their pants around their ankles. Not once in the last thousand years had a sup made it past their wards without permission.

My lips curl at being the first mad enough to try it. Then again, tonight was twenty-five years in the making siring enough soldiers and keeping their numbers hidden from our enemies. We hit them hard and fast right after they changed shifts to guard the portal across town. Those leaving the warded area were fresh and those returning were tired. And the guards inside were too careless after centuries of not being hit.

Utter fools.

Licking the witch blood lingering on my lips, I take a step towards the house. Vlad walks beside me. "Find him. If he doesn't feed, bring him to me." I cock my head to the side. "If anyone doesn't feed, bring them to me." Myers is the only one I'm aware of in the Shadow Domain that has the ability to shapeshift, but that doesn't mean he's the only one.

Vlad nods. Given I caught sight of him as he phased in, I know he's not Myers. He might not agree with all I do, but he knows that this Family is only strong because of me. To kill me is to kill it...until Vlad is strong enough to sire good-quality vampires of his own. Colton might be my official heir, but we both know he won't last.

Stepping inside the house, we head for the stairs. A solid door blocks them, and Vlad opens it for me to enter. At the bottom sits another door, solid wood and painted black.

Both of them are soundproofed so the neighbors can't hear our guests' scream, and as Vlad shuts the door behind us, my pace quickens to the other.

As soon as I pull it open, terrified screams fill my ears, pulsing through my cock as the smell of fresh blood hits my nose. I inhale deeply as the band in the corner starts to play, violin bows moved by two naked bloodbanks who have their legs spread. Male and female vampires feast on their pussies, blood no doubt mixing with their saliva. The music jumps and stutters as the two players struggle to keep their attention on their instruments.

A woman screams in front of me as she is held down on the ground by three vamps. They're ripping her white dress to pieces. I left all the new food dressed so one, they stood out more and two, because tearing off the packaging is such a fucking turn on.

I watch them for a moment as one buries his cock inside her as his two mates feed on her wrists. Then he bites her neck, and I wait to see if he rolls over so another can take her up the ass, but when he doesn't, I move on.

My eyes latch onto one of the snacks being attacked by a shirtless, ripped vamp. He has his hand wrapped around her throat and lifts her until her feet come off the ground. She claws at him as he laughs, terror making her blood sweeter, but then she kicks him in the balls. He drops her, gasping, and his mates laugh at him instead. A smile curls my lips as one of the female vampires quickly moves in on the girl, catching the fist swung at her face, then breaking her arm with a sharp twist. Spurned on by her scream, the group around her close in, and she is soon dragged to the ground and filled with multiple cocks and fingers.

A man fucks her from the back as she lies on top of the woman, who is scissoring her hard, her hands full of the snack's breasts. Leaning up, she sucks a nipple into her mouth and moans. Two men, one on either side, force the snack's hands around their veiny cocks. They rock their hips into her as they each fist her hair and take turns yanking her lips against their pre-cum heads.

The man behind her pulls back, looks down, rearranges his cock, and then thrusts in hard. Given how the female vampire's lips pop off that creamy titty with a scream of pleasure, I can only assume he's now fucking her as he shoves his fingers into the girl's cunt.

Tears streak down the snack's face, her broken arm not cared for at all, and I can see the fight fading from her eyes. All hope gone. I doubt she'll survive till the morning. Either they'll kill her, or she'll do it herself.

A roar of frustration mixed with a crowd of laughter has my head turning to the right.

"Watch it, Max! She'll stab you!"

More laughter follows, but the bulk of bodies is too thick for me to see through. As I make a beeline for them at the back wall, the crowd parts, hurriedly moving bodies falling over pulled down pants. Doesn't matter if they were feeding or fucking, if they're my men or the snacks, they all scamper away.

I arrive just as Max, a silver fox turned in his fifties, pins a lass to the wall, one thick, veiny hand around her throat, one clasped around her wrist. She still has a grip on a steak knife, keeping hold of it even as he slams her arm against the wall repeatedly.

But my eyes are on her long black hair. It's down to her waist.

Just like Sau's.

I lift my eyes to her face and grin.

Green fire glares back at the man growling in her face.

I can picture Sau so clearly as she stared at me, willing me to die with her in their kitchen, and my cock grows fully hard.

I stride forward just as Max slams her whole body

against the wall. The crowd starts to hoot and holler, but then one of the vampires on the sidelines catches sight of me and she nudges the woman beside her. Both quiet, and that instant silence spreads like wildfire through the line as they turn their heads and jump. Stepping back, they part for me, but Max is too focused on his meal to notice.

Just as he jerks the woman's head to the side so he can bite her neck, I grab a fistful of his own head, my claws digging into his flesh, down through that soft part of his skull.

He starts to throw an elbow back, an instinctive reflex that might have saved him from anyone else. But I simply catch it with my other hand, crush his joint together like a ball of clay, and then toss him across the room.

While still holding on to his head.

His neck tears with a delightful squelch, his arteries spraying free as his eyes instantly lose focus. His headless body hits the wall, then drops with a *thud*. The crowd has gone silent, as have the two violinists. Even the terrified snacks have stopped screaming.

As Max starts to dissolve into ash, I release his head and step towards the woman with the long black hair.

Her back pressed against the wall, she trembles, her knees bent in a half-cower. But she still stares at me in defiance. Still grips that knife with a hope that it'll save her.

Smiling with all my charm, I walk towards her slowly.

She doesn't move, her gaze on mine, her brain faltering on what it should do. I stop in front of her and lift a hand to her cheek. Max's ashes leave a smudge across her skin, and I rub the last of him across her lips.

She trembles as she swallows, the pulse at her throat working hard. Leaning in, I whisper in her ear, "Stab me."

She sucks in a sharp breath, no doubt fearing what will happen if she does.

But I can feel her other thoughts whirling.

Feel it in the calming of her tremors.

In the straightening of her spine.

*What do I have left to lose?*

Jerking her arm forward, she slams the knife into my side, but it catches on my rib cage, nicking the bone. Her hand tightens around the handle to yank it free again, and I let her, delighting in the pain, in the proximity to Sau's fire.

It's not as good as the real thing.

This little snack can't do anything to really hurt me, her reflexes too slow, her power too little, her *fire* not hot enough.

I *burn* to have Sau in her place, my hands on her body, my cock ramming inside her cunt as she breaks around me.

But she is out of my grasp tonight.

"Again," I growl as I hold lackluster green eyes that widen instead of narrow. But at least she slams the knife back into me, the sharp pain making my cock throb.

My hand tightening on her cheek, I sag against her and groan. My balls grow tighter with every stab of her knife, my body healing too fast for me to bleed out but not too fast to stop the delightful buzz that comes with buckets of one's blood pouring out at their feet.

Ripping my pants apart with a sharp claw, I dig out my cock, then haul up her dress. She screams as she stabs me again, more feverishly, more hopeful that she can stop me.

"That's it," I groan as I grip my cock in my hand. I lift her whole body by her face until her pussy is hovering over my tip. My cock is pulsing hard, my balls drawn so tight with anticipation. But I wait for her to swing back the knife again. And as it enters me, I enter her, burying my cock deep inside her cunt.

Groaning, I fuck her hard, delighting in her screams, in the pain in my side, in the bright green eyes I can see so well inside my mind. Imagining Sau between me and the wall, I ram my cock inside her faster. Harder. *Deeper.* Until my hips no longer just *slap* against her. They *pound*, a crushing pace that fractures her pelvis. Then crushes it completely.

And still I thrust into her, blood pouring out of her pussy, the brick wall behind her cracking around her body as I ram into her harder. She no longer stabs me. She no longer screams. She just hangs limp, her pale face crushed between my fingers, parts of her pelvis sticking out of her skin and cutting me with every thrust.

Imagining shadows swirling around me, I hiss with a need to come. The feeling of death embraces me, makes my balls throb. And when I finally explode inside her, I bury my teeth into her neck and moan Sau's new name:

*"Mine."*

# TWENTY-SIX

## HER

### 14 AUGUST 1947

I run towards the light, away from the monsters all around me. I'm pulled back to Earth, my breaths ragged, my skin glistening with sweat. I look frantically around me, trying to blink my eyes into focus so I can see where I am, if I'm too late, if *Leon* was too late pulling me into his shadows.

*Caden!*

I want to scream his name, to get an answer before I can see, but I do not have the courage to. What if he does not answer? What if he can't, having been torn apart by the monsters I called forth?

My body shaking, I almost wish my vision to never return.

But it does.

And he is *here*.

In our bedroom. Sitting on the bed in front of me.

The door shuts as Leon leaves, and I fall forward into my husband's outstretched arms. "I'm so sorry," I say. "I'm sorry."

"Shhhh." He runs a hand down my hair as he holds me to him. "It's okay, Sau. Everyone's okay."

"Molly?" I croak, every muscle in my body tensing to hear his, 'I'm sorry, but she's gone.'

"Even Molly," he says, shocking me, and I look up into his eyes, expecting to see a lie. But his smile rings true.

"I want to see her." I start to pull away so I can stand.

"You need to rest. What you did –"

"No, I need to see her. *Please*, Caden," I beg as he holds me still.

"I promise you she's fine."

"But *how*? There were so many bloodsuckers..." My throat tightens at the memory of the one who phased in first, who stared at me with such sick joy in his dark-gray eyes. His short black hair and pierced ear, the hard cut of his jaw, the pure, chilling *glee* – he'll stay with me for the rest of my life. Shivering, I try to focus on Caden's sudden pride.

"Molly's magic triggered at the threat of her life. She said the vampire tried to bite her, but her skin hardened like stone. So he dropped her. She only passed out due to tapping into her power so early."

I suck in a relieved breath. "And the others?"

"I created a shield around them."

My jaw drops into an O. "You did that while fighting?" The amount of power that would require... I always knew Caden was strong. It is why my father had me marry him, but that level of magic – No, the ability to *control* that much... My hands fist as shame fills me. I barely tapped into mine, and I lost control nearly instantly.

He nods. "Which is why it flickered from time to time, allowing a few to break free." His face grows grim. "But I wouldn't have been able to keep that up for long." When he cups my cheek, I lean into his touch. "You saved us, Sau."

I swallow and glance away briefly before looking at the space between us, but he is so close, I can't inspect him thoroughly. I do catch the smell of blood though. My heart twists. "I nearly killed you," I whisper.

"You did no such thing."

My heart breaks at his lie. I want to believe him, but the memory of his scream, that horrible, twisted cry of agony where he believed he was going to die... I hear his mouthed, "I love you." His acceptance of that, his want to protect me from my own guilt even as he suffered *because of me*...

But before I can open my mouth and tell him just how much he means to me, that I love him too, more so than even before, the door bangs open and the smell of copper hijacks the air.

"Myers!" I shout as he staggers in, one hand clutched to his side, soaked and dripping red. But even if his palm managed to stop the blood from leaving him there, he is covered in a dozen more wounds. A bite on his shoulder. Claw marks across his chest. A knife still embedded in his thigh. There isn't an inch of him free of blood.

"I know...you don't know how to control...your magic," he says as he drags one foot in front of the other. Caden stands and hurries to him, catching him just as he falls. "But I figured...might as well try...on a dying man."

"No!" I scramble out of bed, my muscles moving on pure adrenaline despite the screaming aches building all over my body. "You're not dying!"

"Sau," Caden cautions as I draw near. "You could make it worse. I'll get Louise."

The woman who failed to save my brother after he lost his arm. Myers might have all of his appendages still, but I can't believe he's in any better shape than Luther was.

"No," I say as I drop to my knees beside them and hold

my hands out over his side. "She can't handle this..."

"You've never done anything like this."

"I healed my tongue." I don't know if I actually did. If it was me or Caden reattaching all that was severed. But I have to be able to do this. I was told *everyone* was okay. I know Caden meant just those who'd been in the kitchen, but I want him to also have meant Myers. He is the last of Caden's family. He is my family too.

He stares at me, and I will him to believe in me. I need my husband's support in this, though I will do it without. Myers is fading quickly. I can feel his life leaving him, feel his body shutting down as the blood rushes from him in so many places.

So many...

Too many...

*I can't do this.*

I jump at the feel of Caden's hands on mine. He holds them both, and I only then realize just how much they're shaking.

"Breathe, my sweet Sau," he murmurs, his voice calm and showing none of the panic hammering away in my chest. "Feel the magic inside you. It's strong, and it's a part of you. Just like your breath, it fills you, but it moves like a phantom dancing beneath your skin."

I swallow as I turn my concentration inwards, trying to feel it moving. At first I don't feel anything other than the rapid thudding of my pulse and the ticking clock that is Myers' life. Panic explodes at the thought of him bleeding out while I play savior. This isn't the time to be learning. I open my mouth to shout for Louise when I *feel* it.

That quick two-step in my chest, a flashy twirl that demands my attention. *Don't call her. Use me.*

Pressing my lips together, I concentrate on following those footsteps down inside me. It is like...feeling a breeze inside a cave you have been lost in for hours. That slight brush against your skin, raising hairs even though you're not quite sure if the wind is really there. If it's real, or if it's just hope. It is that shattering of a broken heart. That desperation to win the bet. The gut feeling that something is wrong. All abstract things that aren't physically firing across your nerves but you feel all the same. Magic is like nothing I can properly explain, but it feels like *me*.

For the first time, I embrace it, joining it in its waltz rather than simply throwing open the floodgates and letting myself get sucked up in its current.

My hands start to glow with a bright light, and Caden straightens as he holds me. I can feel my power seeping into him, feel the wounds he's hidden under bandages and a change of clothes knitting together beneath dried blood. I gasp as an acidic taste of…infection?…fills my tongue and churns my stomach.

He tries to pull away, guiding my hands to his brother, but I twist my wrists to lock my fingers with his. That tentacle secreted a poison inside him. It's filling his blood, pumping through his heart, killing him without him even knowing. I latch onto it, my body shaking.

"I'm fine, Sau."

I ignore him, knowing he's not.

"Save my brother!"

Almost there…

I dig my nails into his hands, holding on for one more moment before letting him go on a gasp. My body sags forward, shaking from the utter exhaustion pounding me from all sides.

My husband pulls away. "You've overtaxed yourself." I flinch, hearing the accusation and guilt and rage beneath his calm tone. *Why did you heal me instead of him?*

I try to tell him he was poisoned, but he stands without giving me the chance to explain. Or perhaps he already knew and decided that his brother should be the one to live…

Tears blister my eyes as he runs for the door, shouting for Louise. I sag beside Myers, breathing hard as sweat runs down my forehead and my shaking hands lie cradled against my chest.

"It's…okay," Myers says, his gaze on mine before the light – his *life* fades away.

I choke back a scream of denial as I place my hands over his wounded side, and I go back to that ballroom inside of me, demanding another dance. The magic comes swiftly, but it doesn't take me around in a gentle waltz. It is a blaze of energy –powerful movements that leave me breathless and all too aware that I am not the one leading this dance.

My hands glow bright as my magic burns through me. Caden screams for me to stop, but I ignore him, pushing every ounce of my magic out through my fingertips. I can save Myers if I just connect to him, so I open myself up completely, binding our bodies together.

His eyes jerk open as he gasps.

But before I can smile, I scream.

My skin tears. My bones break. Gashes of flesh are ripped off me, mirroring the wounds on Myers.

"Sau!" I hear my name called from a distance as my head rolls back and I fall forward, my body seizing even as the magic continues to flow between us.

My hands are violently ripped away, and the sudden severing of the flow of power causes me to gasp as the world resettles around me. I tremble, my body slick with sweat and blood and in so much fucking pain. I whimper.

Caden cradles me in his arms as Myers sits up in front of me. I look at him, relieved that he at least is safe.

"What happened?" I ask, my voice a croak as I struggle to sit up on my own.

"Your magic turned on you, Sau. You pushed yourself too hard. You should know better than that."

I vaguely remember Father's warnings. How the magic will eat us alive if we let it. Shivering, I swallow at the close call, but I do not regret trying. "Myers was dying..." I say.

Caden looks at me grimly, then over to his brother, who is rotating his shoulder and pulling apart the tears of his shirt to look at his side. A red wound still mars his skin, but it is no longer bleeding. I put a hand on my same side and wince at the flash of pain. A warm wetness coats my fingers, but it has nothing on the joy radiating inside me. I saved him.

For once, I *caused* something good.

I didn't *fail* him.

I didn't *bring* more pain.

I.

Did.

Something.

*Good*.

Tears clogging my throat, I smile at him.

"Thank you," he murmurs. "But you are too valuable to this Family to risk your life for mine."

I shake my head. "You *are* this Family, Myers. We all make up a part of it."

"Do we know how Aleric got in?" my husband asks, his jaw tight, no doubt hating the thought of having to choose between the two of us.

"Aleric or all of the Blood Fangs?" Myers grins, and I suck in a breath, recalling those dark-gray eyes. I've never seen the head of the vampires before, but I know without a doubt, he is Aleric. His name resonates inside me, and I shiver.

"This isn't the time to be a smartass," Caden snaps.

His brother draws back, looking more horrified than when he staggered in here on death's door. "If there's ever not a time for a joke, then go ahead and kill me."

"I might," my husband growled.

Myers laughs but only for a moment. "Katie's checking on the wards. They looked fine to me, but she's a lot more specialized in things like that. Leon is with her. Pity he doesn't have Delun's soul magic."

Neither does Jonathan. Like his older brother, he was blessed with super strength and speed – gifts that most definitely saved their lives tonight. Even with their dad's protection, witch children shouldn't be a match for grown vampires; bloodsuckers are a lot faster and stronger than we are.

Realizing he said Katie's name, I ask, "Katie Wilks? She escaped? Is she okay?"

The two share a look before Caden says, "Yes. She used her hypnosis to make Aleric think she died."

Before I can ask if he hurt her badly, my husband rises to his feet. "How many did we lose?" he asks as Myers copies his movements. He offers his hand to me, and I stand slowly, my legs swaying under the protest of my muscles.

All humor leaves Myers face, and I hold my breath, my stomach churning.

"Too many," he says, his eyes flicking to me. He doesn't want to say the actual number in my presence. Thinks I'm too weak to handle it. Before I can correct him, Leon runs into the room.

"Werewolves!" he shouts. "The whole fucking pack has been spotted making their way here!"

A sudden bubble of laughter chokes my throat. Who ever would have thought that I would miss the nightmares I was trapped in for the last thirty years?

At least in them, I was the only one who was ever hurt.

# TWENTY-SEVEN
## HER
### 14 AUGUST 1947

"How far out are they?"

"Which direction are they coming from?"

"Did the fucking vampires tell them?"

"Are they working together now?"

"Shit, if they are –"

"No, they would've attacked together."

"Unless they want us to think that so they can have a plan B if tonight fails."

"Tonight *will* fail for them."

There's the first break in conversation, but nobody is feeling the confidence of Caden's statement. Even he does not look like he believes his own words.

My throat closing, I shake my head. "I need to talk to him," I rasp just as the conversation starts up again, the men talking about positions to take, soldiers to order.

"What about the women? Katie will be a damn good

asset."

"As will…"

Their words drown out as I remember Antonio's pain that night in the woods. He lost his mate and his children. He never got to hold them. I lost thirty years and Olivia and so many kids I never got to hold either.

We are the same now.

I understand now.

His pain.

His destruction.

His need to find life in the death of his enemies.

In *me*.

"Let me talk to Antonio," I say again, louder this time, my pulse thrumming.

Utter silence descends, but it's different this time. It's a shock of surprise, an instant denial that hasn't yet passed their lips but is clear on their faces.

"No," they all say at once.

"But –"

"Get everyone mobilized," Caden directs, and the other two move instantly. Gone from the room in a second.

"I can stop this," I start, but my husband grabs my arm and hauls me away from the door.

"He might've tried to talk peace with your dad before, Sau, but –"

"He did?" My mind reels. "When?"

"It doesn't matter."

I dig in my heels. "When?"

He turns to face me as we stop in the middle of the room even though he could easily pull me along. "Three months before our wedding."

My arm falls away as I stare at him in shock. Father told me Antonio had laid an ambush then. That he'd tried to wipe us out, to lure us out and catch us with our pants down.

But the white flag had been *real?*

I remember the plea in Antonio's eyes, his voice. A broken man driven to madness.

Not born in it like Father always said.

Not raised in it either.

But made.

By us.

By *me*.

"I need to talk to him," I say again, determined even more. I know an apology won't fix all the pain between us, but it could be a start. We could fight for that peace he wanted all those years ago.

I try to push past Caden, but my body is too weak, too drained, and he easily holds me back. "No. You need to stay here. Let me deal with this."

"I'm not –"

"Thinking straight, I know," he cuts in, and I flinch even as a part of me wants to set *him* straight. But a good girl never talks back to her husband. She never makes a fuss. That is how I was raised, and all those lessons beat into me now and hold my tongue. I open my mouth to push the words out, but he cups my cheek, stopping me.

"Trust me," he says softer, his eyes on mine. "Trust me as your husband to take care of you."

I swallow and glance away. "Antonio wants peace," I whisper. "That's all he's ever wanted."

He brings his forehead to mine, then kisses me gently. "He is not that same man anymore, Sau. He didn't just kill two of our children before you woke. He tortured them."

I flinch, but he does not stop.

"He drew out their deaths for as long as he could. Eric took seven months to die. George was dropped off alive a month after that, so broken I..." My husband swallows, then exhales harshly. "He begged us – begged *me* to make the pain stop." Grabbing my shoulders, Caden shakes me gently, not that he needs to snag my attention. He has it fully, my eyes tearing over the words he doesn't say.

How Antonio made a father kill his own son.

I tremble beneath his hands, able to imagine it so well. I know the twisted sense of justice Antonio is capable of.

Someone rushes into the room but halts right inside the door. They're blocked by Caden's bulk, but I don't look around him to see who it is, too trapped in my husband's wet gaze. Despite how strong he might be, he needs me in this moment.

"I love you," I whisper, cupping his cheek. There are no easy choices in this life, and I can't begin to imagine the guilt he carries on his shoulders... The haunted screams of our children. The knowledge that the only way he could help George was by killing him. My heart breaks for him, and he pushes into my palm.

"Come back to me," I say, wanting him to know I do not judge him at all. That as much as I love my children and mourn the loss of all those I'll never know, I do not hate him for doing what was asked of him.

Such a choice would have broken me.

But he kept himself together for the rest of our kids.

I could never hate him for that.

"Just come back to me," I repeat, then lean forward and kiss him. It is passionate and hopeful and desperate. And over far too quick, pulled away by a chorus of howls way too close.

He pivots on his heels. "Protect them with your life," he says to Katie Wilks, the person at the door.

Then he disappears, leaving me, and my heart clenches over the thought that this is the last time I'll ever see him.

My throat closing, I tear my eyes away from the now empty doorway and look at Katie, who's standing beside it. "Where are my children?"

"In the basement." She gestures towards the hall, and I

nod. That is our safe room, and it's warded with different spells than those that guard our streets for just this reason. "Are they okay?"

She nods.

"Are you?" Her knuckles are bloody, but there's not another scratch on her that I can see. Still, if Aleric had her for a while, she would have suffered greatly. Perhaps there are deep wounds under the long sleeves and gown of her dress.

She smiles slightly. "I won't let anyone get to you."

"That's not why I was asking."

"Come on. We don't have a lot of time." Katie gestures again, and I smile. She's just like my father was. Just like my husband and Myers. She probably won't say she's hurt or dying until she passes out.

But I don't push, feeling the pressure of time. Howls and screams spur us out into the hallway. The house feels eerily empty as we rush through it, everyone either dead or gone. My throat tightens as my hairs stand on end, my pulse pounding with every *tap, tap, tap* of our shoes on the hardwood floor.

We take the stairs down, Katie at my back. Despite being a woman, she moves with the same lethality as the men. I've only ever seen her dressed to the nines, wearing the confidence of an upper class lady born and bred to money. But now she reminds me of a street runner, her eyes darting everywhere, her movements a hair trigger away from exploding into action.

I wonder if she does more for the Family than just run our Floridian hotels and lure targets into staying in them. But now isn't the time to ask.

We reach the basement, and I run in to gather up my children. I take Ryo from Bonnie's arms as my two girls cling to me. I check them over between kisses and hugs of comfort, relieved to find no open wounds or broken bones.

Molly is absolutely free of even tiny scrapes and bruises. She trembles as she tells me she has her magic now, and pride fills me alongside pain.

Regardless of tonight, she will be leaving me soon to start her own family.

Florida still allows a child of any age to marry as long as they're pregnant. Burying my anxiety over her near future, I hug her close and concentrate on surviving tonight.

"How are the wards?" I ask, turning to Katie Wilks after passing Ryo back to Bonnie. I want to do nothing more than hide in a corner with a blanket over me, but only an idiot thinks they can hide from a werewolf. Only a coward tries.

*I am a Shadow*, I remind myself even as my wounds throb from the memory of that night in the woods. My hands shaking, I clasp them together.

"Strong," she says. "Your dad strengthened them every day, and Caden has continued to do so since."

My heart twists at the memory of my father's last moments. He was so strong.

But Antonio was stronger.

Who will win between him and Caden?

My pulse pounding, I walk towards the door. The sense of power radiating off them pushes against my body. The wards have been activated, allowing only those of Shadow blood to pass through. And Katie. Caden must really trust her to have given her passage through the wards.

I glance over my shoulder at her, wondering if she has the answers I seek, if she knows my husband better than me. "Can Caden kill Antonio?" I ask.

Bonnie and Molly suck in a breath.

"Yes," Katie says firmly, but I can see the lie in her eyes. She's worried for him.

Swallowing, I turn from her, my hands shaking as they remember the tearing of their flesh. The wet *squelch* of tendons and muscles ripping down a spike.

*"All you know,"* he seethed as he stalked towards me as I lay sprawled out on my stomach, *"is how to spread your legs and be the good little whore your father taught you to be."*

My throat burning with the contents of my stomach, I lunge for the open door and slam it shut. The wards don't need it to be closed, but I do. I can't face Antonio Garcia even inside my mind. My request to speak to him was infantile and stupid.

I can barely think about that night without struggling to breathe. My chest feels like it's caving in.

Falling against the door, I then collapse to my knees.

My breathing quickens, and I bite my tongue so I don't scream. Instead, I whimper as I remember all that pain. The claw in my open chest. The cock choking me. The heavy hands holding me down as he shoved inside the hole he'd torn through my pussy.

Is he hurting Caden right now?

Or either of my two boys?

Is he torturing them? Making them suffer?

Tears burn my eyes as my head rests on the heavy oak door.

I should open it and run out there and let the monsters loose.

But my legs are trembling too much to listen.

And my breaths are coming too quickly.

And my body is screaming from phantom pain as I am thrown back into those woods.

Helpless.

Alone.

And terribly afraid.

# TWENTY-EIGHT

## ALERIC
### 14 AUGUST 1947

I phase onto the edge of the Shadows' street, just inside the weakened protective wards and those that hide us from the humans. A black gift-wrapped box sits in my hands, Sau's name scrawled on it next to a white ribbon stained red. Hopefully, she actually lives long enough to open it given how much death swirls in the air, its rich copper stench filling me with excitement.

Witches lie on the ground like dropped fast-food bags, their severed heads and limbs wayward wrappers, their intestines a tumbled array of greasy fries. Wolves lie next to them, burned to a crisp, their heads cut off, their hearts ripped out of furry chests. It takes a lot to kill a werewolf, and the air hums with dark magic that reeks of sacrifice and blood offerings.

I am careful not to step too close to any of the bodies as I make my way down the street. The magic clinging to the dead wolves can easily transfer to me, and the witches are known to boobytrap their own corpses with their final breaths. Try to get close enough to tell if they're dead, and *boom!* A final act of vengeance.

Ahead of me, the street lights up with fireballs, flames, and streaks of magic. Wolves dart across the roofs of the houses, trying to get behind the line the witches have drawn across the tarmac; it hums with dark magic rather than the shimmering blue of a protective shield. A blurred white form roars as it races along the line, massacring anything that dares to try to cross it. It is bigger than the wolves and stinks of rot. An eknor demon perhaps, called forth from the plane of Halzaja. A manifestation of Rage.

If it stayed still long enough, I would be able to see its paper-white skin and bright-red blood vessels clear across its steroid-pumped body. They have a head of various-sized horns, and their eight black eyes allow them to have a nearly 360-degree view of the world. They can also see in both more colors than humans when something's in focus of their two main eyes, as well as in black-and-white in the peripherals so they're not overwhelmed with visual stimuli, making their reaction times terrifying...but they're also kind of cute, much prettier than those that are a manifestation of Gluttony or Greed, and my arousal heightens as I wonder if it's female or male. Not that it matters. They both have holes, and I can imagine they fuck like a demon.

My lips curl. I have to remember to save that pun for later. Colton will undoubtedly get a kick out of it.

Or he would if he ever took that stick out of his ass.

Perhaps I should tell Destiny to stop going so hard when she pegs him.

My grin spreads wider as I keep to the shadows, happy that I am downwind of the werewolves. Although Antonio might not care that I am here, too focused on tearing apart the Shadows, there are a few of his pack that will try to kill me as soon as they get the chance.

Although we could work together to kill the witches tonight, Antonio is my enemy as much as Caden's, and if I get the chance, I'm going to gut him like the pig he is.

I hate that I can smell Sau's fear for him, and *no one* gets to terrorize Sau but me.

I bare my fangs as I spot the alpha in the middle of the street, facing away from me. I can phase to him and rip his head off. Werewolves are fast, but I can kill him before he even knows I'm on him...

But then I will die just as quick, ripped apart by the rest of his pack.

There are over two dozen of them with him, and I am not foolish enough to think I can phase away before one of them manages to grab me. Then all it would take is a few bites, a werewolf's saliva being venomous to my kind.

My eyes drift to the blood-smeared line drawn across the pavement. The demon still rushes across it back and forth, slicing out at the werewolves as they keep darting forward trying to wear it out. They rush between houses and jump off roofs, looking for that narrow opening as they dodge fireballs, lightning bolts, and shots of magic thrown by the witches safely on the other side. Other lines run parallel to it, with their own demons, protecting the entire area in a square.

I shift my gaze to the house in the middle of the zone. Knowing Sau is inside it, my cock hardens.

But taking her tonight will ruin the game.

The anticipation.

The build-up that I love.

But gods, it'll feel good...

My gaze shifts back to Antonio as he jumps away from the line, clutching a wound in his stomach, blood seeping through his fingers. He growls, unable to talk in his wolf form, but it's not hard to discern his meaning: *I'm going to kill you.*

After all, they can't hold the demons here forever.

Leaving them all to it, I risk instant death and phase across the line.

I pop up slightly further down the street but way, way higher, and now I'm free-falling hundreds of feet onto the roof of the Shadows' house. I hit with a *thud,* curling my body around the box, making sure it doesn't break in the fall.

Multiple bones, however, do get broken, including my right forearm as it shoots through my skin in an open fracture. I'm also pretty certain I'm bleeding internally. Still, a grin curves across my lips due to my guess being correct. Magic requires strict parameters, and a ward rarely covers the sky over a hundred feet.

Granted, if anyone was watching, they could kill me in the time it takes me to heal (anatomy doesn't care how powerful you are; broken kneecaps are broken kneecaps), but nothing good ever comes if you don't take a few risks.

Shoving my bone back into my arm, I then take out the flask of blood from inside my waistcoat and drink half of it, letting Sau's pathetic copycat heal my broken bones and torn muscles and ligaments. Placing it back inside my inner pocket, I jump from the roof.

The backyard spreads out before me, piles of ash here and there – all that remain of the sired who died during our attack. Soon, the wind will pick up and carry them away, leaving no trace. Colton will undoubtedly let me know who they were, so I turn my attention to the house itself.

I step through the splintered doorway, the door having been blown off by the witches when they chased us, and take a deep breath. My cock jerks at the smell of my girl, but instead of heading to the basement where she is, I go down the hall to the master bedroom.

My eyes narrow on the messy bed, the two indented

pillows. Caden might be her husband, but I know she doesn't love him, not like she will me.

When I break her to make her stronger.

When I fuck her until she can't think of anything else but how good I make her feel.

Leaning over the pillow furthest from the door, I inhale and immediately roll my eyes. It smells like her all right. Caden is such a fool, thinking she needs the protection of his body as she sleeps. He sees her as weak, beneath him, not as the queen she is.

But I will show her.

Show him.

Sau Shadow isn't a delicate dandelion that will blow away in the slightest breeze. She's the thorns of a rose, the acid of a Venus flytrap, the berries of a belladonna.

*She is mine.*

Yes.

Soon.

Soon, she will be.

Placing the gift in the middle of the bed, I straighten, then make my way to the ensuite. A mirror hangs above the sink, and I look my reflection in the eye, snickering as I always do when I see it.

The vampire who started up the rumor that we don't have them was a genius. Or perhaps is, depending on if they're still alive. It's such a simple way for us to prove our 'humanity' to anyone dumb enough to not think it through. Of course we would have a reflection. Light hits us. We're not invisible. It baffles me how well that rumor grew, but it is one I've used more than once in all fairness.

Picking up Sau's toothbrush, I bring it to my lips. My cock hardens as I rub it across them, imagining the taste of her, how it'll feel when I finally sink my teeth into her skin.

A groan pulling from me, I quickly undo my pants with my other hand, then grip my cock, rubbing my palm up and down it as its head pokes out between my fingers. The friction gets me going, the thought of Sau on her knees as she gags around me, with tears running down her face, gets me *hard*.

Breathing roughly, I step away from the sink until I can see my hand. It wants to be around her throat, inside her wet pussy, up her ass as I slam my cock inside her. I'm going to fuck her in every way, all day, until she's too exhausted to scream, to stand, to run. Just lying still on her back, whimpering and moaning as I force another orgasm from her.

No more fight left in her.

Just utter, delicious surrender as she begs me to never stop.

Groaning, I rock into my hand, my hips pumping as I watch myself in the mirror, the thick girthy head of my cock poking out between my fingers. I rub her toothbrush across my lips and pick up speed until precum coats the end of my dick. I pump myself harder, getting the slick salty line to run down and hit my hand.

I envision her on her back, broken and bleeding but so desperate to come, she doesn't even feel the pain. Or perhaps she revels in it like I do, gets turned on at the sting of a cut, at the heavy *thump* of a fist.

My head falls back as I see her fighting me, feel her nails digging into my neck and face, her elbows in my ribs, her teeth on my hand as I smother her with a palm.

A low growl rumbles from me as my balls grow tight, but I don't let myself come. Releasing my cock, I breathe out raggedly as I lower her toothbrush to the end of my very sensitive tip. I hiss in a breath at the contact of it sweeping through my precum. I coat it liberally, working it into the bristles. Then I wipe off the edges, the excess so she won't notice before she puts it in her mouth.

After a quick wash of my hands, making damn certain I

leave no trace on the sink, I shove my cock back into my pants and do them up. The last thing I want is for some witch or werewolf or demon to grab it when I make my exit. As I can't phase out of here, having only been able to enter because I dropped in over three hundred feet, I'm going to have to cross that demonic line.

Whistling a merry tune, I make my way back out into the hall. Flashes of color flicker through the windows as the werewolves and witches continue their fight. Booms and screams and roars shake the walls, and my whistling is broken up by soft chuckles. They're each fighting so damn hard right now, and I'm just about to waltz in and take the one thing they want the most.

Sau.

Fucking.

Shadow.

Opening the door to the basement, I peer down into the dark. I inhale deeply and smile, knowing she's down there. I take a step forward, my foot landing heavy on the stairs so she can hear me.

*Thump...*

*Thump....*

*Thump....*

Does she think I'm Caden coming to retrieve her?

Or Antonio coming to kill her?

My smile spreading, my cocking twitching against my thigh, I reach the bottom step and stop.

I don't need to touch the door to know that doing so will most likely kill me. This is their safe room, and the best defense is a lethal attack.

So I lean my shoulder against the wall adjacent to it and cross my arms and ankles.

"Sau, love," I coo. "Come on out of that room, or I will kill everyone at the portal while your beloved Caden is preoccupied."

# TWENTY-NINE

## HER

### 14 AUGUST 1947

My head jerks up at the sound of the voice coming through the door. It's a deep, rich timbre that causes me to shiver – a statement, not a threat. Aleric didn't just retreat from here, his ego bruised, his plans disrupted. He went to hit us somewhere else.

My legs shaking, I stand. I can't be the cause of any more deaths. There are thirty-odd people protecting the portal at all times. Some witches, some humans that don't even know the significance of the area they defend.

How many of them have families?

Wives?

Children?

I look at Molly and Bonnie and Ryo behind me. My two girls are frozen with their eyes on the door. My little boy is quiet for now, but his face is starting to bunch. He's about to cry, and my heart breaks as I think of all the children who'll sob for hours, wanting their daddies who will never come. Because of me. Because I hid behind a door for 'safety' even though *I* wanted to take my own life not even two months ago. It's madness.

I turn back for the door. And this madness has to end.

Antonio wanted peace once.

Maybe Aleric does too.

Deep down, somewhere, he has to be fed up with all this fighting like I am. Maybe I can reach him.

And if not…maybe my death will end this madness. Maybe I can bring some *good* to the world.

"Sau," Katie hisses as I reach for the door. "Don't."

"He can't get in if I step out, right?" I ask, my hand on the knob. "You and my kids will be safe?"

"You step out that door, and Aleric won't have to kill me because Caden will do it himself."

I turn to look at her over my shoulder, wondering if she's telling the truth or just a lie to get me to stay. I know it is the smart choice to not open the door, to not even entertain what Aleric wants, but it isn't the *right* choice. It isn't right that I'll get to live when all those other people, *my* people, those of the Shadow Domain my family has sworn to protect, will suffer in my place.

"I'm sorry," I say as I release the door handle and take a step back. "You're right. I'm not thinking clearly. I don't want you to get hurt either."

She relaxes – only barely. She's not comfortable with Aleric on the other side of that door, but she's happy I'm being smart.

And I am…

I take another step away from the door, and she turns her attention back to it. She can't attack him with her hypnosis while the wards are up. They wouldn't be much use if magic could get through them.

"It's going to be fine," I tell my kids as I look Bonnie in

the eye. "He can't come in. Right, Katie?"

"That's right," she says. "Your father strengthened these wards himself. Aleric can't get in even if he burns the whole house down. We're safe."

I nod, thankful. Then I take a deep breath...

And turn into my shadows before Katie can make me want to stay with her hypnosis.

She screams at me to stop, tries to run in front of the door to block me, but I simply go around her and under the crack of the door.

I solidify on the other side, my heart jumping at the sight of Aleric pushing off the wall, his eyes narrowing both in surprise and...pride?

Before I can decipher whatever it is the vampire is thinking, whatever it is he might want with me, I grab his hand and pull him towards the stairs. "Hurry before Katie opens –"

I gasp as he picks me up, cradling me in his arms, and then I'm at the top of the stairs, his speed causing the world to blur. The door opens behind me, but I know Katie won't step out of the room. She won't leave my kids on their own. Stuck between two hard choices, she'll protect the truly innocent.

Tears burning my eyes at the thought of never seeing them again, I look at Aleric. "What do you want?" I ask as he steps out of the door leading into the hall.

The world blurs again, and when it settles, we're out on the street. My heart jumps at the sight of Caden. Aleric's people are most certainly at the portal, waiting for his command, and if he dies here, will they slaughter ours in revenge? Continue this cycle of death and more death and more *fucking* death until we're all so damn numb from the madness?

Until we're broken like Antonio is? Consumed by a need to inflict pain on those who've wronged us?

My eyes shift from my husband, who looks dead on his feet even with his back to me, to the alpha of the Death Hunt, who hangs back as the rest of his pack races for the end of our street to escape before our wards trap them here forever.

Facing Caden, he bares his fangs, his nose scrunching as he growls. His ears lie low against his head, and he takes a step forward but stops at the line as a Rage demon blocks him, a towering pale monster with a whip-like tail, its end black with poison.

"Let's end this," Caden shouts as he too steps forward, but before he can dismiss the demon he's called forth, Antonio's golden eyes shift to me. The rage on his face intensifies, and I cower instinctively, fearing that night in the woods, fearing what he can do now that he's had thirty years to perfect his craft.

The arms around me loosen as I'm dropped to my feet. But before I can run to Caden, a hand wraps around my shoulder, claws digging into my skin. My head is yanked to the side, Aleric baring my neck just as my husband spins around, his eyes snapping to me. "Sau!"

"Caden!"

"Antoniooooo!" Aleric shouts mockingly as he lowers his fangs to my neck. My hairs rise at the brush of his breath, and I instantly freeze. If I call upon my magic again so soon, it will most likely kill me for him. And I need a chance to talk to him, to try to negotiate some sort of peace between our Families.

Antonio snaps his teeth, saliva flying everywhere as he runs back and forth across the line like a rabid dog. The Rage demon follows him easily, telling me he is at least over a thousand years old to be able to match the speed of a werewolf. My eyes flick to Caden again as my mouth drops open, awed once more by just how powerful he is to have been able to summon what is most certainly an archdemon.

And not just one, I realize as I turn my head to look at each border of our safety zone.

I briefly wonder if he can force Antonio and Aleric to stay in place while we all have a chat, but the answer stares back at me in the green of his eyes. He's absolutely terrified, and I know, that in this moment, he can't even stop Aleric from taking me. Blood trickles down his chin and nose, clear signs that his magic is killing him.

Still, he raises his arms, willing to sacrifice his own life to save mine.

My heart breaking, I want to beg him not to. He is a thousand times more of a person than I'll ever be. A better parent. A better leader.

But Aleric cuts in before I can. "Ah, ah, ah," he says, damn near singing. "You're going to let us pass through the barrier, or we" –he grazes his fangs across my neck as his tone swears a promise– "will join each other in death."

My heart jolts beneath his teeth. "Let him, Caden," I say, my words moving the distance I wish I could. They reach him while I am stuck here, in the cold embrace of our enemy.

"I'm not losing you again, Sau."

My eyes soften as I implore him to listen. "Our children can't lose *you*."

His eyes widen, the rest of his face going momentarily slack. "They're alive?" Caden breathes as he eyes Aleric in disbelief that he left them alone.

I nod, hoping he makes the same choice Katie did so they don't lose both their parents in one night. Their mom taken, their dad killed trying to stop it.

Howling, Antonio runs straight at the line. He's about to crash into the demon, clearly not giving a fuck if he dies trying to get to me, when a streak of black fur rams into him from the side. They roll across the ground, the new wolf yipping and growling, as if they're trying to talk sense into their alpha. Our wards are nearly back up again; I can feel them charging the air with power.

I jumped as soon as Antonio moved, his sudden motion terrifying me, and Aleric's teeth sank a bit into my skin. He groans as he presses his fangs deeper, and his tongue licks me, but he doesn't bite down all the way. He doesn't drink. He simply sighs against my neck and pulls back up.

"If you want the chance to save her, Caden, I advise you deal with Antonio while we cross."

Scooping me up into his arms, he runs straight for the demon. The world blurs so fast, it makes my eyes sting, and I'm forced to squint to see anything at all. The demon spins, his black eyes locking on to us as his tail whips behind him lazily. A cold sneer curls his lips, revealing two rows of long needle-like teeth.

Just as Aleric reaches him though, the demon vanishes, Caden having released him just in time. Antonio pins the subordinate who attacked him, then turns to my husband. I scream, drawing his attention as we blitz past. He turns to us, but then we're gone, Aleric having phased now that the ward is no longer stopping him.

My scream shifts into coughing and then vomiting as I'm dropped onto the floor somewhere new. The world no longer blurs but spins, my head reeling. I fall to my hands and knees, then vomit again, a cold sweat glistening on my skin.

Phasing is not easy on the body. Only those born with the ability are able to handle the stress, so by the time I manage to breathe without shuddering, Aleric is standing in front of me, his dark-gray eyes on my ass. Heat burns in his gaze, and I drop mine quickly in disgust...only for it to catch on his clear erection on the way down. He's *big* and not far from my face.

"Ugh. I was just vomiting," I croak, turning my head away, disgusted enough for the both of us.

"Beauty doesn't leave, love, just because one's sick." He

crouches down in front of me and grabs my chin with gentle fingers before turning me back to face him. "Does your *loving* husband not show you that?"

Jerking out of his grasp, I clench my fists as I try to stand. Hitting him wouldn't be a great start to negotiating for peace.

"What do you want with me?" I ask as I stumble back, my legs still floppy beneath me.

Standing, he reaches inside his jacket, and I tense, wondering what horrors he's going to pull out.

"Here." He offers me a plain flask, and I stare at it, my brain trying to decipher what my eyes are seeing. "It's just water. To wash your mouth." He unscrews the lid. "I would've brought wine, but I didn't think you'd drink it if you couldn't be certain about what it was."

"There are a lot of poisons that are tasteless, odorless, and –"

He raises it to his lips and drinks without hesitation. The Adam's apple at his throat draws my attention as he swallows. Once. Twice. Not a little sip, wary of ingesting too much poison. But a hearty gulp that tells me what he says is most likely true.

Still...

"Why?" I ask, staring at him as he lowers the flask and offers it to me once more.

"Because I'm a gentleman."

I snort. "You kidnapped me!"

He takes a step towards me, his dark-gray eyes flashing with humor. "No, you came out on your own and then grabbed my arm to run away with me."

My eyes narrow. I can see why no one has sat down with him to discuss peace negotiations. Talking to him at all is a chore. "After you *coerced* me by threatening my people," I remind him.

He cocks his head to the side with a smug smile. "Was it

coercion or was it a lie?"

"You didn't."

"Didn't coerce you or didn't lie?"

My mouth drops open as utter rage for myself hits me. "I'm so *stupid*."

His smile falls. "No, Sau. *Naive* isn't the same thing as stupid. Besides, it's not your fault Caden keeps you locked away in some ivory tower, which by the way, isn't even very nicely decorated, to keep you ignorant of the world."

I stare at him wordlessly. Out of all the ways I thought this would go when I slipped out of the basement, this is definitely not one of them. Though to be fair, I don't even know what this *is* really. He isn't trying to kill me. He's not torturing me or cutting off parts to send to Caden to twist him into doing whatever he wants.

He's...complimenting me? Was thoughtful enough to bring a flask of water for after we phased away?

What.

The.

Fuck?

My mouth opens, then closes again, my thoughts still awhirl.

"Drink," he says again, offering me the flask.

Wordlessly, I take it. Sniff it and then raise it to my lips when I don't smell anything suspicious. The cold liquid hits my mouth, and I swoosh it around to get rid of the vile taste of my vomit before swallowing.

I tense, expecting to die or at least go into a seizure of intense pain.

But there's nothing.

It's just water.

And I'm still entirely fucking baffled.

"Why?" I ask again. "Why am I here? Is this a peace offering?"

He laughs, warm and delightful. "There's that naivety

again. No... After tonight, blood will run through our streets like never before. Antonio will wonder if we're creating an alliance to take him down, so he will attack my Family for the first time. He will hit harder, probably kill quite a few of my sired." He shrugs nonchalantly, as if they mean nothing to him. "Might even kill Colton and a few born ones." He grins. "That'll be a favor.

"But no... We're not creating an alliance." He stands up straight and tends to the cuffs on his sleeves. "We're going on a date."

My mouth drops open.

And I laugh.

# THIRTY
## HER
### 14 AUGUST 1947

Rolling my lips in, I manage to stop laughing, but as soon as I look up at him, I start off again. The cycle runs round and round, and every time it begins again, I laugh harder, louder until tears start rolling down my cheeks, and *I can't breathe.*

Gasping with my arms wrapped around my waist, I struggle to stop again. But it's not just him I'm laughing at anymore. It's the whole fucking messed up situation. He pretended to threaten all those people for a *date*? He scared my kids and my husband just to *kidnap me for a fucking date?*

"I'm married!" I rasp between the laughter, but it isn't jolly and hilarious. It is wild and panicked because I'm so fucking *angry.*

His nerve! His fucking *nerve!*

As if I am a mouse for some cat to play with.

Lifting my head, I clench my fists hard so I don't swing them into his arrogant face. "I just lost my daughter and you want...a fucking *date*?"

Laughter pours out of me now in an uncontrollable current. I can't stop the madness from flowing. More so, I don't care *to* stop it. My dad isn't here to be disappointed in me. My husband isn't here to witness my unladylike and unShadowlike behavior. My children aren't here to be scared of mama going crazy. It's just Aleric and me in an empty building of some sort that I haven't even looked around at.

"You can't bow to death when you wade through it as often as we do." He shrugs. "Besides, you have two more, so it's not like it's been a great loss."

I finally stop laughing.

I finally stop trying to fight hitting him too.

Screw peace.

Screw negotiating.

Screaming like a feral alley cat, I launch myself at him, my hands going for his very chokeable throat.

---

Holy shit, she's the most beautiful woman I've ever seen. Her face is twisted in not just anger but *vengeance*. Her lips are curled, and it's so cute that she doesn't have any fangs. Her eyes are narrowed into green slivers that stand out even more against the red flush of her cheeks. A vein throbs at her temple. Her nostrils flare. Her scream turns into a growl, and I want to kiss her. To gather her up in my arms –

Her fist connects with my throat.

Gasping, I stagger back, bending in half out of reflex. Throats, like kneecaps, don't care how powerful you are. A damaged windpipe is a damaged windpipe. There's no way to muscle up that part of your neck.

Her knee connects with my lowered face, breaking my nose and making my eyes tear. The shot of pain slamming through me reverberates with a deliciousness that stirs my cock, and I groan.

Or rather wheeze as my throat has yet to heal from her attack.

I "trip" over my feet and go sprawling onto my back. I want her to hit me while I'm down. I want her to straddle me, hover her pussy over my chest as she pummels me with her little fists. Like a little kitty cat. A little pussy cat. Before I yank her up my chest to sit on my face.

Another groan is pulled from me as I imagine her taste so well.

But she doesn't follow me down to the ground.

She simply stands there.

And kicks me.

In the ribs.

In the head.

In my groin.

Such delicious pain spreads through me, an arc of fire that matches her fearsome little growls and hisses. Right now, she's just a little kitty, but she'll soon grow into the lioness she's meant to be.

Under my guidance, I will break her.

Then I will rebuild her.

Granted, and then she might become strong enough to kill me, but well... What a fucking way to die that would be.

A bloody grin spreading across my lips, I grab her leg and yank her down on top of me. I roll, pinning her under me. My cock presses into her lower belly, and I thrust my hips forward as she continues to fight me, her nails raking across my face, her little body wiggling, trying to throw me off. But all she's doing is making my cock harder, my breaths faster, my control closer to snapping.

The blood from my broken nose rains down on her,

painting her a beautiful red, and I lick my lips as I feel another bite of her nails that zings straight down to my cock.

I want to fuck her.

I want to tear off her dress and bury myself inside her until she squeezes me as she comes. I want her hating me. Fighting me. Making me work for it even as she's begging me to fuck her faster. Harder. *Don't stop!*

Groaning, I lean down to kiss her. She pushes against my face, her slender palms trying to force me away, but she doesn't have the strength. I break through and trail my lips across her cheek to her ear as she turns her head to avoid me.

"If you don't want me to fuck you, Sau, then *stop me*," I hiss.

Reaching between us, I grab her left breast. She gasps, and her strength momentarily abandons her, her hands going slack against my head. My cock throbbing at her involuntary reaction, I force my thigh between her legs. She arches just a little as I rock against her, shame and desire filling her eyes, and a sudden realization hits me.

My beautiful little fighter isn't being properly fucked by her husband.

Pure primal emotion fills my chest, so strong and quick that it hits me harder than any of her punches and kicks. I want to please her. I want to get her off with our clothes still on. I want her to know that when I finally fuck her, she's going to be a soaking wet mess of pure ecstasy.

Grabbing her chin, I yank her lips to mine.

---

His mouth crashes down on me, stealing my air as he kisses me with a fervor that's almost bruising. His hand trails back down to my breast, cupping and teasing me through the fabric of my dress. With each rub of his palm against my nipple, bolts of desire fly through me, and I squeeze my eyes shut, trying to resist them, to kill the current I shouldn't be feeling.

But Antonio's gold eyes stare back at me in the depths of my mind, and those dirty, secret dreams I had of him and his pack in my coma just makes me even more wet.

Even more disgusted with myself.

*Caden loves me.*

And I love him.

I shouldn't be feeling this aroused when my husband does all the right things…

Shoving Aleric's lips off me, I spit in his face. But he catches it in his mouth. A wicked smile curls his lips as he swallows, and my pussy kegels involuntarily. I shouldn't find that hot. I *don't* find that hot.

Holding my gaze, he finally grasps my nipple with his fingers and pinches it between them. My body shakes from the strong bolt of desire that arcs through me. I kegel again and pray that he can't tell.

But his nostrils flare as his eyes narrow, and I know he can smell me. That as much as I try to hide it, he *knows*.

He knows that I get off on violence. Of being afraid. Of being taken against my will.

I tremble beneath his hands, choked by a desire good wives shouldn't have. Aleric stares down at me, his eyes heated, his lips wet from mine. His cock throbs against me, and he rocks his hips, pushing it deeper into my dress.

A small whimper escapes me as a wet heat slides down my thighs.

And in that instant, he snaps.

Crushing his lips to mine, he forces his tongue inside my mouth. He tastes of blood and sin, of dark desires best left hidden and ignored by the good wife that I am. I ball my hands into fists when he grabs my chin so I can't bite his tongue off, severing it as I did mine.

He forces me to kiss him. To taste him for the split second it takes me to throw my knuckles into his cheek. But it is enough to brand his touch onto me. To make my stomach twist as I'm forced to be someone else's whore.

His head snaps sideways, his lips leaving mine, and he hisses in a breath right before I hit him again, throwing my magic behind it. Something *cracks,* and it takes me a moment to realize it wasn't his jaw.

For now the pain comes, flying down my knuckles and up my arm. He chuckles, then grabs that hand in his and crushes it, cracking even more bones, causing even more pain. Tears burning my eyes, I bite my cheek and go to punch him with my other hand.

The world blurs, and the next thing I know, my back is being slammed against a wall, my head spinning as I gasp for breath. He grabs my hips and lifts me up. I try to kick him in his groin, but he steps in quick, so I only clip his shin. The tip of his cock pushes through the thin fabric of my dress, and I gasp, fear spurning my arousal as he dry humps me against the wall. His fangs elongate past his lips, and I remember how they felt inside my neck.

An invasion.

A violation.

A *promise* of wicked things.

"You're being such a good girl," Aleric growls as more desire pools between my thighs. "You're getting all nice and wet for me." He inhales deeply, his breath tickling my neck, and I push at his shoulders, but he doesn't move. My fingers curl just slightly, gripping his shirt as if to hold him to me when his fangs drag across my skin. He groans. Applies just the tiniest bit of pressure. "When I sink into you tonight, Sau, it's not going to be here."

Pressing his body hard into me, holding me up with just his hips, he grabs the top of my dress, and it *riiips,* the sound of it tearing making my pulse jump wildly beneath his teeth. His groan is a lot more strained this time, his shoulders tense and trembling beneath my fingers.

Lifting his head up, he looks down at my chest, hidden only by my red rayon satin brassiere, dyed to remember the blood of our fallen. His eyes flash a dark red beneath the gray, the beast within struggling at the forefront of his control. "So gorgeous..." he murmurs as I freeze beneath his stare. "So *delicious...*"

Ripping apart the last of the fabric covering me, he quickly dips his head and fastens his lips around a nipple.

I cry out, arching against him as my fingers dig into his shoulders. My head falls back at the sharp pleasure riding through me. I squeeze my eyes shut as shame chases hard on its tail, nipping at its flying hooves, making it more *excited,* though, rather than scared.

I hate how my body's reacting. I hate the intensity of pleasure radiating out from his lips, his tongue as they caress my breast, sucking and claiming and licking. His teeth scrape me hard enough to cause pain, and I cry out, my eyes snapping open as my breath leaves me in rapid pants.

My fingers clenching him hard, I tremble as I watch him move his mouth to my other breast. He licks it slowly, raising chills across my skin as I anticipate the claiming of his lips.

"You want this," he murmurs, and I shake my head.

"No."

"Look how hard your nipples are." He flicks his tongue across it, and I bite my lip as electricity arcs through me, a delicious buzz that makes me hate myself. I shouldn't be feeling this. I don't *want* to feel this. How can my body be betraying me, betraying *Caden* so much? He loves me. He's accepted me despite all the muck on my skin left by Antonio and those who've raped me. *He loves me*, I tell my body, desperate to get it to stop reacting to Aleric's touch.

But the vampire sucks my nipple into his mouth, and a whimper instantly lodges in my throat, mocking my piss poor attempt to control it.

"So. *Fucking*. Hard," he murmurs as he lifts his eyes to mine, and the flicks of his tongue as he speaks have my thighs clenching together, desperate to stop my arousal from leaking out.

His nostrils flair just as I can feel the wetness staining my panties, and he breathes in heavily. "You smell fucking *delicious*," he purrs as he licks his way up to my neck. "I bet you taste even better."

He digs his fingers into both cheeks of my ass and lifts me high. Panicking, I cup my hands and slam them over both his ears, the blow from my broken hand awkward and painful but still solid. He grunts as he staggers to the side, nearly dropping me. My arms flail as I start to fall, but he drops to his knees right below me and catches me on his shoulders.

I grab hold of his head instinctively for support, my fingers curling in his short black hair and pulling hard at his scalp. He groans, and then I yelp as I realize *where* his head is.

It's right between my thighs.

And my dress is bunched up at my waist, shoved up by him sometime during my fall.

"Gods, you smell so fucking *good*," Aleric rasps right before he leans forward and kisses me right on my inner thigh, just below the seam of my panties.

My head falls back.

My fingers dig into his hair.

I'm lost to a wave of ecstasy I've never felt before. My pussy is so sensitive to his every breath. My fingers tingle, even the broken ones beneath the pain – a sharp mix of pleasure. Further pressure builds inside of me, and I know

I'm going to come tonight.

But I don't want to come...

Not with him.

I don't want him to be my first.

"Stop," I rasp, not knowing what else to do. He is much stronger than me. Much faster. And if I use my magic when I'm this drained, it'll kill me.

Perhaps that will be for the best.

Perhaps I deserve to die for betraying my husband in this way.

"Don't tell me to stop," he says as he looks up at me from between my thighs. "Not when you want this so fucking much."

"I don't," I whisper, and his eyes darken as he smirks at me.

"Then how come you're so wet?" He licks the tip of one fang, and my eyes snag on the movement. My breath hitches. My pussy clenches. "You're not the pure, delicate flower Caden thinks you are, now are you? You're not the innocent white lily that needs to be placed on a pedestal. You're the black rose who craves the dark, who hungers for the moonlight denied her."

He reaches a hand up to grab my breast, and I don't do anything to stop him.

I hate that I don't.

But I can't move.

Can't think past the desires he's forcing me to address.

"Does he know he's not taking care of you enough? Not fucking you like you need to be fucked?"

"He loves me."

He snarls, then digs his nails into my breast. Raking down, he leaves five ugly bloody lines running across the entirety of it, and I flinch, but with my back to the wall, there's nowhere for me to go.

"You're going to give these to me as a trophy tonight," he

says as he reaches between us with his other hand and presses a finger against my pussy lips, on the outside of my panties.

"Never," I say.

"You are. Otherwise, I will kill every Shadow Domain at the portal. You want to save them, don't you?"

I clench my jaw, my body shaking as I'm reminded why I came with him to start with. He might have joked that he was lying, but he's also the sort to have lied about that. I can't risk it, risk *them.*

"That's a good girl." He smirks, a cruel tease on his lips. "A *stupid* girl but a good one. But you give me these panties to keep" –he presses his finger deeper into my pussy, the tip sliding between my lips– "and I will pull my men back."

My jaw is so tight, I can barely breathe. I want to tell him to go fuck himself, but what is my pride worth in the face of thirty-odd men and their families?

"If I give them to you," I say, my rage building at how he barters people's lives so effortlessly, "you will leave my *entire* Family alone. You will not kill or maim any of them ever again."

"Is that all it will take to get you out of your panties?" he asks humorously, and I feel like he's slapped me in the face.

Grabbing my ass with both hands, he leans back. My breath catches in my throat as we fall together, then flies out as my knees bang hard into the concrete floor. I yelp as pain radiates up them, then clench my teeth so I don't make another noise. He lies on his back beneath me, his head still between my legs. Blood trickles out of his left ear from where I slapped him earlier and now pools out of the back of his head from the fall as well. But there isn't any pain in his eyes, just pure pleasure.

"Deal," he purrs as he kneads my ass. "Now take off your panties and wrap them around my cock."

# THIRTY-ONE

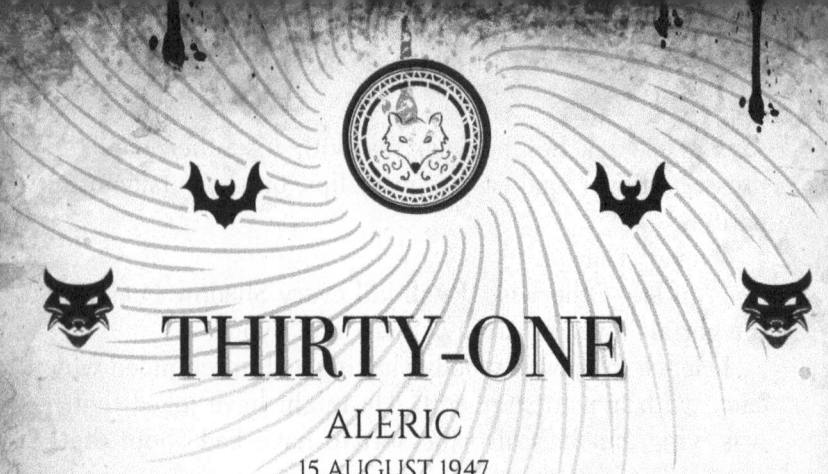

## ALERIC

### 15 AUGUST 1947

As she stands, I slide my hands down her legs, trailing goosebumps along her skin. The skirt of her dress starts to fall, covering her, and I frown. "Hold your dress up at your waist," I snap, "or we don't have a deal. I want to watch you take them off."

She glares down at me as I keep both my hands around her ankles. I can see the fire on her tongue, the want to tell me to go to hel, but instead, she simply bends down and gathers up the fabric in her good hand.

As she does so, her boobs sway, and I lean up to suck one into my mouth. She jerks up before I can properly lavish it with my tongue, and I smirk as I lie back down. She might act like she's cold towards me, but I can see the hardening of her nipple already, smell the strengthening desire in her pussy.

I lick the tip of a fang, impatient to taste her already.

"Take them off," I say, delighting in giving her orders, in controlling a woman of such fire.

Placing her broken hand across the bunched fabric, holding it as best as she can with her forearm pinned to her stomach, she reaches down with the other and quickly pulls down her underwear. I groan at the sight of her wet hairy pussy. The lips of them are closed...for now, but they will soon spread beneath my tongue.

"You're practically dripping," I rasp as I stare up at her soaked thighs. "When's the last time you came?"

My lioness blushes, and my cock jumps at the words she doesn't say. "You've never...?"

Ignoring me, she tries to turn so she can complete the second part of our deal, but I grab hold of her left ankle with my right hand. "Keep your feet planted here."

"Then how –"

"Bend."

She tenses, no doubt imagining what I'll be able to see. Her standing over me, her legs spread as she bends down to wrap her underwear around my cock.

"You can kneel if it's too far for you," I tease, stroking my thumb across her skin. My cock jumps at the idea of her pussy being that close to my face.

She starts to bend down, her legs ramrod straight, and I am torn between looking up to watch her pussy spread for me or looking at her hands as she digs my cock out of my pants and wraps her red rayon fabric around it. My gaze flicks quickly between the two before landing on my cock. I'll have all the time to stare at her pretty open pussy in a second.

She undoes my belt, struggling with her one hand, and I see the moment she decides to drop the skirt of her dress and obscure my vision. "You do that and I'll have to keep myself entertained another way," I murmur, leaning up to kiss the back of her knee.

She tenses, her hand on my belt stilling. Then it pulls sharply, tugging and yanking on the strap of leather until finally it's free, and she's undoing my button and pulling down my zipper to fish out my hard cock.

I lift my hips for her to tug down my under shorts. My cock springs free as soon as the elastic passes them, and I glance up to see her pussy clench. A drip of her cum trails down her black curls to her thigh, and I growl low in my chest, needing to have her on my tongue already.

"I want my cock inside them," I say, tearing my gaze back to her hand. "I want it to touch the same spot your pussy rubs against."

She does as I say, no doubt hoping that's the last thing I'll demand of her. But as she tries to straighten, I slam both my forearms into the back of her knees, forcing them to bend. She hits the ground, her palms slamming beside my shins, her pussy over my chest, and I grab her hips to haul her back to my face.

She starts to turn, no doubt to try to stop me, so I wrap an arm around her ass, banding her to me, lift my head, and slide my tongue between her lips in one long lick.

Gods, she tastes so fucking *good*.

She moans, her thighs clenching as her upper body sags against me. Grabbing her good hand with my free one, I wrap it around my cock, on top of her underwear, pulling the fabric tight against my head. I groan, knowing I'm touching the same place her pussy does, feeling the slick wetness rubbing against my tip. My precum mixes with hers as I use her to pump myself, my hips lifting as my tongue begins its second stroke.

She jerks above me, her pussy clenching, and I lick her again, long slow strokes that build her sweet taste on my tongue. She squeezes my cock hard, digs her nails in as I jerk her hand up and down. The sharp cuts of pain make my balls grow tight. I'm already so close to the edge, the build-up of her fighting me, of her inevitable surrender having pushed me to the cusp of orgasm.

I groan into her pussy lips as she tries to jerk her hand away, no doubt realizing that her little nails are doing nothing to stop me. She grunts, pitiful attempts to hide her whimpers as she struggles against my grip. I push my panties-wrapped cock through her fist, my hips lifting with every thrust. My pleasure building. My need to fuck her hard and fast at war with my desire to make her come for the first time.

Straining my muscles, I keep myself beneath her, keep my hand on hers rather than shoving it into her hair and yanking her mouth down on my cock as I roll her under me so I can pummel her deep and hard until she no longer breathes.

I groan at the imagination of her choking around me, at the spit rolling down her chin as she gurgles and gags.

"Fuck, Sau," I rasp as I finally bury my tongue into her pussy. "You're going to make me come already."

She clenches around me, and my cock jerks as I realize she's just as close. Just as on the edge even though she's fighting it. She's such a dirty little whore deep down, and the knowledge that I'm the only one who knows this has my balls drawing tight enough to hurt.

I see her.

The real her.

Not the fake white flower she's forced to pretend to be, molded by her fucked up family and her dumb-as-fuck husband.

At the thought of that asshole, I growl and kiss her pussy with my lips and tongue. She cries out, unable to hide her arousal as she presses into my face, clenching my tongue in her demand to be eaten to completion.

Perhaps, I'll fuck her in front of him one day. Show him how wet she gets while she's riding my cock and screaming my fucking name.

Removing my arm from around her waist, I trail my fingers up her thigh and to her cunt. Pulling my head back so I can watch my fingers, I shove three of them into her at once, knowing she can take it. She's so utterly soaked. So fucking turned on.

She screams, her head falling against my muscled thigh as she comes around my fingers. I groan at the feel of her clenching me, at the flood of desire squirting out around me, spraying my face and chest. She absolutely drenches me as she shudders on top of me, having come so hard she can't breathe. Her breaths are more like rasps, her chest heaving as her pussy continues to spasm around me.

I pull my fingers out and push them back in, not giving her any time to come down off her high. Her wet pussy squelches around me as I pump into her fast and hard, the noises of her sexy cunt driving me mad.

She jumps as she whimpers, but I band an arm around her waist again, releasing my cock, and hold her still as I ram my fingers in and out of her.

"You're so fucking wet," I say as she soaks my hand, her cum dribbling down my arm and setting in my hairs.

She makes a choked, angry, half-broken noise before leaning forward and biting my cock. Her teeth sink into me deep despite her lack of fangs, and pain explodes down my shaft and into my balls, my back, shooting down to my feet.

Groaning, I release her waist to grip her hair, holding her little teeth in me as I come inside her panties, right where she rubbed them wet with her pussy. Such delicious pain she's giving me. Such a fucking turn on that I can't help but return the favor.

Leaning forward again, I continue to finger fuck her hard as I kiss her. Then I lick her once, twice, my cock still pumping out cum into her underwear. As she tries to jerk her head to rip out a chunk of my flesh, I pull my fingers out of her and sink my own fangs into her lips.

She releases me on a painful cry that only arouses me further. My cum falls down my cock, pooling on my balls and making her underwear stick to me. The coppery taste of blood mixes with the musky sweetness of her, and my head grows dizzy as I feed on her with deep sucks of my mouth. The taste of her slides down my throat and settles in my belly, making my cock hard all over again.

Dragging her underwear off me, I fist her hair and fight her protests to line her mouth back up with my cock. She snaps her teeth over me, and I groan at the hot spike of pain and pleasure radiating from the tip. Shoving hard into her, scraping past her teeth, I finally roll her beneath me.

She opens her mouth instinctively when my cock hits the back of her throat, but it doesn't help her breathe as I fuck her mouth animalistically, grunting and groaning as I continue to feed on her pussy.

I pummel into her, finding pleasure in the tightness of her throat and in the sharp cuts on my dick. She might not be able to use her magic right now, but it pulses strong through her blood, a heady taste that spreads through every inch of my body.

My balls draw tight as she starts to hit me with both her fists, no longer seeming to care that one is broken. She just wails at me with a choking desperation as I continue to fuck her hard and fast.

Her blood courses through me, the magic inside it a drug that heightens my own senses. Dozens of new smells assault me even though all I want to detect is hers. I start to push all the others to the back of my mind when I catch a scent that makes me still momentarily.

*Fucking dirty wolves.*

One in particular – Antonio.

The fucker must've been tracking me, running through the city since he escaped the Shadows' street. I can smell him not far away, maybe a block over at the most. He'll get to the door in a few minutes, tear through it, and run through the gym to here, cutting our fucking date short.

I growl as I lick Sau faster. I want to get her off again before he reaches us, and I know she's close; the bite of a vampire triggers a surge of dopamine in their victim, and she's lifting her hips even as she fights me, at war with what she wants.

Removing my fangs from her lips, I shove my fingers back inside her and curl, searching for that special spot that's a bit firmer than and of a slightly different texture to the rest of her pussy. She jerks when I find it, and I hammer my fingers against it, going faster and faster until the pace mimics a vibration.

Just as she starts to clench around me on the tremors of her orgasm, I pull my fingers out of her pussy and my cock out of her throat. Scooting back, I sit beside her head, then haul her back against me as she gasps for air, spit flying from her mouth.

"Antonio is about two minutes away from reaching us," I say as I wrap one arm around her to grab her opposite breast, fondling it leisurely. The other goes between her thighs. Pushing two fingers back inside her, I vibrate them against that special spot once more.

Her breaths come out in harsh pants as I lean forward to whisper in her ear. "So you have one minute and fifty seconds to come if you want to live. I won't stop him from killing you. But if you come for me, I'll phase us away."

She sucks in a breath, her body going ramrod straight.

I tense, half-expecting her to just tell me to go to hel and accept the fate I've forced upon her. But then she leans back against me and lets her thighs fall apart.

Her submission makes me groan, and I am seriously tempted to phase away now so I can fuck her all week long. But I don't just want to slide my cock inside her wet pussy.

I want to break her.

A wicked grin on my lips, I release her breast to grab her chin. Turning her to face me, I kiss her softly as I vibrate my fingers inside her.

Squeezing her eyes shut, she lets me do with her what I will, no longer fighting me. Even her lips part, but I don't sweep my tongue inside.

"Antonio's on the other side of the door," I say calmly. "You better hurry up."

Smirking, I still my fingers.

Her eyes snap open. Then widen as she finally realizes what I mean. A split second of refusal flashes across her eyes, but then full terror wins out as Antonio reaches our street. A witch's sixth sense has always been such a pain before, as it was in her kitchen, allowing Caden to save himself, but in this moment, I welcome it.

She starts gyrating against my fingers, using me to get herself off.

"I've never seen anything as fucking beautiful as how you look right now," I say, watching the panicked fear on her face, then the bouncing of her breasts as she drags her pussy up and down my fingers.

"Fuck...you," she hisses.

But she doesn't stop seeking her pleasure.

Doesn't stop using me, and my cock presses into her ass, desperate to trade places with my two fingers. My breaths turning heavy, I struggle to not take over and fuck her until she screams my name. I want her to *choose* this. To know that however much she claims she resisted, in the end, *she* got herself off on *me*.

A second later, the door bangs free of its hinges, and she jumps. I lift my head in surprise. I assumed Antonio would try to come in silently, creep in, and take us out close up. Instead, he's rammed through the door and is charging across the gym, still in his werewolf form.

My pulse spikes from the sheer power and rage pulsing off him. My cock twitches at the thrill of the gamble.

"Fifteen seconds," I say, my head heady. It'd be three if he didn't have to twist and turn past all the equipment and jump onto or go around the boxing ring in the middle.

Antonio's paws pound across the floor. His eyes latch on to her, and he snarls.

Her head snaps to him as he enters the ring, and she jerks her hips faster. Reaching a hand up, she grabs her breast and plays with it. Her other hand rubs her clit.

She's so fucking hot.

...until I see the changes on her face.

Her fear turns to arousal.

Her eyes grow half-hooded as she keeps them on the fucking wolf. He's only a few paces away from us now, but I don't doubt she'll come in time.

Her head falls back, her lips part, and –

"Eyes on me," I growl as I yank her head to mine.

She comes on a shuddering cry, squeezing my fingers as her gaze locks on to me. Antonio's breath reaches us as he snarls and lunges forward, his claws outstretched to swipe across Sau's throat.

Grinning, I phase us away right at the last second, so godsdamn close I can swear I can feel the brush of his claws disrupting the air even as we land on a side street not far from the Shadow Domain.

Removing my fingers from Sau, I push her away from me as she heaves, her body shaking from her orgasm and the strain phasing always causes.

Popping my fingers into my mouth, I suck them clean on a moan. Dear gods, one of these days I'm going to have to find a way to keep her scent with me.

Lowering my hand, I dig her underwear out of my under shorts, do up my pants over my hard throbbing cock, and crouch down at her feet as she lies on her belly, still unable to move.

Grabbing her feet, I slide her legs through the holes of her underwear, then tug them up all the way. She tries to stop me, her hand swatting at me half-heartedly, but my fierce lioness is too utterly drained to do me any harm. When they're fully settled on her, I push my fingers against her pussy, pressing the globs of cum left on the inside of her panties into her.

A groan pulls from deep in my chest as I imagine what she'd look like with my cum dripping out of her. My cock twitches in its demand for me to take her hard and fast.

Instead, I stand and start to walk away, whistling "The Entertainer" by Scott Joplin.

"Why?" she asks, and I stop to turn to look at her. She climbs to her feet, her eyes on the street where her home resides...for now.

"Why am I letting you go rather than keeping you locked up in my basement?" A cocky smile spreads my lips as I walk back to her, my eyes on the marks I've left on her naked breast. I stop right in front of her, then lean in, my breath a whisper across her ear. "Because you're going to *choose* me, Sau. You're going to want *me*."

"I'll never want you."

"Never is a long time to live." I twirl my finger around a strand of her hair. "I *never* thought I'd find someone like you. Antonio *never* thought he'd join us in this madness. Caden *never* thought his perfect, pure wife would get so turned on by violence."

I nip her earlobe, and she tries to shove me away, but her arms tremble too much with the truth of that last accusation.

"You're delusional," she says, her words just as shaky as the rest of her.

"Crazy?" I lift my head to look her in the eye. "Maybe. But delusional?" My grin widens. "No. No, that would mean

I have no chance." I tug on her hair. "And I most definitely have a chance, don't I, Sau?"

She opens her mouth to say something –yes, probably– but I yank *hard* on her strand, ripping it out of her scalp. Blood pools on her head as she clenches her teeth to stop her scream.

"An exchange of trophies," I say, lifting her hair to my mouth and running it across my lips. Then I pivot down the street as the sun begins to rise, whistling a jolly tune.

Today is going to be a good day.

I can feel it.

# THIRTY-TWO

## HER

### 15 AUGUST 1947

Trembling, I grab the flaps of my torn dress and try as best as I can to cover my breasts as he leaves me alone on the street. No one is out here at this hour, but I still feel like I'm being watched. Judged.

My throat tightening, my knuckles turn white as the full force of my self-disgust hits me. My lips wobble as tears burn my eyes. I came for the first time with another man – with *him*. And not once but twice, the second time having been under my own actions.

How can I ever face my loving husband?

I want to sit down and cry, not caring that I am a Shadow and *we don't cry*. I don't deserve my last name. I should just wait here until Antonio finds me again and let him rip me to pieces.

My tongue feels heavy in my mouth, and I run it over my teeth.

*"Promise me, Sau. Promise me you'll let me show you the world."* Caden's voice rumbles in my skull, making me equal measures happy and ashamed.

"He loves me," I whisper.

He loves me even though Antonio stole my virginity.

Even though I failed as a mother.

Even though I hate myself now.

"He loves me..." I look in the direction of home – not the house but *him*, my vision blurring.

"He loves me."

I shuffle forward, my knuckles white, putting my trust in him to take care of me. "He loves me."

The words become a mantra, guiding my feet forward, giving me the strength to keep going, running away from the darkness sharp on my heels. He is the light in this hel, and I stumble on trembling legs towards him.

"He loves me.

"He loves me...

"He loves me..."

Someone calls my name as soon as I reach sight of our street, but I don't turn towards them. It's not the voice I want. "She's back!"

Men rush towards me.

"Shit! Someone grab a healing wand!"

"Mrs. Shadow!"

Voices blur as they crowd me, and I bite my cheek to stop from whimpering when they block my path forward. A wand is waved up and down me, but it can't fix what's truly broken. The claw marks down my breast might be gone and my hand might be usable again, but the *pain* lingers. The shame.

The memories of how I came around Aleric's fingers.

I shake my head as a shirt is offered to me. It doesn't smell like Caden, and I don't want anyone else's touch on me. Someone's arm wraps around my shoulders, and I flinch away, whimpering.

"Sau, it's me," a man murmurs, his voice comfortingly familiar, and I turn to him to see it's Caden's younger brother. Throwing myself at him, my face hits his chest with a resounding *thump*. I close my eyes as he embraces me, hiding me away from the crowd.

"Where's Caden?" I rasp, digging my fingers into his shirt, only to find its gone. I start to shake as I pull away, hating the contact of another's skin. He wraps a white shirt around me, and I bite my tongue to stop my protest. No one argues with a reaper.

"Let's get you inside," he says as he guides me through the crowd of guards.

"Where's Caden?" I ask again, panic starting to set in about why he's not telling me.

Antonio was covered in blood when last I saw him. I try to remember what he looked like when I saw him in the street, but all I can remember is his gold hateful eyes. Most of my attention was on Caden, thinking I was going to see him for the last time.

"Myers..." I beg, my entire body trembling as I imagine my husband headless and torn apart by that fucking wolf. "*Where is Caden?*"

He glances down at me, and there is so much weight in his eyes. "He's alive," he finally says, but that offers little comfort due to the tone in which he says it.

"Is he...okay?" I swallow hard, trying to steel myself for what I'm about to find, so I can be the strong rock he needs me to be, the pillar that every female Shadow is supposed to be for her husband.

Sighing, he stops just outside the door to our house. The door itself is gone, and I search the inside hall for any sign of life. Caden is in there somewhere.

"He saw you, Sau," he says, and my gaze snaps to his, and I pray he doesn't mean what I think he does.

But my world is collapsing in on itself, choking me as it squeezes me tight in the grip of its palm. And I *know* what he means.

"No," I cry, the word as broken as I feel. "No." I shake my head. "*No.*"

"He was too weak to help you with his telekinesis, but he didn't want you to suffer alone." He glances away, but I can't take my eyes off him, wishing he's lying. That this is some cruel joke because he secretly hates me for whatever reason.

But there is too much pain on his face. Pain for his brother, who he loves so fucking much.

I pull away from him, still shaking my head. "*No.*"

My body feels foreign, *wrong*, and I drag my nails down my arms, gauging thick red lines as his shirt falls off my shoulders. At the sight of my naked breasts, at the memory of the vampire's mouth on them, I stumble back, clawing at them too. "*No!*"

"Sau –"

"No!" I scream, shoving his hands away as he tries to grab them.

I don't want him to stop me. I don't want him to *save* me. Caden never should have kept me alive in my coma. He shouldn't have helped me reattach my tongue. He should've let me die. I'm just a *disease* that needs to be cured.

My legs give out from under me as I scream, but he catches me in his arms. Dragging me into the house, he tries to calm me down. A good wife never makes a scene.

But I'm not a good wife, am I?

I'm a horrible, sick, twisted person who came while she was being raped. *Twice.*

A sob rips from me as I try to claw at any part of me I can reach.

Myers' hands close around both of mine, and he shoves me face-first against a wall, trapping me with his body just to pin me still. "Don't –" He grunts as he's flung off me, and his body hits something with a hard *crack*.

"Don't fucking touch her."

I spin at those words, at the voice of my husband, and see him standing in the hall. I take a step towards him, then stop, not sure what to do when I feel this disgusting. I go to claw at my arms, needing the comfort of pain, but there's something in his eyes that stops me.

*"You promised me, Sau."*

My lips wobbling, I take a step towards him. He opens his arms, and I run, tripping over my feet to get to him. I fall against his chest, and he stands rigid for just a second before his arms come around me. Then he lifts me into the air. My legs go around him, and Aleric's cum presses into my pussy, making me stiffen. I whimper as I try to push off him, but he just holds me tighter.

"I'm so sorry, Sau. I'm so sorry I let him take you."

I cry, burying my head into the crook of his neck, not caring for once that I'm being weak, an *embarrassment* to the Shadow name. "I'm…sorry I…"

"Shhhh," he says as he turns to head down the hall. "It's not your fault your body reacted, sweet girl. It's just anatomy."

I shake my head, crying. Snot runs down my nose and past my lips. "It *is*…"

"It's *not*. Listen to me." He presses his lips to the top of my head and drops his voice. "Our mother was in love with another woman when she was forced to marry our father. So he raped her every night to 'fix her.' She hated him with all she had and tried to kill him multiple times. But that didn't stop her from…'screaming' every night. Our bodies aren't always connected to our minds, sweet girl. It's not your fault."

I tremble against him, the guilt inside me so fucking strong. "But –"

"No buts. You didn't want it, did you?"

I shake my head.

"Then that is all that matters."

Tears burn my throat as I cling to him. He's too good for me, but I am too selfish to let him go to find someone who will be good to him. Who won't just be a disease that wears him down.

I need his love for me when I am too broken to love myself.

Entering our room, he heads straight for the ensuite. He stops in front of the shower and puts me down inside the ceramic tub, but I grab his arm when he reaches for the tap.

My heart racing, I work my tongue around my mouth a couple times before I manage to choke out the words, "His cum...I have it. You can use that...to kill him?"

His jaw clenches as his eyes narrow on me. "He *raped* you? I only saw right up to the moment he phased."

I shake my head, grabbing hold of my anger rather than my shame. "The idiot gave me back my underwear."

His eyes dip down, anger flashing in them, and I flinch away, knowing that my husband watched me cum on the vampire's fingers. Watched me fuck them to save my own pathetic life.

His eyes soften as he exhales, but he doesn't look at me. Perhaps he can't in this moment. Not that I can blame him. I can't look him in the eye right now either. I don't deserve his love.

My hands shaking, I reach beneath my dress and pull down the rayon satin covered in Aleric's cum...and mine. My cheeks hot, I hand them over to my husband.

He turns them inside out.

His nostrils flare.

His eyes narrow.

And his knuckles turn white as he clenches my panties in his fists.

"You got so fucking wet," he says, his words heavily strained. "Was it Aleric or Antonio that made you act like a whore?"

I flinch, drawing away from him. "Caden?"

He holds up my underwear in one hand while the other snaps forward and grabs me roughly by the arm. "Answer me. Was it Antonio or *Aleric* who made you wetter than a whore?"

"I... You said..." I yelp as his fingers tighten around me. "You're hurting me."

"That's what you like, isn't it? You like being raped?" He hauls me forward, and my knees knock into the white ceramic.

"No." I grab at his fingers, trying to wrench them off me. "Why are you doing this?" I beg. He just told me it was okay. He just made me believe it wasn't my fault. I suck in a breath, trying to breathe past the panic lodging in my throat.

"I heard his words to you, Sau. I saw how he raped you, but I didn't *feel* how wet you were. I didn't fucking know you were loving his fingers inside you."

"That's not true. I *didn't*."

"You must've squirted all over the place to soak these this much." He shakes my underwear in my face, his own twisting in pain and jealousy. "This isn't just coming, is it? It's fucking *loving it*."

"No... Caden, I didn't." I shake my head. "You said it was just anatomy."

He pushes me against the wall, then further tears apart my dress, Myers' shirt having fallen off in the hall when I ran towards him. "Stop."

"Don't say that when you let them fuck you and I'm your fucking husband."

"I didn't –"

He shoves my panties into my mouth, and my eyes

widen as he steps into the tub with me.

"You want me to fuck you like they did?" he snarls as he strips off his shirt. "You want me to *beat* you? *Rape* you? Not give a fucking damn about what you want?" He tosses his shirt, then slams his fist into the wall beside my head, and I jump, terror ripping through me with not a molecule of arousal.

Caden isn't supposed to scare me.

He isn't supposed to hurt me.

He's my husband.

I shake my head, trying to push out the panties so I can tell him I don't want this from him, but he places a hand over my mouth. His other yanks down my dress, tearing apart the zipper as he forces it off my hips.

"Spread your legs," he snaps.

I squeeze them together and jerk my head to the side, but his grip over my mouth hardens until he's holding me still and I'm unable to express my lack of consent.

"Open your fucking legs like the whore you are."

"*Please*," I mumble, but between my panties and his palm, even I can't understand the gurgle that comes out of my lips. I try not to taste the dried cum on the fabric, but it's everywhere and adds to the sickness in my stomach.

His magic wraps around my legs and jerks them apart *hard*, shooting pain down my muscles and ligaments. I don't think he's snapped or torn anything, but I feel like he's breaking something else inside of me.

He strips off his pants and under shorts with his magic. His cock is hard and throbbing.

"Please, stop," I beg. I don't want this.

I don't want this from my husband.

He's supposed to be safe.

He's supposed to love me when I can't.

"You're so fucking wet all down to your knees," he hisses, his face twisting more with rage. "Now tell me if it was

Aleric or *Antonio*."

I plead with him with my eyes, but my husband isn't even looking at my face, his gaze on my spread pussy.

"Aleric's cum is all stuck in your curls," he growls, and his fingers move jerkily with his magic.

I scream against my panties as Caden rips out all the hairs on my pussy at once.

My knees buckle as agony shoots through me, and tears roll down my cheeks.

"Now how do you think I should clean the rest of you?" he asks as my black curls, blood and skin on one end, float down to the tub.

The memory of how he cleaned me with the bottle assaults me, and I stare up at him pleadingly, having slid down the wall a bit from the pain.

"I know..." he says, holding his hand out to the open door. There is no mercy in his eyes, no love, and I wonder if he's just doing what I deserve.

I failed him as a wife.

He must've suffered so much watching me with Aleric.

This is nothing less than what I deserve for being such a whore. No longer fighting him, I open my heart to him. I'll let him do whatever he needs to to work through his own pain.

I'll love him even when he doesn't love me.

A glowing pink vial flies into his hand, and he uncorks it before I can get a good look at it. My pulse spikes as I wonder if it's some sort of acid to burn Aleric's touch off me, but he drinks it instead of pouring it on me.

Wary confusion hits me for just a moment, but then my eyes bug wide as his cock transforms right in front of my face. It elongates and thickens until it's girthier and longer than my forearm from fist to elbow. Thick ridges run all the way down its length, and at the upper side of its base is a fleshy hook about the size of his thumb. It pulses as I watch it.

I spit my panties out now that he's no longer holding his palm against me. "That won't fit," I rasp.

My eyes widen as another vial flies into his hand. He chugs this one too, then tosses them both at the sink on the other side of the room, the glass shattering across the floor.

He grunts as a second penis grows out right above his balls, this one shorter and thinner than the other but not by much. There's an extra flap at the base of it about the width of a tongue, and my pussy clenches at the idea of it working like one.

But even still, I shake my head because there is no fucking way one of them will fit, let alone both of them at once.

"You can't..."

"I *can*. Because his stench is all over you, and I'm going to make sure you don't even *remember* what he feels like."

He wraps my fingers round the larger dick, needing to use both of my hands so I can actually reach all the way around him. I whimper in anticipated pain even as I start to salivate and my pussy starts to throb.

"David took your mouth's virginity from me, and Antonio damn well took your pussy's. But I'm going to take your ass' first, Sau. I'm going to break it in until you can't stand."

My breath hitches as my eyes stay on his two new throbbing cocks. "Are you going to hurt me?" I ask, my heart twisting. I'll let him do whatever he wants, whatever he needs to to get this filth off me, but... But I want... I can't find the words to say even to myself, my lack of experience making me unable to untangle all the feelings inside me.

I lift my eyes to him when he doesn't immediately answer.

His jaw clenches as he glares at me. His face is twisted in jealous anger, and when he grabs me to yank me up and turn me around so I face the wall over the foot of the tub, my pulse spikes with fear. But a vial of pale-blue liquid appears wordlessly at my lips, and I drink it down quickly. It tastes like cum with a hint of chocolate.

I groan instantly, my body shuddering and developing a sheen of sweat as heat floods through my insides. My stomach grows, making space, and I gasp as he grabs my hips and hauls me backwards.

His hand between my shoulder blades shoves me down, bending me at the waist. He slides one cock between my ass cheeks, not going in, and the other between my pussy lips.

"Who has this pussy been fucked by, you dirty fucking whore?"

I flinch, my pulse pounding, surging shame all the way through me. "Please," I whisper. *Please don't make me say it.*

"Who have you let fuck your pussy?" he snaps.

"I didn't let any–"

His hand slams down on my ass, and I grit my teeth from the pain as it resonates up and down my legs.

"Who. Have. You. Let –" He hits me with every word.

"Antonio!" I cry out, my shoulders shaking as I squeeze my eyes shut, remembering how the werewolf fucked the hole he'd made in my pussy.

"Who else?" he seethes, two simple words that are weighed down with the shame of all my sins.

"Bert," I whimper, hating his name on my tongue.

"You spread your legs for all of his friends too, didn't you?"

His fingers dig into my hips, ten pinpoints that radiate his rage. His *pain*.

"I don't know." The words are broken, but I refuse to cry over them. My lips wobbling, I turn my head, my own pain pulled to the surface, drawn out by his. "You were supposed to kill them all for me!" I shout. "You were supposed to protect me!"

His face twists with agony and a mirroring shame to mine, but that doesn't stop him from slamming his hand down on my ass.

"I've loved you for forty-two years, Sau, since you were a baby in a crib. I didn't just see you as some whore to carry my children like my father did my mother. I *loved* you." His voice cracks as he spanks me again, but his hand lingers this time to knead away some of the sting. "I love you, sweet girl. Why can't you love me back?"

Tears burn my eyes as I stare at him in shock. "I *do*." How does he not know that?

"But why should I believe a whore," my husband asks, "when even her lips have been around more cocks than just mine?"

He holds my gaze, the pain in his eyes increasing mine until it becomes hard to breathe. He truly doesn't know I love him. I almost killed him with my shadows. Then I *left* with Aleric willingly. He watched me come all over the vampire's fingers when I've never come with him. I heave in a breath, never tearing my eyes off him. "I love you, Caden. Only you. The others..." I swallow, my throat tight, but the sheer desperation in his eyes, his *need* to hear me say it, pushes the words out. "I don't know why I came with Aleric, why violence...turns me on."

I choke on the admission, hating how dirty it sounds when Caden has only ever offered me safety. But I can't hide the truth from him anymore...or me.

Reaching back, I grab one of his hands on my hips and squeeze. The fact that he doesn't jerk away from my grip gives me hope that he still loves me despite the filth that has wrapped itself around my soul. He can't clean it off. There's no pretending anymore that he can.

"I love you," I whisper. "Only ever you."

Dragging his hand down my hip and over his cock, I

press his fingers to my clit. "This pussy is yours, Caden," I say. "This mouth..." I pull his fingers to my lips and kiss them. "It's yours. My ass...it's yours." Tears burn my eyes from the rawness of this moment, and I clutch his hand to my chest, right over my heart. "I'm yours, Caden. Only ever yours."

His body shudders as he holds my gaze. "Then spread your legs for me, sweet girl, and let me get him off you."

I obey immediately, spreading them wide even as my body tenses over the idea of both his cocks penetrating me at once. Even with the potion he gave me, I don't think they're going to fit.

He draws back, lines up both cocks, then hesitates, too sweet to hurt me despite everything he's feeling.

So I take a deep breath, force myself to relax as much as I can, and then slam back hard and fast. I cry out as I impale myself, my knees buckling until I'm held up only by the thick, pulsing cocks inside of me. Instant regret fills me as the pain radiates everywhere, and I try to squirm off him, but he grabs both my hips and holds me still.

"Fuck, Sau," he hisses. "I can't pull out now." Panic fills me as a knot thickens near the head of the cock up my pussy.

"It hurts," I whimper as I'm stuffed so much, I feel like I'm being torn apart, like it's crushing all my organs and leaving no space for anything else. My hands touch my stomach, and I can feel the outline of his cock. "It *hurts*," I say again, but all he does is groan.

Both of his cocks jerk inside me, radiating sharp spikes of pain, and I cry out before he wraps a hand around my throat.

"Shhhh," he says as he bends down to my ear, going deeper inside of me, splitting me in two, making the pain intensify. My eyes, pussy, and ass burn as he shuffles his legs around mine.

"You can take it, sweet girl."

I shake my head. "It's too much."

"Just relax... Daddy's got you." Something flicks up and down the outside of my pussy lips, and I gasp at the shock of it feeling wet. And *good*. I moan as it rubs across my clit. "That's it. You're being such a good girl relaxing for me."

He reaches forward to fondle a breast, pinching my nipple until it hurts. A delicious current flows through me, and I start to pant.

Finding pleasure from pain doesn't feel so shameful when he's the one doing it. My legs shake as I want to beg him to hurt me more, to fuck me like I need it, but the words still sit heavily on my tongue over worry that he'll judge me like I judge myself for wanting such horrible things.

So instead, I silently spread my legs wider, hoping that he knows without me asking.

His hand slams down onto my ass, and I jump, then stumble, my legs nearly too numb to hold me up, his two cocks feeling like they're cutting off circulation. "Did I tell you you could make demands?"

My mouth drops open as my palms hit the wall to catch myself. "Sorry," I rasp, my heart going a thousand beats a second as excitement courses through me.

"You do not get to ask me for anything. No, tonight, you're just going to *take* –" He pulls out until the knot of his cock hits the rim of my vagina and lodges there. The ridges up my ass popped out one by one, sending jolts of pleasure all through my body. "*It all*," he growls.

I scream against the wall as he slams all the way back in, my fingers digging into the ceramic tiles.

He moves mercilessly, not giving me time to adjust, just pummeling in and out, his ridges scraping my ass, his knot moving deep inside my pussy before knocking at the entrance, unable to leave until he comes. That tongue thing flicks mercilessly at my clit. The sensations are too much, too intense, and I am quickly reduced to a sobbing mess of, "Please," and "Thank you," and "Oh my fucking gods!"

"That's it," he says as he rams in deep, his breaths hard and fast. "Thank me for tearing apart your ass and pussy, sweet girl."

"Thank you for –" I cry out as he slaps my ass with both hands and grabs the flesh between his fingers.

"What was that?" he growls, squeezing me hard as he slams into me over and over and over again, using my ass as two handles to take what he wants without mercy.

I'm breathing so fast I can't actually suck in any air. I'm shaking so hard, I'm surprised I'm still standing. My body is being jerked back and rammed forward, and my head hits the wall every so often, but I can't feel the pain beneath the pleasure of his two cocks.

"Thank you, Daddy, for *what*?" he hisses as he bends down to my ear, still hammering away inside of me.

I moan, my tongue not wanting to do anything other than fall apart in blissful screams. But I force it to work, force it to say, "Thank you, Daddy." I pant hard, my back arching as he slams balls deep inside me, his knot hitting me so deep, it feels like he's all the way up my womb.

I cry out as my orgasm jumps right to the edge, and my entire body shakes with the need to come on *him*. On my husband. My sweet, loving Caden. "Thank you, Daddy, for fucking me so *good*," I pant between ragged breaths.

"You like my cocks inside you?"

I nod feverishly, my pussy clenching around him.

"You like how they tear you apart?"

I nod faster.

"You like how they're going to fill you up until you can damn near *taste* my cum in your mouth?"

My eyes widen at that visual, of him shooting so much cum, it dribbles out my lips.

"Yes," I pant as I push my pussy and ass down on his two cocks, moaning at the knot pulsing quickly inside of me, telling me he's on the edge of his own release. "I want you to fill me that much. You feel so good. I need you, Daddy. I need you to come in me."

He groans as he reaches down to grab my thigh. He raises it up, putting my legs at ninety degrees to each other before he hammers into me wild and fast and so fucking hot, I come within seconds.

Screaming, I squeeze around him, begging him to go faster, to ram into me harder. I'm so fucking stretched, I can't feel anything other than his cocks. They make up my entire world in this moment, and bright lights explode behind my eyes as I squeeze them shut. My pussy pulses over and over again, my orgasm ripping through me with the force of a knockout blow. My body spasms as I jerk beneath his thrusts. My lungs struggle to suck in enough air, and I'm damn near on the verge of passing out due to lack of oxygen.

And still he continues to fuck me, hard and fast and wild like an animal that can't be sated.

His grunts turn into roars. The tongue thing at the base of his cock swirls all over my pussy lips and pays brutal attention to my clit. I jerk, my breaths raspy and shallow as the sensations shooting through me toss me back over the edge, and I come again. *Hard.*

So hard, my vision starts to fade to black as his knot explodes inside me, filling me up with so much hot cum, my stomach starts to actually balloon to where it looks like I'm five months pregnant.

Groaning, my body rippling with ecstasy, I pass out.

---

I come to with him still ramming into me, my back now

against the adjacent wall, my legs over his shoulders, and the shower on, cascading steam around us.

"That's right, sweet girl," he says as he slams into me, his eyes on mine. "This is my pussy. This is my ass." He grabs both cheeks, then reaches up to pinch my nipples. "These are my tits. I can fuck you even if you're unconscious, can't I, sweet girl?"

"Yes," I pant, moaning as his hands go back to my ass, bouncing me up and down his cocks. The one that was in my pussy is now in my ass, and its knot slides up and down me, stretching me so tight. But dear gods, it's the other one that has me a complete soaking mess. The hook on the base of it is curled just right to hit that special spot with each tensing of his muscles. "They're all yours," I wheeze. "*I'm* all yours."

"That's right," he growls as he presses his hips hard into mine, holding me up with just them so one hand can rub my clit and the other can band around my throat. My eyes widen as he begins to squeeze me.

I could barely breathe to begin with, but now I can't at all, and I grab his hand, my pulse spiking, terror and pain and pleasure all mixing into one.

"You want to breathe?" He leans in and kisses me on my lips, all gentle and soft despite the hard fucking he's given me. "Then come for me, sweet girl. Show me that you're mine."

I dig my heels into his shoulders, but the position is too awkward to bounce myself. I grab at his chest, my fingers scraping down it as I search for a purchase somewhere, *anywhere* so I can come, so I can breathe.

But my head grows heady, and desperation claws at me.

My vision narrows. My lips undoubtedly grow blue.

Yet all he does is kiss me gently.

"Come for me, sweet girl. Come for me like you did for Aleric," he hisses – the last words I hear before I pass out in a panic.

---

I choke for air as I wake. His hand is still around my throat, but the pressure is off completely, and I gasp in great lungfuls of air as my eyes fly to his.

"Come for me," he growls as his fingers start to tighten again and his palm presses down with an even pressure.

My eyes bug wide as my air is cut off again, and I kick my legs to try to find purchase.

"Show me you love me," he says, his eyes flashing with a pain that hurts me.

Placing a hand on my pussy, I rub myself as I look into his eyes.

*I do.*

*I love you.*

*Only you, Caden.*

He groans as he slides out of me, then back in, soft and leisurely as I rub myself fast. His lips find mine in gentle caresses that contrast so erotically with the tightness of his hand around my throat.

I try to kiss him back, but my movements are sluggish, and my head grows heady. Unconsciousness beckons to me, but I fight it off, needing him to know that he is my everything.

He loves me when I don't.

He is every single star in my night sky.

Holding his gaze even as mine narrows, I come all over his two cocks. And then I pass out.

---

This time, I'm on my feet, held up by his hands on my

biceps as we stand in a puddle of thick liquid that has a much different consistency to the water rushing out of the shower head.

I look down, and my eyes widen at the rivulets of cum swirling around our feet, at the slickness running down our legs. There's so much of it... My stomach is flat again, no longer swollen with his seed. His cock has transformed back into its normal self, both the potions having worn off, and it now hangs soft between his thighs.

"I'm sorry," he says as he pulls me close. "I shouldn't have called you a whore or accused you of enjoying being raped. I..." He trails off as he kisses the top of my head. "That was my insecurity to bear, not yours."

My eyes mist as I rub my cheek against his shoulder. "I love you, Caden. I'm so sorry I ca–"

"It's not your fault, sweet girl. It's just anatomy."

I swallow as I hold those words to my chest. He holds me tight in his arms, and the water flows over us, as if it's baptizing us despite the stains on our souls.

I feel closer to him, and I wrap my arms around his waist, loving the feeling of his skin. For once, I don't feel tainted by Antonio or my uncle or any of those men he let rape me while I was unconscious.

Or Aleric...

"I love you," I say, swallowing hard.

"I love you too. You're perfect, Sau, so utterly perfect."

I lift my chin, and he kisses me, our tongues dancing soft and slow. When he pulls back, he turns me on my feet so I'm facing the spray of the water. Then he lathers my hair, his fingers kneading my scalp. I close my eyes as he tends to me, taking care of me in every way.

I reach behind me and grab his cock, just holding it in my hand, wanting that connection between us. It stays soft, no demand to be pleasured, no expectation of getting something more.

## MADNESS BEHIND THE MASK

Trailing his hands down my body, he washes me as I lift my head to the spray...

...and smile for the first time.

For my husband still loves me.

As long as we are together, no one can ever hurt me.

# THIRTY-THREE

## ALERIC
### 26 OCTOBER 1947

The whore at my feet is dead. Unsurprising, really, given I'm holding half her spine in my fist. The choking got a bit out of hand.

Or rather, got a bit out of her neck.

I grin as I bring it to my lips and lick the blood off the bone. Bits of torn ligaments, muscles, and nerves hang from it, and I suck a bit of muscle into my mouth to feed on before dropping the whole thing on top of the black-haired whore.

She was a poor imitation, just like all the others have been over the last two months.

A growl rumbles low in my throat as I'm reminded once again that the thing I want is currently in possession of another man.

I bet the fucker even hid the gift I left her.

*He better not have destroyed it*, I think with another

growl. That vampire hunting kit held the first stake to have ever stabbed me. I was so surprised some idiot had actually thought that would be a good idea when guns and bows existed, that I'd kept it.

I was so looking forward to seeing it in Sau's hand, even more to having her shove it between my ribs as she tried to kill me.

My cock hardens despite its recent release, and I glance down at the open hole I ripped in the imitation's neck. My office door isn't locked, and I have a meeting in about two or three minutes, but...it would be *such* a waste of a deep-throating opportunity if I didn't...

My cock twitches as I bend down.

"Father," Colton says as he opens the door.

"You can talk, but I'm not stopping," I say as I grab the dead whore by her long black hair and drag her over to my office chair. I settle into it, facing him, but by the time I look up, the door has been shut again, and he's no longer here.

Smirking, I bring her open throat over the head of my throbbing cock, but the door opens again, this time with a bang, and I sigh heavily as Vlad fills the doorway. Unlike my namby-pamby of a son, he will not be so easily gotten rid of.

"Put your cock away," my underboss snaps as he drags in a man behind him.

"She was bad at giving head anyway," I say as I shove her to the floor and push my cock back into my pants.

Colton steps in slowly behind them, his gaze held way higher than my face. I don't bother looking at him either, my gaze on the witch Vlad's brought in.

His hands are broken, bloody messes, and I lean back in my chair as I stare at him across my desk.

"You were supposed to get Sau past the wards today," I say as I hold his two black eyes. *We had a date.*

"Caden isn't letting –"

"Caden... Caden... Caden..." I hiss, hating hearing that fucking name, especially as a blockade to something *I* want.

Not for the first time, I regret not keeping Sau locked up in my basement or chained to my bed. But there isn't any fun with breaking someone who has nowhere else to run.

I want her to run.

I want her to find protection in all those dumb little places she thinks she can.

I want her to think that she is safe from me.

A cold grin spreads across my lips.

For that is the best time to break them – when their hope is high. And she *will* break. And she *will* run back to me because I'm the only one who really sees her for *her*. Who can free her from the trapped cage her Family has locked her up in.

I will have her beg me to help her. To take her in under my wing and under my body. And then I will kill her. My cock jerks at the anticipation of sinking into her soaking wet pussy as the last of her fire leaves her eyes.

"Let's try this again," I say as I stare at the witch in front of me. Christian Boyle is a falcon – one of the eyes and ears of the Shadow Domain and one who has been in my employment for the last three months. "You came to me, begging for my aid, offering to feed me information in exchange for me killing those who were blackmailing you. I held up my end of the bargain because you came to me when Caden was killing Sau's uncle and told me that would be a great time to strike. And it was, I'll give you that. We didn't have to deal with David's illusions, and Caden was nicely distracted. But..." I trail off as I lean forward. "But... since then, you failed to let us know that the dear old witches have decided to branch into human trafficking. And what is our top commodity again?"

He swallows, his busted lip still dripping blood. "Sex and blood trafficking," he says shakily.

"Exactly. So even someone as thick as you must be able to see how concerning it is that our main competitor is trying to muscle their way into our operations, and the snitch I have *graciously* allowed to live *failed to tell me in advance.*"

"It was a sudden decision on Caden's part," he blurts. "There was no warning, no word. He just –"

I raise a finger and wiggle it back and forth. "Ah, ah, ah. What is the thing I hate most, Colton?" I ask, not taking my eyes off Christian.

"Excuses," my son says tightly; he never did care for these sorts of meetings.

"Exactly. So let's try this again, Christian," I say as I stand and walk around my desk to stop in front of him. "Tell me without giving me some sniveling excuse, why you've failed me yet again?"

Sweat glistens on his brow. His pulse beats wildly at the base of his neck. But my eyes stay on his, watching as terror lights them until they're shiny and red. My fangs elongate as my cock hardens at the sight of his fear.

"I... I... I'll get her out," he blurts, his eyes dipping to my fangs.

"That is not the question I asked."

His face pales. His Adam's apple bobs. "I... I'm sorry. *Please*... I...I won't fail you again."

"Not. The. Question."

"Because I'm a coward!" he blurts, his heart racing as he flinches away from me. "I was scared of what Caden would do if I tried to take her out past the wards. He never lets her out of his sight anymore."

My eyes narrow. Such a distasteful way for my girl to live, stuck in his shadow when she needs light to *grow*. "Even when she goes to take a shit?" I ask, and his gaze snaps back to me at the sudden question.

"Uh..."

The smile I give makes him flinch again. I can see his little brain running as fast as it can as it tries to figure out what I mean.

But the guy is a fucking idiot, and my patience wanes before he figures it out.

"If you don't know," I say, "then you haven't watched her close enough, now have you? And what use do I have for an informant who is so utterly *useless*?"

"I'm sorry!" he whines. "I'll find out. I'll –"

I grab him by the throat, haul him forward, and sink my teeth into his neck. The sweetness of his blood isn't comparable to Sau's, and the poor imitation I am stuck with *yet again* makes me growl as I crush his vocal chords in my fist.

He gurgles, jerking beneath my attentions, the rush of dopamine flooding through his system no match for his utter terror. Our bites aren't magic; it won't get rid of any underlying emotions, and I take pleasure in the panicked gasps that flow from his lips.

Pulling my teeth out of him, I drop him to the ground, then step on top of him on my way out of the room. "Cut him up and package him, but leave the box with his head open."

"And the woman?" Colton asks, his voice tight.

"Pass her around. It'll be such a shame to waste that neck of hers." I lift a hand as I walk down the hall, and Vlad follows me, leaving my son to deal with the mess. I lick my lips, cleaning it of the witch's blood.

"He could've had more use," Vlad says.

"Oh, he will." I smile as I think about the note that will accompany Christian's body when it's delivered back to the Shadow Domain. "Sau wants a treaty, so I will give her one."

"Under what terms?" There's no concern or anger in his voice. Vlad doesn't have a personal vendetta against the Shadows. His Family married in, and dealing with them is simple business. He doesn't care if they are dealt with through blood or pen.

My smile stretches. "Why, through marriage, dear boy. What else?"

# THIRTY-FOUR

## HER

28 OCTOBER 1947

---

Every morning, I go to see Ryo in the nursery, fixed and decorated anew, and am reminded of Olivia. She used to smile at me, making soft noises as drool dribbled down her chin whenever I entered. I'd alternate between who I picked up and cradled to my chest first. This morning, it is Ryo.

Just like it was yesterday.

And the day before that.

And the day before that.

Just like it'll be tomorrow.

And the day after that.

And the day after that...

My chest aches as I hold him to me. He's more quiet now. Although too young to understand death, he misses his sister and cries for her often. He is so lonely in this big old room, but I'm terrified of giving him a new sibling to grow up with. Terrified of losing him or her too.

My throat tight, I turn to Caden as he sits at his desk. He had it moved in here not long after we shared that night in the shower, not wanting to be away from me for a single moment, and I not wanting to be away from Ryo in case he 'just died suddenly' too.

His first birthday has come and gone. Caden assured me that babies are less likely to die for no reason after that, but...

"Does he look okay to you?" I ask as I walk over to him with our son in my arms, balanced on my hip.

Caden glances up at me, but his pen stays poised on the list he's making. Then his gaze turns to Ryo, and he pulls a silly face, sticking out his tongue and widening his eyes. Ryo laughs, carefree and happy, and my husband smiles. "He does."

He waits for me to pass my own judgment, but instead of just trusting his opinion like I normally do, this time, I frown. I turn Ryo to face me, staring into his eyes, trying to figure out if he's about to take his last breath right here in my arms.

Pushing his chair back, Caden pats his knee. He doesn't sigh even though I'm certain he wants to. I've asked him this question six times already this morning. Yesterday, I must have asked it a hundred times before bed.

"Come here," he says, and I obey immediately, wanting the comfort of his touch. I settle on his lap, my legs in between his as I sit side-on on his thigh. He takes Ryo from me, and my pulse spikes at his absence. It's suddenly hard to swallow even though I know Caden loves him. It's there in his eyes, in how warm they are whenever he looks at our children.

*Except Leon*, a little voice says, but I understand why he doesn't. Leon is a soldier now and will be taking over the Family in a couple years. He needs to be treated with the respect of an heir, not just the love of a father.

"This little man is going to grow into the healthiest Shadow. Aren't you, son?"

Ryo giggles when Caden rubs his head against his belly, making playful noises. Squealing, he pulls at his father's curly red hair, his cheeks just as rosy in color. Healthy. *Alive.*

I swallow past the clog in my throat, willing my heart rate to slow.

*He's going to be fine,* I tell myself. I breathe out with a nod, a small smile on my lips when my husband turns to me. He hands Ryo back without me having to ask, and I hug him close to my chest. "I love you, Ryo," I say as I kiss his cheek.

"Mama." He grins so carefree, and my smile broadens, turning genuine in its warmth.

Caden reaches around me to pick up the piece of paper on his desk, then leans back in his chair, holding me to him with his other hand. I take comfort in the feel of his body protecting mine even though I ignore him for the most part, my attention on our son as I play with him while Caden works.

But eventually Ryo falls asleep and my gaze turns to the piece of paper still in my husband's hand. His eyes are a bit glazed, his thoughts outside of this room, but when I shift on his lap to get a better look at the words, he turns to me. I duck my head immediately, remembering how Father would always chastise me for being nosy.

"It's a list of the capos coming to dinner tonight," he says, offering the paper to me.

I glance at him, then the sheet. "You've been looking at it for a long time," I tease. "And here I was thinking you already had their names memorized."

He chuckles, but it's without the warmth he normally gives me.

My stomach starts to sink, the hairs on my arms rising. I

hold Ryo tighter to me as I wait for him to speak.

"I wanted to wait until she was older," he says slowly, a sigh heavy in those words. "And I hoped her marriage would be to someone outside of the Family to strengthen our reach, but..."

My stomach twists. My tongue feels too heavy. My eyes fall back to the page, reading each name over and over again. *No.*

"But that *night*," he says, and he doesn't need to clarify. I know the one he means. When the vampires attacked, then the werewolves. When I was violated yet again. "Left us greatly weakened. We lost a lot of our soldiers, and we need to strengthen the inside of this Family. Rebuild it."

"She's only eight," I whisper, but there isn't a tremble to my words. Nor any grief. I keep that deep inside like a good wife should. *But she's only eight.*

"She's started her ascension. That makes her a woman."

I close my eyes briefly. I knew this day would come. It happens to every female Shadow. It happened to me. I would have been so happy to be married off so young. Jade definitely would have bragged about it. But now... After all I've been through. After learning what it means to be a mother in this family... To lose a child... To fear for them every day they go out? I'm left awake every night, terrified that I've just seen Leon or Jonathan for the last time.

"She won't go to someone we can't trust," Caden says softly.

He doesn't promise her love.

My mother didn't have it.

Nor did my aunt.

Nor any of the women of the Shadow family in the last five hundred years but one.

*And me*, I say mentally, taking a bit of comfort in that.

"Who have you picked?" I finally asked, turning to him.

"I haven't yet. That's why I'm still staring at this damn

piece of paper." His jaw tightens, and his next words are flat and so damn controlled. "I do not doubt that some of the capos were loyal to David. Or failing that, they *knew* what he was doing and waited to see how it all played out before they pledged their loyalty. Myers is in the middle of weeding David's associates out, but..." He hesitates. "We might never know who they all are."

My hands trembling, I clench them into fists, careful not to press my anger into Ryo. "And yet we must pick one to marry our daughter."

He nods, not sugarcoating it in the slightest. This is the reality of the world we live in. I used to be so proud of it...

Now all I want is to run from it.

Or watch it burn.

Shaking the thoughts away, I look at the piece of paper again. "Tell me about them."

"Kallum Zafira has been with this Family a long time. Your father spoke highly of him, spoke of his solid loyalty and his bravery. We haven't always agreed on everything, but he has a strong sense of morals that I respect."

"But...?" I ask, knowing there is one.

Caden sighs. "But he is already so damn loyal. Molly's marriage is to gain *more* of it, and I don't see how their alliance can do that."

"So you can mark him off the list then."

"Not quite."

"Why not?"

"Because offering her to someone else might *turn* his loyalty. There's only so much a man can get overlooked before he starts seeking shows of appreciation elsewhere."

I frown. "Can we give him something else to show that?"

"Perhaps. But he is rich. Greatly so. Each capo gets a percentage of the money they bring in, and his district is flourishing. He's also not a gambler or a drinker, so his money isn't squandered as fast as he makes it. There isn't much he doesn't already have," he says.

My frown deepens.

"But that was a good idea," he adds, kissing the side of my head, and my lips reverse the direction they're in.

"Who else?" I ask, nodding at the list as I pat Ryo's back.

"Vance Marshall. He's the youngest capo on the list and was only promoted a few years ago. He's smart, sly, and will go far if he lives long."

"But...?"

"He's probably not going to live long."

"Why not?"

"He's a necromancer."

I suck in a breath. Necromancers are incredibly rare. "He was born as one or he learned?" I ask. Anyone can learn to bring back the recently dead, but it takes decades of training, and it has a very low survival rate considering to bring someone back, you have to one, give up a piece of your own finite soul, and two, venture into Purgatory to get them – a place that makes the Plane of Monsters seem cute and the perfect place for a family day out. And, of course, the only way to train to survive Purgatory...is to constantly go to Purgatory.

A person who learns it rarely ever lives long.

But a person *born* to necromancy lives even less. Their magic isn't limited to only bringing back the recently dead. Nor is it limited to 'healthy' corpses. Necromancy can never bring back people who lost their head or had their heart ripped out, but a born necromancer can bring back those who lost whole limbs or still have lethal poison in their veins.

The issue isn't that their magic kills them. It's that their bodies do.

Or rather...the black market buyers who want their bodies.

A necromancer's head goes for sixty thousand dollars in

today's market. His heart, seventy five. A single finger only goes for three, but there are ten of them. The man's a walking bank, and I don't want Molly anywhere near that level of danger.

"He's learned," he says, and I breathe a bit easier.

"What's his innate magic?"

"He's human."

My eyes widen. "And he *learned* necromancy?"

"Which is why I don't think he'll live very long. He's too smart for his own good. Got the balls of a rat though, I'll give him that."

I silently agree. "What about Garrett Madison?" I ask, looking at the next name on the list.

He sighs. "He volunteered to fight in both World Wars, and is a respected hero even by a lot of the other Families across America. He has an admirable sense of honor and has the innate ability to go invisible, making him a damn good assassin – not that he does much of that anymore, but that is how he rose through the ranks. Solidifying our connections with his family will be no bad thing."

"So what's the problem with him?"

His jaw tightens. "He has a long beard."

I blink. "What?"

"And he prefers to cycle rather than drive."

I glance at him, confused.

Then a smile breaks out across my face as I realize he's just finding excuses not to marry our daughter away. I wiggle on his lap, snuggling deeper against his chest. "He sounds awful."

"Quite," he says, so deadpanned I laugh.

Caden sucks in a breath, then turns me around with his telekinesis until I'm facing him. He looks deep into my eyes, something he does every time I laugh, and my heart squeezes with love for him.

He kisses me, careful not to squish Ryo. My mouth

opens, and his tongue sweeps inside.

"I love it when you laugh," he murmurs against my lips.

"I love you."

Ryo takes this moment to wake with a little cry, and I shuffle back until I'm on my feet. "I think he's hungry," I say, only to immediately gag at the smell coming out of him.

Caden stands. "I'll grab a nappy. Put him on the desk."

I do as he says, then step back. One of Ryo's favorite things to do, it seems, is to hold in a fountain of piss until someone changes his nappy.

Caden stands beside me as Ryo cries, using his magic to change and clean him. As expected, a stream of piss shoots out a second before the new nappy goes on, and I shake my head with a small smile. He always fucking waits.

His wails sound louder.

No doubt he's annoyed that he didn't get to piss on someone's face.

My grin widens.

*What a little shit.*

But at least he is alive and healthy.

My smile falters.

*If only Olivia was too.*

# THIRTY-FIVE

## HER
### 28 OCTOBER 1947

Our living room fills with five capos, Leon, and Myers within seconds. When being late is a show of disrespect and being early is a sign of not being busy enough, you learn to be right on time.

Not one of them looks at me, their eyes passing over me like I'm just another object in the room. A lamp with its light on dim. A cushion discarded from the couch. A book on math or science that people leave around just to make themselves look smarter to any guests who happen to catch a glimpse of it.

I stand beside my husband, a smile plastered on my face as he talks about everything but business and the reason they're all here. But though he doesn't mention our daughter even in passing and though none of them ask about her, I can feel her presence in the room. It's in the buzz of expectation, in the puffing of chests, in their reaffirmations of loyalty, the mentions of their successful endeavors. Kallum boasts about how he killed a dozen of sired vampires and one wolf that night. Garrett marvels over how he's already doubled last month's drug sales, and there are still three days left, with Halloween being a major day for moving product. That's a bit too close to business talk though, a bit too pushy for the rest of the capos, and Vance jokingly accuses him of being the buyer for half of those sales.

The room erupts in laughter. Garrett smiles in good humor, then fires back his own sting about Vance raising the dead just to fuck them, and if that technically counts as masturbation considering he has to give them a part of himself.

A smirk curls the necromancer's lips. "Why would I bother raising them when I can just fuck them as they are?" he asks.

My eyes widen, but the room erupts once more. Myers says something in Caden's ear, then disappears into the dining room. My husband's jaw ticks once, and I start to ask him what's wrong, but then he's smiling and joking with his capos and our son, and I don't want to interrupt.

Mother told me all the time a good wife never talks to her husband's guests unless spoken to first. And even she was never allowed at the dinners, so when Caden told me I was to join him tonight, I thought he was mad. What would his capos think, him needing me by his side? "It is a sign of weakness," I said.

"It is a sign of love and respect," he replied.

I still don't think I should be here, but I am happy that I am. I want to get to know my potential son-in-law before he – whoever *he* is takes my daughter away.

My eyes fall on Leon. And I want to try to get to know my firstborn. I've been trying so hard to close the gap my coma caused, but every time he visits, I am asleep. Every time I enter a room, he seems to leave. Our conversations are heavily stilted. The only time we've ever hugged was when Olivia died.

I've tried to apologize for all the moments of his that I missed due to my cowardice, but his strides only ever get longer then. An "I have to go," always slips out of his lips before I can ever get anything out of mine.

And so the distance grows.

Even tonight, when we are finally in the same room for more than a couple of seconds, Leon doesn't look at me. Doesn't acknowledge me at all.

I try to tell myself he's just practicing for when he's Boss. That a Boss can never show his weaknesses in case they're used against him, but then Caden catches my eye, and he smiles. Acknowledging me. Loving me. Not caring to hide that I am his weakness.

My throat closes as I smile back. I wish his love was enough to heal the pain of our son.

But it isn't.

The bell rings for dinner, and the mood changes in an instant, going darker, heavier as silence reigns and eyes dart around in fast lines.

"Ethan is tied up at the butchers in town," Caden says with an easy smile. "Let us eat without him."

The tension eases immediately. Ethan is the sixth capo, the one missing, but his tardiness isn't a sign of disrespect like we all assumed at the ring of the bell.

Caden walks towards the dining room, then to the head of the table. Eight places are already set, two at the ends, six in the middle. Silver domes hide the beef stew that's been prepared for us. Although the war's over, meat is still rationed, and my mouth waters at the thought of such a treat. I hesitate right after entering the room, not sure where to sit, but a line of servants usher us all in, showing us to our individual chairs. I sit to Caden's left, Leon to his right. My cheeks burn at the rank given to me, higher than the capos even though I shouldn't be at this meeting. If we are to strengthen ties, surely this isn't a good idea?

Unless it would cause more strife to claim one should sit at the Boss' side, above the rest.

Before I can think too much on it, the servants all lean forward and lift the domes in front of us off at the same time. The delicious smell of beef stew makes my mouth water, and I –

"What is this?" Kallum suddenly shouts.

My pulse jerks as my head snaps to him. His blue and white China bowl is empty. His face is red. He starts to stand, but Myers' hand on his shoulder shoves him down. Before Kallum can even turn his head, before I can even wonder how Myers got there so quickly, the reaper shoves a knife through the side of the capo's neck and rips it out the front, spilling his blood into the bowl.

Kallum gurgles and gasps. He raises a hand, his fingers twitching, but no magic builds before his life ends. Utter silence fills the room, fills my stomach too. No longer that hungry, I lean back from the table and the smells of meat and blood.

Myers wipes his blade on Kallum's back as the other capos and Leon turn to Caden in various states of unease.

My husband chews politely with his mouth closed, a silver spoon in his hand as he eyes them all. When he swallows, he scoops up more stew. "Kallum was a traitor," he says before he takes a bite. He makes us wait as he eats, not rushing in the slightest. The tension of the room rackets with each pass of his teeth, but no one moves or says a thing.

"He backed David," my husband says, putting down his spoon. His fingers close around his butter knife. "And he took what is mine."

I suck in a breath, my eyes flying back to Kallum. He was

a trusted capo of my father's, and even *he* violated me?. I want to reach forward and pick up a knife, then go over and stab him repeatedly in the back like he did me. Like he did this *Family*.

Instead, I keep my seat, my hands clenching beneath the table as Caden begins to butter his slice of bread. He looks over at Leon, then casually points his knife at him. "Now Ethan Jenson wasn't a part of David's little gang."

Leon holds his gaze, but his face is a bit white, his body a bit tense. The entire room is still on edge, and I wonder if there are any more traitors around this table.

"But he knew about David and Kallum for two years," Caden continues, dipping his bread in his beef stew. Once. Twice. He raises it to his mouth and takes a bite. Chews. "And he never said a thing to me or Myers. Hedging his bets. Seeing how it all played out. Now, normally, son, we would kill him without hesitation, but..." He takes another bite of his bread.

"But we are low on men, and he is a great asset to this Family. A strong witch. A good capo – well, good in the financial sense. His *loyalty* needs work."

Leon doesn't move, but there is a sense of unease to his stillness rather than the confidence of an heir.

"So, son..." Caden puts down his slice of bread on the small plate beside his bowl. "What do *you* think we should do with someone like that?"

Silence reigns for just a moment before Leon lifts his chin. "We should kill him. His actions, or lack thereof, hurt Mother."

He glances at me then, so much pain and guilt in his eyes, and my throat twists at the sight of the burden he carries on his shoulders. I want to tell him it wasn't his fault, that I don't blame him anymore than I blame his father for failing to protect me. David fooled us all, but now isn't the time for it. Later though, when we have a bit of privacy, I will make sure he knows I love him.

"Then you should be the one to do it," Caden says. "For your mother."

My stomach fills with sudden nerves. What if he's not ready for this? Ethan is a capo. He's experienced and has surely fought for his life multiple times before. What if he kills my boy?

My head jerks to Caden, but before I can ask him to please not ask this of our son, Leon nods and says, "For Mother."

Strong.

Final.

The words of a leader willing to prove he's worthy.

Caden's hand comes over mine, and I turn mine up to grip his fingers. He squeezes me as Leon stands.

"I shall do it now," he says. "He is at the butchers in town?"

"Tied up in a pretty little bow," Caden says, and my eyes fly to him. I thought I heard regret in those words, a cry of pain, but when I look at him, there is nothing but cold indifference on his face.

Inclining his head, Leon turns to leave.

The door of the dining room swings shut behind him.

Caden stares at it for a moment longer, then turns his attention back to his bowl. Picks up his spoon. "Garrett," he says. "You requested more incubus potions for your district? How many do you need?"

Conversation starts up all around me concerning the increase of demand for sex potions like the ones Caden and I used in the shower now that more and more soldiers are returning from across the seas. Discussions about who might be good replacements for the two capos are also had, and underlying it all is their silent brown-nosing for Molly's hand.

No one even glances at the dead man on the table as we

eat, but my eyes keep going back to the closed door.

*Please, gods,* I pray, *don't let that be the last time I ever see my son.*

# THIRTY-SIX
## ALERIC
### 28 OCTOBER 1947

There is a delicacy to torturing one's mind, to breaking them so completely, they are reborn. You can't break them too fast, too hard. Otherwise, they'll shatter, cave in, fall into a coma in an attempt to hide away from the world. You can't break them too slow, giving them little fractures that will allow them to grow stronger, handle pain better rather than breaking apart at your feet.

You have to fuck with them *juuuust* right.

You have to get her attached to you just a little, give her her first orgasm.

Then you have to take away all her things, break them one toy at a time as she's helpless to stop it. When she's forced to think about the next toy in line. About all the ways she *could* save it, maybe...before she fails.

She'll start to think about you. Obsess about you. And that is when you'll own her.

When you should give her a little morsel, a bit of hope that she can save her favorite toy as long as she pleases you. Does what you want without question.

And Sau'll do it. She's too soft, too willing to sacrifice herself for others. For the witches at the portal. For her husband. *Her children...*

My gaze lands on Leon as he hurries through the dark, quiet streets of St. Augustine. He looks skittish, like he already knows death is coming for him even though he can't see me from my perch. His head keeps turning to look behind him. His heart beats faster and faster in his rapidly rising chest.

For a moment, I smile, thinking I spooked him even more than expected when I mailed him four boxes of Christian with the note: 'I know what you did. Caden is about to too' clamped between his teeth.

But then I catch a whiff of someone else on this street.

My fangs elongate as the hairs on my neck rise.

*The fucking reaper is here.*

My gaze flies back to Leon as he turns his head to look behind him.

A shadow moves in front of him. Dark and dangerous and fast. A glint of metal catches the moonlight. Seems like Caden already knows and has ordered Myers to kill him.

In a blink of an eye, I'm gone from the roof and down on the street between Leon and Myers. He whips his head around as his uncle's knife lands in my back, perfect for a strike to Leon's heart. His eyes barely have time to widen before I grab him and phase again, the knife ripping out of my skin.

As we land halfway across town, I sink my teeth into his neck to heal myself. He tries to slam his fist into my side, but it misses me, too offset by his disorientation. Blood gushes down my throat as I swallow, its sweet, rich taste exploding across my tastebuds.

I phase again. Releasing his neck, I dart to the side just quick enough to avoid his spurge of vomit. He falls to his knees, swaying as his world spins. Stepping behind him, I grip his shoulder and vanish again, this time reappearing in the bathroom of my home. With my free hand, I grab the back of his head, fisting his red curls as he kneels in front of me, and aim him over the open toilet.

He heaves, the sick smell of an upset stomach pouring out of his lips. "It's hilarious, isn't it?" I say as I hold him over the bowl. "One of your ancestors made a deal to walk through the Plane of Monsters unharmed, yet still you can't handle phasing." Every hop opens a portal to that place, but we're in and out in a blip, moving too fast for the monsters to get us...most of the time. Occasionally, an unlucky bastard has really bad timing and ends up trying to step through a set of teeth to get to their destination. Then they reappear in this world, torn to shreds and half missing...if they reappear at all.

Leon groans as I yank his head up. With my free hand, I flush the toilet and smile. "It's almost as funny as this."

Shoving his head forward again, I force it all the way into the bowl. Water squirts around his head, filling it in, and soon he can't breathe. Grabbing his arm with my free hand, I raise it to my lips and sink my fangs into his wrist.

I drink deeply, holding him down as he desperately tries to fight me. But between the awkward angle of his body, his lack of air, his life draining down my throat, and the crushing disorientation of our trip here, he can't get in a good blow even with his super strength and speed. Maybe if I were human...

But I'm not, and soon, he stops moving entirely.

I swallow one last time, then release his arm as I yank his head up. He gasps, spitting toilet water, and I stand, my hand still in his hair. Yanking him backwards onto his ass, I whistle "Ole Buttermilk Sky" by Hoagy Carmichael as I drag him into my bedroom. I haul him into my special torturing chair, which faces my bed so I can sleep to such sweet dreams, and strap his arms and legs down with bands of leather embedded with small sharp blades that stab through his skin with ease. They're not tight, so he can struggle if he wants to, can kill himself if he wants to.

But I've found people rarely like to take their own life. No...they beg and plead, asking me to do it for them, their cowardice about the underworld they'll end up in making them desperate to cling to the living. It's an entertaining tango to watch, them torn between wanting to die and wanting to live. Them trying to convince themselves to do it, to end all their suffering...and then cowering from the pain. The knowledge of what waits for them if they do.

I wonder what kind of man Leon is.

If he's the optimistic sort who thinks the underworld will be better than here.

Or if he's able to keep his head even under torture.

I snicker.

Regardless of what he is, he won't be keeping his head.

Or his hands and feet.

Lifting his head, sweat beading across his pale flesh, Leon spits at me. I catch it in my mouth, swallow, then lean forward and whisper in his ear, "Delicious."

He jerks from me, and I rock back with a laugh.

"Fuck you," he seethes. A pathetic smile curls his lips, a little baby seal trying to look fierce under the shadow of a club. "You think you can blackmail me about telling my father what I did?" He laughs bitterly. "He already fucking knows."

"Blackmail you? For what?" I shake my head, my eyes laughing. "You want to kill Caden. That aligns fine with me. Hel, I might've even been tempted to back your little coup had I known about it before. You're an absolute wet sod. The Shadow Domain would've crumbled under your leadership, especially considering you marked the man who is the sole reason it's still alive." I laugh out loud, my whole body shaking.

"Delun was strong, but he had too many feelings. If he'd just stayed inside the church and let Antonio take those pot shots, he wouldn't have died. But he rushed out like a fool, taunted by petty revenge."

"His father ate Delun's wife!"

I wave a hand. "Yes, yes, as I said. Petty revenge."

He tries to swing for me, I assume, given the wild jerk of his left arm that instantly stills beneath the cut of the blades through his wrist. I wait for him to decide if he wants to try again, if he thinks it's still worth hitting me with the hacked off stump of a hand.

But he just grits his teeth, pain wetting his brow. I sigh. They just don't make them like they used to.

"But Caden..." I continue. "Caden knows the logistics of death. Hel, he sacrificed your siblings at the portal, didn't even come for them when I tortured them in front of his scry."

I lick the tip of a fang, remembering how they tasted, how they screamed for dear old dad to save them. He watched the whole thing, how I butchered them one at a time, how I made them beg for the other one to live. Such close family, the Shadows. All so willing to die for each other. It's fucking good fun playing with them.

Which brings me to the purpose of dear old Leon.

"No..." I say as I stand from my crouch. "No, I never planned to blackmail you."

"Then why did you send Chris to me?"

"Because I wanted to know if it was true and not just some wild words of a dying man. You should never trust the desperate," I say sagely. And Chris was most desperate when he came to me, begging for protection. Only a fool would do so without knowing why, so when I went to kill those he'd asked me to, I had a little chat with them first.

I grab the pruning saw I left on the dresser, then the block of granite beside it. Turning back to him, I watch his eyes widen as they latch onto the large sharp teeth of the saw. "So what was she like?" I murmur as I run the blade across the rock, sending out a chilling screech.

"What?" Leon asks, the word high-pitched and raw. A tremor runs through him. Blood drips down his wrists and ankles to pool on the floor.

"What was your mother's cunt like?" I ask, dragging the saw across the granite again, dulling the teeth so they will drag and tear more than cut.

"I didn't..."

Another *screech* has him jerking on the chair. He tugs an arm, then grits his teeth, the pain of the blades keeping him still.

"I didn't..."

"You *did b*ecause David Shadow wanted to make sure you only ever saw her as a thing and not your mom." *Screech.* "So how did it *feel* sliding your cock into her dry cunt?"

"What do you care?"

"I want to know what I have to look forward to."

"Fuck you."

Holding up the saw, I look at the rounded teeth. Then smile. Dropping the rock on the ground, I step to the side to grab the first box in the pile near the chair. I place it in front of him. "Last chance to tell me, boy. Save yourself a bit of misery..." I lay the blade across his forearm. The smell of piss hits the air, and I chuckle. Whistling "Ole Dan Tucker," I slide the dull teeth across his skin. His jaw clenches; he starts to shake. I add more pressure, jerk it harder. He flinches away from me, then instantly stills, the knives in his wrist confusing him on what to do. A moan escapes his lips, then a scream on the next run of the blade.

"I didn't!"

Blood squirts from both sides of the saw.

Flesh gets embedded into its teeth.

"I didn't!" he screams again, but I know he did.

Christian might not have said. Nor did Kallum's second before I drained him dry and stole the ledger David had hidden in Kallum's office inside a dirty magazine. But I can see the guilt on Leon's face, the shame.

The *need* to confess his sins before he dies.

Not that I will give him absolution.

"Did you come in her?" I ask as I rake the teeth across bone. He screams when the blade digs in, and I yank *hard* in an attempt to free it. It rips through his bone, snapping the radius entirely, and he slams his head back into his chair as he cries. He heaves, his head now dropping low, his shoulders shaking. Sweet slickens his red curls flat against his head.

"Did you come in her?" I ask again.

"Yes," he whimpers, tears rolling down his cheek.

My fingers tighten on the saw as I line it back up with the cut. "Did you like her cunt squeezing around you?"

"*Yes.*" The word comes out choked and raw, and my jaw ticks as an unexplainable rage crawls at my chest.

I hack at his flesh viciously, slicing the saw across him. His arms vibrate against his binds as he thrashes. The tool is nearly ripped out of my hands, but I tighten my grip. His radius *snaps* from all the force, and blood gushes free. Both of his hands hang limp, shredded so only slivers of flesh keep them attached. He's bleeding out, dying quick.

So I bite my wrist and force my blood between his lips. My blood will not save him. In fact, it will kill him, but it'll do it slowly, much slower than the saw will, and in the meantime, it will keep him alive.

As his screams vibrate across my bedroom, I start to whistle "Badineie". The saw meets the wood of the chair. I nudge his arm into the open box, then turn the blade to his thigh.

For three hours, I hack him into seventeen various-sized pieces, feeding him my blood to keep him alive. I'm covered in his rivers of life, drenched in the sins of mine. Licking my lips, tasting that oh-so-sweet copper, I go to stand behind him.

Rage still clawing at my chest, I line the saw up with his throat. Lean down to whistle in his ear. The blade's gummed up with flesh now. It's just my sheer speed and strength that's cutting him. He gurgles, unable to scream but still so clearly able to feel pain.

I hack through his skin, through his vocal chords, and spine. Gripping his hair, I stand and yank his head back to do those final cuts. He stares up at me, his dull green eyes so wide in pain and terror. "You took what was mine," I hiss. "Tell me, was it worth it?"

But of course he can't say.

He barely has a neck anymore.

Just a sliver of flesh.

Growling, I drop the saw, rearrange my fingers in his hair, and *pull.*

The sound of a wet tear rips through the room, rips through his flesh too. I have the urge to throw his head at the wall, but instead I drop it onto his chest. It rolls down his butchered body and lands in the box placed in front of the chair.

I stare at him for a moment, the rage swirling inside me unwanted.

This isn't revenge for her.

This isn't *her* fucking game.

It's *mine.*

And this rage, this *need* to cut into him further for hurting her more than any of the others in that damn ledger could...

That fucking rage has no place here.

All this is is a calculated move in a game that will take decades to complete.

Pursing my lips, I begin to whistle. I pull off my shirt. Use it to wipe the blood off my hands. Then I stride across my bedroom to my bedside table, open the drawer, and pull out David's ledger and a pen.

Opening it up, I cross the last name off the list.

And now the real game can begin.

# THIRTY-SEVEN

## HER

### 29 OCTOBER 1947

My throat is closing. My heart is stopping. I cannot breathe. *Something is wrong.*

I thrash in my covers, needing to get free. Caden is awake in a moment, out of bed and on his feet, between me and the door, protecting me from a threat he can't see. Can't feel.

But *I* can feel it. I can feel my baby boy dying right now. "Leon!" I stumble out of bed, my breaths heaving.

Caden doesn't turn to comfort me over my panic for our son. His arms raise instead. His fingers twist, magic buzzing between them. He's reaching out with his power, searching...like a predator trying to find his prey in the high grass of the savannah.

My eyes widen.

My heart trips into my stomach.

Tumbles further down into my feet.

*No.*

*No!*

But everything is snapping into place now.

Caden's cold shoulder to our firstborn. Leon's heavy guilt. His refusal to be anywhere around me, unable to meet my eye, to bear my touch. A hand reaches to my throat as I take in the lethal stance of my husband. If Leon burst through that door right now, he'd kill him.

*Maybe he already has.*

*Myers left not long after Leon.*

"What did you do?" I ask, my love for him climbing up an edge crumbling into the sea.

He turns, his hands lowering as he realizes my scream wasn't in terror of our son attacking us in the middle of the night. But still his body is guarded, his defenses up. "Sau..."

"What did you *do*?"

"I don't know what –"

"Don't lie to me!" I charge forward before I even know I've moved. My hands are suddenly on his chest, pushing him back. "I can *feel* him dying!"

His eyes widen. "How do –" Then they bunch. "Sau, I am sorry. I didn't know... If I did..."

"You didn't know what?" I demand, needing him to spell it out, to not leave any doubt, any assumptions in my mind. I want him to look me in the eye and confess the sins of a father.

"I didn't know you'd be able to feel when he died. A connection like that – the magic, it's incredibly rare."

I stumble back, shaking my head, the last of my hope dying. *That* is what he has to say? That is his excuse for killing our son without telling me?

"He's *our son*!" I wrap my arms around myself, hoping Leon can feel my embrace, my love in his final moments.

"Sau..." Caden reaches for me.

I smack his arm away. "Don't touch me!" Pain claws at

my chest. A howl wants to rip its way up my throat. "At dinner – you weren't asking about Ethan, were you?"

Shame fills his eyes as he holds my heart in his throat, in the words that will soon pour forth. "No."

"You let him decide to kill himself!" I gasp, desperate to breathe. "He didn't even know. He didn't even..."

"He knew, Sau. It was there in his eyes. He knew all too well what I was asking. It was why he never went to the warehouse."

"You let him run?" Hope blossoms. "He's..."

He shakes his head at the same time I remember who left the room soon after.

Myers.

The reaper.

The killer of traitors.

"He's his uncle..." I say, my heart crumbling beneath that weight. "How could you ask him that?"

He glances away, so much guilt and shame in his eyes. Barely a whisper, he admits, "Because I couldn't."

I stare at him, my chest heaving. The reaper doesn't kill unjustly. He doesn't get involved in the politics. He's entirely neutral in his protection of this Family.

But Leon is his nephew.

My son.

Our firstborn.

I can't... "Why?" I ask, the broken word wrung from my lips with what feels like the last of my strength. "What did he do?"

But I know what he did.

And Caden knows I know.

Ethan was accused of knowing about the coup. David wouldn't have been able to take the throne with any of my children alive, so if Leon knew...if he knew and said nothing...

"He didn't just know, did he?" I ask, torn between my

love for him and my hatred for those who raped me.

He hesitates for a moment. Then his shoulders sag, all pretenses crumbling beneath a collapsing cliff edge. "He was involved with David all the way."

Bile churns up my stomach. "Involved like...they were *together*?"

"No..."

My eyes bunch. I shake my head. I know what he means. Knew it as soon as he said it, but I needed to hope. Needed to pretend... That incest was better than my own son selling me.

"Did he...?" I can't bring myself to say those other words.

Caden crosses the distance between us and gathers me in his arms. "Gods, no, Sau. He wouldn't do that. He's still our son. No. No, he wouldn't have."

I don't want to look too deeply into his repeated words, like he's trying to convince himself. Like he doesn't really know but refuses to believe.

I just cling to his strength on silent tears, too broken to know what to feel. He killed our son. But our son helped all those men rape me...

Leon doesn't...didn't love me.

But Caden does.

And I hold on to that, using it as the only light through this path of darkness. "How...?" My throat closes as the pain of Leon's death resonates inside me. I know he's gone now. I never felt the pain he lived through, but I felt the dying of his soul.

And now I feel nothing.

"How do you carry on after..." I squeeze my eyes shut and think about all the other children we have lost.

"I think about you."

A tearless sob escapes me.

"And all our other children." He runs a hand up and down my back. "Think of Jonathan, Sau. How much your firstborn needs you."

I shudder, hating that the title of heir has moved so easily, so quickly, erasing Leon's life like it never was.

But I think about Jonathan, about how he's going to lose his laughter, his good humor. How the weight of his new responsibilities might crush him...twist him like it did Leon? I want to save him from such pain. I need to save him.

I need to stay alive to protect him.

"Think of Molly and Bonnie."

My two girls who will one day be married away. Who need to learn what it means to be a woman in this Family. Of our responsibility to breed. Of the weight of carrying on our family name, of giving heirs capable of winning this war between the gangs of St. Augustine.

"Think of little Ryo."

Just a baby who's lost his closest sister.

They all need me.

More than I need the absence of life's misery.

"Think of me, Sau," Caden whispers, vulnerability in every word. "I can't lose you again. I *can't*. I won't..." He trails off, but his statement is solid in its clarity.

My children are my weakness, their deaths the pain that will push me over the edge of oblivion.

And I am his.

Clinging to him, my chest becoming lighter despite the weight of guilt and grief, I nod. "I love you, Caden. I love you."

"I love you too, Sau. I love you so fucking much."

A moment of silence stretches. I press my cheek into the crook of his neck. "Please don't hide anything like this from me again."

He tenses beneath me, then pulls back. Before he can voice whatever flashes in his eyes, though, the bedroom door swings open behind him.

"She knows, Myers," Caden says without turning to look

to see who's entered.

"*You* don't know," he says, his voice strained and full of jitters.

My husband spins around. I step to his side so I'm not looking behind him.

Myers is as white as a sheet, his hands trembling.

"Know what?" Caden asks.

My heart plummets.

A part of me already knows. I just don't know who took him to get to me, if it's Antonio or –

"Aleric took Leon."

Caden stumbles back until he collapses on our bed. "It was supposed to be quick," he says. "He wasn't supposed to suffer."

"He could still be alive..." Myers starts, but I shake my head.

Then I stumble back too and sit on the bed with my husband, pulling him into my arms. He trembles, drawing strength from me even though I don't feel like I've much to give.

He did this.

Caden's choices led to this.

His attempt to handle it all on his own.

But I can't hate him in this moment.

I can't hate him more than he clearly hates himself. "I'm sorry," he says over and over as he clings to me.

Myers stares at me in silence. I want to hate him for being willing to kill our son.

But he is an uncle as well as a reaper.

Caden is a Boss as well as a father.

And I...I am a victim as well as a mother.

Opening an arm to Myers, I mourn in muted misery. He stumbles towards us. Collapses on his knees in front of us. He loved our boy just as much as we did.

Leon might have had to pay for his crimes...

But not like this.

Not under the hands of that psycho.

---

The post comes early at our house, so I've been up every morning for the past couple of days, waiting for the mailman to arrive. Aleric always sent us the bodies of our loved ones when Father was alive. I do not see him doing any differently now.

He might be trying to woo me now, to make me *choose* him as he claimed, but he isn't going to send me flowers and chocolate. He isn't going to ask me to a dance. Isn't going to take me to the movies or a picnic under the stars.

No...his so called *gifts* will come in the twisted forms of his mind. Like the butchered body of the man who hurt me. He won't care that it's my son. Won't understand the devastation that will cause. *I am an alpha lion. See me provide.*

I'd rather see him rot in Niflhel. Perhaps, I will join him down there just to make sure he does.

"Sau."

My heart kicks up into my throat as the U.S. postal van comes into view. The dual-toned, white top machine heads for its first stop at the end of the street.

I watch, one hand clutched to the front of my dress as a man with brown hair and glasses gets out to deliver a box to Henry Yales, a soldier who lost his leg to a werewolf during that night our wards were down. His wife answers the door. The box is handed over. The mailman walks back to his van.

He gets in, starts to drive towards our house.

I hold my breath, desperate for him to stop and finally put me out of my misery. I hate waiting for this delivery. I hate getting up every morning, terrified this will be the day I see Leon one last time. But I also hope he just keeps driving. That there aren't any boxes for me.

Aren't any twisted gifts from that fucking psycho.

He passes one house.

Two...

Three...

"*Sau.*" Caden entwines our fingers, but I don't look at him, my eyes glued to that damn white top monstrosity.

"*Breathe*," he says, and my burning lungs start moving even though I wanted that pain.

*Needed* that pain to get me through this.

"You promised me," he murmurs.

Promised I wouldn't kill myself. Wouldn't hurt myself. That I would stay here with him despite all the pain life threw at me.

I tear my gaze away from the van and look into my husband's eyes. He's been through all of this on his own. I had eight dead children before I woke. All of them might not have died tragically – perhaps sickness took them or they died during their ascension or maybe they just died in their sleep like Olivia, but some of them must have left this world at the end of the Blood Fangs. I should ask him one day, what happened to them all, but not today. Not when the grief is already so strong, I am struggling to keep that promise to him.

Squeezing his hand, I nod at him.

*I promise.*

Then my eyes are back on the van.

My breath frozen once more in my throat.

He's at the house next door.

He isn't stopping.

My throat tightens as I'm torn between two desires.

Stop...don't stop...stop...don't stop.

He stops.

Walks around to the back of his van and reappears with a box.

I roll my lips in to stop my scream. I squeeze Caden's hand harder, and he squeezes mine. Together, we watch the man from the window. He lugs up one box. Then another. Then another...

By the fifth one he notices us staring at him like ghosts, and he jumps, nearly dropping the box.

I stare at him without moving.

He stares at me.

I can practically hear his heart thumping past the door. Then he places the box down on our doorstep, hurries to his van, and comes back with a sixth box. He sets it down, then straightens. He doesn't go back to his van. Doesn't retrieve another body part of my son.

With a trembling hand, I reach over to the door and pull it open.

"I just need a signature from a Sau Shadow," he says. He can't be much older than my boy.

But his eyes are so much softer, his face so less stern. He didn't grow up in war. Too young to be drafted. Too lucky to be born or lured into one of the three gangs.

I take the pen from him, and for a moment, I want to stab him in the neck with it. Give Death him rather than Leon.

My fingers clench around the pen.

My eyes dip to his neck.

"Sau," Caden murmurs, and I jolt.

Signing my name quickly, I then hand the pen back to him. He wastes no time leaving.

My eyes fall to the pile of boxes. They don't look big enough to hold my boy.

"Maybe he's not in them," I say.

"We don't have to open them."

I stare at them for a long moment, the door opened only a crack, as if opening it wider will invite all the bad things in.

But then I pull it open all the way.

Caden starts to use his telekinesis, but I shake my head as I pick up the first box. It's a lot lighter than I thought it'd be. I remember Leon's bulk, his heavy form, his body thick with muscles.

*Maybe he's not in them.*

I tell myself that with every box I carry from the porch into David's room. I don't want to open them in view of the street...and maybe seeing Leon in David's quarters will remind me enough of his sins that it won't hurt so much seeing him.

A foolish wish – as foolish as *maybe he's not in them.*

When all of the boxes are inside the gutted room – the renovations to the place not yet done, I stare at them once more.

"We don't have to open them," Caden says again. "You can just take them into your shadows. You don't need to give him the chance to hurt you."

A humorless laugh escapes me. "He already has."

Kneeling down, I pull out the small knife I have picked up every morning for the last few days, and cut open the box in front of me. With shaky hands, I part the flaps and find scrunched up paper inside. There isn't a smell yet, but my nose wrinkles all the same. My heart in my throat, my ears, in every part of my body, shaking me with every pulse, I pull out the packaging.

Another box, this one covered in dark stains, sits inside it. Scrawled across it in even more blood is a message:

*No one ever gets to hurt you but me.*

I swallow down the bile and hurriedly open the lid. A sharp gasp leaves me, but I trap down the scream. I don't let it out. Don't give him that victory.

Even as my eyes land on Leon's dick, both of his balls separate and spaced out above it – morbid eyes in the face Aleric arranged for me – a bit of intestine curved into a mouth screaming in pain.

I fall back on my heels, a hand pressed to my lips. I will not cry. I won't.

Caden wraps me in his arms, but he can't protect me from the chill running down my spine, can't stop me from seeing the butchered body of my boy. My eyes fly to the other brown boxes, and I know they all have messages inside them.

*Look what I did for you, Sau.*

Tearing myself out of my husband's embrace, I grab the next box and cut it open. Rip out the paper on top.

*You're welcome.*

*For you, love.*

*You still owe me that date.*

*You should've got a bloodoath from me.*

The mockery of those words slaps me across the face, and now I'm damn near vibrating with rage. As if Aleric would honor a fucking bloodoath. As if he wouldn't enjoy the magical pain he'd get from breaking it.

As if he dares put the blame on *me*, on my naivety in thinking I could argue for peace when I traded my panties for his word.

His fucking *word* that he wouldn't hurt my Family.

A broken laugh escapes me as I grab the last box and tear it open. But I don't rip out the paper. I don't yank out its insides in a mad frenzy. I just sit there laughing, unable to tell in this moment, if the rage I'm feeling is for him.

Or me.

For being so fucking stupid as to believe we could ever have peace.

"I want him dead," I rasp as I glare at the final box. "I want his fucking head on a spike. I want..." My knuckles whiten on the knife as my whole arm shakes. "I want his *son* in exchange for ours."

Lifting my eyes to Caden, I beg him to give me this.

But his eyes only hold pain. Not rage. Not *vengeance*. He shakes his head as he stares at me. "If you go down this road, Sau, you can't come back –"

"I don't care! He butchered our son! He cut him into little pieces. He arranged him like some...like some..." I gesture wildly with the knife, pointing at the box that's been opened all the way. "Look at what he did!"

"I know, Sau. I *know*." He pulls the blade from me, then takes my hand as I try to reach for it. "But killing Colton won't bring Leon back. It won't make Aleric suffer. The only thing it will do is give him what he really wants."

"He wants me!" I scream as I jump to my feet, unable to stay sitting down. "How is killing his son giving him that?"

"Because he wants you to be like him, Sau!" He rises, and I flinch away, slapped by his words. His jaw clenches. His voice quiets, but it's no less hard in its honesty. "He wants you to be like *him*. Please, Sau. Don't go down this road."

I stand there shaking.

Hearing what he's saying.

But hearing what my heart is too.

Would it really be that bad to be like Aleric?

A man unaffected by the deaths of those around him? A man who can't be hurt by the pain life wishes to inflict?

Tears burning my eyes, I close them on a rough exhale. I will not cry. I will not give him that pleasure.

"Take Leon into your shadows," he says. "Let our boy rest in peace."

A choked cry escapes me. "A poor fucking choice of words."

He doesn't say anything.

There isn't anything to say.

It wasn't fair of me to point that out, accusingly, as if he meant it. He most definitely realized as soon as he said it. Probably hates himself for doing so. But he is a grieving father, his thoughts numb like mine.

Except mine aren't entirely numb.

There is a voice in the back of my head still, or perhaps in the bottom of my heart, that wishes for Colton's death.

An eye for an eye.

A son for a son.

Opening my eyes, I look at my husband. "Please," I rasp as I bare open my soul. "Give me Colton's head."

His jaw clenches, but he doesn't say anything.

And I don't wait for him too, unable to bear his refusal. Not now. Not when my son is in six boxes in front of me. Turning from Caden, I open myself up to my magic. My eyes fall onto that final box, and I hesitate.

"Open it," I say, not having the strength to grab the knife and do it myself.

He opens it with his magic, pulls out the paper, and reveals a dirty magazine.

Scrawled on the front cover, across the boobs of a lady with long blonde hair and puckered lips is a message:

*I killed more than Myers.*

I'm too tired to decipher its meaning. But Caden seems to understand as he's over there in a heartbeat to pick it up with his own hands. He flips it open, and a grim line straightens his lips.

"David's ledger," he says.

I close my eyes, knowing Leon's name is in there. "Get it away from me."

He sends it out of the room with his telekinesis, but he doesn't leave my side. He stands with me as I spread out my arms, pouring shadows forth from my palms. Sweat glistens his brow, no doubt as he remembers nearly dying because of me the last time I did this, but he doesn't move, doesn't waver in his position beside me.

He loves me.

More than his own life.

Holding on to that, using it to combat my grief, I pull

every box of Leon into my shadows.

"I want to learn to fight," I say as the last one sinks into the darkness swirling around our feet. "I want to be the one who tears Aleric's head from his fucking shoulders."

"You're too valuable to be on the front lines," he says.

"Then bring him to me alive."

# THIRTY-EIGHT
## HER
### 3 MARCH 1949

I draw my shadows into Aleric's silhouette, building them up until they stand taller than me, taller than Caden, at *his* height. The darkness swirls like smoke in a breeze that's constantly changing until I solidify it into his shape, his bulk. I remember everything about him – the way his hair falls across his face, the cut of his eyes as he laughed at me, the size of his fists, his biceps. The feel of his teeth, his fingers –

Grunting, I swing my fist into the shadow's jaw. It goes straight through the poor imitation of the monster I want to kill, but Caden won't let me spar with anyone. The men all need their rest when they're not on duty. I hate it, but I get it. Our numbers are still low a year and a half later; unlike the werewolves and the vampires, we can't make more of our kind overnight. They need their downtime so they stay sharp when out on the streets.

So I am forced to fight this damn fucking thing that doesn't move unless I make it. I'm learning nothing, but at least I get to take out my frustration, get to practice some of the punches and kicks I begged Caden, Jonathan, and Myers to teach me over the years.

I force the shadow to swing for me, and I duck under its arm, then lash out at its leg. There's force behind my blow, but there's nothing solid to hit. And still I train for hours, wanting to be ready for when Caden finally brings him here to me.

*But it's been over a year*, a little voice says as I punch Aleric's shadow straight through the chest to rip out his heart. *Perhaps it's time I use myself as bait. Draw him out...*

Caden will never go for it though. Nor will Myers or any of the capos. I'm too damn *valuable* until one of our children makes it to the age of twenty-two.

Scowling, I drop 'Aleric's heart' and then dismiss the shadows with a wave of my hand. I hate this. This feeling of being trapped, of being useless. Of being *safe* behind our wards. I've not left this street since Aleric kidnapped me.

Perhaps it's time I did.

Perhaps it's time I sought him out rather than waiting for him to come to me.

Caden is out...

Myers is too...

Not giving myself time to talk myself out of it, I sink into my shadows and race towards the end of the street. I know where the vampires' nest is. If Aleric doesn't find me wandering the city, I can just make my way there.

But I know he will notice as soon as I step past these wards. It's been over a year since I've seen him, but I have never been more sure of an outcome.

Slipping through the natural shadows, evading the eyes of the guards who will most definitely reach out to Caden if they see me, I make it to the end of the street. My heart thunders inside me, but I don't stop. Don't slow. I just dart through the wards and come out the other side. I travel a few more blocks down, outside of the patrol of our guards, before re-materializing into flesh in an empty alley.

My body shakes. My breathing is rapid with fear. I lean with one hand against the wall of the building, the other to my chest.

I'm outside the wards.

I'm in the fucking open.

With no protection.

With no guards.

The world is closing in on me in its utter vastness, and I'm struggling to breathe.

A dark feeling hits me like a sucker punch, raising the hairs on my nape and dropping a weight in my stomach. I twist around, then scramble to the side, but I'm not fast enough to evade the hand reaching for me.

Antonio grabs me by the arm and tosses me against the wall. He's in his human form, but I know he can still kill me easily. My back slams into the building. I try to sink into my shadows to run, but he grabs my hand and twists. *Crack!* The entire thing is bent back the other way. Bones snap out of my flesh, and I cry out on a small whimper, my mind tossed back to that night in the woods.

I can't stop him from grabbing my other hand. I try to kick him, headbutt him, but he just envelopes my fingers with his, then crushes them all together. His other palm slams across my mouth as I scream, muffling my cries for help. My knees give out from the pain until it's just him holding me up, his palm squeezing my jaw. I feel a tooth crack, my jaw fracture like a spider's web.

"You should've stayed in your fucking home." He jerks my head forward, then slams it back into the wall. Pain explodes in my skull, but even it can't override the agony in my mouth as multiple teeth pop out like kernels in a fire. I kick him. I claw at him with the bones sticking out of my hands, raking the jagged edges across his face. He doesn't move, doesn't blink. Just glares at me with those damn golden eyes as he keeps the pressure on my jaw.

I aim for his eyes, the pain of my exposed bone nothing compared to the fear of dying in this alleyway, of Caden never finding me, Leon never getting justice, my children losing their mother all over again, the Shadow bloodline potentially dying with me as my twin girls are infertile.

He slams my head back into the wall, on my vision, the swing of my arms, and I miss his eyes with a gurgled cry of broken teeth and bleeding gums. He leans in closer, as if he needs to watch every last twitch of my muscles, spot every shade of terror in my eyes as his palm crushes the lower half of my face into mush. But he keeps my nose free, keeps me breathing. Killing me so quickly won't do for his rage.

Whatever peace he used to hope for, whatever life he wished to give his mate and pups has been ripped away from him. *By me.*

My eyes flutter as the pain makes me start to pass out, and the last thing I see is the twisted, painful triumph in his eyes. Is my death healing him like I believe Aleric's will me?

Before the answer can be found, I'm dropped to the ground, and he flies through the air. Hope fills my chest as my ass hits the pavement, and I watch as Antonio gets run over by a car. Its engine is off; there's no driver inside. Knowing Caden must be here, I roll my head to the side.

My heart jumps at the sight of him. He's so fucking angry, and I know half of that is aimed at me. For doing something so stupid, for leaving the wards only three days after he finally got comfortable enough to leave my side.

Movement to his left catches my attention, and I see Jonathan running towards me. I want to scream at him to get back, to not get this close to Antonio even if his father has him pinned under a car, but my mouth doesn't work. He skids to a stop in front of me, down on his knees, his hand fumbling in an inside pocket of his jacket. He pulls out a healing potion, one of the ones I made for him, and raises it to my lips. He curses as he tries to figure out how to pour it down my throat. My mouth feels like a tin can that's been stepped on and squished, and by the look in his eyes, it probably doesn't look much better.

"Sorry," he says as he tilts my head all the way back. Agony ruptures on every nerve, and I instinctively flinch away from him, but he fists his hand in my hair and holds me still. Placing the vile on my nose, he pours its contents down them, lighting up my nostrils with a burning pain that makes my eyes water.

But the potion works quickly, and a small cry is finally able to leave my lips. He ducks under one of my arms and hauls me to my feet.

An animalistic growl comes from beneath the car. I turn my head towards it just in time to see it get tipped onto its side. The crash is loud, but no human runs into the alley to see what's happening. Caden must've erected a shield around it, hiding us from their eyes.

A flash of red fur darts towards us, and Jonathan tries to move in front of me just as I try to drag him back. The car slams into Antonio, knocking him to the side.

"Run!" Caden shouts.

Jonathan and I turn back around. We take one step, but then he's wrenched away from me, pulled by a man who's just suddenly appeared. Grinning at me, Aleric throws my boy at Antonio, trying to force Caden's attention.

But my husband whistles a high note. Jonathan shifts into his shadows. Aleric spins towards me, his arm out, but I'm suddenly flying through the air, pulled along by Caden's magic. Just as the vampire looks like he's about to phase to me, a bright light explodes in the alley. I close my eyes instinctively. My body keeps moving. Up, up, and then sideways at speed, flying in the direction of home.

---

"What in Hel's name were you thinking?" Caden yells as I sit on the couch in our living room as Louise tends to my injuries. Healing potions, like premade wands, can only do so much, each body too uniquely different when magic needs to be exact. A few of the teeth that regrew have come in sideways, and Louise straightens them, her hands alight with white light. She keeps her eyes down, a blush of embarrassment for me across her cheeks.

My jaw ticks. "I was *thinking* someone finally needed to do *something*!" I say, trying my damnedest not to shout back. A good wife doesn't scream, and she most certainly doesn't tell her husband to shut the fuck up. Father would beat me for the thoughts in my head. I love Caden, but right now I want to throttle him.

"Do 'something?' Like what, feed him your face? Die at his feet? Decorate him in your intestines and teeth?"

The rage blisters beneath my tongue. "I was trying to lure Aleric out –"

"And did you just forget about Antonio? You *know* he's been watching this fucking street since you woke up from your coma."

My cheeks burn. My eyes flash. I'm not the idiot he's painting me as. "Of course not! But I thought –" I stop, biting my tongue.

"You thought what?" he snaps.

Louise's eyes widen as she rolls her lips in. She knows I fucked up. I hate that she knows I fucked up. "I'm done," she says, then mutters a soft, "Good luck," beneath her breath before she hurries from the room.

"You. Thought. *What*?" my husband snaps as soon as the door closes.

I clench my teeth, not wanting to say the words.

"You thought Aleric would just come for you," he says for me, and I flinch. He's making it sound wrong, like I'm obsessed with him, like I want him to come get me. Like I think there's some tight bond between us that's tying us together, a bond stronger than what I share with Caden.

"I just wanted to draw him out!" I yell, unable to keep the rage in any longer. "I just wanted him to finally die!"

"By dying yourself? What made you possibly think you could win a fight against Aleric?"

I open my mouth, then snap it shut again, realizing he is right. The only way I would win is if Aleric didn't want to kill me. Which would just sound crazy...even if that is exactly how I feel. Like he might beat me up and break my bones, he might leave me crippled and wanting to die, but he won't ever actually *kill* me.

Because of that bond...

I look away, my cheeks hot with so many emotions I can't name. "I just wanted him to die," I say. "It's been *over a year*, Caden. Leon –"

"Leon let you get raped and tried to kill me! I don't give a fuck about Leon!"

"Caden!" My head snaps to him, but he doesn't flinch, doesn't look embarrassed or ashamed over the words he uttered.

He just crosses the room to me and grabs my hands. "I care about *you*, Sau. I care about Jonathan. I care about Molly, Bonnie, and Ryo still having their fucking mother."

I flinch, but he squeezes my hands, keeping me to him.

He opens his mouth, then closes it again, but there are so many words on his face. A thousand of them. A full on story.

But I can't read any of them.

"I can't lose you, Sau. I can't..."

I swallow hard in the face of his raw honesty.

"Promise me you'll never go after him again."

Desperation bleeds into my voice. "Then bring him to me. *Please*. It's been a year and a half, Caden."

"I've been trying, Sau, but he's paranoid as fuck and our paths rarely cross."

"What about Colton?"

His lips flatten. "We've talked about this, Sau."

"No, *you've* talked about it," I snap, pulling my hands away. "Leon was my son. I don't care if you don't care about him anymore. *I* do. I need to get vengeance for him so he can rest in peace. We failed him, Caden." Tears burn my throat, making my words hoarse. "We failed him as parents. *I* failed him. If I was just there for him, maybe…" I swallow hard, but my next words still crack. "I should've been there for him. I should've guided him as he grew up."

"His choices aren't your fault, Sau."

"Yes, they are. Because I'm his mother. I should have been there to love him."

Pain fills his eyes, and he pulls me into his arms. I press my cheek against his chest and let him hold me, comfort me even though I don't deserve it. My actions killed my firstborn. I can never forgive myself for that.

I can only try to get him justice.

"Please, Caden. Bring me Colton if you can't bring me Aleric."

His arms tighten around me. He exhales slowly. Then he kisses the top of my head.

"I will, Sau. I will."

---

It takes him six months to get me Colton, but now I'm staring at his bloody corpse. He brought him to me dead because it was too risky to bring him alive. At first I was angry with him, wanting to kill Aleric's son myself, to find a bit of relief from the pain and guilt constantly at war inside me.

But now that Colton's on the floor of our living room, staring up at me with lifeless eyes, I can't bring myself to even hate him. He looks so much like Leon. They don't share any physical features, but there's an essence to him that reminds me of my own son – a boy taken too soon, a son killed for his parent's crimes, a victim of a war that will never stop and has no meaning.

A tear rolls down my cheek, the first one I've shed in years. And it's over the son of my enemy.

"Did he die quickly?" I ask.

"Yes. He would've phased away otherwise."

Another tear joins the first.

"Sau...are you okay?"

"I thought... I thought this would make me feel better. I thought it would..." I swallow as tears clog my throat. "I thought it would feel like getting justice. But it just *hurts*. It just... I killed him and for what?" My vision blurs as I keep my gaze on Colton's face. He doesn't look peaceful. He doesn't look in pain either. He just looks lost. Gone. Murdered for no fucking reason.

"You didn't –"

"But I *did*," I cry. "You might've dealt the killing blow, but you did it for *me*. And I did it for what? I killed him for nothing. It's not going to bring Leon back. It's not going to end this war and protect our other children. It's not even going to deal a blow to the Blood Fangs or upset Aleric. I just... He's dead for no fucking reason other than my selfish, stupid desire to kill him. I'm supposed to be a healer... I wanted peace..."

"Sau..." Caden wraps an arm around my shoulders, and it's only then, when his body seems to be vibrating beside me, that I realize I'm shaking. "There are no easy choices in this life, and there's no easy way to deal with the things we've done and come to regret. But his death doesn't have to be meaningless."

"*How?*" The word is raw desperation ripped from the bottom of my heart. I just want it to stop. All the pain. All the deaths. This vicious cycle of seeing who can hurt the other the most.

Caden turns me to face him, then tilts up my chin. "By fighting for him, Sau. By fighting for all the soldiers who are expected to die for the whims of their leaders. He had a wife who died trying to protect him –"

A sob escapes me.

"–and a child on the way."

I jerk away, horrified over what I've done. Over the entire family I've just killed. "No."

"You need to know this, Sau. You need to realize that these aren't just vampires dying – faceless enemies who deserve it. These are *people*. These are husbands and dads and mothers and children.

"We fight when we need to protect ourselves, and we don't hesitate when we do." His eyes drop to the dead boy in front of us. "But a life should never be taken without seeing them for the person they are."

"I didn't see Colton," I whisper.

"No... you just saw a vampire and the son of a man you hate."

His words take root inside my chest, burrowing into my rib cage, wrapping their tendrils around the bone and digging their feelers into my heart. I want to fight for him.

I want to fight for all the soldiers who have died for this pointless war.

I want to fight for the future of my children, so they don't have to live with the pain and guilt I've suffered.

That my father and mother suffered.

That their parents did too.

"So why did you do it?" I ask Caden, needing to know

more than I do. Needing to grow up from the stupid, naive child that I still am despite the decades I've survived.

He looks back up at me, a sadness in his sharp green eyes. "Because you asked me to."

My heart breaks even as it grows.

I want to fight for Caden too.

I want to fight for my husband who is clearly so tired of this war. I pull him into my arms and hold him tight. But…is it foolish to think I can break a two thousand year cycle? Am I just being naive, wanting to try to bring us peace?

# THIRTY-NINE
## ALERIC
### 25 SEPTEMBER 1949

"Oh, Murder Victim Number *Twenty-niiiine*...it's time for your *appointmeeeeent*."

Her fear calls to me, telling me exactly where she is. The slam of her heart against her rib cage leads me down the hall. I track her through the smell of her sweat, the sound of her harsh breaths, the strong beat of her heart that calls to me on a sense humans don't have.

I stomp my feet extra hard so she can hear my every step. I phase in front of her, just out of sight any time she takes a turn I don't want her to take, making her spin on her heels or dart through a door. I'm herding her to my bedroom, to my ensuite, to the bath that is nearly full.

I received such wonderful news tonight. My son's dead, as is his wife, but that's only okay news. The *wonderful* part is that they died because of Sau. My little lioness is growing her claws, and I'm growing hard at the idea of her dragging them down my back.

Up ahead, Murder Victim Number Twenty-nine bolts into my room. I give her a second before I open the door behind her. She throws a vase at my head, then yanks open the ensuite door. I phase into the bathroom, keeping myself in the corner so I can see the fear in her eyes.

She screams for all she's worth, but her gaze isn't on me. She probably doesn't even see me at all, her attention on the seven people hanging upside down above the red-splattered, white cast-iron, enameled bath with brass feet. Their throats are slit. Blood pours from them in various speeds, the one to the left running the slowest, only a few drips now, the one to the right still gushing a bit in its freshness.

She's frozen in horror, but only for a moment. Then she slams the door shut and flips the lock. She backs away, trembling and mumbling some sort of prayer. I wonder if she'll plan on hiding or if she'll try to take down the last free meathook in the ceiling and stab me with it. If she stands on the edge of the tub, she can reach it, and it's on a pulley, so she can easily remove it.

But my bath is getting cold, and I cannot be bothered waiting. So I step up behind her, my footsteps now utterly silent.

She backs into me, screams, then turns, and I laugh as she trips over her feet and crashes into the floor. Her arms come up as if they're enough to shield her. "Please...please let me go! I won't say anything. I won't tell anyone!"

"I can get your silence with you dead. The first rule to bartering, kid, is to offer something I don't already have or can't easily get." I reach down and grab her leg. She kicks me with her other foot, but she's young, probably still in school, and has no real weight behind her blow.

I haul her up upside down, then reach over to grab the last free hook. Number Thirteen is basically empty, his drops no longer dripping, just pooling on his face, waiting for gravity to do its thing. Once she's up, I'll lower him to make way for one of the other humans down in the cell.

"Wait!" she screams as I pull the hook lower, the sound of its cord going through the pulley an ominous creak. "I can get you more victims!"

I pause. Glance down at her, a smile curling my lips. Oh, I do like this one. I cock a brow. "Oh?"

"Yes," she blurts frantically. "I know where there's a drug den. No one will miss them."

I chuckle. "Now why would I kill my own clients?"

Her mouth opens and closes in her panic. I press the meat hook against her calf muscle, running the metal up and down her leg.

She screams. "Wait!"

I stop, delighted with her willingness to sacrifice others so easily. "Yes?"

"I'm a prostitute. I can get you johns."

"Before or after you fuck them?"

"What?"

"I want to know if you're asking me to be your pimp? If so, I want a cut of the money."

"You're getting their lives!"

"Kid, look around you. I'm filthy rich. You don't get this rich by passing up opportunities."

She glances around as she hangs from my hand. The amount I spent on renovating this bathroom was more than the average worker makes in a year. She doesn't need to know about stone quality or the cost of artisan craftsmanship to realize that. It's in its spaciousness, in the details carved into the doors of the sink –two Chinese dragons making the African blackwood come alive– and the mirror hanging above it –an art piece of birds and foliage carved into the blackwood edges. It's in the light fixture, in the white marble sink, and the gray stone of the floor.

Taking this all in, she huffs out a breath, looking vastly

more annoyed at the fact that she'll have to give up some of her hard-earned money than she does about dying. In fact, she looks like she's considering telling me to stick my offer up my ass and hang her.

"Fifty percent," she grumbles.

I laugh. "Kid, you think I don't know how much a pimp makes? I'm not from the fucking Shadow Domain. Eighty and you'll attend my parties at least once a month."

She chews on her lip, fear still so strong in her eyes even though she's trying to hide it. She ran through the basement when I released her from her cage and told her to run. She saw the whores getting passed around in the orgy going on down there, how they were slapped and beaten without a care to their health. Multiple men in their holes. Constantly going around. Some clearly dead yet still being used.

She hesitates, then her eyes shift over to the bodies hanging over the tub.

"Fuck you," she says.

I grin, and slam the hook into her calf. She screams as I haul her up to the ceiling. She thrashes, trying to get free, trying to bend up at the waist to get her leg off the hook. But I'm tying off the other end of the pulley, and now I'm on her, slitting her throat with the knife I left on the sink.

She gurgles, her eyes widening, her hands clasping over her neck, as if she can stop the blood pumping out of her severed arteries. She hangs limp a few seconds later, and I look at the level of the bath. It's a *bit* low, but that was a damn good finish, and I'm certain the other two in the cell won't be as nearly as fun to chase. The whole time I was dragging people out, they sat, cowering in the back, unmoving as they clung to each other. Besides, there's only about a gallon in a body. Two more won't really make much of a difference.

Stripping off my shirt, I drop it to the gray stone floor, then remove my pants and the rest of my clothes. I step into the bath with one foot just as the door bangs open. I sigh. "Vlad."

He answers by barreling into me, grabbing hold of my throat as he tackles me out of the bath. Blood splatters across the bathroom, and I try to calculate how much I've just lost from his little play. I really don't want to have to bring up one of those sniveling boys. My back hits the wall as he presses into me, his fangs bared in my face.

"They killed my sister," he growls, "and you're having a celebratory bath!"

"The bath isn't for her. It's for Sau finally demanding blood."

"Through the death of my sister!" He jerks me forward only to slam me against the wall.

"Through the death of my son. Destiny just refused to let him die on his own. Jumped on the pyre with him and all that."

"She loved him."

"A foolish thing, aye."

His eyes flash red as he goes to rip my face off with his teeth. I headbutt him, breaking his nose, then grab his hair and yank his head to the side. My teeth slip into his neck. His fingers squeeze around mine, hoping if I can't drink, I can't drain him dry. A quick action that makes me respect him even more.

But I don't need to feed off him to kill him. I ripped open his artery, and as I lift my head, his blood squirts out across the room.

His eyes widen as his fingers tighten around my neck even more, compressing my arteries, refusing to let air get to my brain. But Vlad's strength is failing fast, and he drops to his knees, his hand falling from my throat.

I squat down over him, lifting my wrist to my fangs. Biting deep, knowing he needs a lot to heal from that wound, especially since he isn't one of my sired and my blood won't heal him as miraculously, I let two great big rivers flow into his goldfishing mouth. He refuses to drink for a moment. Then instinct kicks in, and his lips fasten around my flesh.

"The next time you attack me, Vlad, be smarter about it. Bring a gun or something."

As soon as the inside of his neck starts to knit back together, the flesh still ripped open wide, I yank him off me. I'm not stupid enough to let him drink to full health, especially given it will drain me.

"You said...there would be peace...with a marriage." He scoots back, using the bath to lean against as he sits up.

I stay crouched near the wall, my dick between my legs, the air cold on my balls. "And there will be. In time. A pity your sister won't see it, but..." I pause, holding his gaze. "You will. And with Colton gone, I can name you as my heir."

"Did you set her up to die?" Vlad asks, and my eyes soften. As much as I do not care for my own actual son, the vampire in front of me has earned my respect a dozen times over.

"I'd never hurt anyone you cared about."

He stares at me, the silence pulling tight between us. The honesty I've never spoken before. Then I shrug and stand. "Then again, I promised Sau I wouldn't hurt any of her family either and well..." I flash a grin, then lick his blood off my lips.

His eyes harden, but he doesn't attack me for playing with him. Whether or not I set Destiny up to die along with my son doesn't matter. Vlad isn't strong enough to kill me. Nor is he sneaky enough for a paranoid fucker like me.

"Now, get out so I can enjoy my bath."

I step past him, daring him to try to attack me now that I'm so close, but he doesn't. Perhaps he took my advice to heart about being smarter the next time he tried. Stepping into the bath, I settle into the lukewarm blood that still drips from the corpses above me.

He rises to his feet, then leaves. The door slams behind him, and I smile at his need to get in one last word. It's so unlike him. He must be really hurting over her death.

Staring at Little Miss Fuck You, I wonder how Vlad will react if he ever finds out she's still alive. I doubt she will reach out to him as long as I'm still here, thinking it'll be too risky. That I might come for Colton for making a fool of me, for running away from his responsibilities...

Never knowing that I set it up for them to 'escape' this cruel life. Caden might be logical and ruthless, but he has always had a soft spot for cowards like my son. Who want a different life away from the fields of blood. A few words here and there, a reminder that Myers is a shapeshifter, a mention of the alley behind the library being the old spot to parlay – a tradition even Delun honored when Antonio first tried it all those years ago.

And Caden...his disgusting need to protect Sau at all costs, even from herself, made him an easy fiddle to play. I could use his lie to turn her further against him, force a deeper wedge between their marriage...

But I won't.

I'll let Colton have his happy ending – my one gift to the grandchild I'll never meet, who's currently growing in Destiny's womb. Perhaps when they finally find a place though, I'll send them a postcard.

A smile curls my lips as I lean my neck against the rim of the bath and turn my thoughts to why I'm celebrating in the first place.

The game has fully started. Now it's time to wait out her paranoia, trick her into lowering her defenses before I absolutely annihilate her.

Twelve years sounds like a good idea. That's a special number to a witch, divided by three and all that, one set for each of her four children. A fitting number... And it'll let them grow up. Give them a taste of life before they die. Plus, then they'll be old enough to leave their little nest, the warded street, and it'll make it so much easier to kill them.

Closing my eyes, I start to plan my next move.

*Eeny, meeny, miny, moe.*

Which of her kids will be the first to go?

# FORTY
## HER
### 13 OCTOBER 1961

*Twelve years later...*

The sun is so beautiful as it crests the horizon, bathing the world in its warm oranges and yellows, spreading out its rays to hug the world. I feel *good*. My children are safe; all of them but Ryo are married. Molly to Garrett. Bonnie to an outsider from New Hampshire. Jonathan to a lovely girl called Delilah. She's three months' pregnant too. And my husband is in bed asleep – the first lie in he's had in years.

We are not anywhere close to peace. Antonio Garcia still wishes to rip my head from my shoulders and feast on my heart, but his rage seems to be dwindling. Perhaps nearly killing me triggered something in him. Made him realize it wouldn't be the great big ending he wanted, the justice, the giving of peace...

Whatever is going on in his head, he's turned a vast

amount of his attention to actually leading his pack now rather than just using them for revenge. Their empire up north has just crept into North Carolina, and there are rumors that he's going to take control of the entire range of the Blue Mountains.

They're still running strong in St. Augustine and other parts of Florida, but I wonder if they'll eventually move their base north. Away from me. The start of a new life.

If it's possible for Antonio to find peace after all this time, after what I did and what he lost, perhaps then so can the rest of us. I'm not naive enough to think we can exist alongside each other without any bloodshed at all, but maybe this war can end. Maybe all the deaths can just be over territory or the clashing of business rather than mindless killing.

Maybe the next generation can grow up with only ever hearing stories of the nightmares that used to be.

Sitting on our front porch, looking at the warm rays of the new day, I dare to dream.

---

The door creaks open behind me, and Caden steps out. The roasted smell of coffee wafts through the breeze.

"Morning." He kisses the top of my head. Sitting down beside me on the bench, he offers me one of the two mugs in his hands. I take it with a warm smile.

"I thought you were going to sleep in?"

"So did I, but Vance just scried me. The Mattos twins are arriving early."

Normally, such meetings would take place in our home, but Ashely and Aaron are the succubus and incubus who supply us with a large amount of our potions, and they aren't a fan of the sticky Floridian summer heat.

Even though it's October.

Such soft skin, northerners.

So Caden is going up to Vance's territory in Raleigh, North Carolina, for four nights. Two to spend with the twins – taking them out on the town to strengthen our alliances, and two to spend with Vance, making sure his territory is still running smoothly given his deteriorating condition. Vance summoned an eknor demon last week, and it managed to break his circle and bite him on the shoulder before he banished it. The infection is spreading, black inky lines running through his veins, and there's nothing I or any healer can do to stop it. He'll be dead in another week.

He should be on bedrest, but he's as stubborn as he is lethally curious. I wouldn't be surprised if he discovers a way to come back as a ghost or a zombie – two creatures that don't even exist.

"When are you leaving?" I ask.

He glances at his watch. "Six minutes ago."

"Caden!"

He shrugs. "I'm not going away for four days without spending the morning of with my wife."

I scoot closer to him. He transfers his cup to his other hand, then wraps that arm around my shoulders.

"So what are your plans today?" he asks.

"Once Delilah is up, I'll see if she wants to make some combat potions. The stash is running low." Ever since she learned she was pregnant, she's been sleeping over at ours whenever Jonathan is out at night. He turns twenty-two in twelve days and will take over as Boss then. He's been out strengthening connections and has been taking over more and more of his dad's responsibilities. The transition is going smoothly, and we are both so proud of him.

"Sounds good. Do you –" A black car pulls onto the drive and Myers steps out. Caden sighs and finishes the rest of his coffee. "Sorry, Sau, but I have to go."

He places his cup down on the glass table beside him,

stands, then leans down to kiss me. He tastes of coffee with less sugar than mine. My chest squeezes at the thought of not lying next to him tonight.

"I love you," I say.

"I love you too."

He gets into the passenger seat as Myers settles back in the car, and I watch them drive away.

I fiddle with the ring on my hand, thinking about the thing that has been on my mind for the past few days. I love Caden, but he isn't my lifemate – the other half of my soul that the gods ripped apart at the start of creation and flung into the Seven Planes for me to find.

Everyone has one, and Caden's is out there somewhere too. So maybe what I'm thinking is foolish. Maybe he'll turn me down and break my heart as he does, holding out hope that in a later life, he finds the one he's supposed to be with.

But maybe...

Maybe he feels the same as me and wants us to be tied to each other through our souls as well as through our hands. Maybe he wants to spend literal forever with me, finding me through our connection every time we are reborn.

As witches, we've the ability to create our own version of a lifemate through a blood bond, which combines blood and sex magic in order to bind our souls together across every timeline. But it comes with a high cost – you have to let your partner do a sexual act that will destroy you.

The djini that gifted witches with this ability had a cruel sense of humor. Or perhaps they were just cruel. But that is what happens when you try to barter with one who cares for you as little as the gods do. We are nothing but toys to play with.

I spin the ring round and round my finger, chewing on my lip. I know what sacrifice Caden must make, and I know the sacrifice that would be demanded of me.

Caden would have to watch me come...with *Aleric*. He

understands rape. He understands anatomy. He has been the rock anchoring me when my self doubt wants to tear me away, telling me I'm a horrible person for coming on his fingers. But there's a darkness to Caden's thoughts, a twisted voice that tells him I am drawn more to Aleric than to him. I can see it in his eyes, feel it in his soul. He'd be jealous watching me with anyone, but he wouldn't be broken. He wouldn't be the level of devastated that the binding requires him to be.

And I...I would have to let Caden *rape* me. Not like in the scenes we do, where I have a safe word to call out if he goes too far. He'd have to push me past that, force me until I'm begging for him to stop, until I'm terrified of him and what he'll do next. Until I fear he might kill me. I'd have to turn my sweet loving husband into a monster.

My ring goes round and round.

I want to be able to find Caden in the next life and all the lifetimes after, but... I don't know if we could survive the ritual. If I could see him in the same light after. If he could see *me*.

And that is the djini's true entertainment: a binding of souls that grow to hate each other.

My heart plummets into my stomach. I don't ever want him to hate me. I just want –

"Mrs. Shadow?"

I start at the creak of the door as Delilah comes out. Maybe it's the negative thoughts already swirling around inside me. Maybe it's the hard clench nausea already has on my stomach. Maybe it's *why* I'm thinking about blood bonding at all – how there's a fear building inside me that these last twelve years are about to explode, and I might lose Caden forever.

Whatever the reason, I am absolutely terrified when I turn to face my daughter-in-law.

That terror only amplifies at the sight of her pale face.

She's still in her nightgown. It's not unusual for her to not get dressed when Jonathan is still out. She is a foreseer, catching glimpses of past and present and future at the whims of the gods. Sometimes we can change the course of things she sees, sometimes not, but the weight of one's sight is crushing. Very few foreseers live long lives, driven to depressive suicide. And none of them manage to stay sane for long.

Her arms are wrapped around her stomach, and she wobbles towards me, looking ill.

"Delilah, are you ok–"

She holds up a hand. "I'm bleeding."

There's no blood on her palm. None on her anywhere I can see. But my heart jumps into my throat as I jump to my feet.

"Where?" I ask, my fingers sparking with my healing magic, ready to act as soon as I know where to focus it.

She touches her throat, and I shake my head. "There's no blood there, Delilah. Are you having a vision? Are –"

I stop, the blood draining from my face as I catch the glint of the knife she has in her other hand, still pressed to her stomach.

I'm rooted where I am, torn between jumping back for my own safety or rushing forward to save her and her baby from herself. "Delilah," I whisper, trying to keep my voice calm, "put down the knife."

"*I'm bleeding*," she repeats, her eyes glassing over, the desperation in her voice leaking out onto her face. "It won't stop. I can't get it to stop."

"I can," I blurt, raising my hands to show her my white light. "I can stop the bleeding. Just put down the knife, okay?"

"You can't stop it." Delilah angles the knife across her stomach. "No one can stop it."

"Delilah. Delilah, look at me." I wish Caden was here. I

wish I could call him back. His telekinesis could keep her blade steady while we calmed her down, figured this out. Foreseers shouldn't be disturbed when they're having a vision. Doing so could kill them. In this moment, she's being touched by the divine, and the gods don't take too kindly to being interrupted.

"He's dead," she whines, so much pain in her words, on her face. Tears streak down her cheeks. She's trembling, the knife shaking. "I can't stop the bleeding."

"I can, Delilah. I promise. I'm a strong healer. I've even healed a guy after he stopped breathing. You remember Johnny?" I'm not a necromancer, but I can bring one back to life before they fully pass over, just like human doctors do with their medicine. "And if not, we can get a doctor. I can get a whole team of doctors."

It's risky bringing them in. We might have to kill them after if they witness any magic or any 'wrong' anatomy, but I'll risk it for her and my grandchild in her belly.

"Just put down the knife, Delilah. Please. Just put down the knife."

She looks at me. The glassiness in her eyes fades for a moment, replaced by so much sadness and pity. "I am so sorry, Sau, but you'll have nine sons to love."

She raises the knife to her throat, and I tackle her on a hope and a prayer.

The blade clatters on the floor a second before we hit. My hands go over her temples, white light building in a foolish notion that I can heal her from any godly damage that might be dealt.

She gasps, then starts to scream in agony, and I realize I can smell blood. A lot of it.

Terrified one of us is stabbed, I pull away, directing my hands down. Her body is fine; there's no cut or stab wound through her gown. As is mine.

So where –

And then I see it, the first lines of red seeping through the fabric over her thighs.

My own cry escapes me.

She's losing the baby.

My hands go to her stomach. I feed my magic through, seeking the damage to try to find it. Is it with the mother or the child?

I can't figure out what's wrong.

I don't know why her baby's dying.

I can't save my grandchild.

"He's dead," Delilah sobs, covering her face with her hands. "He's dead. He's dead. He's dead."

Her words slap me across the face. My entire world feels like it's collapsing, a star going out, a species at its end. "Who's *he*, Delilah?" I ask, my own panic rising as the baby is – *was* a girl. "Delilah, who is he!" I scream it this time, needing to know who else I'm about to lose.

I lift my head to peer down the road in the direction Caden just left in and catch sight of a vehicle stopping in front of our house. It's a two-tone van, the top half of it white.

"No," I whisper even as I keep pushing healing magic into Delilah's body, trying to fix what I can't. "*No.*"

"He's dead," she cries. "He's dead, he's dead, he's dead."

The delivery man gets out of the driver's seat. He goes around to the back, pulls out a cardboard box, and heads up our drive.

"No."

Flashes of Leon's body slam into me, and I fall away from Delilah, my own grief making me forget hers. "No."

The man starts to walk up our drive, not seeming to care that Delilah's still screaming bloody murder. That I'm on my knees, shaking like a leaf in a hurricane. He just puts the blood-stained box down in front of me, then goes to his van to get another one.

And another.

And another.

"Mrs. Shadow?" the man says, smiling at me, his eyes vacant but bloodshot, some sort of magical drug coursing through his veins. "I just need you to sign here."

He holds out a pen and pad to me.

"*He's dead!*" Delilah wails, and I finally know who 'he' is. There aren't any official labels on the boxes. Someone just popped them into his van this morning, right after they forced him to take a Mad Hatter – one of our potions that will make a person be more open to suggestions. Like delivering blood-stained boxes and not seeing anything wrong with it. A delivery of the stuff got intercepted by the Blood Fangs last week…

"Mrs. Shadow?"

Numb, I take the pen and mark a line, not bothering to properly sign it. But that's all he needs, all he's been told to get, and he turns on his heels and leaves.

"Has she lost the baby?" someone asks, but I don't look up to see who it is. His voice is fuzzy and far away, unable to properly pierce the fog choking me as I stare at the three cardboard boxes.

Jonathan is dead. My firstborn has once again been stolen from me. By *him*.

*"Has she lost the baby?"* Those words float around my head again, having run a lap and come back, flashing in their importance. *"Has she lost the baby?"*

My head snaps up. I'm on my feet, my heart lodged in my throat. Bonnie is now my firstborn, and she's a girl. Just like I am.

I run past the boxes and down the drive, not caring that the pavement hurts my bare feet. My daughter's life is in danger because she has a younger brother. Because she's a girl standing in front of a male getting the throne. And they'll kill Molly too – anything to 'break the curse' that comes from having two sets of female firstborns.

*It's been twelve years,* I want to cry. I was able to keep them safe for twelve years, and now I'm losing them all at once.

No. No, I won't. I'll get there in time. I'll get them to pack a bag. They'll live a life on the run, but they're both infertile, so maybe that'll keep them safe. Keep them from being hunted in fights for whose offspring is the true heir. Ryo can marry and continue the line. My two girls can be left alone. They can live. They can live.

"Molly!" I scream as I bang on her door. It swings open under my fist, terrifying me. She always locks her door. "Molly!"

I run inside, dashing through the house even as a little voice tells me to give up, to go check Bonnie's before it's too late for her too. Caden is away. I was preoccupied. Any witch worried about the curse would strike hard and fast before either girl could get away.

But I can't abandon one child over another.

I can't be asked to choose.

So I run through the house until I find her still in bed, her throat slit, her eyes closed. I rush forward with white light flowing from my hands, but I can't bring back the dead. I can't restart her heart and get her breathing again.

Asking for her forgiveness for abandoning her, I race out of the house and down the street to Bonnie's.

I'm too late for her too.

Her throat is slit just like her sister's, but her eyes are open and her body is crumbled on the floor in the kitchen. They came up behind her and killed her before she knew they were there.

Dropping to my knees, I cradle her body to my chest.

"I'm so sorry," I whisper into her hair. "I'm so sorry."

I hold her for a long time before taking her into my shadows. Then I walk back miserably to Molly and tell her my goodbyes too.

Without the blood staining her body and the bed, she could almost look peaceful.

*Peaceful...*

The word mocks me.

A twisted cry of pain escapes me.

*Peaceful.*

I wanted peace.

But Aleric...all he wants is death and pain.

Cradling Molly in my shadows, I rejoin her with her sister, then walk hollowly back to my house. I might not be able to do anything for my girls now, but Delilah needs me. She needs –

I stop at the start of my drive.

Delilah no longer screams.

No longer cries in pain for her husband and daughter.

She no longer moves at all.

She just lies in a pool of blood, her own throat slashed, a bloody knife loose in her fingers.

*"I'm bleeding."*

*"Where?"*

*"Here."*

She saw her death by her own hand.

No...

By *Aleric's* hand.

He caused all this.

He *did* all this.

My body shaking, I let the rage build.

*I'm going to kill that fucking psycho.*

I don't care if I have to sell my soul to do it.

# FORTY-ONE

## ALERIC
### 13 OCTOBER 1961

Sau's coming for me. I can feel it – an electric current along my skin. Ducking under the fist of one of my three opponents, a female sired vampire with red hair, I glance at the gym's closed doors. That flash of distraction costs me, and her foot slams into my chest. My back hits the steel wall of the cage.

Throwing my arms up, I catch the spinning kick to my face, freezing her leg for the split second it takes me to kick her in the groin. She might not have balls, but she has a pelvis, and when that *cracks* so loud it can be heard over the roar of the crowd, she drops to her knees on a scream. I step forward and snap her neck. Then pivot and send my heel into the man rushing me on my left. He falls backwards. I continue to spin, jump, and snap my other foot into the cheek of the man on my right. His neck snaps from the force, and he's out before he hits the mat. With one man left, he moves more hesitantly, fear making his reactions slow.

Normally, I would play with them, drag out their pain by breaking multiple bones before I "kill" them, but my attention is already off the fight. Their pain can't please me like *hers* can, so I dart forward and drop to my knees. He panics, not sure if he should kick me or run, and by the time his brain sends out a signal to do *something*, I take out his legs. As he falls, I reach up and snap his neck.

The crowd goes wild.

The bell sounds, and I roll over to the woman, taking her head again in my hands. Wrenching it around, I rest it in its correct position, then do the other two. I turn for the door of the cage. As soon as I'm out, five others rush in. Three to grab my opponents' bodies. Two to fight to the "death" against each other. As sired vampires, they'll heal in a few hours.

The bell rings with the start of a new match, but my attention stays on the gym door. My lioness is about to blow through it with the fierceness of a fury of vengeance.

My cock gets hard.

The sweat and blood of the gym, the same one I took her to on our first date, fills my nose and gets my adrenaline pumping. Soon her blood and sweat will mix with ours, and she will be baptized in the chaos and reborn anew.

The door doesn't bang open.

Shadows simply pour beneath it.

For a moment, I think she's brought her whole damn brood. That somehow she managed to stitch them all back together and resurrect them because the amount of black that crawls across the floor like octopus ink is too much to come from one person.

But then she forms in front of the door alone, her face so beautiful – twisted in lethal fury, in deathly desires, in cold-blooded vengeance. There's no sign of the coward who wishes for peace like Caden tried to make her be. There's no want to talk this out in her gaze. Sau Shadow just wants the world to burn – just like she did that very first night we met.

It takes the sired vampires a moment to notice they're chickens in a pen with a fox. Their eyes are on the match. Their focus is on who is going to be the last man standing in this room when all the fights are over, but they don't yet understand it won't be any of them.

They don't yet understand that Sau, heartbroken mom and dark phoenix about to rise, is about to kill them all.

And then they do.

She moves with none of the grace of a seasoned fighter, acts with no cold efficiency. She simply launches herself at the nearest vampire, his back to her, and stabs him in the neck with a blade she pulled from inside her jacket. His blood sprays out all around him, and the temperature in the room suddenly changes. A hundred heads whip in her direction.

Teeth become bared. Two try to grab her, but Sau turns into a shadow and hustles back before she reappears. She doesn't seem to want to kill them with the monsters in her magic. She wants to do it herself, feel every last life fade by her own hands.

My cock gets so hard it hurts.

I need to touch her.

I need to shove my cock inside her as she stabs me in the side, screaming out all her rage.

So I phase to the cage standing proud in the middle of the room. The vampires previously inside it have already exited to join the fight, and I am alone, easily spotted on the higher floor, with no one crowded around me.

Her eyes fly to me. She screams my name, so furious, so beautiful, so damn *hot*, I nearly come in my pants. As is, precum trails a thick line down my head.

She shadows over to me, ignoring the other vampires.

"No one comes in," I say right before she starts to form in front of me. I phase directly behind her, then punch her in the kidney. She drops like a stone, curling her body in on itself instinctively. There are a lot of weak points in our bodies, a lot of places where a strike can cause crippling pain regardless of how you train.

I crouch down in front of her as she gasps.

"Rule one, never fight clean. Honor will get you killed."

I fist her beautiful black hair in my hands, then pivot on my heels as I stand. Using the momentum of my spin, I throw her at the wall of the cage. The vampires on the other side, their fingers between the criss-crossed wires, shake it and hiss. A few rake their claws at her, and she rolls away from them, barely getting the required distance before collapsing with a painful gasp.

"Rule two." I pick up the knife she dropped, then twirl it in my hands. "Don't give your weapon to your enemy. That's just dumb."

I dart forward as she tries to rise, half-bent with one arm wrapped around her stomach. I slide the knife into her side – once, twice, three times in rapid succession.

She gasps as she stumbles back, trying to get away from me. I grab the back of her head, holding her still, and stab her two more times before she even tries to punch me back. The knife slides into her hand, straight through her palm, and then I kick her away, wrenching it out.

The cage rattles as she hits it. She gasps as sharp claws reach for her wounds. She jerks away, dripping blood all over the mat.

Flipping the blade into the air, I grin at her. "It's about time we had that date."

"You *killed* them," she hisses as she presses her hands to her wounds, white light flowing from her fingers.

"Yes, and you should thank me."

She looks like she wants to kill me.

"They were dragging you down," I clarify.

"They were my children!" She rushes me. I throw the knife at her face, spinning it harder than needs be so the handle hits her eye rather than the blade. As she staggers off course, I walk over to her. The rattling of the cage adds a wild beat to the screams demanding blood and pain.

Raising my leg, I slam my foot down into the side of her knee. She screams as her bones snap, dropping her.

But the rage stays in her fiery green eyes, overriding the pain. "They were my *children*!"

"So you've said."

"You're a monster."

"No," I say with a smile. "I'm Aleric."

Grabbing her hair, I yank her head back. "Rule three –"

"Fucking die," she hisses, and my cock throbs over the fury alight in her eyes.

Her shadows shoot forward, wrapping around my leg before I can move back. The adrenaline of death caresses my balls, squeezing them tight in its grip. I yank her to me and take her lips before she can protest. But she doesn't push me away. Doesn't kiss me back though either.

All her thoughts are simply on opening herself up to her magic, of becoming the dark phoenix the world will learn to fear.

With my tongue stroking hers, I see my end in her eyes, and I've never been more turned on.

# FORTY-TWO
## HER
### 13 OCTOBER 1961

I wanted peace.

I wanted the fighting to stop. The mindless killing.

I was willing to ignore, if not quite forgive and forget, the pain he'd caused me. My rape. Leon's death. I was willing to let it all go so I could focus on raising my other children. On watching them grow up, become mothers and fathers in their own right.

I wanted peace.

But I will settle for revenge.

Opening my mouth further to his kiss, I let Aleric think he is winning me over. That I am choosing him. That I'm just so fucking *turned on* to care anymore about the death of my children. I kiss him back. I let my shadows slowly dissipate, stretching them out thin until you can barely tell they're there.

And then when he groans, when he lowers his defenses

due to them being crushed by his huge fucking ego, I clamp down on his tongue and rip my head to the side. His lips leave mine.

His tongue does not.

Not until I spit it free.

His blood runs down his chin and mine. His eyes are wide with pleasure, and although that pisses me off, at least he can't make some stupid quip. He can't mock me. Can't belittle me. Can't say a damn thing at all.

"You took my children from me," I seethe, my heart twisting as all their deaths flash in front of my eyes. "So I will take all of yours."

His vampires hiss as they shake the cage, but they can't get me here. They can't break through the wards I put up as we fought. They can't get out of this gym either.

He laughs, and there are words on his tongue – the half that's left. Turning from him, I try not to think about how little he cared when Colton and his family died, try not to think how it *felt* when I stared at his lifeless body, how disappointed Caden was in me, how I've carried that guilt for the last twelve years, mourning a child that was not even mine. I look at the vampires around us, and I see *them*.

They are not just things I can use for my revenge. They live and they breathe and they hope and they love.

And now they will suffer.

Not because Aleric cares about them but because they give him power. Because they make up the majority of the Blood Fangs, and today, the entire gang is going to end.

I'm going to have my peace.

I'm going to have it without my children…

Tears want to fall down my cheeks. For them. For me. For taking this path I won't be able to come back from.

But I'm not like Aleric. This won't be mindless killing. This will be for the greater good.

For peace.

Opening my shadows up, I call the monsters to them outside of the cage.

And then I bring them out.

---

"This is the end for your Family, Aleric. I put my wards around this entire building before I came in. No one can phase in or out. And now you must watch them die for your sins."

I don't look at him, don't want to see his indifference. If he makes me think these deaths are meaningless, then I don't know if I'll be able to see this through. And I need to see it through. I need to protect the future kids Caden and I will have. I'm not losing another one. Not one damn more. *I can't*.

So I watch as tears fall down my cheeks, as their high-pitched screams and blood-drained faces humanizes them even more. I mourn their deaths as they are ripped apart by teeth and claws, by pincers and talons, by tentacles and spikes, but I don't close my shadows.

This is needed for peace.

For my children...

A particular movement catches my eye, and I turn my head to the left. A gasp of horror escapes me as I watch a hairy monster with an upturned snout and horns curling out of the top of its head munch on the ripped-off bottom half of a sired vampire. The man's upper half is beneath the beast's hairy bulk, his intestines spilling out all over its angry red cock as it slams into his body over and over again. He begs and cries, still alive, and my heart thunders with regret and horror and a want to save him.

But he quickly fades into dust, finally dying, the curse that came with his siring coming into effect.

The beast howls in outrage, its thick cock pulsing with

beads that ripple up and down its length beneath the skin. Then it grabs the next person it can and impales them on its cock.

"Beautiful, isn't it?" Aleric whispers in my ear, and fear floods my system as I turn. He waits until I'm facing him before he grabs my arms, forces them both over my head, and then phases us. We reappear only a few paces away, the wards I put up when I was tossed into it previously keeping us from passing the criss-crossed wire. Instead, a wall of energy meets my back, lets him pin me between it and his body as mine shakes from his method of travel.

But I see now why he didn't walk. He's missing his left foot, having cut it off, sacrificing it to the shadows, so he could escape.

Clamping a large hand over both of mine, he squeezes my fingers together so I can't use them. Then he grabs my face with his other hand and forces it sideways, forces me to watch the monstrous rape of that vampire. Aleric licks up from the base of my neck to my ear. His tongue is too short, not yet fully healed, but it doesn't stop him from tasting my skin.

"So much power in its thrusts," he says in my ear as he presses his hard cock into my stomach. "Can you imagine how it feels being torn apart from a big cock like that?" He laughs. "Of course you can. I bet Caden uses those incubus potions on himself all the damn time. Someone like him needs to overcompensate."

"Fuck you."

"No, Sau." He turns my head back to face him. His grin is wide, his eyes predatory. "I'm going to fuck you."

My pulse spikes, but my thighs clench, remembering the feel of his fingers. *It's just anatomy. It's just anatomy.*

I try to move my hands, to access my magic, but he just squeezes them tighter. "Rule four," he murmurs with a wicked smirk. "Never turn your back on your opponent."

His hand trails down my neck to the collar of my shirt, and he rips it straight down the middle. He cups my right breast, forcing my nipple to harden between the roll of his fingers.

I hate him. I hate my body. I hate this whole fucking world.

"I'm going to kill you," I vow.

He presses a kiss to the base of my neck. "It would be a pleasure to die at your hands with my cock inside you."

"I should've bit off more of your tongue."

He chuckles. "Rule five, if you're trying to incapacitate a vampire, make sure they don't have any vials of blood on them."

I stare at him, listening to the screams of his dying children along with his laughter. "How can you not care at all about them?"

He lifts his head. His fingers pause, and there is a look in his eyes that looks so utterly *wrong* on him. If he had a soul, I'd say he looked tired of life. Of loving people who die. Of giving up a bit of his soul over and over again until he has nothing left. On him though? All I can say is it looks wrong.

"How can you?" he murmurs.

His dark eyes flicker across mine like he's genuinely looking for an answer. And for a moment, I wonder if we could talk this out. If he could *understand* all the pain he causes, but –

You can't explain love to a monster.

So instead, I just hold his gaze and look at *him* for the first time. Not the person I hate the most, even more than Antonio now. Not the person I'm terrified of for there's nothing worse he can do to me. Not the murderer of my children. Not the careless father who's letting his own die. Not the charming asshole with the ego the size of the stick up his ass.

Just Aleric.

A pathetic, pitiful excuse of a living thing.

And I know the exact moment he sees my thoughts. His eyes narrow. Rage – the first genuine emotion to cross his face twists his lips into a sneer.

He pinches my nipple hard, punishing me, sending that bolt all the way down to my pussy. I stiffen my muscles, trying to fight the reaction of my body, but it remembers the feel of his fingers, his tongue, his lips, and I'm still horribly turned on by violence.

I've tried so hard to come with Caden without the need for pain, but as soon as he's gentle or loving, my libido plummets. There's a dark part inside me. A part I hate. A part Aleric can touch and coax out of me so easily.

*"It's just anatomy, sweet girl."*

Caden's words hurt my heart. I don't care if it's just anatomy. I don't care if he'll forgive me. I won't be able to forgive myself.

I came here to kill him, to bring peace with the death of his gang, and he's just *enjoying* it.

I won't let him enjoy me.

Tears burning my eyes, I picture Caden's smile this morning. How he held the mug out to me. How he didn't want to leave without spending a bit of time with me. I see the sun's gentle rays on his face. I see the love in his beautiful green eyes.

As Aleric tears apart my skirt, I picture Ryo as a baby, that moment he reached for me and called me mama. I feel the same heartache I experienced that day, the utter disbelief and pure joy. In my mind, I watch him grow up. Learn to fight. Learn to sing. He has such a deep, beautiful voice, and I let one of his songs flow through my ears.

*"The sun is only rising,*
*The dew's not even burned,*
*The colors are all enticing,*

*But, Mama, I'm ready to come home.*

*I lie in a meadow*
*Seeing nothing but daisies,*
*I walk through the woods*
*Hearing nothing but crows.*
*I've been around the world, Mama,*
*But all I want to do –*
*All I want to do is come home."*

Holding on to all of their love for me, every hug, every kiss, every moment of laughter we shared these last few decades, I use it to strengthen my resolve.

As Aleric's cock slides horizontally between my pussy lips, I make a choice I can never come back from. One that will mean I'll never see Caden or Ryo again.

"*Alakim vera k'arr,*" I murmur, using dark magic for the first time. Opening myself up to it completely, I let it take whatever payment it wants. It strips off the flesh on my breasts. It disintegrates one kidney. It's killing me, but I don't care to restrain it.

"Stop!" Aleric hisses, but I don't.

*"The sun is only rising,*
*The dew's not even burned,*
*The colors are all enticing,*
*But, Mama, I'm ready to come home.*

Sucking everything into my shadows, killing every last fucking thing in this room, I scream out all my rage and pain. Power flows through me like nothing I have never felt before. The world turns dark as I'm sucked into the very vortex I'm damning them all into, down into the Plane of Monsters where I will surely die. I cannot come back to this world on my own, and Ryo does not know where to look for me. But I do not care.

I will bring peace to this city for my family.
I will gladly sacrifice myself for that.

*"Oh, Mama, I'm ready to come home."*

# PART FOUR:
## FUCKED-UP BOSSES

# FORTY-THREE

## ALERIC
### 13 OCTOBER 1961

I collapse to the ground, my legs giving out. My body is shaking. My breathing is strained. Born vampires are built for phasing. We don't have to learn any spell. We didn't have to make a deal with any djini. It was a gift from the gods.

And yet, phasing hundreds of times, one after the other to keep myself in the air while Sau's shadows covered the floor, eating everything, has utterly wrecked me. My body in chills, I barely manage to roll over and vomit. I spit a couple times after, trying to rid myself of the acidic burn in my throat.

I reach for a vial of blood inside my jacket, but my hand is shaking too much to find the pocket. I'm going into shock, my foot still bleeding out. If I were a human, I would've been dead a long time ago, but phasing helped to keep the blood where it was, momentarily freezing it so I could jump.

My fingers manage to find the small tube of glass, and I pull it out. Popping off the cork, I raise it to my lips and drink Jonathan's blood. A witch's essence works so much better than a human's.

It isn't enough to regrow the entire part of my leg that I hacked off with the knife, but I regain a few inches, and the bleeding stops. That is good enough for now.

I look around the empty gym. All the equipment is gone. I am utterly alone. It was filled with sired vampires for a tournament to see which ones would get promoted up the ranks. All of my "children" were once here, and now they're all dead. Not even dust remains.

Nor does Sau.

I smile at that, having expected to find her body, the dark magic she unleashed having killed her. But it looks like she got away. Lives to fight another day.

My grin widens at the thought of our next fight.

The door to the gym opens slowly at first, then it's swung wide with a bang. "Where the hell is everything?" Vlad asks.

I rise to my feet – well, foot, and hop around to face him fully. "Sau took it all when she killed everyone."

His face blanches as he reaches me. "Everyone?"

"That is what I said."

"Except for you?" There's a clear accusation there, and it's not exactly unwarranted. I did throw the tournament on the same day I sent her Jonathan as a beacon to bring her here. They were all my bait, and they played their part so damn well.

"They couldn't phase. I had to hover for about fifteen minutes."

"So that's why you look like Death came and shat all over you."

I chuckle. That's not unwarranted either.

"Why are you here?" I ask as he ducks under my arm, the same side as my missing foot.

"I saw the wards outside. Thought all the witches had come –"

"So you came in on your own?" My words are biting, chastising in every syllable. "I did not think you a fool."

His jaw ticks, and I know he hoped Caden would be here. That his want for revenge made him stupid. If I had my strength, I'd slap him round the back of the head.

"If we both died here," I say instead, "the Blood Fangs would be easy picking for another nest to move in."

"We just lost over half our numbers. I highly doubt the Crypts are going to sit back and let us regain them."

I tilt my head to the side in agreement. The Crypts is a gang in northern Louisiana, and they've been toeing our borders, testing the waters to see if they'll burn, for years. "Let them come," I say, my fangs extending. "I could use a feast."

Calling me a fool, Vlad phases us home.

---

It's been over a week, and I've not seen Sau.

More worryingly, I've not seen Caden.

No one has. He hasn't left the street, their home, most like, since he got back from Raleigh, North Carolina. And he returned early, pissing off the Mattos twins. My spies say he didn't even meet them, having left Vance to see them on his own.

I assumed Caden came back as soon as he heard about Sau's little rampage and is nursing her back to health. But what if she isn't healing? What if he's in mourning?

I shake my head. *No...no, she's stronger than that.*

We will die together, our blades inside each other. That is how it is meant to be.

She'll heal.

She has too.

So I sit on a rooftop, staring at the Shadows' home, and wait to catch a glimpse of one of them.

---

Something is most definitely wrong.

It's Ryo's wedding day, and neither his mother nor his father are attending. Sau loves her children. She wouldn't miss this unless she was dead.

But she can't be.

She was healthy enough to leave the gym, and no one mentioned finding her body in the streets. She made it home, and she's one of the strongest healers that has been born in generations.

She's alive.

She has to be.

But then where is she?

The question claws at me as I watch her firstborn as he stands at the front of the two rows of pews, waiting for his bride to walk down the aisle. My face is pressed so hard into my pair of binoculars that I'm sure I'll look like a raccoon when I lower them.

I scan the pews a dozen more times, tracking each row, looking at every person, but none of them are Caden or Sau.

"Where the fuck is she?" I murmur as the binoculars roam around the guests again. They're having an outdoor wedding, safe behind the wards of their street. Guards are patrolling the blocks surrounding it so there can't be a repeat of what happened at Sau's wedding. They're fully on guard and itchy, like they fear something will happen, which makes me even more worried.

If they're this nervous, then Caden and Sau should be with their firstborn to protect him.

"Do you want me to see if I can get you an invitation?" Vlad asks dryly as he appears beside me.

"Sau isn't there," I say, not in the mood to joke around.

He grabs the binoculars off me. I start to growl at him, but I trap the noise in my throat so I don't sound like a jealous school boy with a crush.

"Neither is Caden," Vlad says, his words tight.

"Which means there's something wrong with Sau."

"A good thing for us."

This time I do growl. I can't stop it, and his gaze snaps to me. Grabbing the binoculars from his hand, I scan the pews one more time.

Then again.

He yanks them off my face. "They're not just going to appear because you're looking," he says. "And why isn't her death a good thing for us? Especially if it keeps Caden out too?"

I glare at him, my jaw ticking. I know what he's really asking, and I don't like it. *Why isn't this a good thing for you?* As if I'm getting *attached* to her, as if she's no longer just a toy.

Not answering him, I phase to the gym. This is the last place I saw her; it's not been used or entered since. I walk around the place, searching for any sign of her.

I find nothing.

I walk it again.

Still nothing.

My teeth grinding, I narrow my eyes as they fall onto my shadow, cast by the lights in the ceiling. I stare at it, a thought tickling my brain before it suddenly forms in its entirety.

What if she fell into the Plane of Monsters, dragged down with everything else?

My pulse stutters, then slams hard and fast. She won't ever be able to come back. Shadows can only open it from this side.

Growling, cursing her for being so fucking stupid, I phase. The Plane of Monsters flashes in front of me, so dark, I can't see anything other than black. A split second later, it's gone, and I am once again in the bright lights of the gym.

I phase again, trying to keep myself in the Plane for longer, but I'm kicked out in a second, back in the gym and alone.

Maybe a longer distance will give me more time.

It doesn't work like that. I know it doesn't, but that doesn't stop me from trying.

I phase to the other side of town.

The blackness comes.

It's gone.

I phase again, this time to Georgia.

The blackness comes.

It's gone.

I jump from one place to the other, my fury building with each failed attempt to stay in that place, to linger for more than a second. But I know she's in it because I've just caught her scent.

A fleeting drop in the wind that I can't hold.

Can't track.

My heart thundering, I growl like a man obsessed and phase again.

# FORTY-FOUR
## ANTONIO
### 25 OCTOBER 1961

There is a poetic justice to this – killing the last of that bitch's children on his own wedding day, the same way I tried to kill *her* all those years ago. I hope his death is what ends her. I hope it makes her heart finally give out as she lies on her deathbed.

Perhaps then Siome can rest in peace.

Lining up the shot from the spire of a church six blocks away from the Shadow's street, I place my finger on the trigger. Guns have come so far in the last four decades, and I have been practicing hunting with them up in the Blue Mountains. I haven't missed a single shot in over a year. I'm not going to miss this one.

The butt of my rifle presses into my shoulder.

The breeze picks up, and I wait for it to die, my sights on the curly black hair of Sau's firstborn. That title shows everything that is wrong with the Shadow Domain. When their children die, they just wipe them from history as if they never were. Monsters like that, who can forget their own damn children, don't deserve to live.

The breeze dies.

The music starts up as the bride arrives.

Ryo turns to look at her.

His face lights up.

I fire, splattering his brains all over the officiant behind him.

I swing my rifle over to the Shadows' residence, seeing if anyone comes out. The commotion at the wedding is frantic and chaotic. Even at this distance, I can hear all the screaming.

Yet, the Shadows' door stays closed.

No one comes out to see about their little boy.

"Fucking monsters," I mutter as I pull my rifle up and turn away from the Shadows' street. She didn't deserve to be a mother, not like Siome did.

*Not like us.*

My chest tight, I sling the gun over my shoulder. I hope Sau rots away on her deathbed.

But if not, I'll be back to kill her too.

---

The bitch is actually dead.

I watch as the Shadow Domain rips itself apart, once-allies attacking each other on their street. The Shadow bloodline is gone, and Caden is about to be overthrown or perhaps even killed. He was a good leader once, but now he's just a shell.

I doubt he'll even put up a fight.

Not that I care about him. He was never on my list to kill.

Standing at the edge of the Shadow's street, I watch as

witches are mowed down by rapid gunfire. They won't use magic out in the open, and no one has cared to put up a ward to hide their activities from the humans. Any proper fighting will be inside the homes, and the police aren't foolish enough to get in the way of one of our wars. They will wait until it's over before rushing in like the cowards they are.

The Shadow Domain is finished.

Though even if it's not, my revenge is over. Sau and her line is dead.

Turning away from the street, I head home.

But I can never head back to Siome.

# FORTY-FIVE
## CADEN
### 4 NOVEMBER 1962

"Put the damn bottle down!" Myers shouts as he rushes into my bedroom. He throws the covers off my lap, yanks the bottle of whiskey out of my hand despite my protest, and hauls me to my feet. I sway, the world spinning in my alcoholic haze.

Cursing, he drags me to the cupboard in the ensuite. Shoving me down onto my knees, he nudges me in the ass with his foot, forcing me to curl beneath the bottom shelf. "Just hide in here and don't come out."

I start to protest, wanting the comfort of my bottle, but he slams the door in my face. I sit there, unable to figure out how to move my legs. I want the bottle. It helps keep Sau's memories away.

Tears flowing down my cheeks, I reach for the door. I need the bottle. I need its sweet embrace.

The sound of grunts and breaking bones comes from the

other side of the cupboard door. I peek through the slats to see myself on the other side.

No, not me.

Myers just shapeshifted to look like me. He hurries out of view. There's the rummage of fabric against fabric.

I struggle with the door handle before I manage to open it. "What are you –"

He's wearing my dirty clothes, having pulled a vomit-stained shirt out of the basket. The pants are wrinkled.

"Doing?"

"Just stay in there and shut up!" He marches over and shuts the door in my face.

My brain struggles to connect the thoughts. All I can think about is the bottle he took from me. "I want..."

"Oh, for fuck's sake! Fine!"

He comes back a moment later. The door is yanked open. Sighing, he crouches down in front of me.

He doesn't look like I did before Sau died. He looks like how I do now. Haggard bags under bloodshot eyes. Sweat-slick hair stuck to his face. He looks sickly and poor and he's lost so much weight...

With a shaky hand, I take the bottle.

"I love you, Caden," he says, pulling me into a hug. I protest his interruption to my drink, and he looks at me with the saddest eyes.

Then he's standing. The door shuts. And he's gone.

Uncorking the bottle, I raise it to my lips.

The bang of a door slamming into a wall causes me to jerk, and the golden liquid spills all down my shirt. I start to mutter, but a man's voice, loud and angry, cuts me off.

"The great Caden is going to die in his fucking bed. A fitting end for a coward."

My brow furrows as I recognize that voice. Garrett, my once son-in-law, is making a play for power. I promised him a good seat at the table by marrying Molly, but now she's gone.

I raise the bottle to my lips.

They're all gone.

Jonathan is gone.

Molly is gone.

Bonnie is gone.

And now Ryo is gone too.

Killed at his own wedding while I mourned his mother.

I should've been there to protect him.

I should've –

Cruel laughter mocks me – my own demons laughing at my misery before I realize it's coming from the other room. "You're so fucking pathetic," Garret says.

Something hits the floor with a *thud*. "You're not even going to fight back, are you? Too fucking drunk to even stand on your own feet. Let's say we have a little fun then, hmm?"

My brow furrows as I lower the bottle from my lips. My hands shaking, I try to figure out what's disrupting the haze of my months-long bender.

I'm here.

Myers is out there.

But he looks like me.

Is dressed like me.

Probably crawled into bed to look even more like the pathetic man I am.

A slurred curse escaping, I try to rise to my feet.

"You like the alcohol so much," Garrett sneers, "so why don't I give you more of it." Glass shatters in the other room. More cruel laughter hits the ceiling.

I want to yell at Myers to defend himself, to not get slaughtered in my place. He's my younger brother, and I am supposed to be the one protecting him, not the other way around.

I fall through the cupboard door as it swings open. My

face hits the cool tiles, jolting me out of my haze a little bit more.

My little brother needs me.

He's the last family I have left.

He can't die because of me.

I crawl towards the ensuite door and haul myself up its frame. My hands shake on the door handle. I try to twist it, but it refuses to move. An agonized scream ruptures from the other room, and I try to cry out, to let him know I'm coming, but all that spews forth is vomit. The alcohol burns my esophagus, and I sag against the door in a cold sweat.

I'm pathetic.

Weak.

And my brother is going to die because of it.

Because of *her*.

Because she ran into a stupid situation and got herself killed.

Tears fall down my cheeks over all I've lost. I want to die and join her. I want the suffering to end. I want to go back to my bottle.

But first I need to save my baby brother.

Closing my eyes, I reach for my magic. It comes to me quickly, an instinct not even alcohol can rip away from me. I grab hold of the atoms making up the door, inhale calmly even as my brother screams, and then push my power forward. The door rips off its hinges, splinters into five large stakes, and each one buries itself into the throat of the five people hurting my brother.

"You...fool," Myers says as he looks at me with the one eye he has remaining. They scooped the other one out with a broken bottle, and it now lies beside Garrett's body. "They're going to kill me anyway. You should've let my death mean something."

I stare at him as I push some of the alcohol out through my pores. It leaves me shaking and instantly missing the haze I need to survive Sau's death. But Myers needs me right now. I can't fail him like I failed Ryo.

"You're not going to die," I say. "We're going to get you out of here."

"I'm not going unless you are."

"Don't be a fool."

"Like you?"

My eyes narrow. "Myers –"

"I'm not leaving unless you're with me."

"I can't leave. This is Sau's home." *This is where I want to die.*

He struggles to his feet; the pain in his head must be crippling, but he makes his way over to me. "Then protect it for her. She wouldn't want this. This is her legacy."

This is the last of her that's left.

And I'm ruining it. Destroying it.

Falling to my knees, I scream out a sob.

*I'm killing her.*

Myers puts his hand on my back, and I can feel him shaking. I can feel his urge to get me on my feet. I can hear the gunfire outside. I can feel the bodies hitting the ground to move no more.

Reaching into my magic, I offer the five bodies to the void. Their sacrifice lets me pull on dark magic, lets me strengthen the power already inside me. Throwing it out, I erect the ward on our street to hide us from the humans, and then I stop everything.

Every person.

Every bullet.

Every bit of madness.

Walking out of my house – out of *our* house, I pick up the crown I tossed away after my queen's death.

The weight of this Family will forever be mine. I will rebuild it in Sau's honor.

"For you, my sweet girl."

*I will die for you...*
*But right now I will live for you.*

# FORTY-SIX
## CADEN
### 18 APRIL 1963

I stand in the back alley of the library with my brother, Myers no doubt wondering if I'm drunk out of my mind again. I haven't gone a day without a drink, but it's been a long time since I've been that drunk. I'm chasing the buzz not the emptiness. Just something to take a bit of the edge off the broken pieces of my heart.

The Shadow Domain has been reduced to only a few hundred members, but although that is a great fall from the thousands it used to be, it's still a lot higher than the forty-five it fell to after the coup, triggered by Ryo's death.

The Death Hunt has left us alone, no doubt thinking we would kill ourselves while they focused on building their empire to be the new fucking Rome. The Blood Fang, oddly, has ignored us too. Talk on the street says Aleric declared us off limits in October. And now he wants to meet for a parley behind the old library. He didn't even protest me bringing anyone. He only asked me to set up a ward to keep us hidden from the humans.

I've only brought Myers though. I'm not scared of him. The ward, however, is up.

He phases in right on time. We arrived early to check for traps and saw nothing.

Aleric's hair is disheveled. His eyes are bagged and red. He doesn't look like he's slept any better than I have these last few months.

"You look like shit," I say.

"At least I'm not drunk and shit."

We stare at each other, measuring each other, but I am the first to break the silence. I have too many things to do to play his bullshit games. "What do you want, Aleric?"

"I need help staying in the Plane of Monsters."

I tense, my sixth sense blaring. "Why?"

His jaw ticks. His lips stay still.

"You want my help, you'll tell me why."

"None of my contacts know much about the place."

"And you think I do?"

"You married in." He pauses, stills, his body tight as if I hold his world in the palm of my hand. "Do you not?"

I stare at him, assessing his rigid stance. In all the time we've fought each other, in all the stories I've heard about him, he's never been this...serious.

"Why do you want to stay in the Plane of Monsters?" I ask again, my pulse thudding between my ears. I know why...I think. But I want to hear him say it. I want this not to just be a desperate grasp of hope.

He glances away, looks at Myers, then turns his gaze back to me. "Because I thought Sau went back to you after she became Reaper of the Sired."

My pulse stops.

Everything stops but the movement of his lips.

"But she didn't. She went into the Plane of Monsters to

# Madness Behind the Mask

kill us all...and she hasn't come back out."

"She's alive?" It's a croak, a whisper, a desperate plea.

My enemy exhales long and hard. "Yes, and I can bring her back if I have your help."

# FORTY-SEVEN

## HER
DAYS DO NOT EXIST HERE

The screams echo on all sides of me as the vampires are ripped to shreds – eaten or fucked to death by things I can't see. Without my sight, all noise is heightened, and I can hear every *squelch* of intestines being sucked down, every crack of bones between their teeth. I try to listen for Aleric's cocky words as he tries to taunt the beasts in his final moment, but I hear nothing other than painful death.

Cupping my hands together as I kneel on hard ground, I call forth my magic, letting the softest light penetrate this place. I don't feel any better for it, any safer as I see the vampires get eaten in this desolate landscape of dark rocks and no vegetation.

"Help me!" a young woman cries, her arm outstretched in my direction. She's missing half her face – her left eye hanging free, her ear missing. "Help –" She screams as a furry black four-legged beast with quills in a mohawk up its back clamps its jaws around her face.

I scoot back quickly – not from terror but from guilt. Colton's dead eyes haunt me as I look all around. I can hear Caden telling me his wife was pregnant. I can see his disappointment in what I've become.

I can hear Aleric's laughter as he tells me how proud he is. How I'm just like him.

"I'm not!" I cry even as all these mindless deaths say I am. All the Blood Fangs weren't in that gym. I swing my arms around as I stumble through the massacre, my feet slipping on the blood liberally coating the jagged rocks, but I don't need to search to know Aleric isn't here. I was a fool to think I could kill him just because I *wanted* to, was desperate to.

All I've done is added to the mindless killing.

All I've done is become Aleric.

Screaming at the top of my lungs, I let the light go out. Perhaps one of the monsters will eat me. Perhaps I'll fall off this damn mountain and tumble to my death.

The gods know I do not deserve to live.

---

I don't know how many days it's been. I don't even know why I'm still alive.

I want to die. I deserve to die.

But there's a drive in me that's forcing me to keep going. A need to correct the wrongs I've done. I cannot bring the vampires back. I cannot turn back time, but I can still bring peace to St. Augustine, to my family as long as I can get out of this place.

So I ignore my desire to stop, to just rest against a rock as I starve to death, and instead, I just keep moving.

Exhausted with hunger, I follow the trail of slime from some slug-like monster. My light isn't bright enough to spot the beast, and I don't want to get close enough so it can. My bloodline might protect me from being attacked in this place, but I'm not so confident the deal with the djini my ancestor made will stop them from crushing me on accident, say it didn't see me due to the lack of eyes. That seems exactly like the sort of loophole a djini would leave in.

So I keep my distance as I follow the slug down the mountain, across a barren rocky landscape I can barely see. I'm hoping that when it eats, it tears its prey apart rather than swallow it whole, so I'll be able to live off the scraps it leaves behind.

My stomach growling, I march on. I want to escape this place. I want to see Caden and Ryo again.

I *will* escape this place.

I *will* see Caden and Ryo again.

I repeat those affirmative statements over and over, pushing hope into my words.

"I will escape this place. I will see Caden and Ryo again. I will bring peace to St. Augustine once I'm free. Because I will escape this place. I will see Caden and Ryo again. I will bring peace to St. Augustine…"

---

I'm going to die here. I stare down at the end of the mucus trail. It stops abruptly with no sign showing where the slug went. I look up, holding my hands above my head to see if it's suddenly levitated. Nothing but black sky. At least, nothing I can see in my thirty-odd foot diameter of healing light.

I want to scream out my frustration, but I don't. That takes energy I don't have.

Dropping my arms, I stare at the slime left by the slug. Then I drop to my knees and scoop up a bit of the mucus. My stomach growling in pain, I raise it to my lips.

As soon as the slimy wetness hits my tongue, I gag and my hands move away from my mouth. But if I don't eat, I won't live, so I squeeze my eyes shut and force myself to swallow.

I immediately throw it up again, my cheeks billowing out as I catch it before it leaves my lips. Although there is enough for me to try again, I know if I don't manage to swallow this mouthful, I won't manage to take another slurp.

So I fight it down, gagging many times before it settles in my stomach. I gag a few more times after too before scooping my hands back through the goop I'm kneeling in.

"I will escape this place," I whisper as I raise the next mouthful to my lips. "I will see Caden and Ryo again." Whatever it takes, I *will*.

---

*Water.* The word is a croak even inside my head, my throat too parched to sleep. I drop to my knees and cup my hands at the shore of the lake. I'm at the bottom of the mountain, and the rocks have given way to vegetation. After drinking my fill, I grab whatever berries and flowers I can find and shove them into my mouth, trusting my healing magic to counter any poisons I might be eating.

My stomach is bloated, and my muscles are weak, but I'm not dead yet.

Falling onto my ass, I stare at the shore, watching the ripples of the lake move back and forth. It's calming me, soothing me, damn near hypnotizing me, so it takes me a moment before I bolt up, my eyes wide.

I can see without using my healing magic.

It's still darker than nights on Earth, but compared to the utter blackness I've been living in, it might as well be full on daylight.

I croak in place of a laugh as I look around. Trees cover all sides of the lake. So alien and yet so familiar to the ones from home. Giant palm-like leaves stretch out above the one I'm sitting under, and I envision weaving them into a roof as I stare at them.

Walking mindlessly won't change anything now that I've found water. And where there's water, there will be animals coming to drink. I need to stay in one place so I can conserve my energy and try to open a portal back home from this side.

Standing up, forcing my aching muscles to move, I start to search for a place to build my temporary home.

---

I'm certain it's been years. It feels like years. My hair has grown from my waist to my ass, and the amount of time I catch it on things makes me yearn to cut it off. But it's my only source of telling time, so I can't get rid of it.

Standing at the shore of the lake, my belly full of some cat-mixed-chicken thing that came to drink, I try to pull on my magic. But it stays trapped inside of me, refusing to come out. The only thing I've managed to do in this damn place is call on my healing light. I can't access anything else – no spells, no wards, no summoning circles to call an eknor demon companion. Just my damn white light.

I know I should be thankful to have even that, but I'm not. I want my shadow magic. I want to be able to open a portal back to my family.

Growling, I kick a rock into the lake. Maybe I should start moving again. Maybe there are people somewhere – poor, unfortunate people like me who got sucked into this place and are doing their best to survive.

But here I have certain water and a much better chance at finding food. It doesn't make sense to go.

And yet I do – too desperate to stay still.

---

Leaving was a damn stupid idea. I'm starving again and dehydrated. The world has gone into its pitch-black cycle, so I am guiding myself with my healing light. A monster growls behind me, no doubt as hungry as I and frustrated that it can't eat me. But I've grown used to the snapping of teeth and the brushing of things across my skin as monsters follow me, only to soon leave once they realize I'm no good as a meal.

But this thing doesn't go. It just lingers right on the outskirts of my light so I can't see what it is. All I know is that it's big. Bigger than a giraffe sort of big. But despite its size, it doesn't register on my other senses. I can't hear it when it moves, its feet silent. I can't smell it even when the wind blows from its direction. And it seems to be able to phase short distances, appearing on one side of me, then the other.

When I manage to find something to eat, I throw a bit of meat at it. It's not a lot – probably too small for it to even bother with, but I can't spare much when I barely have enough for myself.

The thing ignores the food entirely, just staring at me, so I walk over to the morsel and pick it up. Shoveling it into my mouth, I study the beast a bit closer and realize it's missing a leg. I've seen a lot of weird creatures in this place, but none of them have had an odd number of legs.

A lightbulb moment flashes in front of me, and I cup my hands together. Concentrating hard, I build up more light, nearly doubling my usual output. Then I sit down and wait for a different monster to get lured in by it.

It doesn't take long.

A scaly animal with a long tail and an upturned snout

comes up to me. It's about the size of a car, and its mouth is full of needle-like teeth. It bares them at me as it hops around, trying to figure out how to eat me. With all of its attention on me and my light, it doesn't notice the beast creeping up behind it.

As soon as it gets close enough, my monster pounces, attacking it with praying-mantis-knife-like legs. It stabs it through the back, and my heart races at how efficient of a killing machine this thing is even with its missing leg. With the scaly creature mostly dead, my monster starts to eat.

My mouth waters at the sight of so much food, and I inch forward.

My monster tenses, but it doesn't stop eating.

I take another step forward.

It ignores me this time.

I'm right beside the scaly creature now. Reaching out with my sharpened rock knife, I try to cut a bit of flesh off for myself, but the scales are rock-hard and my knife can't get through. A frustrated noise escapes me.

The monster pauses eating to look at me. Then it raises a front praying-mantis-blade-like leg, and I jump back, my heart racing. It slams it down into the flesh where I was just trying to cut it. When it pulls its leg out, it stays watching me, like it's expecting me to do something.

I hesitate for a moment, then stick my knife into the nearly-dead monster's wound and scoop out a bit of meat. My monster makes a weird noise, then lowers its head to pull off more chunks for itself.

My mouth drops open as I stare at it.

Then I laugh in pure enjoyment of finding a friend. Or a pet. Or just a momentary companion. Whatever it is, I'm grateful for its company.

I've been so utterly alone.

# FORTY-EIGHT
## HER
### DAYS DO NOT EXIST HERE

My hair is down to my knees when I see it. My heart jumps into my throat as a flash of familiarity hits me. But then the thing is gone, having phased away, and I am left wondering if I just imagined it in my sleepy state.

Olivia – the name I've given my monster lifts her head as she feels me move, ever alert. She's curled up around me, something I was originally hesitant about given her blade-like legs, but on closer inspection I found them to be more like fangs. Good for piercing, less so for slicing.

She nudges me and makes a series of clucking noises. I rub the top of her small beak, soothing her until she falls back asleep. After I healed her after she got into a fight with another of her kind, our relationship has been solid.

Once she's out, I stand up, careful not to wake her, and walk over to the spot where I thought I saw...someone appear and vanish.

There's nothing here. No trace of anyone at all.

Certain I'm finally going crazy, I shake my head, then head back to Olivia, where I lie down and close my eyes.

Picturing Caden's smile, I yearn for him as I fall asleep.

---

I definitely don't imagine it this time. I'm well awake, not on the edges of sleep, and he was *there*.

I'm not sure who. I'm not sure what. They were gone before I could discern any clear features. I just have that same strong feeling of familiarity.

He feels like...home. Like hope.

I can't leave this spot. He could come back. He could be my way out. Hope strangling me, I sit down and wait for him to return.

---

I run my hands through my hair, brushing it as best as I can. It takes me hours every day, but I have the energy now that we've perfected our hunting technique. And the gods know I have the time.

I try to picture Caden as I brush it. He kept it beautiful while I was in a coma. He loves it, but I can barely recall his face now. My hair is all I have left of him, and I am terrified of the day I'll have to cut it, as stupid as it is.

"Caden loves me..." My fingers still as that statement hits home, and I start, my entire body tensing as my back goes ramrod straight. "Caden... It's Caden!"

Olivia perks up at my shout. She's become used to me talking and has learned a few simple commands as well as my differences in tone. Curious, she nudges me with her head.

I want to throw my arms around her in a hug, but I'm pretty sure if I do, she'll see it as an attack. She might like me, but she's still a wild animal. I have no idea how old she is, how much time she spent alone. Past experiences could easily have her turning on me, and wouldn't that be ironic? Surviving all this time only to die when Caden has finally figured out a way to save me.

"It's Caden," I say as I stroke from between her saucer-size eyes to the start of her beak. "He's looking for me. He's figured out a way to search this place. I have to help him. I have to give him a way to figure out where I am!"

I scramble up, my head swinging left and right to see if there's anything I can make a sign with. Though what will they say? I can't give him a place name. I can't give him directions. And what happens when it turns pitch-black again? The world has been in its "light" cycle for a while. It'll switch back soon. Then any sign will be useless.

No. I can't think like that, can't let the despair win. Caden will find me. He loves me. He won't give up and neither will I.

Turning to Olivia, I pull my knife out of my crudely made pouch of leather. I start to dig it into a rock I pick up, scratching an A into it, thinking an S would be too hard for her to do. Any human letter will be enough for Caden. She looks at me, her large eyes blinking. It takes me a long time, but I eventually get her to copy me.

---

We leave signs with an arrow pointing in the direction we're traveling. I tried to stay in place as long as I could, but we have to follow the movements of our prey.

My hair sits heavy on my head now. When loose, it hangs down to my feet. I need to cut it soon.

*I can't.*

Not until I get out of –

Olivia swings towards me with a cry, lifting a leg to skewer me straight through the head. "What are you –"

The world vanishes. My stomach drops. My balance is thrown off completely, and I squeeze my eyes shut as I fall to my hands and knees. My fingers dig into something soft and foreign as they curl in the ground. A warm hand circles around my back.

"You're okay, Sau. You're okay."

"Caden!" My head snaps up. I try to open my eyes, but the blinding light has me crying out and flinching away. He stands quickly. I reach for him, not needing my eyes to feel him moving, having got so used to the dark. A weird hum starts from one side of the room, something I have never heard before, but it kind of sounds like the radio when it's on but not tuned to anything.

"Leave your eyes shut," he says as he comes back to me.

Then his lips are on mine. His hands are between my thighs. I'm naked, my clothes having turned into rags a long time ago. He spreads my legs apart. There is the pull of a zipper and then his cock is being pushed into me.

I cry out at the sudden burn. "Wait!"

"I can't. It's been too long." He shoves in on a groan. I try to scoot back as the pain spreads, but he grabs hold of my hips and anchors me to him.

He thrusts into me hard and fast, and soon the pain turns into pleasure. "Wrap your legs around me."

I do as he says, wanting this, *needing* this connection I've been without for so long. My heels dig into Caden's ass as my hands cling to his shoulders. I try not to think about how dirty I am. I had a wash in a stream relatively recently, but I've also had multiple meals since then. I don't even want to think about my breath. The raw smell of meat that clings to me.

But Caden doesn't seem to care. He's obsessed with me,

running his hands everywhere. Squeezing my breasts, pinching my nipples, rubbing my clit as he pounds into me. He sits us up right, placing me on his lap. "Come for me, Sau," he rasps, his breath hot in my ear.

I arch my back, pleasure filling me despite the lack of pain. I want this. I need this. "I love you," I say as I dig my nails into his back and fuck him like an animal.

His thrusts falter for a second as he lets me ride him. Then his hands are in my hair, his tongue is in my mouth, and his cock is jerking inside me as he comes.

The feel of his pulsing release triggers my own, and my pussy clenches around him as I scream. My orgasm leaves me shaken and exhausted. But his doesn't. He starts up again, rocking into me. Kissing my neck, then my breasts.

I dig my hands into his hair. My brow furrows at the feel of it. With my eyes closed, I run my fingers through the strands. It's straight instead of curly. Caden has curly hair...doesn't he?

I try to remember, but my memory is nothing but a black world full of monsters. I don't even remember who Olivia was named after. All I know is she was important to me. She was important to *us*. To Caden and me.

Caden...

Caden has curly hair...doesn't he?

"Gods, you feel so good." He groans as he comes inside me again. But the feel of his orgasm doesn't send pleasure through me this time. It twists my stomach and claws at my heart.

Forcing my eyes open, fighting through the agony of the bright light, I look at Caden.

His hair is black now. And straight.

Popping his lips off my nipple, he looks up at me, a smirk in his eyes.

In his dark-gray eyes – the eyes of my enemy.

# FORTY-NINE

## ALERIC
### 25 FEBRUARY 1984

She tries to fight me, slapping her hands against my chest, bucking her hips to throw me off. It just makes me harder. I want to come inside her again. Need to fill her with my cum before Caden gets here.

These last twenty-three years without her have been so dull. All the women I took in her place were nothing but disappointments.

I wish I could have longer with her, but Caden knows where I've gone. He knows I have her. I returned within seconds every time I phased while we searched for her. It won't take a genius to figure out why I haven't this time.

"Get off me!" she yells as she tries to gouge out my eyes. She nearly manages before I twist my head away. Her nail digs a sharp line into my cheek. The pain makes my cock throb. I'm going to come again.

"Olivia!" she screams, and there is a sudden presence

behind me.

I phase away and land by the video camera. A monster stands in front of me, one of its front legs piercing the carpet where I just was, right between Sau's legs. It turns its head to me, and I grab the camera and vanish, this time arriving in the gym Caden and I were working out of.

A fist slams into my jaw. "What have you done?" he seethes, but I can tell by the fury in his sharp green eyes that he already knows. My cock, after all, is still swinging in the breeze and wet with her cum.

"Just giving her what she wanted," I drawl.

He swings for me again, too drunk to use his magic. He's been in a constant booze-state since she left. I let his fist connect with my chest. The pain zings all the way to my cock. The thought of taking him right after his wife – while he watches me fuck her on camera makes me so hard it hurts. I'm not into men, but I am into the pain that will cause Sau.

She deserves to suffer for abandoning me for twenty-three years.

Turning on the playback, I show it to him. His jaw goes slack, his fire doused under his depression as he watches his sweet wife ride my cock in a desperate need for her own release. I set the video camera down on the table. He walks towards it, his eyes never leaving the tiny screen, pulled to it like a magnet.

"This is my particular favorite moment," I say as Sau tells me she loves me. She fucks me hard and fast after that. She comes soon after.

I replay it from the beginning as I step behind him. I push his torso down, bending him at the waist, his body putty as his mind is lost in the haze of the camera. I lean down to his ear as one hand goes around his waist to undo the button of his pants. "Just think of how much you could hurt her when she comes in seeing my cock up your ass."

He doesn't move. Doesn't respond.

And then he does.

His magic wraps around me, catching me off guard and freezing me entirely in place.

"I could tear you apart atom by fucking atom," he says, his words a monotone but vibrating with strong emotions. "I could rip the skin off your body inch by inch. Then tear off your muscles, rip out your bones. I could drain you dry or pull all your organs out of your fucking cock.

"But I'm going to let you go because you brought her back to me." He stops, then turns to look at me, his bright green eyes searching mine. "Is she alive?"

He releases his grip on my mouth to let me move it the tiniest bit. "Yes."

He glances away, a thousand emotions painted on his face.

"Then get out of here. And if I ever see you again, I will do all those things I mentioned."

He releases me, then picks up my camera. He stares at the screen for a few seconds, then throws it across the gym. It smashes against the wall, but the amount of pieces it flies into isn't natural. He's ripped it apart with his magic.

"Go!"

The word chases me as I phase away. But when I land in my house, my hand goes immediately to my cock. The game has started up again, and one day Sau will have to choose.

Feeling her wet heat still coating me, I pump my cock and groan.

# FIFTY

## CADEN
### 25 FEBRUARY 1984

She's having a shower in our ensuite when I get home. Myers is outside our bedroom door, looking worried, but all I can see is his one eye that got taken from him even though he's reforged it with his magic. He lost it because of *her*.

We lost Ryo because I was too busy mourning *her*.

The Shadow Domain nearly crumbled because *she left us*.

She left *me*.

There's part of me that wants to just go in there and tear her apart. Mourning her was easier than dealing with all these new feelings. The relief. The pain. The disgust. The hatred. The love.

The fear that I have lost her.

*"I love you."* She said that to *Aleric*. Because he's the one who saved her. Because, for all I know, they've been fucking each other on the Plane of Monsters for the last two

decades.

Perhaps she was never even there. Perhaps she was in his house all this time, sucking his cock and telling him she loved him.

"Be gentle with her, Caden," Myers says as he stands in front of my bedroom door, between me and my wife. "She looks like shit." His eyes track me up and down. "Even worse than you."

"She's my wife, not yours."

"She's my sister-in-law."

I laugh, but it borders on the edge of insanity. "Get the fuck out of my way, Myers."

His face flattens, that reaper mask coming down. But then he steps to the side, and I go in to see my wife. I fiddle with the two incubus potions I have in my pocket. I didn't stop to grab her a succubus one. I don't want her to feel pleasure. I want to punish her. I want her to hurt like I'm hurting. *"I love you, Aleric."*

I open the bathroom door without a sound. The hiss of the spray covers the soft thumps of my feet as they hit the tiles. I stop outside the shower, but I don't pull back the curtain. I can hear her crying and see her scrubbing her thighs, but I can't find the understanding I always had for her. The unquestioning love.

*"I love you, Aleric."*

Standing here watching her, part of me wants to just leave. Leave this bathroom, this house, this damn fucking city. Leave *her*. But I can't.

Because she is everything to me even when I want her to be nothing.

*"I love you, Aleric."*

I can't get those words out of my head. I can't stop seeing how she orgasmed on him – willingly and without pain.

"The first thing you did when you got back," I say, my

words slow and calm, "was fuck him."

She swings towards me, but she doesn't draw back the barrier between us. The sound of her voice after all this time doesn't stop the pain. "I thought he was you."

"He looks nothing like me."

"I had my eyes closed –"

I laugh, cutting her off. "You expect me to believe that? That after all the years we spent together, you forgot what my cock feels like? My hands? I would know you in the dark, Sau! I would know you if I were mute and blind. If I lost all feelings in my hands, I'd still know the woman I love!" My chest heaves, the pain damn near unbearable.

"I thought you were dead!" I carry on. "I thought my wife was dead instead of fucking around like some damn whore! I mourned you, Sau! I mourned you, and in my grief, Ryo died. Because of you!"

She makes a choked noise, but no words form to soothe away my pain.

"I came back, and three of our children, Delilah, and our grandchild were dead. And you were gone. You went to Aleric all on your own, without taking any of the men with you. Why would you do something like that? Why would you not want anyone to know where you were? Did you fuck him that night? Have you been there all this time?"

She whimpers, but I keep pushing. I can't stop, the dam of my fears and pain blowing open.

"Four of our children died because of him, Sau!"

*"I love you, Aleric."*

"How the *fuck* do you love someone like that!"

"I don't!"

"I saw you fuck him! I heard you say the words!"

"I thought he was you! I promise, Caden." She's bowing in on herself now, her silhouette shaking. "I thought he was you."

"He looks nothing like me!" My voice cracks as I yell

those words. My chest heaves. My hands clench – white knuckles and bleeding moon-shaped grooves. "Maybe I should remind you what I feel like then," I snap.

I yank aside the curtain and step into the shower as I pull out the two vials in my pocket. I drink them both in the time it takes her to turn towards me. Tears streak down her cheeks. I lower my gaze, my eyes on the thighs wet with another man's come. Crowding her against the wall, I lift her onto my hips as my cocks grow and shift under the magic potions.

"Caden, please. Don't –"

I slap her across the face, then pinch her jaw together. "Shut up. I don't want to hear another word out of your whore mouth."

Her eyes widen, sickening me. I hate the sting on my palm. Hate the hatred inside of me. I love her. I swore I would never hurt her, and yet, here I am feeding her my own pain.

Dropping her feet to the ground, I turn her around and push her head against the wall. I can't look at her while I do this. I just need to use her, to hurt her, to get rid of all this pain. Share it on her shoulders.

Lining up my cocks with her holes, I shove in.

She screams, her muscles tearing as I force my way in. I stop at the start of her cervix, barely in past the head of my new cock. It's different to the one I used decades ago. It has backward hooking spikes all up and down its length to clean her out rather than ridges to give her pleasure. I growl as I try to shove in deeper, but it won't go without tearing through her organs. The one in her ass doesn't have any resistance, so I pull out of her pussy and slide it between her thighs as I ram all the way up her ass.

She screams again. Blood runs down my cock as I fuck her. The knotting triggers, growing inside of her, stopping me from pulling out.

I slam in deep and close my eyes, trying not to look at the tear-stained face of my wife.

But instead I see her fucking Aleric behind my eyelids. She rides his cock and drags her nails all down his back as she screams, *"I love you."*

*"I love you, Aleric."*

*"I love you."*

Screaming, I slam my fist into the wall beside her head. My knuckles break. The tiles crack. I slam my fist into it again until the bones are jagged peaks poking out of my skin. Then I grab both her hips, hammer in hard and fast a couple more times.

"I hate you," I growl. "I hate you for what you did to our children. I hate you for leaving me. I hate you for fucking the man who took everything from us. I hate you, Sau Shadow.

"I. Hate. *You!*"

Digging my nails into her skin, I shove her away as I rip my cock free. The knot tears out of her ass, hurting me and hurting her. Blood runs down the two of us, but the agony in my heart wins out.

Nothing else can ever compare.

*"I love you, Aleric. I love you."*

Stepping out of the shower, I leave my wife bleeding in a ball underneath the spray.

And I don't care.

# FIFTY-ONE

## HER

### 25 FEBRUARY 1985

I cry for a long time as all my memories come crashing down on me at once. The names of my children. The love Caden used to have for me. The pain Aleric gave me over and over again. And I remember how I wanted to blood bond with my husband. How the worst thing in the world could be him hating me.

Yet here we are with him doing just that.

I want to curl into a ball and cry for days, but the door to the bathroom opens, ruining my sanctuary.

"Sau?" Myers comes in, but I can't bring myself to lift my head, can't pretend I'm okay when every part of me wishes I never left the Plane of Monsters. At least there, survival was only physical instead of emotional. At least there, I forgot all the people who'd brought me pain, both in their actions and mine.

"Are you okay?" he asks, the question hesitant and not

really after an answer. He already knows it. It's clear in the blood swirling around me. In the shaking of my body.

"He hates me," I whisper as he turns the water off.

"No," he says softly as he lays a towel over me. "No, he doesn't. He's just going through a lot, Sau. But he loves you. He loves you more than anything in the world."

I shake my head, knowing he's wrong. However Aleric managed it, he showed Caden what he did to me, and that severed all the love he had for me. "I thought it was him," I say. "I really thought he'd come to take me home. Why didn't he come for me?"

"He did, Sau. He worked alongside Aleric for decades to bring you back."

Knowing that hurts even more. My husband suffered that vampire's presence, suffered having to be the one who stayed behind, and the first thing I did on my return was hurt him. "I'm so sorry," I say.

"I know."

"But he doesn't." I close my eyes as I struggle to calm my breathing, my thoughts. "How do I fix this, Myers?" My breath hitches. "Aleric came in me twice. What if I'm pregnant with his –"

"It's highly unlikely, Sau. There's only been a handful of hybrids in existence."

"But it could happen." I look up at him, terrified that I could have a little Aleric growing in me soon. Terrified that I've lost Caden forever with that one act because I know I won't be able to bring myself to get rid of it, to lose yet another child.

"There's a potion you can take to be sure," he says. "I'll get you one tomorrow."

"Thank you."

"Now, come on. Let's get you into bed. You need your rest."

He pulls me up, and I wrap the towel tight around me.

He grabs another three towels to dry my hair before he guides me to bed. He doesn't ask if I want to cut my hair, and I'm grateful for that, unable to handle that question right now. I planned to cut it when I got home, but with Caden mad at me… It'll feel too much like I'm cutting him out of my life.

"How do I make it stop?" I ask as he tucks me into bed. "How do I make all the pointless killing *stop*?" Angry tears flow down my cheeks as he stares at me in silence. "I tried by killing all those vampires, but the Blood Fangs are still here. Ryo is dead." My heart twists at the loss of my last child. He died because of Aleric. And me. Because I left my family in an attempt to save them.

"How can I make it *stop*, Myers?"

He looks at me, really looks at me, searching my soul as I lay it all bare.

"I'm tired of having everything taken from me," I say. "I'm tired of not being strong enough to save those I love. I need to end this. I *have* to end this. Tell me how."

He sighs as he shakes his head. "I'm sorry, Sau, but there isn't a way to end this. It's been going on for too long, and you're only one person."

I flinch away from the truth of his words, but I don't care for those statistics. "You're wrong," I say. "And I'm going to show you."

He lays a hand on my shoulder. "You do that," he says. "I would love to see it." He leans down to kiss the top of my head. "Just don't leave Caden again, Sau. He won't survive it."

Standing, he leaves me alone in my grief.

Only, it's not just my grief that's with me. It's rage. It's determination. And as my shadows move across the floor, it's Olivia, too, as she comes through to curl in the bed around me.

"I'm not alone," I whisper as I stare at my hand. Olivia rubs her beak against my palm with a small *cluck*, and I smile. "I'm not alone." I can train a whole damn army.

---

Eight months later, I am standing behind the library under the light of the moon. There is a ward around the street, hiding us from the humans, but it's a bit pointless. There aren't any out at two in the morning. Not here at least. Behind the library isn't the local "cool spot."

But hopefully, what happens today will be the coolest thing to ever happen in St. Augustine.

I shift nervously as I wait for the three men to arrive, not because I worry they will hurt me but because I'm afraid they'll be stubborn, idiotic men who would rather die than listen to a woman.

And if they choose that, then I'm going to have to go through with my threat of killing them, then call a parley with whoever replaces them.

As much as I'm sick of death, I'll do that as much as I need to. Delilah told me I would have nine more sons, but I'm not bringing anyone else into a world with this much suffering.

So the suffering will end today, one way or another.

Caden is the first to arrive, and the sight of him breaks my heart. I have no idea where he's been for the past few months. He walked out of our bathroom and never came back. Myers has kept in touch with him, sent him things to sign off on given he's still the official Boss of our gang, but he refused to share Caden's location. Myers' loyalty is to the Shadow Domain...not to the wife of his brother.

"You look good," I say as he approaches. He's early, a whole fifteen minutes before the hour. I arrived early just on the chance he did.

"You're a liar," he says.

I flinch, then swallow hard. "You look good to me."

An awkward silence descends, crushing me under its weight. Caden's eyes are baggy with the lack of sleep, as are mine, but his eyes look sharper, less twisted in pain. I wonder if that means he's ready to forgive me...or if he's cut me out of his life for good. My breath catching, I lift a hand to my hair. It's twisted in a bun atop my head, still not cut.

"How have you been?" I ask, needing to fill the silence with something.

"Fine."

I roll my lips in, catching my sarcastic comment, then pushing it out anyway, wishing we could talk like we used to. "Now who's the liar?" I tease.

He stares at me, no smile curling his lips, and I wonder if I've fucked up even more.

But then he sighs, and for a second, his shields drop. "I miss you."

"Then come home."

"I can't."

"You can. I can sleep in a different bedroom. We can –"

"Well, isn't this sickening?" At Aleric's sudden arrival, I stiffen, then turn towards him.

"If you find it sickening, then gouge your eyes out."

He smirks as he looks me up and down. "Divorced life suits you."

"We're not divorced," Caden and I say at the same time, and I look at him, hope in my eyes. He holds it for a second, then glances away. "Why are we here, Sau? You must know talks of peace are useless by now."

"No, they're not. But we need to wait for Antonio to get here."

"Then say it so we can end this parley, and I can kill you already."

Caden takes a step towards the newest arrival, then stops. My heart twisting, I turn to look at the alpha of the

Death Hunt.

"I have a treaty I drew up with Myers' help. You are all going to sign it." Pulling the stapled pieces of paper out of my bag, I hand them each a copy. Antonio, unsurprisingly, refuses to take it. "The faster you read, the faster this can be over."

He growls as he snatches it from me. I just manage to release it fast enough before it tears.

"You want me to give up Miami?" Aleric snorts.

"To the Death Hunt, yes, and in exchange, we'll end our sex trafficking operations."

"Including David?" He quirks a brow, and I nod.

"David too. It's time we put aside our grievances. I'll never forgive him for what he did to me, but I can let it go as a show of commitment to this treaty."

"No," Caden says.

I turn to him, but he's right behind me, and he shoves the treaty to my chest. "David suffers for the rest of his fucking long life. I'm not moving on that."

"But I'm okay with it, Caden. I want –"

"He didn't just hurt you, Sau!"

I jerk back, my pulse hammering.

"Ooooh. More trouble in paradise," Aleric teases, but I block him out, all my attention on my husband.

"You said he didn't touch Olivia," I whisper, praying he tells me I have it wrong. That he means someone else in a different way.

"I lied," he says.

"Why?" I cry.

His eyes soften just the tiniest bit. "So you wouldn't blame yourself."

I roll my lips in as a shudder rolls through me. I want to fall into his arms. I want to grieve our girl properly, want to scream and sob over her death being far from peaceful, but showing any weakness here will end this peace treaty before it even begins.

Crying won't bring her back.

Screaming won't fix the pain inside me.

But this treaty will bring peace for all our children after.

Closing my eyes, I exhale. Then I open them and look solely at my husband. "We'll end our sex trafficking, but we'll keep David to do with as we please." I can let my grievances with the Death Hunt and the Blood Fangs go, but I will make David suffer for the rest of his miserable life for what he did to Olivia.

Caden stares at me, his eyes wet, but then he nods. I lift a hand to cover his hand on my chest, the papers between his palm and me. Giving him back his hand, I implore him to keep reading.

"I'm not signing this," Antonio says. "I don't care what fucking things you offer me. The only way you'll get your peace is in death."

I turn to him, having known he would be the hardest one to convince. I stole his wife from him. Killed his three babies before he even got to hold them.

"I'm sorry, Antonio, for what I did to Siome." He tenses at her name, and I let my guilt show clear on my face. "I was a stupid girl raised to believe all werewolves should be eradicated. I didn't see them as people, but I do now. You and Siome wanted peace once. You can honor that today by —"

His hand is around my throat in a second, his claws nearly piercing my skin. "You know *nothing*."

"Release her, Antonio," Caden says. "Or you will not have your fingers when I make you."

I raise a hand up to stop my husband. "You're wrong," I wheeze out, looking into the wolf's eyes. "I didn't know anything then, but I do now. I know the pain of losing children. I've watched people I love die right in front of me. I know the pain you carry every day because I carry it too.

# Madness Behind the Mask

We all do. But it's time to end the cycle." Reaching up, I clasp my hand over his. "You have a little boy now, Antonio. Sign the treaty for him." Myers told me all about his pup. He doesn't believe Antonio loves his new mate, but he does love his son.

He growls low in his throat as his eyes dip to his hand, and I know he wishes to crush my windpipe. Snarling, he releases me and steps back.

"And if we don't sign?" Aleric asks.

I take great pleasure in looking him in the eye when I say, "Then you will die here, and I will hand the papers to your heir."

He laughs, the seriousness of the meeting dissipating.

"You might be Reaper of the Sired," Antonio sneers. "But I can kill you with one hand behind my back."

"Of course you could," I say in complete honesty. I could train for a lifetime and still never match his speed and power. "But you can't kill Olivia."

Holding his gaze, I twirl my fingers until the shadows build beside me. As soon as Olivia's first leg reaches up into our world, he steps back. She pulls herself out with a shrill cry, her head swiveling around to look at each Boss, assessing who she needs to kill.

"Or Jonathan." A dark feline with a row of red quills running up his back and two large teeth hanging past his jaw climbs out next.

"Or Bonnie." A truck-sized spider with a dark-purple pattern on her back.

"Or Molly." A snake-like creature made of feathers with two bright wings that draw the eye as they shake so fast they buzz.

"Or Ryo." A roc flies out, its wingspan large enough to touch both ends of the alley.

"I have a whole army I can call out within seconds. Sign the treaty or die. I'm sure I will not have to cut my way through every member of your gangs before I find someone who will."

The silence is deafening. Antonio Garcia still looks like he wants to rip my spinal cord out through my anus, but he isn't stupid enough to try. Aleric is staring at me in awe, not even bothering to hide his boner. My eyes shift to Caden, wanting so badly for him to support me in this.

He stares at me, a flicker of pride in his eyes before he tamps it down. "Did you bring a pen?"

Smiling hard, I pull a quill out of my bag and hand it to him. He takes it, knowing that it writes in blood. It is a common tool in swearing magical oaths.

I pull out the official treaty document on a clipboard, and he takes that too. Signing quickly, he gives it back to me. With a soft exhale, I turn to the other two.

"Well, if it's going to get me a smile like that, then hand it over." My lips flatten into a line. "Or not," Aleric drawls.

"You would rather die?" I challenge.

"Over a smile from you? Most certainly."

"You're delusional."

He smiles a lazy smile. "We've been over this, love. I'm only crazy. Not delusional."

My cheeks heating, I glare at him.

"Come on," he says. "Show us you're serious about this whole peace thing, or would you kill me over a smile?"

I bare my teeth at him.

"Mmm. That doesn't seem like the one Caden got."

"Fuck you."

"You've already done that, love. *Twice*."

Caden goes to swing at him, but I signal to Molly, and she wraps her body around him in an instant. To strike another on the ground blessed by the Peaceful Goddess Eirine would, ironically, kill you. Antonio was pushing the line. Caden would've barreled right over it.

*For me.*

I smile at that, letting my eyes lose focus as I look in Aleric's direction.

He steps right up to me, then leans in to whisper in my ear. "Seeing you like this reminds me of how you came around my cock. That's better than any smile."

I jerk back, wanting to strike him myself, but I don't. "Do me a favor and don't sign the damn treaty," I hiss.

He laughs as he plucks the quill from my hand and signs his signature above Caden's. Then he offers it to the wolf. "Let's end this already. I have a whore pleasuring my men while she waits for my return, and I don't want her dead by the time I get back."

His jaw ticks as he yanks the quill to him. He signs a name that hurts my heart: *Siome*. And then he signs his under hers.

Straightening, he passes it to me. I start to put it back in my bag, but he grabs my wrist. "Sign it."

"I'm not a Boss."

"He's right," Aleric says. "You're forcing this treaty. It's only right that you sign it."

I glance at Caden. "But he's –"

"Do it, Sau."

Swallowing, I place the quill under his name. Changing my mind, I move it beside his and sign.

A sharp prick of pain emits from my right index finger as my blood is transferred to the page.

When I look up, Antonio is already gone. Aleric phases soon after, though not before blowing me a kiss, and then it's just Caden and me.

"Come home with me," I say, wanting to fix things with my husband.

He shakes his head. "I can't. Whenever I look at you, all I see is him inside you."

He turns and walks away, taking my heart with him. I press a hand to my lips, biting back the pain that wants to escape.

I might have lost everything I ever wanted, but at least St. Augustine will finally know peace.

That is enough.

It has to be.

# PART FIVE:

## A MASKED LOVER

# FIFTY-TWO

## HER
### 31 OCTOBER 1987

*Two years later...*

I'm dressed in a floor-length red open-back gown with a slit that cuts nearly all the way up to my naked pussy. Strappy black heels adorn my feet, and a mask hides my identity. Black fox ears curve up from the top of it, satin rose petals decorate it between the eyes, and my mouth is hidden by an intricate pattern of black lace.

My husband once said he would be able to recognize me in the dark, if he were blind and his fingers numb. I want to see if that's still true. And if it is...if he'll come to me. They say these masked balls give you a freedom to be a stranger for the night. To work things out with your husband or wife without restriction. Touching my hair, I really hope that's true.

My nerves tight, I walk down the deserted alley as the

noises of the night sound behind me – car horns being held down, music blaring from speakers, drunken college students patrolling the streets with high-pitched giggles.

A well-dressed man stands at the alley, in front of a closed door with his arms crossed. Thick with muscles, they bulge beneath his dark-blue button-up shirt. His eyes pierce mine in the dark of night. I don't recognize him, and I wonder if he's human or witch.

Pulling the gold card out of my black clutch, I show it to him. He takes it and flips it over, checking it isn't a fake pass to the most exclusive secret club in all of Georgia. Without a word, he offers it back, then opens the door behind him.

I'm instantly hit by the sounds and smells of sex. The slapping of hips. The aroma of cum mixed with sweat. The groans and moans that spike my pulse and make it beat harder than the bass blaring through the speakers.

Stepping through the door, I swallow down my doubts about having come here. Punishment and Sin is owned by my estranged husband, and although he rarely frequents, I know he'll be here tonight. I just don't know if he'll care that I am.

Exhaling out my nerves, I step further into the club. Soft red light strobes across the place, lighting up bodies dancing on the floor and fucking against the walls. The sofas and chaises strewn about the place are all covered in naked or barely concealed flesh, the wooden tables near them creaking too.

A woman in black lacy lingerie strips inside a gold metal birdcage hanging like a chandelier above us. A double staircase leads up to a balcony that only contains a handful of people. Tuxedo-dressed guards stand with their hands in front of them, their eyes scanning the crowd to keep an eye on any trouble makers.

The rooms behind them are for the VIPs who have

enough money to buy their privacy in this sea of sex. Some doors will still linger open, inviting others into their space. Some will be shut but the blinds of the room left wide so people can still watch. I wonder if Caden is up there, enjoying some bitch who isn't me.

Two years is a long time to expect him to be celibate even if I have. Men, supposedly, have stronger needs.

My pulse kicks as movement on the balcony draws my attention. A man in a skull mask with small metal spikes protruding across every inch below his jaw stands in the middle of it, his hands gripping the rail as he leans over to look at the floor below. Chin-length white hair curtains his face with jagged edges, giving him an air of mystery and sophistication.

He is the only one still fully dressed, and rings glisten on his fingers as the light strobes over him.

And then he's gone, hidden in the darkness.

"Miss?"

Blinking, I pull my gaze away from the balcony and focus on the naked woman in front of me. The only thing she's wearing is a black lace collar – marking her as the property of the club. As *Caden's*. She won't be touched tonight, at least not here. Those that do will have their hands broken and their balls severed.

My eyes on her collar, I want to strangle her with it.

"What color collar would you like?" She holds up a tray of black satin with rows of simple ribbon across it. "The green means you're open to anything and consent isn't needed. Yellow is ask first. Red is don't approach me; I will come to you if interested."

"What's black?" I ask as if I don't know, looking at the two lace collars laid out in the top right corner of the tray.

"Those are for a special VIP."

"But there's two of them. So how are they only for one person?" My voice is strained beneath the light air I force past my lips, jealousy clawing just beneath my throat.

"It's for the women he chooses," she says. Leaning in, she smiles as her eyes roam down my body. "Hang around for a bit, and I'm sure you'll be chosen. He's already here and has a thing for dark-haired goddesses." Winking, she straightens.

After a second of hesitation, I reach for a red collar at the back of the tray, but just as I brush the fabric of one, a strong calloused hand closes over mine. Electricity burns down my arm, jolting my heart with awareness.

I look over my shoulder and see the man in the full skull mask. He guides my hand to the black lace.

"I don't share," I whisper, looking into the eyes of my husband. They're not their usual green, but then nor is his hair his usual red. I'm sure if he talks, his voice will be different too, magic giving him a deeper cover than just a flimsy mask. But I know this is the man I love. I can feel the bond flowing between us.

Wordlessly, he takes up the second black collar and shoves it in his pocket. Then he picks up the one my hand is on and lifts it to my neck. My pulse beating strongly at the base of my throat, I swallow hard as he fastens it to me.

His breath at my ear, he says, "And I'm not waiting to touch what's mine."

Digging his hands into the V of my dress, he cups both my breasts. I lean back on him, my nipples hard against his palms, his cock hard already against my back.

The woman's eyes grow hooded as she watches him play with me, and a spike of jealousy mixes with my want to sneer at her for not being the one he's touching. I don't want her wearing his mark, but in this place I'm not his wife and he isn't my husband. We're just two strangers – one who needs to be punished for her sins, one who needs to punish her so he can finally forgive. I just want him to take that first step so he can come home.

He trails his mask to the base of my neck, and I wrap an arm around his head, digging my fingers into his hair. My heart jerks at the feel of it being straight, and panic momentarily floods me, but his words whisper in my ear.

"Did you really think a mask would hide you from me?"

*I would know you anywhere.*

Tears of hope burning my throat, I turn to look at my husband. Love burns bright in his eyes, albeit wary and full of pain. I'm about to tell him I'm sorry when the woman speaks up. "May I have a taste, sir?"

My eyes jerk to her. She's staring at my naked breasts, now only covered by the palms of his hands.

A low possessive growl comes from him, and my pussy clenches from the deep vibrations against my back. "Since you're so desperate for sex, you can change to green," he says, his words tight with the need to punish.

All arousal disappears from her round face as her eyes fly wide. "Sir?"

"Change it, Sierra. Now."

Swallowing, she shifts the tray into one hand then then reaches behind her neck to undo the clasps of her lacy choker. Laying it down, she picks up a simple green band with a gold clasp on each end. "I'll need help..."

He signals to a broad man with a white and blue mask behind her, who strides over without hesitation. As he helps her with the clasp, my masked man grabs the VIP collar she took off and shoves it in his pocket.

My chin lifts. My back straightens. He's choosing me – as a stranger for the night, at least, but I am determined to bring him home.

As soon as the man has the collar fixed around Sierra's neck, he drops to his knees behind her and buries his face between her ass cheeks. Wet noises and groans spew from his lips as he grabs his hard cock and starts jacking himself off. A woman comes over to eat the tray holder's pussy, and a third masked man stands to the side as he sucks on her breast.

Arousal is back on the woman's face.

I'm pulled away from the trio and through the dance floor. There's no disco here. No line dancing or waltzing. It's carnal grinding, fucking without the actual fucking. My eyes roam around all the masked bodies as they move in rhythm to the music pumping out of the speakers, and my pussy clenches at all the acts that are often only seen behind closed doors.

The bass vibrates in my soul, loosening me up as my masked stranger leads me to the balcony. I want to talk to him, tell him once more I'm sorry for hurting him in my ignorance. I've sent so many letters to him through Myers these last two years, but I've never received one back. I have no idea if he still hates me as much as he did. Or if he hates me more. Everyone knows he isn't the Boss of the Shadow Domain even though he still holds that title officially. They turn to me, a woman over him.

Does that fill him with shame?

Does he hate me for that too?

My father would have committed seppuku no doubt, if Mother did the same.

I stare at the man's mask, wondering why he's come to me tonight. I expected to leave in disappointment. Maybe to catch his eye, only to watch him turn away just like he did behind the library.

He still could. He could use me to work out his anger and frustrations, then dump me like leftovers that have been left to go moldy.

My heart in my throat, I wonder if I could handle that. A fuck that clears up all his rage and pain, only to end our marriage for good rather than save it.

"Ca-" I start, but he turns to me and grabs my throat, squeezing hard. His eyes are electric blue slits of painful fury.

"No names here. We are strangers. I don't love you. I don't want to please you." He yanks me close to him, his unmoving mask so close to my lips. "I'm going to punish you for all your sins. There's no safe word for you here tonight." He lifts his head, his eyes over my shoulder. "If you don't like that, leave now. Because once I start..." His eyes come back to mine. "I'm not stopping until you are broken beneath me."

I tremble beneath the gaze of his skull spiked mask. "I'm not leaving you," I whisper, letting him hear the promise in that statement. He is my husband. I love him.

His eyes lighting with passion, he hauls me up the balcony and into a VIP room. He doesn't pause once, his strides long and quick. Shutting the door behind us, he spins me into the wall. My back hits it, and his hands on my shoulders push me down.

I kneel in front of him, my chin lifted as I look up at his mask, a thrill shooting through me at the sight of its unmoving indifference.

"Raise your hands above your head," he says, his cock bulging in his pants just inches from my lips. The lace of my mask runs down like trickles of water, easily separated with the push of a tongue. I think about them lying over his dick, caressing him as I take him deep, and my pussy clenches.

I raise my arms, and he grabs my wrists, bringing them together before pinning them with one hand.

He digs his cock out with the other and rubs it against the lace of my mask, moving the dangling strands with each sway of his hips.

His words a rasp, he asks, "Do you want me to fuck you like Antonio did?"

"Wha–" I scream as a knife slams into my overlapping palms. My fingers curl automatically over the blade in a desire to try to pull it out, but they're so weak now, their tendons severed that they barely move.

He releases my wrists to grab my chin. Forcing my mouth open, he shoves his cock down my throat. I gag around him, struggling to adjust to the instant invasion as he rocks out and thrust back in.

"Do you think about him when you touch yourself?" he growls, and a flare of fear slams through me. He's so angry, so godsdamn furious and hurt. "Do you think about that night in the woods while you finger your pretty little cunt?"

My cheeks burn as I try to turn my head and force him out, but his fingers dig into my jaw, pinning my face as well as his knife does my hands.

"Or would you rather I fucked you like Aleric?"

Grabbing my arms with one hand, he rips the knife free with the other. Then he hauls me up by my wrists and shoves the blade back into my flesh. I scream as the pain radiates down my arms. My knees want to give way, but I'm held up by his body pressing into mine.

The sound of a drawer opening beside us draws my attention, and I glance down to see him pull out a dildo in the shape of a werewolf's cock when in human form. It's not as thick as the cocks he gave himself in our ensuite, but it's capable of knotting. They're sold on the legal side of the market in comparison to the potions we deal.

He pushes it against my lips. I try to fight him, to talk to him about what he wants from me, but he just shoves it down until I choke. His eyes dip to my throat.

"That's it. Squeeze it like the whore you are."

Tears burn my eyes, then fall down my cheeks as he activates the button on the bottom. The knot swells in my mouth, pressing against my teeth so it can't be removed without knocking them all out.

My eyes widen as my nostrils flare. I can't breathe with it in me. Panic floods through me, triggering my flight or flight response, and I thrash beneath his body.

"If you don't want to die," he sneers as he slides his hand between the slip of my dress running up my thigh, "then you'll come on my fingers."

Just like Aleric made me do as Antonio was charging for me.

My pulse spiking, I spread my legs. His fingers pierce me, going deep, and I ride them frantically as my chest tightens from the lack of air.

"That's it," he purrs as he thrusts the dildo in deeper, moving the knot down my throat before pulling it back to my mouth. "Come for me, Sau. Come for me like you came for him."

My movements turn jerky, the lack of oxygen starting to fuck with my coordination. Desperately, I wrap my legs around him and line my pussy up with his throbbing cock. He removes his fingers, then groans as I sink down onto him, taking him in slowly inch by inch until he grabs my hips and slams me down.

Pleasure rips through me, and I fuck him fast and hard as my vision starts to narrow. My chest is burning now, overriding the pain in my hands, but instead of fleeing from that high, I'm chasing it. A mad dash of desire, a frantic race to my orgasm before I lose consciousness.

I arch off the wall as it hits me, consumes me, wraps me up in its overwhelming embrace, and leaves me in a fit of tremors that jerks my muscles uncontrollably. Hot cum shoots down my throat, a working part of the toy, and the knot deflates so he can pull it out. I gasp for breath, my lungs expanding.

My body is abuzz, lost in that lavender haze, and I'm barely aware of him pulling out the knife in my hands and moving me to a bed. I'm laid down on my back, my arms above me, breathing hard. Cuffs snake around my wrists. Sweat clings to me. He spreads my legs and moves my dress aside. Then he lies between my thighs, and I breathe leisurely, expecting the touch of pure bliss.

Instead, the touch of cold metal on my clitoral hood confuses me. It's like he has it between a pair of pliers –

It pierces me, and I jolt up on a scream. Or I try to, but my hands are chained to the headboard, and I fall back down as the muscles in my shoulders protest.

Pain radiates like fire and acid being splattered across my pussy, and the agony only strengthens when he flicks his thumb across it. The *ting* of a nail hitting metal rings through my panicked breathing, and understands hits me as he chuckles.

The fucker gave me a piercing.

Tears of pain burning my eyes, I lift my head to look at him. "I'm sorry, Ca–" I yelp as he flicks my new piece of jewelry.

"*Sir*," he growls.

I don't mention that he used my name earlier. The pain of the blow, the need to comfort him over my own sins has me biting that back. "*Sir*," I say, looking at his skull mask and the twisted gaze peering through it. "What do I need to do to make you believe me?"

He stretches above me and stares directly down into my eyes. "Stop lying to yourself and *me*. Admit that you knew who it was you were fucking. You simply loved it because you're just a fucking *whore*."

# FIFTY-THREE

## HER
### 31 OCTOBER 1987

"That's not true! Ca—" I scream as he slams into me with enough force to arch me off the bed and disturb my fresh piercing. Pain makes me feel nauseous and sick, and the sweat clinging to me feels like poison seeping out of my pores. Everything in this moment is wrong. I thought he loved me.

I thought, despite everything, he still loved me.

That he wouldn't hurt me.

But all he wants is to express his pain, his frustration only building since that last time in the shower.

"*Sir*," he hisses, and I whimper, crying more for the loss of my husband than the agony of my body.

I have been through the worst life has to offer. I have suffered the deaths of fourteen children. I have been used and betrayed by those I thought loved me. And I am *sick* of being beaten with clubs upon my back.

"Fuck you!" I scream, no longer caring that he's in pain. It doesn't give him the right to hurt me. "I said I'm sorry. I told you I didn't know it was him!"

"You're a liar! Admit it! Admit that you're just a whore who doesn't care whose dick is inside her."

"That's not true!" My words fade on a groan as he rams his cock inside me, thrusting hard and fast until the agony of his piercing and the girth of his cock dragging against my sides makes me lose focus of all else.

"You thought you were so tough forcing us to sign that damn treaty, making us all look like fools. But you're not so tough now, are you? Not so tough when you have my cock inside you and you're squeezing it like a dirty little whore."

He pulls out and shoves back in, making me bite my cheek so I don't scream. My eyes water from the pain of the forced piercing shooting up my spine. It's sharp and wicked, intensifying all the more when he reaches down and flicks it with his thumb, a harsh *ding* sounding as he smacks it with his nail.

I cry out, and my eyes close involuntarily as the agony makes my legs jerk, my body spasm. I clench around him, feeling the large girth of his cock as it pulses inside me, the tightening and relaxing of his pelvic muscles making it move. I start to panic at the feeling of being helpless, reminded of all the times where I was too weak, just a toy for the world to play with. I open my eyes to glare at him, to feel some minute bit of control despite my willingness earlier to give it up. He isn't my husband in this moment. And I'm not his wife. He's just a cruel stranger hiding like a coward behind a mask.

"Not so fucking tough when you're clenched around my cock, are you, Sau? Not such a bitch when you have your legs spread wide for me." He removes his hand from my clit to raise his arm, his palm flat. I tense, expecting the slap to my face, but it lands hard across my breast, swinging it into the other. "Not so powerful when your body is under mine, now is it?" He slaps me again, leaving red marks that'll form into bruises – if he lets me live that long.

I jerk against my binds, glaring at him beneath my mask as my need to escape, to save myself sets in fully. But I can't hit him with my magic due to my mangled hands, can't speak it given how quick he is to choke me. I am defenseless, trapped, and entirely at his dark, twisted mercy.

He thrusts into me, his eyes on mine, peering through the holes of his mask. I clench my ass as he pumps inside my wet pussy so my hips don't lift in rhythm to his. I'm not going to give him anything. Not going to break like he wants me to.

But my body is getting hot as the slaps of his hips mix with the harsh grunts of his breaths. He squeezes both my breasts hard as he slams into me, digging the rough pads of his fingers into my ample flesh. Then he leans down to them, and the anticipation of his metal spikes against my skin makes me shiver.

I bite my cheek, begging my body not to betray me for once, but he must catch sight of my slight trembles for he starts to laugh.

"You dirty little whore." His breath feathers across my nipple. "You're so fucking disgusting getting turned on right now."

"Fuck you. It's just anatomy," I grit out. A lot of assault survivors can't control it, and it's nothing to be ashamed of. Like when the doctor hits your knee, making it kick involuntarily. Caden taught me that, and I hold onto that now.

I clench my teeth as he chuckles, his cock still sliding in and out of me at a rhythm that's going to break me.

"Maybe," he says, then trails his fingers along the underside of my breast, leaving a trail of goosebumps in its wake. "Maybe you don't want my cock inside you." He pulls it out slowly. "Maybe your pussy is just sloppy and wet because of *anatomy.*" He thrusts in hard. "Maybe your body isn't really trembling on the verge of coming around my cock." He pulls out, and my heart beats rapidly at the coming thrust. My lips part ever so slightly as I hold his gaze.

But he doesn't move, just lies there with the tip of his cock inside me.

*Damn you.*

"But maybe," he sneers. "Maybe you're going to squirt around me because you're a dirty little whore who needs a real man to fuck you into oblivion."

He shoves in just as he pinches my nipple hard. I cry out, jerking beneath him, my hips lifting as I'm assaulted by pain. He pulls hard enough I'm sure he's about to rip it off. His other hand flicks my glan piercing, and the two waves of agony crash in the middle of my stomach before rippling out through my entire body.

And on the heels of all that pain is the first orgasm of the night begging me to let it out. I squeeze my eyes shut as I tremble beneath him, trying so hard to fight it back, but he is ruthless, moving his fingers to my other nipple and hitting my piercing again with the hard flick of his thumb.

"You're ready to come on my cock, aren't you? You're ready to know what it feels like to finally be satisfied. You should've married someone stronger, someone who isn't so pathetic. You hate your husband, don't you?"

"No!" I scream.

He leans up and digs the spikes of his mask into my neck. The cold metal causes shivers to run across my skin as he thrusts into me.

Harder.

And harder.

And *harder.*

The wide girth of his cock stretches me, tearing me up

despite how wet I am. He's simply too big, and it's been too long, my pussy unaccustomed to such brutality.

My body grows hot, a blazing heat that spreads from my pussy to my head, and slowly, the pain starts to recede under the crashing waves of unwanted arousal. My hips lift as one leg wraps around his calf. My breaths come out on ragged pants as he lifts his head to look at me. There's no blood on his mask despite how hard his spikes dug into my skin, but I can practically see his lips beneath them curl into a wicked sneer.

"That's it, sweet girl. Take my cock like the gift it is." He grabs my other leg, the one still down, and lifts it to wrap around his ass. It moves without resistance, and when he removes his hand to grab my breast, my leg stays were he put it, opening me up to a new angle.

He rocks into me, a pulsing of pleasure. He grabs my other leg and urges it to join the other. "Lock your ankles around me, Sau."

His words have lost a bit of that biting edge, that anger directed at me, but his feralness and need to own me only increases, shown in the strain of his words and the rapid pulsing at the veins in his neck and temple. In the slower pounding of his cock as he tries to coax me over the edge, desperate to have me come around him almost as much as my body is to do so.

"Fuck you," I breathe even as my leg obeys, my ankles locking around his ass as he thrusts into me, pleasure and pain mixing with every push of his hips.

"Hate me all you want, but you're still going to come for me. You're still going to be my dirty little whore all night long."

He reaches a hand between our bodies as he crushes me with his full weight. Grabbing my piercing between his fingers, he tugs on it gently, but that's enough to send a shockwave of pain shooting through me. Crying out, I arch my back, a pathetic struggle to get away.

He grunts as he tugs it again. Then slides his finger lower. He rubs it against my lips, then lines it up with his cock and pushes in. Another cry is torn from me as my already stretched pussy rips at the additional invasion.

"Stop," I plead as the pain becomes too much.

Everywhere he's touched is sore – my broken hands, my choked and bruised neck, my slapped nipples, the new piercing in my clit, the tearing of my pounded pussy. It's all just too much, wave after wave of pure agony rushing through my body like a tsunami. "Stop," I beg again.

"No," he says as he shoves another finger inside. "You are mine tonight, Sau. However I want you. Whatever I want to do to you" –a third finger goes in, making me scream– "you can't stop me. Not tonight. But beg me all you want. I love hearing the Queen of St. Augustine so fucking weak."

Bringing his legs up, he grabs my hip with his free hand as he sits on his knees. My shoulders dig into the mattress as he lifts the rest of me up. My legs are now wrapped around his back. He thrusts into me with his cock as his three fingers curl back, hitting that spot with merciless attention.

I try to squirm up the bed, away from him as tears burn my eyes, but his fingers dig into me, his strong grip holding me still.

I want to tell him again to stop, but I know it's utterly pointless. Hopeless. Pathetic to even try.

"Stop fighting it, Sau," he grunts, slapping his hips into me. "Just relax and let it happen. Squirt all over my cock as I fuck you hard."

I whimper as his cock suddenly pulls out of me and pushes back in with a tenderness that feels almost gentle despite the pain.

"You like this, don't you? Not some fucking anatomical reaction, is it? You like being tied up and taken by a real man."

He grunts as he sinks deep into me, his fingers flexing fast against my G. My body shakes as my teeth clench.

"Fuck you," I rasp. I don't like this. I like my sweet Caden. I like how I can trust him not to hurt me.

"You are," he chuckles as he keeps pushing against the tears inside me, the slight burn becoming a quiet numb that is slowly fading. "You're squeezing my cock like a good little whore, so desperate, so needy. Your swollen clit wants me to kiss it, doesn't it? Wants me to soothe the pain."

He presses his thumb against the piercing, and my ass muscles clench from the ripples of agony exploding from it.

"Go...fuck yourself," I correct.

"I'd much rather stay fucking you." The humor falls from his eyes as his lips flatten. "Now come for me, Sau. I won't ask again." And the way he says it, a clear threat coloring his tone, has me shaking around his cock.

"No," I grunt as sweat glistens across every inch of my body from the sheer control I'm using to force my orgasm down. I can show him it's just anatomy. I can show him I only want *him*. Not the pain. Squeezing my eyes shut, I shake my head. *No. I won't come. I won't –*

I cry out as I jerk beneath him under powerful tidal waves of pleasure that drag me to the bottom of the ocean. And still more waves come, crushing and crashing over me as his fingers pull out to grab my hip. He picks up his pace, slamming into me as I spasm around him, my legs kicking against the mattress as my back arches, and I scream. It's too intense, too fucking intense. I'm thrashing around on the bed, but he doesn't let up from the brutal pace of his cock inside me.

"That's it. Good girl," he growls as his fingers leave bruises of ownership on my hips. "Keep coming for me, sweet girl. Keep squirting all over my cock." He groans as he falls forward, his mask finding my neck. Then trailing down to my breasts as he pushes them together to cup his cheeks. He rubs his spikes across a nipple, not letting me come down for even a moment, the foreign sensation of metal on flesh forcing me to stay on that high of ecstasy that's draining every bit of energy from my limbs.

I shudder and whimper and scream and beg. And still he thrusts into me, his mask roaming around my nipples, his spikes flicking them back and forth.

He groans behind his mask as he pushes me down onto the mattress and collapses on top of me. His body shakes, the underside of his cock pulsing against the stretched walls of my pussy. He empties himself inside of me, filling me with his scent. His claim. His mark of possession.

"Such a fucking good girl."

I stay still beneath his assault, my body too broken to do anything more than breathe shallowly and tremble. I failed him. I failed to not come under the brutality of the scene.

"You came so fucking hard," he sneers. "I bet you've soaked the mattress all the way through."

I flinch at his callous words, but I can't refute them given how wet my thighs are. How wet his are as they press into my body. My pussy kegels around him, and he groans as he jerks his cock inside me with the tensing of his own muscles.

I whimper as I kegel again, clenching around his still hard cock. I can't move, can't speak. I just lie there with his cock inside me, soaked from the waist down.

I love my husband.

So why don't I love this?

# FIFTY-FOUR

## HIM
### 31 OCTOBER 1987

Fuck. I've never come so hard. Never lingered after finishing in years, yet I'm still inside her, my cock still mostly hard, enveloped in the tight hold of her pussy. Her scent fills the room, arousal mixed with blood and sweat, and I breathe in deeply, imprinting it into memory, along with the damn good feel of her squeezing me.

I lick my way up to her jaw, my cock twitching against her wet grip. She squirted all over me. Fucking soaked the place. Anatomy, my ass.

I meant to punish her, use her, break her for all the pain she caused me. A growl leaves my lips as the furious hatred settles in my heart like a poisonous thorn. I lift my hips and ram into her. She cries out on a whimper, no doubt sore given all the blood. No doubt not ready for another round.

But fuck her and what she wants.

She is my enemy, and I'm going to break her for all her

sins. Reaching between us, I flick her piercing, my eyes on her face, watching the beautiful twisting of pain and fear. She presses her lips together, fighting back a whimper or perhaps even a scream. Still too proud. Still too fucking in control. I want her loose. I want her feral. I want her to stop hiding behind her fucking words of, "It's anatomy."

Rocking my hips, I wait until my cock is fully hard again before slamming in between her legs. Her ass is shoved back into the bed as it creaks. Her pussy's warm cum runs down my thighs. "You're such a fucking whore," I growl as I rope my arms under her legs, "that your pussy has become so loose in your arousal."

"Your dick is just too small."

I smirk as I sit up, pushing her knees up to the sides of her breasts as I bend her in half. I pull all the way out so I can see her pussy unhindered. My cock jerks at the sight of it gaping and pulsing, and I spread it wider with my fingers on one hand, looking further in. It's so damn pretty and pink and so fucking wet.

Lifting a hand, I smack it red, making sure to hit the piercing. She yelps, then tries to kick me in the face. I let her hit me, her muscles exhausted, her strength no match for mine without the help of her magic.

My smirk spreading, I spank her pussy again, putting enough force behind it to feel the sting on my fingers. My little whore whimpers as she jerks this time, instinctively fleeing rather than fighting. I like that. Her broken and bleeding beneath me. The punishment of her sins. The last true Shadow, the great Sau made pathetic because of *me*.

Anger shooting down my arm, I smack her again.

She bites her lip, holding back her scream as her hips jerk sideways. I grab her, holding her still as I hit her again.

She kicks me in the face, then the chest, then aims for the throat. And only then do I grab her ankle and slam it down on the bed. "Can't ever say I'm not a gentleman, Sau,"

I seethe as I push three fingers inside her pussy. "Can't ever say I don't take care of my woman." I press another finger in, pushing deep, so she takes them all the way to the knuckles.

"*Stop.*" Her words are fractured but not fully broken.

Snarling at her attempt to deny me once more, I fold my thumb in and shove my whole hand up to the wrist.

She bucks, her scream breaking on a half sob, half whimper as she falls back to the bed. I push in further, feeling the walls of her pussy trying to fend me off, trying to stay rigid as I force them to tear.

"Stop," she rasps, a desperate little plea that has me stilling.

"I told you you're mine tonight, Sau," I growl as my eyes dip to her stretched across my wrist. My lips part at the sight of her taking me in. I want to push in further, but I can already feel her cervix without fully extending my fingers. They're bent inside her, and I slowly pull my arm back to straighten them as I search for the opening of that tiny hole, the tips of my fingers brushing back and forth across her cervix. But her pussy is so fucking wet, and without being able to see what I'm doing, I struggle to feel it even though I know where it should be.

I exhale a bit of my frustration through my nose before turning my attention to the hole I can see. Pulling my hand out a bit further, I let my thumb slip free and then push it into her ass. She squeezes around my nail. "That's a good girl," I murmur, the words escaping me on a mindless breath.

Flattening my lips, I bite back any more praise. This isn't a night of pleasure. Just a night of punishment and sin.

"You claim my dick is too small," I say as I lift my eyes to her lopsided mask. I want to rip it off her. I want to see her completely, but there's a thrill to keeping our masks on that has me reaching forward and straightening the satin across her eyes.

I smile as I pull my thumb out of her ass and push it back in. "So I'm going to make sure you're all taken care of like the gentleman I am. I'm going to open that door and find the biggest cock downstairs for you."

Her green eyes widen, a flush coloring her cheeks as she subtly shakes her head.

"Yes, Sau. I'm going to let him fuck you raw and then I'm going to find another to join him because you like that, *don't you*? You like coming on other men's cocks?"

A tightness wraps around my chest, anger building under a need to humiliate her. "Then I'm going to find another man. And another. And watch as they all rip apart your pussy."

I pull my fingers out of her and spread her lips wide as I glance at them. "How many do you think you can take at once? Two?" I growl as I rub my thumb across her wet pink lips. "Three?"

"*Please.*"

My eyes lift to hers again, wanting to see her beg. To see her hurt like I hurt every time I think about her with *him*. "Please what?"

"Please don't."

I still at those words, those soft and desperate words of a little girl looking for protection behind a wolf. I hold her gaze, my chest squeezing to the point of lightheadedness.

Then I smirk. "For someone so smart, you're fucking stupid when you're in pain. I already told you your pleas won't work on me, and yet you still try. The Great Sau so fucking pathetic."

She turns her head away, but I can see the first tear slip free of her mask. Can see the increased fear shaking her body. The anger turns into a restless discomfort I don't like, so I move swiftly off the bed and head for the door. She doesn't make a noise as I leave to make good on my promise.

I hesitate in the doorway, as if waiting for her to beg again, to ask me to stay, but she doesn't, so I continue on. Down the hall of private rooms; some doors are open, some not. High pitched moans and cries mix with the music pulsing around the walls in heavy beats that vibrate in my bones. A woman catches my eye as she's fucked hard from the back doggie style. She gestures me in, and I look away distastefully, continuing down the hall to find someone suitable for Sau.

A cold smile curls my lips. I called myself a gentleman.

The word tickles in the back of my throat, then fades as I catch sight of a large cock being jerked in a meaty fist. A muscular man, six-two, six-three stands, stance wide, in an open doorway, peering in, his lips parted as he watches –I glance in– two lesbians.

"Want to fuck my girl while I watch?" I ask, straight to the point. It takes him a second to tear his eyes away from the women scissoring on the bed to look at me.

"She fat?"

My smile becomes more a baring of teeth. "No."

He looks back at the two lesbians, then shrugs and pivots to follow me down the hall. And for a split fucking second, I want to rip his throat out. He blinks dark eyes as his confidence seems to shrink, but then I spread my lips, portraying the easiness I *should* be feeling over punishing her for her sins.

But there's a possessiveness shoving aside my hatred of her, my want to see Sau broken and humiliated.

My fingers twitch at my sides as I stop at our door so he can enter first. "She likes it rough," I say. "Just see how wet she's made the bed."

He glances at me, hunger in his eyes, before ducking through the door and stepping in. I follow behind him, clicking the door shut behind us. To leave it open is to invite all others in, and I don't want anyone with small dicks joining. *Only the best for Princess Sau...*

My jaw tightens as I watch the man approach her. His eyes are on her pussy even though she has her legs closed together. Mine go to her face, and the twisted fear there should make me happy, excited to finally see the great witch break, to mock her for her claims of *it's anatomy*.

But it doesn't.

It fills me with a restlessness to move, a need to step in and be her hero as I rip the man's throat out.

A low growl crawls up my throat, but I hold it back, right below the edge of the cliff it's ascending, its muscles straining, its fingers digging deep as the man, the filthy fucking man, places a knee on the bed and his hands on my girl's knees, forcing them apart.

I take a step forward, then root myself in place.

This is what I want for her. The pain. The humiliation.

The knowledge that it isn't just fucking *anatomy* that made her come all those years ago.

So why the fuck do I want to rip his fucking throat out just for looking at her how she is?

Naked.

Vulnerable.

Fucking *mine*.

I'm on him before I even realize I've moved, my teeth in his neck, ripping out his jugular as she screams. Red paints her mask in long spurts, streaking across closed eyes and an open mouth. I grab his chin and force his head to the side, not wanting him to see her even in his final moments.

His eyes are bugged in horror and pain, and I hope the fucker is suffering. He tried to touch what's mine. Tried to take from *me*. My pussy. My fucking girl. Anger straining my muscles, I tear his head off, the ripping of flesh, the snapping of tendons and bone a song of delight. Snarling, I toss it across the room. Breathing heavily. Wanting to tear the rest of him limb from limb, but then I hear Sau whimper softly.

My gaze snaps to hers, then stills.

Knowledge and understanding slam into me.

He *entered* her.

My own agonized rasp escapes as I watch her clench her jaw and shudder beneath him.

He's still inside her, his headless body between us.

His cock deep in her pussy.

The pussy *I* own.

Anger overrides the pain as I envision him inside her, her *enjoying him*. My muscles tremble with the force of emotions bombarding me from too many sides. Like I'm being curbstomped from all directions, kicked in the head and disorientated.

I don't want to feel anything soft for her. This is a night of revenge, of sweet, sweet revenge, but all I can think about is his cock is still fucking inside her, and she's making no move to throw him off.

A snarl ripping from me, I stand, hoping it is just our combined weight making her still for him, but it isn't.

She still doesn't move.

Still doesn't toss him off.

Why the fuck isn't she tossing him off!

"You fucking whore," I bite out as I reach a hand under her still body and roll her away from me, moving her on top of him. She doesn't move off him, still *enjoying* him in some twisted little power play; 'the joke is one you. I'm into this.' My chest tightens on a wail I don't release, but the pent up anger is making me feral.

"You like his cock inside you, don't you, whore? You wanted to spread your legs for him? Played me like a damn fool."

I crawl back onto the bed and grab her hips, my fingers bruising her skin.

"Fuck you," she chokes out, so I slap her ass hard – all punishment, no pleasure. She is still a fighter, has all her feisty rage, so why isn't she moving off his fucking cock?

"No, Sau," I hiss as I grab my own. "I told you I'm doing the fucking tonight."

*Now* the bitch finally moves, feeling the tip of my cock against her tight and bloody pussy. She tries to jerk away, so I release my cock to grab her free hip, all my fingers forming more bruises, locking her still.

"You like it rough, don't you, Sau? Pretended to cry so you would get the big cock you wanted, making me think you didn't."

"I didn't –" She breaks on a scream as I push in on one deep shove.

His cock is flaccid beneath mine, all the blood pressure having left through his open neck. The coppery smell of the bastard has overridden the teasing of hers, the smell of our mixed scents. He's still bleeding out like a butchered pig beneath her arms that are outstretched and tied to the bed, and I grab the back of her head, fisting her long black hair to yank her gaze over to mine.

"You want to come on him? Go for it, sweet girl, but he doesn't get to enjoy what's mine."

I pull out and thrust back in.

"He doesn't get to hear you scream."

Her eyes hold mine, still so fucking defiant even as they blur beneath a shine that twists the air in my lungs.

"He doesn't get to feel you squirt all over his cock."

I ram into her, growling, then yank her head further back, pulling strands free as I arch her nearly in half.

"He doesn't get to enjoy what's *mine*."

I rip off the lower half of my mask and kiss her bloody mouth as my cock pumps into her. She thrashes beneath me, but my grip tightens on her hair, forcing her to still as I take what's mine. She bites my lip, and I know she's close again.

"Tell me it's just *anatomy* now," I sneer. "Tell me you're not just a dirty little whore."

"I'm not."

"Liar!" I shove her head down, coating her mask in the blood on the sheets. "You like having another man's cock in you. You like to pretend you're being raped, that you're not *into* this when you're soaking the godsdamn sheets and the mattress underneath. Now say it!" I demand as I yank her head back up. She gasps, spitting blood free from her lips. "Admit that it isn't just anatomy. Admit that you liked coming on Aleric's cock!"

I slam in and out of her, dragging the dead man's cock out of her pussy with my movements so it's just me inside her now. Me and my rage and my need to have no lies between us.

"Admit it, sweet girl," I growl as I wrap a hand around her throat. "Tell me the truth so I can forgive you."

I want to forgive her. I want to forgive her for all her lies, for all her pain, for all the choices she made where it wasn't me. "Admit it, Sau," I beg as I slam into her again. I kiss the side of her neck, my chest burning with the need to hear her words. "Admit it."

Sobbing, she nods, finally breaking apart. "I'm sorry. I'm so sorry."

"Sorry for what?" I ask, my words tight, my body still.

"I'm sorry I..." She chokes back a sob. "...enjoyed it."

"Enjoyed *what*?" I growl between clenched teeth. "Say his name."

She shakes beneath me, her walls down, unable to lie to herself anymore, to lie to me. On a wail, she admits, "*Aleric.*"

# FIFTY-FIVE

## HER
### 31 OCTOBER 1987

He collapses against me, breathing hard and fast, the anger all pulled out of him. He's shaking, as am I, and I cry beneath his weight, wanting him to say something, to yell at me, to accuse me, to hit me as he fucks me. To do something other than just shake on top of me like I've ripped out his heart, his soul, his reason for carrying on.

A broken noise comes from behind his mask, and I wonder if he's crying. But then I realize he's laughing, a wild, manic wheeze that's ripping through his whole body.

"I knew you were a whore," he rasps. Pressing his lips against my neck, he kisses his way up to my ear as I lie in shock. "But you're *my* whore," he says. "You will always be mine, Sau. I don't care how many cocks end up inside you, you will forever be mine."

"I don't want any other –"

"Shhhh." He presses a finger to my lips. "Don't lie to me

after that truth."

It is the truth, but I bite the words back, knowing he isn't able to hear them right now. I might feel a bond to Aleric, he might draw me in like a siren's song, but I don't want him. I want my husband.

I just want my husband.

"So what now?" I ask softly. "Will you come home?"

He stiffens.

Then rocks back on his knees, his cock sliding out of me. Reaching a hand between us, he slides his fingers up and down my pussy lips, pushing cum back inside of me.

"Go home, Sau," he says, his fingers lingering on the piercing he just gave me. It's sore and tender, and I try not to wince at the pain just that light touch is giving me. "Don't talk to me about tonight. I'm going to throw these clothes, this mask in the garbage, and I want you to do the same before you leave. There's a shower and extra clothes in the basement, but you don't belong here."

"Neither do you," I say. "Please – *sir*, come home."

He looks up at me, holding my gaze as he rips out my piercing. I scream in pain, my legs clenching together. He raises the jewelry up so I can see a black metal hood with cone edges. Unscrewing one end of it, he places it inside his nose, against his septum. My blood and cum are all over it, and he inhales sharply.

Then he stabs it through his own flesh. "To remember you by," he says before turning to leave. "Now get out of my club and don't come back."

As the door shuts behind him, I don't know which pain is worse – my torn clitoral head or the loss of the only man I've ever loved.

# FIFTY-SIX

## HER
### 1 NOVEMBER 1987

I walk into my house in the late hours of the night, hope flickering in my chest that he's here, that his exit at the club was just the end of his stranger's charade, but he isn't. Falling into bed, I curl around my pillow and mourn Caden's absence. I hoped to heal the part of him I broke tonight, but all I did is make it worse. I told him things I couldn't even admit to myself, truths that were too hard to hear.

"He's never going to forgive me," I whisper. I start to pull on my shadows, to call Olivia to me so I'm not alone, but the sound of the front door opening has me bolting upright. My ears strain for another sound, and at the soft thumps of footsteps, I throw my legs over the bed and hurry out of my room.

My breath catches at the sight of my husband as he stands in the living room, facing me. He's freshly washed, his curly red hair still damp. I want to run to him, but my feet are rooted to the floor. Our masks are off now, and the protection of anonymity is gone. Now it's just a hurt husband and his wife who doesn't know what else she can do to apologize.

"I'm sorry I said those things about you enjoying it," he finally says, his eyes bloodshot with fresh tears. "I know how much you hate Aleric, and I shouldn't have accused you of loving the monster who killed our children." His Adam's apple bobs as he swallows. "I can't imagine what it was like to be in that place for twenty-three years, and for you to get assaulted on your first day back. Even if you... *liked* it," he chokes out. "you were starved of human contact for decades."

"I swear I thought it was you. I lost so much in the dark. I forgot what you looked like. I forgot our children's names. I –" I swallow the rest of my excuses. Knowing them won't stop his pain. "Tell me what to do to fix this," I say, the words a rasp of desperation.

He doesn't say anything.

Doesn't move.

Then he simply opens his arms.

My chest tight, I take a step towards him.

Then another.

And another.

Then I'm running into his arms and throwing myself against his body. He wraps me in a hug, squeezing me tight.

"I'm sorry I hurt you," he says.

I close my eyes against all the pain I suffered tonight at his hands, but if I had the choice, I would suffer it all over again. It brought me my husband back. Nothing I endured at that club hurt more than his absence.

"It's okay."

"It's not. You're my wife, Sau. A husband should never hurt his wife."

"And a wife should never hurt her husband."

"Two wrongs don't make a right."

Lifting my head, I look up into his green eyes, loving that they're back to their normal color. "Can we heal from this?" I hold my breath for his response, feeling it tight in my chest as my world balances on a pin.

Squeezing me, he kisses the top of my head. He doesn't say anything, perhaps not yet sure, but he carries me into our bedroom.

Lost in each other's embrace, we start to heal the first part of each other's pain. No masks on. No shields up.

Just two raw, open souls desperate to go back to being one.

# EPILOGUE
## HER
### 3 OCTOBER 1992

Caden holds me in his arms as we sit on a bench and watch our three boys playing in our yard. We've moved house, started over on the outskirts of St. Augustine – as far away as we can be from Aleric's nest without leaving the city. As much as I never want to see him again, this is our home, my family's legacy, and I'll not let him scare me away.

We might have his signature on a treaty, but I know it will mean nothing if he discovers my secret. I know his obsession with me hasn't waned despite Caden's hope that it has. Aleric once waited twelve years before making his next move in this 'game,' and I fear he's still waiting now. Perhaps for my children to grow again...to leave the safety of this house and all its warded acres.

My heart in my throat, I watch as Varius, our firstborn, shows his two brothers a beetle he found in the grass. He holds his hand out, and Leno, the middle child, places his palm up right next to it, allowing the beetle to walk across his hand. Khalid holds his up next, giggling as the insect's feet tickle his palm. Alternating their hands, they make a train and laugh over something so simple.

I want to just enjoy this moment, to let their happiness seep into me and push out all my fears.

But I can't.

Something is wrong. I can feel it in the pit of my belly, a tight knot that twists with every breath.

Caden's arm tightens around my shoulders as he turns his head to me. "You okay?" he whispers so as not to alarm our children.

"Yeah," I lie. "I'm fine."

"Sau –" He stops, his words cut off by the sound of an engine. My heart jerks as I instantly picture a delivery van, but when I turn my head, all I see is Myers driving down the dirt road.

I force a smile as he stops in our drive and gets out. Khalid and Leno run to him, screaming with laughter. Varius walks a bit more calmly, the beetle still crawling on his arm. He shows it to his uncle, who *oohs* and *ahhs*, then ruffles his hair. But there's a darkness in his eyes, a strain of fear when he lifts his head to look at us.

Caden and I are on our feet in an instant.

My legs grow heavier with every step as my heart slams around my skull. "Kids, why don't you go inside and get some ice-cream."

"Yay!" They leave Myers and race inside. Varius still has the bug.

His smile instantly falling, my brother-in-law turns to his car and opens the back door. He pulls out a cardboard box stained with blood. "This was left on my doorstep. It's addressed to you, Sau."

Caden curses. "Don't open it, Sau. He's just trying to get

a rise out of you."

Ignoring him, I reach for the box.

Open it.

Then suck in a hard gasp as a hand flies to my lips.

For inside is Jonathan's black feline head, the red quills that used to line his back laid down across his eyes, almost like a mask. And in his nose is a black hoop of metal.

"What the fuck?" Caden snaps. "He shouldn't be able to linger long enough in the Plane of Monsters to..."

But his words fade under the rush of blood pounding in my ears. My hand shaking with rage and fear, I reach for the black card inside.

*Enjoy the next few decades with Caden, love.*

*For the rest of them will be mine.*

# WHAT TO READ A SMALL EXTRA SCENE?

Join me on discord.

# WANT TO KNOW WHAT HAPPENS WHEN THE TREATY FAILS?

Read *Cursed to be Mine*.

It opens with noncon somno from her stalker.

# AUTHOR'S NOTE

Hello everyone!

Thank you so much for reading *Madness Behind the Mask*, and for those that voted on what 9,000 SHORT STORY I wrote next, thank you so much for picking this one. LOL. This was a fucking hard challenge, which I clearly failed given it's 127k instead, and I'm not going to lie, I cursed you all multiple times as the 'short story' kept growing and growing…but now that it's over, I am really happy you voted on this one.

Sau's story isn't complete, and I hope you enjoy the rest of the series.

You can continue it now by preordering *Cursed to be Mine* (which takes place long after *Madness* and is about one of Sau's children) or reading it now on my website: shop.mirandagrant.com

Happy reading,

# RESEARCH NOTES

I always dive into the research when I write, and this book was no different. If you want to stay in the realm of pure fiction, skip this bit, but putting light on some of the issues I come across helps me clear the darkness I dive into when I write. A bit of a balance of the soul, if you will. Yes, this is fiction. But there are people who suffer greatly in this world, and I wouldn't feel right if I just ignored that under the argument of *it's fiction*.

So unfortunately, the ages of marriage mentioned in here are accurate. Georgia, USA allowed a woman to marry at the age of ten in 1918. In Florida, up until *2018*, a rapist could could marry their victim if they got her pregnant or got pregnant by him at *any* age, the argument being it was best for that child to have a piece-of-shit father than be raised by a single mother...

As of March 2023, **forty-three states out of fifty** still allow child marriages, and seven of them don't even have a minimum age, making it technically legal for a five year old (the youngest recorded pregnancy) to marry her rapist. And once a child is married, their partners can no longer be charged with statutory rape even at a federal level. They also can't divorce because, get this, *they're not old enough to understand/consent to divorce.*

Over 200,000 children (suspected to be over 300,000 given many states gave incomplete or zero records to the study) were married in the US from 2000-2015. Personally, I think it's a great deal higher than this given when California made it so underage marriages had to be documented, they jumped from there being fewer than twenty since before 2019 to *nearly 9000* in 2021 alone.

The vast majority of child marriages concern girls, but roughly 15% concern underage boys. "The youngest wedded were three 10-year-old girls in Tennessee who married men aged 24, 25, and 31 in 2001. The youngest groom was an 11-year-old who married a 27-year-old woman in the same state in 2006." (independent.co.uk 2018)

Of these, only 14% of them were married to other minors. In 88% of cases, the older party would have been charged with statuary rape if they didn't marry their victim; one was a 74 year old to a 14-year-old girl. The US is so well known for this that it is a **hot destination for pedophiles to travel over there** *to marry their victims.*

So if anyone wants to know more or knows of a child bride/groom in America who needs help, please visit **https://www.unchainedatlast.org/forced-and-child-marriage-survivor-stories/**

May we make the world a better place.

1. https://www.cfr.org/blog/its-time-end-child-marriage-united-states
2. https://www.unchainedatlast.org/united-states-child-marriage-problem-study-findings-april-2021/

# SPOT ANY ERRORS?

Please let me know by emailing me at:
**authormirandagrant@gmail.com**

# WANT TO IMPACT THE REST OF THE SERIES?

Drop me a review! Tell me what you loved and want more of or what you hated and want less of.

# WANT TO LEARN ALL ABOUT WIPS AND NEW RELEASES?

www.ingramcontent.com/pod-product-compliance
Ingram Content Group UK Ltd.
Pitfield, Milton Keynes, MK11 3LW, UK
UKHW021301070225
4502UKWH00048B/712